DARK
STARS

Also Available From Titan Books

NEW TALES OF
DARKEST HORROR

DARK STARS

EDITED BY
JOHN F.D. TAFF

WITH A FOREWORD BY JOSH MALERMAN
AND AN AFTERWORD BY RAMSEY CAMPBELL

TITAN BOOKS

Dark Stars
Paperback edition ISBN: 9781789098983
Electronic edition ISBN: 9781789098990

Published by Titan Books
A division of Titan Publishing Group Ltd
144 Southwark Street, London SE1 0UP

First edition: March 2022
10 9 8 7 6 5 4 3 2 1

This is a work of fiction. Names, places and incidents are either products of the author's imagination or used fictitiously. Any resemblance to actual persons, living or dead (except for satirical purposes), is entirely coincidental.

The authors assert the moral right to be identified as the author of their work.

A CIP catalogue record for this title is available from the British Library.

Printed and bound in the United Kingdom by CPI Group (UK) Ltd, Croydon, CR0 4YY.

This book is dedicated to all of the teachers who spend their time nurturing talent, imparting wisdom, and gently nudging people toward fulfilling their potential.

I am deeply appreciative of all that you have done for me and continue to do for others.

CONTENTS

FOREWORD
BY JOSH MALERMAN

Horror is having a moment.

Maybe it always is, I suspect that's true. But right now? This is *our* moment, any and all writers, anybody alive and doing it. And maybe even some of the dead ones, too. From teenagers trying their hands at their first short stories to men and women a hundred years old who still thrill at getting it down on paper: horror is indeed having a moment. And us twelve, the twelve writers between the covers of this book?

We're part of it.

Thing is, there's a pandemic afoot. For that, we couldn't get a photo of the twelve of us together. Sorry about that. We couldn't fly to one place let alone stand arm in arm, our smiles to be seen. I like to imagine it, though, Alma Katsu somewhere in the middle, the rest of us fanning out from there. John Taff quietly staring the camera down, proud and at ease, for having brought the group together in the first place. In this photo (that does not exist) I imagine myself and Caroline Kepnes with drinks in our hands, John Langan and Chesya Burke on the verge of laughing from a joke one or the other made. Stephen Graham Jones, Gemma Files, Usman Malik all seated on the porch rail, the darkening sky behind them; some blood and shadow in the air. In this photo (that does not exist) Priya Sharma is mixing paint in a plastic cup, prepared to paint eyes on the rest of us. Livia Llewellyn is pointing at Ramsey Campbell, who either just spoke or is just about to speak, seconds away from saying something the rest of us will cheer.

But . . . no photo. And that's okay. What do writers do to mark the occasion when there's no camera in sight?

We write it down, of course.

Dark Stars is our photo, a snapshot of the twelve of us at this moment in horror, this moment horror is having.

It's everywhere. Yes. Horror is on your Christmas tree and in your cereal. It's on your shoes, your jacket, your hat. It's in your Twitter handle and, for us lucky ones, it's in your dreams, as there's no shortage of imagery (obscure and not) in your numerous daily feeds. But I'm not even talking about the ubiquitous state of the genre; I'm pointing a bony, bloody finger at the books, the stories, the scripts, the tales. Horror is something like black taffy these days, enough elasticity to stretch across any room (even the word "room, feels a little confining while discussing the modern state of horror: *Is* it a room actually? Could be something else), and you'll find that elasticity here in the pages of this book. Most of us writing today grew up when horror was having another moment, the holy/unholy 1980s. We were drawn to the paperbacks with black spines and red titles as if they were needles and the rest of the store was made of hay. But our book life didn't start and end there, most of us didn't build a home in horror and never leave town. We ventured out. We read the classics. We read self-help books. We read adventure novels and romance novels and books with no plots and books with titles that sounded more profound (at the time) than *The Darkness* or *The Dead*. We stretched our reading and, for that, stretched our eventual writing with it. You'll find it everywhere in the new horror releases these days: more than a mash-up, modern horror has *reach*. Diversity helps that, of course. Diversity in writers, diversity in readers, diversity in language, cover art, titles, pen names, real names, places of birth, countries of birth, countries we call home, states of mind we call home, too. And while none of this is to suggest the best horror stories of any era were so bland as to be singularly horror and nothing besides, we're currently stretching things more than they've ever been before.

Let's stretch that photo (the one that does not exist). You take one side, I'll take the other, and we'll pull. And the twelve of us pictured will actually stretch, becoming elongated things with elongated faces, our expressions no longer determinable, the purpose of our gathering completely impossible to guess at. New monsters, we say. Even us, even as we write them, even as we read them, too. And there's John Taff, still eyeing the camera, still in control, still saying (without speaking), *I knew this was a good idea.* Because John has not only experienced previous moments in horror, but he read the books that acted as snapshots of those eras, too. Kirby McCauley's *Dark Forces* comes to mind. So does Paul Sammon's *Splatterpunks.* And John, aware as anybody that horror is in motion, that horror breathes (horror is one of the only genres that can flourish when it doesn't breathe, too), John said, *Somebody get a camera.*

Say cheese.

I can't speak for everybody else in this book, but I've never been one to zero in on the "marketplace." Before having anything published (but after signing with my agent) I received an email detailing current trends in the publishing world. It scared me silly, the idea of actually following these trends, strategizing in any way according to them. It wasn't that I frowned upon someone who would, it's just that it seemed to be the opposite of what I was feeling: an unchecked enthusiasm for all things unsettling, all things that go bump in the (day or) night. I wasn't looking to tap into any modern taste, I just wanted to freak somebody out. I wanted to touch the same darkness our predecessors touched, and I hoped it was still there. But this hope was foolish, no? For isn't it up to us, our era, to *create* that darkness? I suspect my peers in this book feel the same. It's the kind of thing you can feel in a person's writing. And what would you rather be presented with? A skilled storyteller with the passion of a stone, or a person who can't stop themselves from telling you their story, what happened, all "talent, be damned?

I think somewhere therein lies the moment horror is having. Did Poe feel the same? I suspect he did. His words are fire. I find similar smoke in the *Weird Tales* writers of the twenties, thirties, forties. And there's no doubt Beaumont, Serling, Bradbury, Nolan, Matheson rode their own electricity all the way to the page. Can you feel Shirley Jackson's urgency in her stories? I can. You can, too. We talk often about the fear of the unknown, how it will forever rank First in Fear, but let's take one step *into* this concept: rather than leaving the unknown to the confines of the story itself, let's wonder as to the unknown of the people who are writing it. The best way to really scare somebody is to surprise them, to come suddenly from the shadows you, yes you, created. The worst thing an era can do is ape the one before it. Where's the unknown in that?

Readers, meet Gemma Files. Stephen Graham Jones. Usman Malik. Chesya Burke. Livia Llewellyn. John Langan. Alma Katsu. Ramsey Campbell. Caroline Kepnes. Priya Sharma. John Taff. Me. Some of you have no doubt read many if not all of the names found within. Some of you, if not all, are in tune with the moment horror is having. But for those of you who are not, who are coming to the genre today, by way of *Dark Stars* . . . welcome. My biggest hope is you don't entirely recognize the style, the storytelling, the spirit within. Any of these stories could be a movie. Any of them could be told across a campfire, bottle in hand. But all have been written down.

Because horror is having a moment and we all feel compelled to mark it.

Now, let's stretch Time, just enough so we reach the days immediately following the pandemic and the current state of things. Let's stretch Time so that the twelve of us featured here find ourselves at a convention. We're all in the lobby of the hotel in a fine city (any city will do right now, and usually does) and we're talking horror. Maybe we're offering opinions on one another's stories or (more likely) we're ecstatically discussing how wonderful it is to be at a convention again, face-to-face, attending panels, buying books, surrounded by like-minded people after spending a good deal of time with ourselves. And when the talk turns to how each of us managed to endure our own private lockdowns, the conversation will invariably touch upon the very book you hold.

How did the genre flourish in such times? Because there was no stopping it. Where did we, the readers and writers, find solace at such a troubling moment in history?

Why, through books, of course.

And through seeing our names in print and sharing a table of contents with one another, some of the brightest voices in a genre that's well and alive. And at that convention, I hope someone approaches us with a camera. And I hope they say, *Hey, before you dozen go your own ways, while I got you all together, let me take a quick picture.*

And we all line up. Alma maybe somewhere near the middle and the rest of us fanning out from there. John Taff smiling at the camera.

And just before he hits the button, our cameraman says,
Say cheese.
Then: *Wait, you people write horror.*
Scream it instead.

Josh Malerman
Michigan 2021

INTRODUCTION

I had the idea for this anthology a few years ago, when Josh and I were brainstorming projects we could work on together. Because, I mean, who wouldn't try to pin Josh Malerman down with projects to work with him on? I'm not crazy, you know. Working with Josh is like grasping the live end of an electrical cord, with all the ensuing energy and none of the imminent death.

The idea was to come up with something that could follow on what *Dark Forces,* that seminal eighties horror anthology edited by Kirby McCauley, had done. Namely, bring horror to a wider audience.

That sounds ridiculous, right? Horror needs a wider audience with people like King and Straub and Rice and Barker? With the popularity of television and movie properties such as *Bird Box* (Josh!), *Us, The Haunting of Hill House* (or *Bly Manor*), *Hereditary, Midsommar,* and *Lovecraft Country?*

Okay, how about bring a wider *spectrum* of horror to the audience?

Ahh, there, *ding-ding-ding.*

Dark Forces succeeded in showing that horror was much more than a dark-alley genre. It wasn't just the lowbrow backwater many literati (and many of my college English professors) proclaimed it to be. In classes, I was often told that, according to Henry James, my taste for the works of Edgar Allan Poe was "the mark of a decidedly primitive stage of reflection."

In all deference to James, suck it.

Dark Forces didn't so much *prove* that horror could be soaring and literary as *remind*. Poe, yes, but Mary Wollstonecraft Shelley, Bram Stoker, Wilkie Collins, H. P. Lovecraft, yes, even Henry James all proved that well before *Dark Forces* was published.

But McCauley's *Dark Forces* reminded readers that this quality was a fundamental bedrock of horror. It featured writers like Stephen King, sure, but also Joyce Carol Oates and Isaac Bashevis Singer and Ray Bradbury.

So, I didn't feel the need to readdress that. Horror can be literary. Check!

What I wanted to show—okay, really *remind* readers of—was horror's vast *range*, the huge canvas that it can paint upon. The numerous, diverse voices that are writing horror, reshaping it, making it their own. Range is important to me as a writer, and I wanted to flaunt the range of this genre to readers.

Yes, horror can be literary. That's important. But what's even more important, especially now, is that we acknowledge just how *expansive* horror is. That horror can push more boundaries than just about any other genre and in ways other genres simply don't . . . or can't. That horror can stretch anywhere from the quiet, literary side all the way to bloody guignols, and all points between.

Within these covers are stories that run the gamut from traditional to modern, from dark fantasy to neo-noir, from explorations of traditional horror tropes to unknown, possibly unknowable threats. It's all here because it's all out there now in horror. I've said many times that we appear to be in a kind of Golden Age of Horror. We've gone from a time, say sixty or seventy years ago, where there were just a few successful authors out there writing horror—say Shirley Jackson or Richard Matheson or Ira Levin or William Peter Blatty or Robert Bloch— to a positive fiesta of horror authors too numerous to name, yet too good to ignore.

That's what I wanted with *Dark Stars,* and that's what I hope I've been able to bring to you. Some already have it, but every one of the authors in this book deserves the attention of and recognition from readers.

I've taken nearly six hundred words to sum up, but the idea of *Dark Stars* is simple. And it's this: expand your horizons, not just about what horror *can be,* but what horror *is.*

John F.D. Taff
Southern Illinois
March 2021

THE ATTENTIONIST
BY CAROLINE KEPNES

The first time he calls, I'm not there. I'm not home to answer. I'm down at the beach. It's 1993 when alone means *alone*. The beach by our house is small and stupid if you ask my sister. It's just a pond and it's just me. I don't know that he's calling. I don't know that someone out there is thinking of me, trying to find me.

That is all I want, to be wanted, pursued, and I'm getting what I want and I'm not there to know it.

Reg is home. She doesn't come to the beach because she doesn't like to be away from the phone. Once I heard my dad tell my mom that Reg has *the soul of a beauty and the body of a worker*. My mom told him he was terrible, but she also laughed. Reg is hopeful, hungry. Her eyebrows grow so fast that she has to pluck them every day and she picks up on the first ring because that's who she is. The ringing phone is Reg's favorite sound in the world and the irony is that to answer the call is to silence those bells. It's a big day for Reg. The last night of the county fair and she wants to go but not just with me, with boys. The phone is a promise. A beacon of hope. Boys, knock on wood, if she's lucky.

"Hello?"

That's how she always answers. Her voice lifts as if the telephone is such a mystery. The caller is no dummy. He hears the longing in her voice. He probably knows how she is. *The soul of a beauty and the body of a worker*. He probably senses that she fantasizes about making out with a guy on the Ferris wheel, any guy, please, someone.

"Hello," he says. "Is Maeve there?"

You'd think Reg would be upset that he wants me, not her, but we're sisters. In her head we're a monolith. What's good for me is good for her. So she's cutesy and perky, treating every word like a barren cupcake with so much potential.

"Well . . . Actually . . ." See how she spreads out the words? Frosting on her cupcake. Creamy, or maybe sloppy. "Miss Maeve isn't around right now . . ." And see that? See how she calls me *Miss Maeve* as if that's a thing she calls me? It isn't. He has Reg all figured out by now. Maybe he can see her through our bay window in the front of the house. Maybe he can't. But he wouldn't be surprised to know that she's wearing these cutoffs that shrunk in the dryer. They're tight. They cut off her circulation and leave red marks on her belly, but she wears them so that if some man called and asked what she was wearing she could be like, *tiny cutoffs and a tube top.* She's not a liar, my sister, and she wouldn't say she was wearing the shorts if she wasn't and all summer she's been hopeful—*What if we met brothers? What if a new cute guy moved into the house across the street*—and all summer I've been real—*We don't know any brothers. That house is condemned.*

I'm embarrassed for her. Younger but older than me, the voice of reason. Impossible to imagine her on this planet before I came into the picture. But there she was and here she is, the happiest she's been in weeks as the lights dim in the theater of her mind and she twirls the phone cord and licks her teeth.

"Well," he says. "That's too bad. I was hoping to catch her."

She lies down on the sofa. Legs in the air, opening and closing. Bare feet. Can he feel her offering her body to him? God, she hopes so and she picks up a bottle of nail polish and shakes it. "Sorry to break your heart . . . Is there anything I can do to help?"

To this day, she cries when she gets to this part of the story, like it's her fault, the way things went down. She's ashamed of her own desire. Her fantasy. Her excitement about stealing him. She couldn't help it. He reminded her of Davey.

* * *

Real quick, let me tell you about Davey.

Three summers before the summer I'm talking about, Reg was the one working at the club and she liked a member too. A guy named, well, Davey.

She had good reason to think the feeling was mutual. They kissed at a party on a beach. There was a fire pit. She thought he kissed her because of the flames. *Everyone's beautiful by a fire.* Davey knew what she looked like in the daylight and he told her he'd call. But he never did. Then his family moved, I don't know where. I just know that Reg was different when the waiting gave way to this weird form of horrific acceptance.

It was about the rejection. It wasn't about him. He, too, looked best by the fire. He was good but not great, but being so foolish was hard on Reg. She thought she was stupid. For months she was annoying and tense. Her whole body looked different, like someone turned some screws and tightened every joint. She got skinnier and hairier. Not enough to be sent to some hospital for girls, because like she said, *I can't even do an eating disorder right.* All of her sentences were like that, framed to highlight her failure as a human.

All of this for him. Stupid Davey who was only cute if you waited until dark and lit a fire.

Anyway, it was a year and a half later, almost Christmas. Reg was helping Mom clean out all the places you forget need cleaning. She and my mom got these little pads you put under the legs of heavy furniture. They managed to move the dresser in the front hall.

And Reg saw something on the floor.

A tiny scrap of paper.

Reg, Davey called 508 . . .

Reg screamed so loud that she woke me up. I ran into the living room.

"What happened?"

"What *happened*?" Reg was always that way. A bull digging in. Repeating what you said to remind you that you asked for it, as if all of your words were just food in her mouth, repurposed and regurgitated. "Well what happened is that Mom destroyed my fucking life."

"Reg, calm down."

"For sixteen months I have hated myself and thought I'm stupid and ugly and insane and deluded and probably fit to be institutionalized."

"Reg, stop it."

"For sixteen months I have been sure that I oughta be locked up, throw away the key."

"Do you hear yourself? Where is this coming from?"

Reg cried now. Real messy sobbing. There were no words for a while, and it wasn't the kind of crying where you go and hug her. Mom looked at me—*Do you know what this is?*—and I lied to Mom and shook my head. *No.*

Reg blew her nose on her shirt. "Mom, how did you let this happen?"

"Let this happen . . ."

"This is from Davey."

"Dave . . ."

"*Davey.* Davey Lane. From two summers ago."

"Was he here? I don't remember a Davey."

That was mean; it's Mom's house and she knows her way around. She knew that none of us had ever had a boy over back then, same way as now.

"No . . . you don't get it."

Mom laughed. "Well, what else is new?"

"Mom, it's not funny. This message is from Davey Lane. You took this message and I liked him and he said he would call and until right now I thought he never *did* call and I have made myself crazy wondering why for almost two years and I can't believe you did this to me."

"Me? Well that's ridiculous, Regina."

"You ruined my life."

"Oh I did, did I?"

"If you had put this message in a safer place like maybe on my bed or on my desk, if I had seen it, I would have called him back and had my first boyfriend. I would be a whole different person by now. I would be confident, I might even have a boyfriend . . ."

"Most of these things don't last, Reg."

"Well, I guess I don't get to know if mine would have, do I?"

Mom made a visor with her hand in that way she does when you can see her actively regretting her decision to have kids, wondering what it would have been like if she'd had boys. "Reg, you don't have to be *this* dramatic. It's one damn boy and if you knew him so well, I'm sure you would have mentioned him at some point or bumped into him since."

"Impossible. He moved away."

"Well, then good. It wasn't meant to be."

"You ruined it. This is my *Mystic Pizza*. I am living in *Mystic Pizza,* but now it's too late. My Charlie thinks I hate him."

Even I knew that Reg went too far with that *Mystic Pizza* crapola and Mom wasn't into movies, especially movies like that, but she knew enough to know when one of us was going into what Dad called clunker mode. He always meant that to be funny and it was and it wasn't and my mouth hurt. My head hurt. The house was too quiet. Too full of women—not me though, I was just a girl—and Mom put on a Carol Brady tone. "Alright, Reg," she said, like she had all the power. "Let's get this floor cleaned up."

But Reg grunted. "Make her help you."

Her was me and Mom was blunt. "She's sick. You know that. Come on now."

It was true. I had strep.

Reg started crying again but these tears were different. Mom went to her. She squatted on the ground like someone in church about to pray. "Reg," she said. "All you can do is see this as good news. He called. So that's good."

"He's gone."

"But he called. So now you know that he liked you. Yes?"

"Yes, but."

"No but. That's all that matters. He liked you. Many boys will like you."

Reg rolled her body onto the sofa, almost into it. Mom stood up. "Regina, no."

But Reg wouldn't let us look at her. "It's too late. I'm too messed up in the head."

This time, when she started crying, Mom kicked the coffee table. "Oh, for fuck's sake, Regina. It's not my fault or his fault if you're this much of a mess over one boy you barely knew one summer several years ago."

"Two years. Not even two."

"Well so what? You shut yourself down? You mope and melt over one damn boy? A boy you barely knew? Let me tell you something about men, young lady. Men go after it, okay? Men try to get what they want, if they really, really want it. They don't call once. If he liked you, if he was worth your tears, one unreturned message wouldn't have deterred him. So enough, okay? Enough!"

Mom left the room and soon she left the house—*I'm going to the grocery store*—and I sat down in the big chair by the sofa so Reg would know I was there. The front hallway looked so weird with the giant dresser in the middle, like a brown beached whale bear. I said that to Reg, and she laughed and rolled over so she could see the dresser, too.

Her face looked different, like the car right after a wax job and you know it will only shine like that for a day or so. "Funny," she said.

"Are you okay?"

"Yeah," she said.

"Do you wish you never found the message?"

She was staring at the dresser so intently. Maybe that was for my benefit. Maybe she wanted me to think that she was evolving before my eyes. "Mom's wrong."

"What do you mean?"

"Davey did like me a lot. See, Mom likes jerks. Jocks like Dad. Guys who are pushy and won't take no for an answer. But Davey was sweet. He didn't write a poem for me or anything, we never got that far, but he was pure. His feelings for me were so strong that he couldn't call again, you know?"

She seemed so sure of herself and I was young. I believed every word. "Wow," I said. "Are you gonna call 411 and find his main house?" She looked at me like I wasn't making sense, so I tried to be clearer. "I mean his real house, where he lives during the school year and all that."

Reg laughed like I was younger than I was. She was always a little mean when she was happy. "His summer house is just as 'real' as his family's *winter* house," she said, and she didn't look at me. She was too busy hatching a plan, making things seem better than they were, squinting at the wall like a professor. "No," she said. "I can't call him. That's what makes it a tragedy. Only boys can call girls. Only boys can go after what they want. You call a boy, he knows that you want his attention and he can't help it. If he liked you before, he likes you a little less now that he knows that you like him."

"That's not fair."

"No," she said. "But that's the way it is. And there's more."

There was God in my sister. Knowledge. Light. "What?"

"When you know that a boy is obsessed with you . . ." See that? Now Summer Davey the poet was *obsessed* with her. "Well," she said. "Attention from boys is the best drug. You get his attention and suddenly, you don't need a lot of other stuff, you know? You don't really need him, only his attention."

She was on her feet now, headed toward the dresser. I offered to help, and she waved me off and then she wiped down the dusty floor until it was shining like a freshly waxed car. She was Hercules. She moved the dresser back to its spot on her own and she clapped her hands. Proud. I swear she was taller. Leaner. Even prettier.

She was like that for a while. My dad made jokes about this new *cocksure* Reg and my mom gave her extra money so she could get highlights in her hair, hoop earrings. No boys called the house, but this was the house that Davey had called. She was the one that got away and she never let us forget it.

Six months later, things changed. She stopped wearing earrings. She said one of the holes was infected and she didn't want to freshen up her highlights. She went back to being the Reg she is now, the Reg she was before. Gloomy. Screws all over her body, tighter than ever. You'd think that me and Mom and Dad would have been upset, but in some weird way it was a relief, like oh right, *this* is Reg. Housebound. Attached to the phone.

One day after school I asked her what was wrong.

"I miss him," she said.

"Davey?"

She nodded. "I think I'm dying . . ." All of Reg's favorite books were about pretty high school girls dying. All of her favorite movies were the movie versions of those books and that enraged her because the girl in the movie was prettier than the girl in the book, because when Reg read the books of course she became the dying pretty girl.

I asked her why she was dying and she answered without hesitation. "Male attention deficit disorder," she said.

"Wait," I said. "I have that."

"No, Maeve, you have ADD. Attention deficit disorder. That's different. Doctors have that figured out and you take your pills and you're fine. I have a deficiency of *male* attention. MADD is different . . ."

Now it had a nickname. MADD. "I never heard of that."

"Because it's a thing we're not allowed to talk about, even with Mom. You can only find out about it from a sister."

"How do girls without sisters find out?"

"They don't. That's why girls without sisters are so mean . . ." That was a dig at Gretchen, her best friend. Gretchen had three brothers and Gretchen could be mean. My mind was in overdrive. I was ten going on seven. The type of kid who would have gone back to believing in Santa in a heartbeat if presented with a shred of evidence. A plate of crumbs.

Reg started talking. She said the first time she had MADD was the summer she met Davey. She liked him but he didn't like her back. Finding the message helped, the proof that he *had* in fact liked her. But old attention wasn't new attention. Attention was milk. It was eggs. Better fresh than stale. Time was passing, wreaking havoc on her body. She was growing out bangs. Fighting MADD, a nasty disease. "See," she said. "Without male attention, your body stops producing certain life-or-death hormones. If no guy likes me or looks at me within the next ten days . . . I'm a goner. Bring on the casket."

There was nothing I could do, nothing Mom could do, nothing Dad could do. No doctor could help. Boys had all the power. But I didn't want her to die and I grabbed her precious cordless. She laughed. "No," she said. "Don't tell me to call Davey. You know I won't and also . . . Mom was right. He never liked me. Let's just forget about it . . ."

She was agreeing with Mom—MADD was a *disease*—and I wanted to help her, save her. Your teeth hurt and you go to the dentist, but you need attention and there's no such thing as an *attentionist*. "You can't just give up," I said.

"Alright," she said. "It's like this. As it turns out, Davey never liked me. Ever. He only called this house to get Gretchen's number. I was a fool to be so happy about finding his message because I actually thought he was out there pining for me and . . . I don't want to talk about it."

This was bad news and she was rolling over into the wall, into herself, but I was emboldened. Maybe I was the attentionist. "Okay," I said. "But that was a long time ago. Maybe you should call him anyway."

"He never liked me."

"But you're awesome. Maybe he likes you now."

"No," she said. "Remember when you found out Santa is fake? Well that's what this is. All that retroactive attention I thought I was getting . . . it turns out I never got it and I know I never will from him or any guy ever so just do me a favor and leave and let me die because there is no point. None. I am mad and I have MADD and that is all."

I left. I went to my room and marked the countdown to my sister's death on my wall calendar. Those days are still vivid in my mind. Mom and Dad and Reg acting like everything was normal. Reg bought hair clips that changed her life—*My bangs are off my face, hallelujah!*—and she didn't die. I knocked on her door on the eleventh day.

"What?"

I opened the door. "It's been over ten days."

"Huh?"

"You have MADD," I said. "You told me . . ."

She howled and laughed because I had actually *believed* her and how could I be so smart and stupid all at once? MADD wasn't real. I turned red because *yes it fucking was* and she shook her head at me. So young. So dumb. She called me *Kiddo* and that was a new one. I didn't like it. I didn't want to be *Kiddo* and I didn't like her either. I had given away something without meaning to and I didn't know what it was. She was different. Vicious. That's how I knew MADD was real. Slower than she'd said, but real. In her movies, the dying girls are just like this, prone to mood swings and viciousness.

She had to tell *Gretch* about this—they were back on good terms, friends again—so she went and got on her bike to ride to her house. On the way there, she hit sand. It wasn't a smart fall. It was dumb. Her head was banged up and she broke a leg in the bad way, and she was home for a solid month with a cast. But this was good, you see. For the first time ever, boys came to our house. As friends, yes, but they brought flowers, they ate all our chips and signed her leg. She got so much attention. None of them liked her like that. It was just a thing to do. They came together and they left together like she was a movie. And the boys. One of them took a big poop in our half bathroom and clogged the toilet. Boys with big lumps in their throats and legs that shook so hard you could see the coffee table tremble if you looked closely. They filled up our house with their smells. They had no attention spans, their eyes moved around so much it made you dizzy, but their presence was attention.

It's why Reg healed.

Their attention was consistent as the sun, lingering after they left, the stench in the bathroom, booted footprints on the front hall doormat. Reg had no permanent damage from the fall and the doctor said she was lucky, but I knew it was me. I saved her. Me, the attentionist behind the scenes. I drove her out of the house, onto her bike, and she was good for a while, back at school. But then her group of friends splintered into nasty little duos. No more groups of kids and so many family-sized bags of chips expiring on top of the fridge. And why do they call it family size when what they really mean is friends?

Honestly, I'm sure of it. Not one boy in our house ever since.

So, do you get it? Do you get why Reg *needs* for this guy on the phone to be the start of a new chapter in our lives (her life)? She is coy: "Who should I say his calling?"

And he laughs but she talks over him. "Wait," she says. "Don't tell me."

"You're the boss."

"I know who you are."

"Oh you do, do you?"

"Yep."

"Okay. Then tell me who I am."

"You're Tony. Tony from the club."

"I'm Tony and you are."

"It's Reg," she says. And that is something that has never shifted. Reg loves her name, the full version, *Regina like the pizza place,* and the short version, *probably the only "Reg" you know.*

"Well, hello, Reg."

"Well, hello, Tony."

I know we just got back in it but real quick, let me tell you about Tony.

Tony is my "crush." He's a member of King's Landing, you know, where Reg worked for two summers and never got a boyfriend out of it. Dad laughs when he overhears us talk about the boy members of the club. *You sound like soldiers talking about war.* That's what we are, according to Reg, soldiers of love!

I work in the snack bar. Five days a week. Tony plays tennis at the club. Also five days a week. He drinks Arnold Palmers that he puts on his family's tab and Tony only lives here in the summer. He has blond hair and a good serve and he could be a hot mean guy in the movies that we both actually love—*The Karate Kid* and *One Crazy Summer*—and that's where me and Regina fall in line together.

We know you're supposed to love Ralph Macchio and John Cusack. But we love the bad guy. The spoiled preppy in his Corvette. The ruthless bad boyfriend with all his boys blindly following him to the dark side.

Mom says we're demented. *You can't change people, especially men.*

But Reg and I have a secret. We don't want to change them. We like their evil.

We're not kind and popular like Elisabeth Shue and we're not cool girl guitarists like pure Demi Moore and we freaking know that, you know? We don't want the underdog. We just don't have it in us. We want that preppy jerk with the money. When Dad sees us swoon at a blond bully, when he overhears me talking about Tony, how he said his Arnold Palmer was *especially sweet* today and how that means that *I* am especially sweet, Dad shakes his head at Mom, at us—*Send these clunkers back to the shop!*—and that's only fuel for the fire. Reg and I are equals this summer for the first time. I'm at the club, on the ground, and she's at home—summer school means she can't work—and she's the veteran to my soldier. I go to battle, into theater, and I return in my uniform. Smoldering. Spent. And then we analyze. We strategize.

"Well he did it," I told her, one random day.

"He asked you out?"

"He requested that *I* make his Arnold Palmer No Ice."

All rich boys and all rich men, they all want Arnold Palmers (no ice) and Reg crossed her arms. "You specifically?"

"I know it's not a big deal but it's the way he said it. His voice. I want a CD of him just saying *Hey Maeve, Arnold Palmer no ice.* That alone would be enough."

Reg was the senior officer and she didn't like that. "Let me pluck your eyebrows," she said. "You look like an animal."

And then a few days later, she must have done a good job with my eyebrows because Tony was bold. He hopped the counter and winked. *I won't tell if you won't tell.* And then he spiked his friend's drink with a nip of vodka. *Vodka.* It was the closest we'd ever been, physically, and it had to mean something.

Same way it had to mean something a few days later when he said *Have a good weekend, Mary.* He called me Mary so that I could correct him—*Actually it's Maeve*—but of course I blew it, blurted a lame *You, too* and Reg said we're not hot enough to play hard to get and I told her I freaking know that.

It's hard to be losing the war. To keep fighting. But we pull through. Just last week, Tony called me Maeve and his voice was buttery, warmer now, as if there was heat beneath the butter. Reg said this was good and Dad said we were starting to spook him. "Scarier than *Poltergeist*," he said. "Clunkers in heat. Didn't your mother teach you anything? You can't control things. Especially these . . . never mind."

Never mind indeed and what does he know? Nothing.

Tuesdays are my Mondays and Reg is always up first, in the kitchen frying eggs. I am slow to rise, I hate the start of a new week, but last Tuesday, she said this was her purpose in this summer life, to *egg* me on, and we laughed so hard—war can be fun—and then she was serious. "I feel it my bones," she said, same way she did every Tuesday all summer. "This is it, Maeve. This is the week Tony asks you out. Trust me. I know it."

So now you get it.

Reg wants this for me. For us. She is putting on lipstick as if Tony can see her. And she is focusing so hard that she forgets he's there and he coughs.

"Hello? Reg, are you there?"

"Sorry, Tony." She says his name to make it official. God how she has waited for this moment.

"That's okay. So yeah. I'm not up to much today. I was just trying to get ahold of Maeve . . ."

My sister goes weak at the knees because of that language. *Get ahold of Maeve.* "Sorry, Tony, but you can't get ahold of her here. She's at the beach by our house."

"I didn't know she lives by the beach."

"Well, not the beach-beach, but the pond."

"Which pond?"

"Jacque's Pond. Do you know Sonny Boy's Lane? It's by Osef's Path . . ."

It's a side note but it has to be said. The names of the roads in our neighborhood are ridiculous. Pond names. All possessive, as if at some point a hundred years ago, Sonny was out there with a stick screaming *This is My Lane* and Osef was a few feet down the way screaming back, *This is My Path.* Ocean people are much better at naming roads. Tony's an ocean person. His street is named for nature—*Shore Road, By the Bay Drive*—and you get it, don't you? This is a big deal for Reg. Selling the lake to an ocean boy. So, of course when he asks her to slow down so he can take notes, she obliges.

"Thanks," he says. "I had no idea there were ponds around here."

Regina gulps. That was so rich boy of him. Saying *lake* not pond. She craves that mean fire but it burns. "Cool," she says. "Hey, what are you doing right now?"

"Um . . . I believe I'm talking to you, Reg."

Oh, to hear the truth and know for sure that you are not delusional. What is happening in her head is happening in the world. She is talking to a boy. A boy who likes me (and down the line, maybe her!). "I'm so stupid," she says. "But yeah. Maeve is down at the lake so you should surprise her."

"Oh really?"

"She's all alone down there, too. It's a pretty hip spot."

The lake is not "hip" but her heart is so loud in her chest, working overtime for her for me. "I don't know," he says. "Are you sure she'd be into that?"

"Oh God yes and it's really so cool. I mean not cool like . . . well it's just deserted so you can do your own thing and nobody bugs you."

"Well," he says. "I guess I better get ready."

"Yeah," Reg says, and she is going for it now. Applying mascara. "You should get ready because she won't be there forever. It is the last night of the fair and all . . ."

Tony laughs and thanks Regina for the help and she hangs up the phone and does jumping jacks. She wants to look and feel her best when our new life begins. She sees it all so clearly: My Tony shows up at the pond. He surprises me. We swim in the freshwater together. We make out on the dock. We swim back to shore. We slide into his Beamer in our damp suits and we make out again before we start the quick drive to my house where Regina just *happens* to be waiting in the bay window. She's wearing her cutest cutoffs and her most flattering little T-shirt. It *is* the last night of the fair—she bats her eyelashes, *oh right, totally forgot*—and Tony has a friend—all rich boys do—and later that night, the four of us strut through the white shell walkway to the 1993 Budleigh County Fair. We're on the first double date of our life (lives?) and we both get fingered by rich boys on the Ferris wheel and our dad was wrong.

We're not clunkers, not anymore.

While my sister is picking out which cutoffs are *just right,* I'm in the lake alone, treading water, swallowing more than I mean to.

I still don't know that Tony called. I have no way of knowing. I'm not psychic. I'm breathing heavily the way I do, not getting anywhere, going in messy circles around the dock like some half-assed lazy shark. I climb the ladder onto the dock and the wood is cold. Ponds are moody. There's a little clique of clouds that won't leave the sun alone—I should have gotten the nerve to climb up here earlier—and I lie on my back, the way you do for the pediatrician, with my arms flat, as if I am bracing myself for a cold hand.

This is the most alone you can be in the world, and it's also the loneliest after a few minutes, when nobody whistles or jumps into the water. But I don't let it get to me. I always stay up here until I'm dry. I'm strong that way. I'm the one with discipline.

I close my eyes and go into my fantasy world.

It's a do-over, of course. It starts in early July. The first day at work, the first time I make an Arnold Palmer for Tony. In my fantasy I'm better at flirting. I do what Reg says you have to do and let him know my door is open.

And because I made myself vulnerable, everything in my life is more exciting. Adrenaline pumps thorough my body and I come to this beach and swim out to this dock and I attract better things. A boy is visiting his grandparents—step-grandparents, to explain why I've never seen him, why this is all new to him—and he sees me on this dock and I'm strong. He can practically smell my adrenaline. I call him Kevin in my head, and he changes into his swim trunks and can't get into the water fast enough, can't get to me fast enough. In my fantasy, I'm a relaxed person, so I'm sound asleep on the dock—browner than I am in real life, legs a writer could describe as *sinewy*—and then I feel-hear something.

Drip. Drip.

I yawn and blink and yelp when I see him. Standing on my dock. He is wet. Dripping. He's nowhere near as cute as Tony, of course he has wrong red hair and you just know he's nice, as kind as Ralph Macchio. I could never love him. But I let him touch me. I let him try and make me love him and I love this process. The stakes are low. I am in shop class, learning how to maneuver my way around a real live boy. Learning the physical things in a safe way. This is how it feels when someone wants you more than you want them. This is how it feels to be the loved one. And this is how MADD works. I use the attention I get from Kevin to make Tony want me even more.

It doesn't make me a monster. It makes me someone who knows what she wants.

At the tennis club, I'm thinking about nothing but *KevinKevinKevin* and boys know this. They feel you the most when you stop caring about them, when you don't yearn. So that's why Tony can't stop thinking about me. *MaeveMaeveMaeve.*

And Kevin is a guy who is willing to get his heart broken, so when I do it, when I tell him that I can't see him anymore, he doesn't implode in a bad way. He writes songs about me and years from now, he becomes a famous rock star and you know what? He's better off because of that summer that I broke his heart. My attention calcified his bones. Sharpened everything in him so thank God for me, after all.

Me.

And about Tony . . .

Well, Tony and I fall madly in love. It's hard to picture if I think too hard but there are some things I see clearly, on mute. In montage form.

Tony beside me, a hand clamped over my mouth because I'm too loud and happy about his other hand. The thing Reg swears feels good, as if she knows for sure.

I see us in a Guns N' Roses video. I am leaving a bar—it's a fantasy, we go to bars—and I am livid. Hurt. He was flirting with someone else and he chases me down in the rain. *In the cold November rain.* She meant nothing and I am everything and he can't live without me, he *won't* live without me and he is a terrible person and before you know it, I'm kissing him, cupping his perfect face in my hands.

You are my terrible person.

Tony's lips are on mine, his hands are hungrier than Kevin's, sturdy, not so nervous, larger than I imagined, bigger than *Kevin's*—remember him?—and that's the best part of the fantasy, the fact that I get to break Kevin's heart, that I feel *awful* about knowing that I will hurt him. I am a good person. Kevin was training wheels to prepare me for the real thing and that's not my fault. That's the fault of this big mean beautiful clunker of a world and then I hear it in real life.

Drip, drip. Drip.

That's the hook of that scary story someone tells you at a slumber party when you're a kid, when the dark is the scariest thing in the world. But I'm not a kid. I have a job. I'm fourteen years old and I'm on a boring dock on a boring lake in my boring neighborhood and the sun is out and what is that sound?

Drip, drip, drip.

Before I open my eyes to investigate, the dripping stops. Cut off by the roar of an engine, an engine with a bad esophagus. A painful exhausting whinny that sets every square inch of my dry skin on fire. What was that? Who was that? But I'm too late. All I see is the back half of a blue loud pick-me-up truck going, going, gone.

And the drip? Well it was me. I got my period.

I climb into the water and swim to shore and my body is all revved up and my teeth chatter as if it's cold—it isn't—and my head hurts and my hands tremble and I have to laugh. I'm not a soldier of love, of anything. I scare so easily? I was the drip, and the truck was just some landscaper, no doubt, or some old man who stopped by the lake to pick something out of his teeth. He probably didn't even see me. I'm ridiculous and chubby—too many Arnold Palmers, as if drinking what Tony drinks was gonna get him to like me—and I am traumatized for no reason. I don't want to listen to Reg tease me about my period—*You're such a dork, Maeve, seriously*—so I sit on the picnic table like a sea monster. A lake monster.

This is almost officially the summer that nothing happened and no one is here and I like my bathing suit enough, so I take my T-shirt and shove it in there to catch the blood and I walk up the cruddy path, onto the street, and on the way home, I start a whole new fantasy for the fall. In this one, I get a job in a bookstore and I don't have to wear ugly stiff blue shorts at the bookstore. I wear blue jeans that *love me, they get down on their knees and hug me.* Tony comes back for Thanksgiving and he barely recognizes me because I'm talking to *another* boy, the autumnal version of Kevin, a homeschooled boy whose parents just died—which will make it all the more terrible when he falls deeply in love with me, when I have to break his heart and leave him, just like his parents, if you think about it . . . In this fantasy, Kevin commits suicide—as it turns out, there is no getting over a girl like me—and I am bawling at his funeral—the guilt—and autumnal Tony is caressing me, wanting me to stop—*It's okay, Maeve. He loved you. It's not your fault*—and I'm walking faster now and you know what?

I am cool. I adapt. Just as plucky as a sick girl in one of Reg's dumb movies.

It's okay that Kevin dies in my fantasy. It's okay that Reg and I failed to meet boys. Nothing good happened. But nothing bad happened either. The dark and the light need each other, and my house looks different to me now, small as ever but now it seems like it settled on this little hill to fool people into thinking it's bigger than it is.

Reg in the bay window. All dressed up with no place to go and flipping the pages of *YM*. Clutching the cordless phone, pretending to be on with a friend—I can tell when she's lying—and acorns are raining on our driveway—we have too many trees—and suddenly I'm not so happy. I hate the wad of T-shirt turning red in my bathing suit. I blame Reg for it. I hate my fantasies and I hate the both of us for being two sides of the same worthless coin. *Clunkers.* She's too needy—can't even sit on a couch and just *be*—and I'm too good at meeting all my needs in my head. She goes to the mall, to the real beach and looks for it at least, but me? I spent the whole freaking summer alone in the pond and what a lie.

I'm not independent. I was never alone.

I was passive, waiting for Imaginary Kevin to see me, flashing a vacancy sign every time I saw Tony so that he would know he can have me if he wants. How I threw myself at these boys with my routine, rolling out the red carpet—no, it's a doormat—and no boy even noticed me, did he?

I carry on up the driveway, a wounded warrior, and Reg spots me finally and she leaps off the sofa and tosses the *YM* as well as the phone and why? Why is she mad at *me*? She had two years on

this planet in this house when it was all hers. Maybe that's why
we can never be friends. She was born before me, she is a loner
at heart, and maybe her "male attention deficit disorder" isn't so
much about boys as it as about me. The baby who challenged her
for Mom and Dad's affection, for their attention. Some people are
meant to be a big sister and some people are not. Reg is not. She
yanks the door open and blasts into my face and she is louder
than loud, always.

"What the hell, Maeve? Where is he?"

"He who?"

"Don't be a dick. How did you manage to screw this up and
what is that bulge . . . Oh my god you little freaking pig. Look at
you! Of course you screwed this up! Did he see you like this?"

I follow her into the house and run into the bathroom because
I am a pig but I am not a pig and she is out there ranting and it
feels good to clean myself up. I splash cold water on my face. I am
younger but older. Calmer. And I walk into the living room like it's
half mine, which it is, okay a quarter, but mainly I walk in there
like someone who figured it all out. I know that we are clunkers. I
know if we were entrees at Friendly's you wouldn't put us back in
the oven, you would just toss us and start from scratch.

"Alright," I say. "What seems to be the problem?"

"Well obviously the fact that he's not here."

"He who?"

She groans. "'He who'? Are you serious right now? Tony as in
your Tony. Duh! 'He who?' I mean you say that like you know all
kinds of Tonys. Your Tony, *obviously*."

Only in this house is he *my* Tony and I blush. "From the tennis
club."

My sister is a crazy person—why would Tony be here?—and she
clenches her fists and growls and she flops on the couch and she
goes into the sofa the way she did the day she found the message
about Davey.

"Reg," I say. "I'm sorry. But I don't get it. Why would you think
Tony would show up at the pond?"

She waves off a fly that got in because the screen door takes a long time to close, because flies like it in this house. We're bad about taking the trash out, so now it's gonna be me and Reg and this fly. The house is odd in this moment, the way it was that one time that Mom got a cleaning lady. Something is different here and yet nothing is different. Reg is crying and Dad is away on business and Mom is off helping her friend May paint her new apartment—Fake Aunt May: the original clunker—and the fly clips me—I smell like blood—and Reg stops crying. Finally. She rolls over.

"Sorry," she says. "I just . . . I really thought this was it."

"I know," I say. "But why did you think Tony was coming over?"

"Because he called."

I picture him at the front desk of the club, making up a story to get my phone number, and I tuck my hair behind my ear like a girl in a bikini. "What do you mean he called?"

"Just what I said. I told him you were at the pond, I gave him directions and he said he was gonna surprise you." The fly buzzes her nose and she doesn't swat. "But I guess *that* didn't happen." My sister is not a person. She is a praying mantis. All folded up. Defensive. "Whatever," she says. "He probably flaked or found something else to do."

"I can't believe he called."

"Well, he did. And I told him you were at the beach and he said he was gonna go there and surprise you and I figured . . . well, it's the last night of the fair. Whatever."

"I didn't even think he knew my name."

"Well, he does," she says, and my mind races back to the beach. *Drip drip drip.* The blue pick-me-up truck. But no. Right?

"Wait, Reg, I still . . . Did he really call? Cuz I barely know him."

"You make it sound like you flirt all day."

"Well I mean . . . I know I flirt with him but . . ." I don't know how to tell her what I know. That there is no light without dark. That I never met Kevin and because there is no Kevin there can be no Tony. "Reg, are you sure it was him?"

"Am I sure it was him? He said it was him! What kind of a stupid question is that?"

"I just can't believe he called."

"Well he did. And you're right about his voice. Wow. Super sexy."

She's sad—she got dressed up for the fair, the last night of the fair—and she's mad—she hates that I'm still soaking it in. Happy and not manic. She hates that it's enough for me to sit with the knowledge that he called.

Tony called. He really did.

And she should know that part of being a clunker means that accepting the good news is wonderful but awkward at first, like squeezing into jeans—blue jeans, like the ones in my fantasy, my fantasy that might just come true—and I know how to be ignored. But the idea of Tony calling, the upturning of all the logic that only just got cemented in my head, it's still wet and now I'm stirring it before it's too late.

Tony called. He really did.

"Where did you put it?"

"Where did you put what?"

"His number."

She swallows. "His phone number?"

She doesn't have to say it. I know that she forgot to get his number. She bites her tongue and she's so mad at herself that I can't be mad at her and I tell her it's okay and I try to touch her elbow but she pulls away. The tears she cried before, those were tears she was in charge of, tears she willed, but the tears in her eyes right now are something different entirely. They have their own agent and she can't control them. "It's ironic," she says. "If you were more like me, you would have been home when he called, and if I was more like you, I would have been down at the lake and I would have gotten to walk home and see you on the phone with him. That would have been nice, sis."

It's no good when she calls me "sis." It's rare. I see the wheels turning. She's blaming herself, on her feet stretching, pulling her body out of her tight shorts, pausing at the Dresser of Dave's Lost

Message, she's doing that for my benefit—*It never works out for the clunkers*—and dragging her feet. The fly is pumped up, as if he senses the comparison—his life is sweet, he has a house and we are just sulking, doomed—and I grab a flyswatter—I have to do something—and I take a shot and miss. My armpit hurts. I tried too hard and that's what I do isn't it? I ruined her fantasy and now she's all dressed up with no place to go and I love my sister. I wish she had a place to go right now and I chase the fly and miss, as I apologize for ruining everything, for not being here to answer the phone, for ruining our one shot at summer fun. (If I called it love, she would *kill* me.) I will never get the fly—he's so happy, he's free—and I toss the flyswatter.

I sit on the couch by the bay window and squeeze the pond water out of my hair onto the cushion. Mom would kill me if she could see me right now and it's only five. The night ahead is long and empty and I look around our house. Mom always said it's a friendly house because there are three ways in—the bulkhead basement door, the front door, the back door—and twenty-seven large windows. Dad says it's a clunker, an energy sucker. It doesn't like to get warm in the winter and it hogs all the heat in the summer but Reg and I side with Mom. The problem is that all the ways to enter serve to remind you of the reality that no one wants to pop over.

Maeve sinks into Dad's chair. "You could call 411."

"You know it won't help. Rich people summer houses are never listed." But then I feel bad and I pick up the cordless as if I'm reconsidering.

It's too little too late and she scoffs. "Nah, the fair is stupid anyway." She is waving the white flag but then she wraps her hand around her wrist, tiny and tan. "Then again . . . if you really wanted to find him . . ." This is about her now. "You could always call the club."

I balk because she bit my head off when I made the same suggestion to her and she says this is different. "Tony likes you, Maeve. He called. I know this."

I shrug. "I don't feel it in my bones."

No, she's on a tear—that was a mean dig on my part—and she says that I think she's a dummy and a liar and I say no and I wish there were three of us instead of two and she grabs her precious cordless phone out of my hand but the phone is dead. She growls and pounds her feet into the kitchen and it's one of those moments in life. As she reaches for the landline phone on the wall, the one with the big fat fun oversized digits, it rings. She looks at me and I look at her and now I'm on my feet. Is it him? Is it him?

I want to explain the deal with the phones in our house.

We have three of them. Reg's cordless is always dying—she's irresponsible, always holding the phone, wanting someone to call, which means that the phone is perpetually dying—and then there's the main phone in the kitchen, and, of course, the rotary phone in my parents' bedroom.

All summer, I have begged for a phone of my own, but my parents said no because look at Reg. She wanted a phone so badly but on the rare occasion that she talks on the phone to Gretchen—always and only Gretchen, and less every week—Reg can't use *her* phone because it's always dead. It's a dumb argument. I am not Reg. I wouldn't let my phone die every day. I wouldn't perpetually squeeze it to death.

But the point of the story is the phone wars got ugly. Mom and Dad lock their bedroom door when they go out because otherwise Reg will loaf on their bed and watch *The Karate Kid* and leave the tape in the VCR which annoys Dad and eat a whole bag of chips, which annoys Mom. She is that type of teenager, she just has to be near a phone at all times, you know?

And on this day, we are home alone, so Mom and Dad's bedroom is locked. We only have access to the one phone, the kitchen phone, which is ringing.

*   *   *

I am never allowed to answer the phone because that's Reg's favorite thing to do, to say hello, to experience that nanosecond of suspense and endless possibility when the caller could be anyone, the mean blond bad guy from *The Karate Kid* or Damien Andresen who graduated from our school four years ago and was both too hot and too old for both of us.

I don't really get it. I don't like to answer the phone. The phone rings again and Reg shakes her head—not yet—and the phone is white and modern. Oversized "fun" digits on squares. Reg fought for this phone because she thought it was cool. Mom caved and bought it over Memorial Day weekend before summer started, but the phone doesn't have magic powers.

Is he in there?

Is he really in there?

The whole pond is in my stomach, in my gullet, churning, and Regina grabs a pillow and squeezes it. "Okay now."

I obey. "Hello."

"Hi, is Maeve there?"

"This is her . . ." Holy shit. Holy shit. And holy shit because he sounds different on the phone. But so do I, I bet. I lick my lips. "Tony? Is that you?"

Reg does a one-handed cartwheel while maintaining her hold on the pillow—how?—and he laughs at my question and I sit in a chair because maybe then I won't sound so nervous. He's quiet for a minute, and I don't know his phone voice. I only hear him say *large Arnold Palmer extra ice.* My sister looks at me—*What's he saying?*—and I nod a lot—*yes it's him, hold your horses*—and he sighs.

"Oh Maeve," he says, and the blood outside of my body turns hard and cold. It's not Tony. Tony is younger. Dumber. Simpler. "Your sister is pretty stupid."

My face is red. That was vicious. The opposite of a phone call. "Sorry."

"You will be sorry, Maeve. See, I called to talk to you, not her."

She is now dancing with the pillow, the pillow that is a dance partner, a man, dipping her. I cross my legs and block my eyes. I can't look at her. I whisper. "Who is this?"

He laughs and he's not Tony and my leg is shaking. His voice is cold and he says he saw Reg do a cartwheel and I can't scream for help—what if he's watching?—and are the doors in our house locked? How did that fly get in? The bay window has curtains but they're tied back—Reg hates them closed because what do we have to hide?—and have I ever seen her this happy? She's now the woman in the *Here I Go Again* video, she's dancing on top of a car and he is laughing. "You can thank her for me," he says. "But I don't want her. I want your little poulkies."

"I don't know what you mean."

"Yes, you do, Maeve. Dirty piggy. I saw you on that beach. Bloody pig . . ."

The pick-me-up truck was him. The pick-me-up truck was him. I stutter and gulp and Reg is dancing and why do I have to be me? Why can't I be her?

"I didn't know I'd get to see where you *live,* little piggy."

That is what he calls me: *little piggy.* This is the first man who ever wanted me so bad that he had to do something about it, he had to pick up the phone and call me and this is what I am to him. A pig. But who is he? I go through every Arnold Palmer at the club but I only pay real attention to Tony and he is still calling me a pig and I am sitting here taking it and he clicks his tongue. I think. "Tell me something, little piggy. Did you wipe all that nasty blood off those poulkies?'

Regina transformed again. Now she is Janet Jackson. In *Control.*

I gulp. I can't kill him over the phone. What are *poulkies*? And I can't tell her the world is a bad place. I don't want to tell her goddammit because this is the day that Tony calls. This is the day our lives get better not worse and we need to cure our MADD and he will not ruin this day for her, for me. No. I lower my voice. "Who the fuck is this?"

He laughs again. That laugh. The anti-Tony. "This is the man who's gonna get those poulkies and eat them for lunch."

Reg is spent, in dreamland on the sofa, hugging her pillow and where are our parents? Where is our housefly? Why didn't we ever get a dog?

My skin curdles. Our housefly got out. A door opened. Was it him?

"Calm down," he says. "I'm not coming back tonight."

Thank God but fuck God because why do I sigh with relief and I can't trust this man, this monster? What is a *poulkie*? What? Reg leaps off the couch and grabs the cordless—she intends to charge it so that she can eavesdrop—and I know my sister and she will sit by that phone until it charges and I have to act fast. Smart. Now.

"Okay," I say. "Why did you drive away today? I wanted to see you."

"I'm not stupid."

"I know that."

"Well, little piggy, I was on my way, but you're bleeding too much."

The blood stops flowing in my body but that's absurd. No, it doesn't. It keeps going. He was here for a fact. He saw me. He knows. "Well I washed up. You could come back tonight."

"Nah," he says. "I don't want that fly to get back in. You girls get a good sleep tonight. Kiss those poulkies for me, piggy."

The lying starts as soon as he hangs up the phone, as soon as I hang up. I lock the side door and Reg runs in and wants to know everything and I am a good liar. I tell the truth of my fantasies, the truth I know so well, how Tony has been building up the nerve to call me all summer, how he's leaving to go back to Boston.

"Well wait," she says. "Are we going to the fair?"

I pull on the string, the string that lets the curtains close. "I wish. But he already left."

"God," she says. "He really likes you."

What are *poulkies*? "You think?"

"'You think'? No. I *know*. He waited to call until he was gone for the winter and that means that he's in this for the long haul. He wants to get to know you from a distance and that's the ultimate show of respect. It's kinda Victorian, even. He feels a genuine connection. He's going to keep calling all fall . . . Maeve, the boy is courting you! And that's the opposite of some summer boy who

uses you, you know? It is so much better this way. It's romantic. I
knew it when he called, now that I think of it."

It is so hard to—*poulkies*—speak, but I have to—*poulkies*—try.
"What do you mean? How did you know?"

"Well Tony . . . he was confident, you know? And not in that silly
way that boys get . . . he was someone who is sure of what he wants."

"But he told you he was coming to the beach."

"Yes," she says. "But this is better, Maeve. Trust me. I know."

It's absurd and she knows nothing about boys, no more than
me, and I hate my sister. She's supposed to be older. Wiser. She
hugs me and she goes to plan her fall wardrobe—*I bet he has
friends who will come down with him on long weekends!*—and I am
so full of envy and love. She gets to think I am loved. She gets to
believe that we are getting what we wanted.

He calls a lot, sometimes twice a day and I don't know his real
name—he won't say, obviously—but my whole family thinks he's
Tony because he says he's Tony.

When Dad answers, they chat about fishing or sports and then
Dad calls out my name in this singsong way, *Oh Maevey dear, it's
your boyfriend* . . . and oh if you could see my mom, just so happy
for me, *I knew one of you girls would meet someone nice working at
that club eventually.* And Reg . . . Reg is a different person. She's not
glued to the phone since it became a thing that I need, a thing that
connects me to Tony, Tony being the doorway to all boys, especially
wealthy boys. City boys. Boys you'd think girls like us would think
are too good for us but nope. We are confident in this house.

Dad got so sick of me complaining about the lock on the
bulkhead door being busted that he and Mom spent a whole
weekend fixing it. Tony was mad about that.

*But don't worry, piggy. I'll find a way in to cut off those poulkies
of yours and eat them when I'm good and ready.*

That's where we are now. In November. *Poulkies* are Yiddish for
thighs and as far as I know, the club where I work—*worked,* never

going back obviously, never—well, there were only two Jewish families as far as I know, and I don't think it was either of those Arnold Palmers.

Strange the way a mind is. I want the caller to be from the club, I want him to be someone who knows My Tony. I want the validation of someone from that place picking me. Choosing me, to teach Tony a lesson, that he was wrong to never call, to never try, and then again this is insane because the caller is a pervert. A sadist. He calls me piggy and once in September a few weeks after he first called, he got into the house when we were out.

I should say he got *back* in, but I'm trying to survive. To not break.

In September, when he got back in, he left a small dead pig in my bed.

Do you know how hard it was to not scream? To clamp my hand over my mouth and become the intruder himself? Silencing me so as to not ruin everything for my family? I put the pig in a plastic bag and brought it to the pond and dumped it in the woods and the next day when he called, he said I looked especially fat and stupid when I was at that beach alone, illegally dumping a pig.

"I'm gonna find you," I seethed. "I saw that pig and they use pigs like that in science class and if you work at my school . . . so help me god, I will find you."

He laughed. "Oh Maeve," he said, "there are plenty of fish in the sea, plenty of schools, too."

My stalker is not someone who finds me beautiful. And that's another reason I don't tell Mom and Dad and Reg. It's bad enough to know that my thighs are *poulkies*. It's bad enough that my "relationship" has made them all so fucking happy in strange ways. Mom is busy fixing up the house—*We can't wait to meet Tony!*—and Dad doesn't call us clunkers anymore. He's not so old school that he needs to find us boyfriends or anything. It's more like he just wanted us to be appreciated by his brothers, so that he would feel like less of a failure as a man.

I could totally be wrong. I doubt myself a lot these days, I do.

Reg though, she's doing so good. She has a boyfriend. A guy named Kelly. And if you could see them together . . . he's a truly shy person. He looks at her while she's talking and you can see him when he comes over for dinner, he looks like he's making a list in his head, tallying up all the things he loves about her, even though she's not making a list about him in *her* head. And sometimes she winks at him and he gulps his root beer so fast that it dribbles down his chin and she has to catch his eye and send him a signal— *wipe your chin*—and that's how nervous he is, so focused on her that he can't even feel his own chin. It's an act of bravery, that's what love is, and hate is cowardice.

And I'm attracted to a hateful coward, so what does that say about me?

Sometimes he tells me that I am a hateful little pig, useless and fat, not worth the price that my *poulkies* would get at the deli and sometimes he talks so much, so intensely that I believe him because of this basic disbelief that I can't fathom. He calls me every day, sometimes twice a day. When I'm not home, when I'm in the world, I search every road every parking lot for his blue pick-me-up truck.

Pickup truck.

But then I go home and take his calls. I keep the lie alive and I can't have it both ways, and I don't go the police. I listen to him.

Remember how I fantasized about Kevin's suicide? Remember how I let Tony spike that guy's drink? It's a lot to carry but it would be harder to share the fucking load with my family, you know? I can't even follow through with the thought of them finding out that Tony doesn't love me, that the man who calls just wants to *slice off my poulkies and eat them while I bleed to death on the floor* because if this were one of Reg's movies, my "stalker" would be someone who loves me, someone who is crazy but convinced that I am the most beautiful woman on the planet, someone who says that if he can't have me, no one will. And then I remember how those movies end. How the bad guy is bad even if he does think you're beautiful and I give up and I set my alarm.

"Maeve!"

It's Reg downstairs and she is on her knees, staring at the news.

It's our town and they're dragging a man out of a house and I know that I know because of all the love songs that teach you how you'll know when you know. The twisted paradox of fate.

That's him. Mine.

"This is fucking sick," Reg says. "This guy lives like five miles away and he was harassing like a million girls our age."

It stings to know it wasn't for me, not just for me, and it stings again, the double awareness. I am someone who wants attention. I am not the brave girl who called the police. I am the one who wondered what he looks like, if he was hot, if *I* was crazy.

As it turns out he is handsome. In an aristocrat kind of way. His family were members of the club a few years ago, but obviously he's also vicious and violent. Bad.

Mom comes into the living room. Our house smells like Thanksgiving already and she gathers me and Reg like she's Marmee in *Little Women,* like she can protect us. Reg takes to that kind of love, the smothering kind where you're meant to have some inner child who's bright eyed and alive inside of you; but I don't like it. Not usually.

Today is a different story. I let Mom hug me. I let the tears make streaks on my skin. I wasn't enough for him. I was quiet and loyal and I looked up *poulkies* in the dictionary and I tried so hard to make something good out of it, something good for us, for him and I still wasn't enough. They trot out girls with blurry faces on TV, girls who were harassed by this pervert and Mom is holding me hard. Angry hard. "Thank God my girls are okay," she says. "You don't get over a thing like that. Around it . . . sure, but when a nightmare like that comes your way . . . well, I'm just glad my girls are okay."

I curse those blurry girls—I said it, I mean it, am I going to hell?—because my family was doing better, if you leave me out of the equation and those girls ruined everything for us. Thanksgiving is a blur. I'm just like those girls on TV. Blurry. Here but not here.

Carl doesn't call again—obviously—and I cry a lot for what I am sure are all the wrong reasons—I tell Mom and Dad and Reg that Tony dumped me. Reg seems relieved. She says I was starting to seem *like some nervous lapdog.*

And a few days later, I'm in my room. I'm hiding. The phone rings. Dad's at work and Reg is busy. She has a date tonight—see how good my fake love was for her?—and Mom picks up on the third ring. It's the police. I'm not there but I'm close enough to hear the almost professional tone in her voice.

Yes, this is Mrs. Halsey.

I pick up the cordless. It's a risk but I have to hear it.

The officer is calm and polite, but he sounds like a person at the Salvation Army giving things to the needy like he's trying so hard to bury his relief at being him, and not my mother, not us. He tells her about Carl—still can't get over that name—and he says that Carl placed *one hundred and fourteen* calls to this house, and he asks if my mother ever spotted an old blue pickup truck in the neighborhood and she doesn't know, she can't say, and now he can't resist being kind of a dick.

"You might want to have a talk with your daughters," he says. "It's clear to us that this man was stalking one or perhaps both of them."

My mom is a woman who is used to men being nice to her, treating her with reverence. Childbearing hips. Warm eyes. This cop is so different, so disgusted, and my poor mom is awkward, obsequious. "Well, thank you, Officer. Thank you so much."

The line goes dead and there's a snap, the sound of Mom pulling the receiver off the wall, breaking the cord and then the phone hits the wall. *Bam.*

The first person I think of is Reg, poor Reg, she loves that phone to death, more than any object or person in this house because for her, it represents hope, the magic on the other end of the line. In a matter of seconds, she is in the kitchen, screaming. And Mom is louder than I expect her to be.

"I am asking you this once. Was it you?"

"Was what me?"

"Was it you talking to that . . . that filth."

"Mom, what the hell?"

Mom's voice drops to a whisper now and it's clear that she knows it's not Reg. It's me. She's telling Reg about the call, and I already know about the call, so I'm not missing out. There's nothing Mom knows that I don't. While Mom does all the talking, I smell coffee—she's making a pot—and there is something comforting about the blur of the quiet, like the backyard when it's snowing and there might not be any school tomorrow. I feel safe.

And then Reg starts it and she's Reg, so she's loud.

You mean that was never Tony on the phone?

No, of course I didn't know. What the hell? What the fucking hell in hell? All this time, she was . . . she was on the phone with that pervert?

Jesus, Mom, no. No, I will not keep my voice down because what the hell? What is wrong with your freaking offspring?

I'm not mad at Reg. I hear the guilt in her voice. I can't imagine being the older one. The lead clunker. The one who gave the pervert directions to my beach, and in this moment, all I think about is how good I am, as a person, how much I can't wait to forgive my big, dumb sister. On she goes, filling in the blanks, as if she knows I'm up here listening. I could have told her the truth. But I didn't. I could have been a victim and she could have saved me but instead I'm just a liar. So, of course she's still yelling.

You want me to talk to her? I don't know what to say. You're the mother. And obviously there is something wrong with her because if he called a hundred times or whatever and she didn't say anything then she must have liked it . . . Mom you saw the news. You saw the kinds of things he said to those girls . . .

Mom is flustered, going for the broom.

Okay. So now you want to know why didn't she say anything? Because something is wrong with her, Mom. She must have liked it. And you can't sweep it away. How many times did you answer the phone? What about Dad? What about me? She lied to us and we all talked to that animal. You realize that, right? He could have come in here and slaughtered us in our sleep!

Oh that's classic, Mom. Blame me. Tell me I'm being melodramatic and make it about me watching too many movies. Classic. Sure thing, Mom. Nice try.

Yes, I know she's the victim, okay? But she's also . . . a person can be two things at once, even your precious baby girl Maeve. Face it, Mom. The girls on TV told their parents. They went to the police. Your daughter . . . whatever. You know exactly what I mean and everyone is going to know and think we're a family of freaks.

Mom is crying now, wilting, she is spinach on the stove and Reg opens drawers and slams them shut, *bing bat, bing bat.* There's something comforting about the sounds of my family. This is the sound of their love for me, their fear. Mom sweeps up the shards of plastic as Reg tinkers with the broken phone, trying to fix it. Loving someone is knowing them and I knew Carl, the first man to really know me, same way I know Reg. She loves the phone because she values the possibility of connection more than the connection itself. That doesn't make her a bad person. Just wary. *A family of freaks.* She hates me right now, she can't help it, and I love her right now, I can't help it. You're always angriest with the people you know best. Perverts are out there no matter what and there's never going to be a world without a man in a blue pick-me-up truck fixing his devil eyes on all the attention-seeking young girls who become angels in his orbit, if they survive, which I am, I will.

Mom, no. I'll go up after you. But wait. I need you to push on this thingamajig while I turn the . . . yes, hold your finger right there. Harder.

Reg might fix the phone after all and maybe it's good that I lied. The truth is out and I'm free now. I can't wait to forgive her. She'll say it's all her fault and I'll tell her that I only lied because I wanted that damn phone to come through for her. We both failed each other and we will never mess up again and the next time Dad calls us a couple of clunkers, Reg will tell him we don't like that word, and he will stop. Forever.

Mom sneezes and Reg blesses her and then Mom asks a question.

What do I think he said to her? How do I know? I'm not a pervert. I don't know what a pervert would say. Probably told her he was gonna slice up her poulkies or something crazy and sick.

Am I hearing things? Did she just say poulkies? That's his word. It's my word. Not hers.

Ugh, Mom, I don't know what "poulkies" are. They're thighs or something. It's some Yiddish I heard on TV or something.

That was two *or somethings* in a row and Reg is lying. She heard it from *him*. I want out of my room. I want out of my skin. She knew. *Poulkies.* Reg knew. I can't live in this house with her. She knew that no one loved me, not in the normal way, not in the *Tony* way. She probably laughed at me, her stupid little sister, and I'm no good either. I sat there listening to Carl, lying to my sister. I don't know what's worse. Him or her or me or it. *Poulkies.* I let him fill my ears, as if it was my job to listen, to let him pay attention to me, like when you go to the dentist and your job is to sit still and open your mouth and let him do his job. I didn't go to her and she didn't come to me. She's had time to think, to study me and learn what I look like when I'm lying. I can't look at her—it's over—but it's us. Does she even love me anymore? Who could love a girl like me? And then the worst part. Will I ever love her again?

No, Mom, you can't go see her yet because I need two sets of hands. Pass me that screwdriver and pay attention because the phone is fixed but not totally fixed and you're gonna have to know how to fix it when I'm not here to do it myself. You ready?

The answer is yes, of course.

You have to be ready to live your life even if you're not, if you don't know how. I don't ask Reg how long she knew. In those first months after they take Carl, she keeps her distance from me too. One night, *Dirty Dancing* is on and my dad starts to say that those girls remind him of me and Reg and his voice trails off because no, even he knows we're not close like that, not anymore. No more clunker jokes from Dad and we go through an ugly time. It's embarrassing, the whole world of your town knowing that you are a girl who sat there and took it. Perverted by association. Nobody looks at me and sees a victim. They see an enabler. The phrase you learn in school is *fight or flight*. As if those are the only choices. As if we're all so quick to throw a punch or make a run for it. Some of us are slow. We just need a minute to think. They should tell you that it's fight or *freeze* or flight but I guess that's too long and clunky and it's no surprise that the freezers get the short end of the stick, as if we don't count. I wish people were different, but it's a useless wish. They aren't.

Still, I try to do better. I show the police where I dumped the pig at the beach, which allows them to add charges against Carl, my first boyfriend and no, Maeve, *no*. In that part of the story of our lives (my life?) nobody really cares. It was a dead pig. Not a person. So what? Get over it, Maeve. You're starting to sound like you liked it.

The pond is never the same after that and I don't go back.

But you go on, don't you? You hate the people you love and you fight the hate with love. I think one day I'll confront her.

Why didn't you tell me you knew about Carl? About poulkies?

But it's hard to picture how that plays out.

I can't even get a montage going and I'm a writer by trade now. Some days are just never coming no matter how many years go by and here we are now, twenty years later.

It's Thanksgiving and it's my turn, my house, and my weapon of choice for this occasion is . . . a pig. Dead and stuffed and glistening on the dining room table with eyes that follow you around the room. Reg has no clue. She's not a vegetarian but she's squeamish and traditional. She wants turkey and she doesn't know that she's not getting what she wants. She's parking in my driveway and I'm outside, holding the door, and she says I look good and I say that she looks good and she makes her same old joke about how no matter what she does, she always looks older than me—yawn—and I smile for her kids. They run around to the backyard and I shuffle Reg into the house. I close the door and she freezes up.

"What's that smell? Is that . . . is that a turkey?"

"No," I say with a little laugh, a little snide but tempered as I lay a hand on her shoulder, helping her wiggle out of her coat. "We thought it might be fun to get a pig!"

She is facing the front door. She can see me as I maneuver her coat off her arms. "Ah," is all she can say. "A pig."

"Yes, Reg. Poulkies for all. Sounds good, right?"

I leave her alone with that word, that word I didn't know was still in me after all this time. I don't stand there waiting for her to respond. She's a big girl, a grown woman, and she knows where to find me when she's ready.

A LIFE IN NIGHTMARES
BY RAMSEY CAMPBELL

"Time you were up and gone, Maurice."

The boy thinks his mother sounds as if she's wishing him away. "Can't I read a bit longer?" he pleads.

"You'll have to do plenty of that at your new school," his father says. "Off to bed now and we'll come to see you're tucked."

Tomorrow isn't why Maurice is nervous. The new school should be a stage of growing up. As he trudges into the hall he hears his parents sigh, and thinks they're relieved to be rid of him. The plump carpet on the stairs feels like a bid to comfort him while every step takes him further from his family. The white tiles of the bathroom remind him of a hospital, and an unseasonable September chill makes him shiver. He doesn't need to see how small and young his face looks, a nervous specimen trapped under glass. He soaps it and dries it and brushes its teeth, foaming at the mouth until he finishes spitting almost as discreetly as his mother calls polite. He stands over the toilet until he's afraid his parents will wonder why he isn't yet in bed. The prospect adds to the blockage, and his struggles to relax ensure he can't. At last a drip looses a downpour, and once it runs out he has to make for his bedroom.

When he switches on the light all his books take shape to greet him. They're in order on the shelves except for an alien invasion novel splayed face down on the bedroom chair. He often reads in his room, but never after dark. He drapes his trousers over the back of the chair and drops the rest of his clothes beside it, and once he has donned his pyjamas he can only crawl into bed.

His outfit feels too small for him, and so does the bed. Is that because he'll be a senior tomorrow? The thought doesn't stop them resembling forms of imprisonment, and he tries not to fancy that the footsteps on the stairs suggest warders on their way to lock a cell. Why does his mother have to pin him down so tightly with the blankets? She settles a dry kiss on his forehead and then frowns at retrieving the items he abandoned by the chair. "It's past time you acted your age, Maurice."

The bathroom light cord clatters against tiles as his father joins her. "Less of the leaving lights on, son. It's not you it's costing money," he says before relenting. "Now get yourself some shuteye and dream about big things."

"Can you leave the door open?"

"We don't want to keep you awake," his mother tells him.

"Just get your head down," his father says, "and before you know it you won't know where you are."

He shuts the door, and their footfalls descend into remoteness. In a few minutes Maurice hears the mumble of the television, which means they're more distant than ever. If he shuts his eyes tight, will this fend off the dark? He's desperate for any light to show him there's nothing in the room to justify his indefinable dread. Before he can grow too afraid to move he sits up in bed.

A trace of a glow under the door to his left outlines a dim sketch of a chair and lends the shelved volumes the look of blocks of coal. The window is beyond his desk on the opposite side of the room, and he wishes he'd opened the curtains as far as his parents might have tolerated. The light switch is beside the far edge of the doorframe, but the thought of setting foot in the dark makes the bed feel more like a refuge. Why couldn't he have kept someone with him until he fell asleep? He might have asked to hear a story if that wouldn't have been pathetically childish. Perhaps remembering a favourite will keep him safe somehow, and he recalls a tale of a cottage in a forest, where some power hid the occupants from monsters in the trees. He's feeling reassured enough to lie down when he glimpses a hint of light outside the window.

It's glistening on the pane—no, on an object beyond the glass. When it stirs he thinks the curtains have lent it the appearance of movement, but the window is shut and besides, he can't hear any wind. Then how can the edges of the curtains be shifting on both sides of the window? An intrusion is disturbing them. Objects are creeping around the frame, two bunches of them—long thin fingers eagerly growing longer.

Maurice backs away an inch, all the space he can find. Grinding his shoulders against the headboard feels like a desperate attempt to squeeze out a cry for help, if not to compact himself into invisibility or somehow to flee through the bedroom wall. He achieves only a feeble shriek like the last gasp of a balloon. He can't tell how long he has been clenching his eyes shut to ward off the sight of the questing fingers by the time he hears his mother. "What were you dreaming about, Maurice?"

They're at breakfast, but he's afraid to bring the night back. "Just a dream. Can't remember."

"So long as you know that's all it could have been," his father says.

"You and mum were in it. You were really real."

"I should think we were," his mother says with a reproachful look.

"It'll have been nerves, son, but you haven't got an earthly reason for them."

Maurice wants to think his new school won't give him any. He manages until his mother insists on zipping his coat up as if she's bidding farewell not just to a habit she's embraced throughout his childhood but to him. His parents wave goodbye from the doorway framed by obese bay windows, where their stance looks as artificial as the symmetry they're part of. As he turns away his mother murmurs "I hope the big boys don't give him too much trouble."

The bus stops at the far end of their road. Under a sky the colour of sunless rain the houses and equally motionless cars seem less real than the future toward which he's hastening. By the time he reaches the stop his coat feels far too fat and hot. At least he's able to find a seat on the bus once the driver has dealt his pass an unwelcoming look. Several passengers are wearing the black St Maurice's uniform, and more pile on at every stop. Some tower above Maurice as if they mean to daunt him into giving up his seat. Are they the sort of big boy his mother had in mind? As he avoids their eyes the bus passes a cinema, which is showing a film of the book he left on his bedroom chair.

When the bus halts beside the school it disgorges dozens of boys to swarm between the towering grey stone gateposts. Maurice feels reduced to less than himself, a negligible element of the swarm. A boy at least a head taller than Maurice is positioned by the left-hand gatepost, and points a clipboard at him. "Name," he says as if he's trying to condense the word.

"Maurice." Most of this sticks in his throat, and he coughs to dislodge it. "Maurice."

"Another one, are you?" If this is any sort of joke, the prefect dismisses it by adding "Last name."

"Maurice Roston."

"Roston," the prefect says like a rebuke for wordiness and ticks a listing on the clipboard. "Scuttle off," he says without looking up.

The grey school building stretches two extensive storeys wide on both sides of a central entrance reserved for staff. Maurice thinks it looks as though it's blocking anyone's escape. Pupils use a door at the left-hand end, where a prefect even taller than his counterpart at the gates wags a finger to detain Maurice. "Hands up," he says. "Your coat and goat. Other hall."

Although Maurice can't believe he heard this, his hands struggle to comply. "What do you mean?" he pleads.

"Not mumbling, am I?" The prefect jabs his finger at the corridor beyond the door. "Hands up your coat," he says, "and go t'other hall."

When Maurice ventures into the school, nearly tripping over the stone sill that generations of footfalls have trodden askew, he sees boys hanging up their coats in a capacious alcove. At last he manages to snag a stubby protrusion with the slippery strip his coat keeps refusing to proffer, and then a noise like the bumbling of a mass of insects leads him to the assembly hall. A prefect who would dwarf his colleagues is lurking just inside. "Sitter the frump," he says to Maurice.

Maurice is close to protesting that he doesn't need a sitter until he grasps what he's been told. As he makes for the front row the hundreds of boys fall silent, isolating his footsteps and inhibiting them. In a moment every boy grows taller, a process that produces a thunderous rumble. They've stood up because the headmaster has strode onstage, and he watches Maurice dash to the empty space at the near end of the front row. His unblinking gaze rests on Maurice while he says "Welcome to our community, all you new men."

Maurice doesn't feel much like a man, though at least he's grasping the headmaster's words—those, at any rate. The headmaster talks about the transition of the school, surely the tradition, which must be what he said. Now he's telling the boys how they have to make sure everyone looks up to them. Armies looked up to their patron saint Maurice, but Maurice thinks the headmaster's directive sounds like urging his listeners to grow lankier, invoking the big boys he's meant to beware of. "Remember you're all Morris Men," the headmaster appears to urge, and Maurice clutches at his knees to prevent his feet from performing an impromptu clattery dance.

At first he's glad when the headmaster's departure releases the audience. Most of the boys march out, leaving just the front rows occupied, and the prefect who sent Maurice there moves in front of them. As he reads out names from a clipboard their owners leave the hall, having apparently understood whichever phrase he adds to each, and Maurice can only hope he'll grasp his. "Roston," the prefect says at last. "To beater."

Maurice isn't sure he wants to comprehend, but risks asking "To what?"

"To beat her," the prefect says, staring so hard at him it feels like a physical dismissal.

Just in time Maurice thinks of a solution. He'll loiter outside the hall and follow whoever is sent on his way next. He stands up, feeling pathetically small, only to find every bench is unoccupied. How can he have been at the end of the list when he thought it was alphabetical? "After your room," the prefect says, and Maurice has to understand there are four words in the order.

The corridor is deserted. The grey metal of the sky shutters windows higher than his head. Is the fire door ahead of him muffling sounds from the classrooms? When he hauls it open, a task requiring both hands and all his strength, it shows him another silent stretch of corridor. Stone stairs lead upwards to his left, and as he wonders whether to use them he sees a sign on the wall beyond them.

2α, 2β, 2γ . . . Each is followed by an arrow, and the second of them tells him where to go. Reading the Greek letter feels like regaining more language than he knew he had. Two Beta can't be in this section of the corridor, since every room is full of unoccupied desks facing incomprehensible traces of words on blackboards. He sprints to the next fire door and heaves it open. Beyond another group of classrooms, the tallest prefect yet is guarding the far end of the corridor. "Found it," he calls.

At least that's clear. The corridor has magnified the voice and brought it closer. Or is it approaching because the figure has already begun to stride towards Maurice? Its legs really shouldn't be so long, nor the arms that it extends to him. He lets the fire door thud shut and turns to flee, but a lanky shape has crept into this stretch of the corridor. As it stalks fast towards him, a fact becomes inescapably plain. "Found it"—that wasn't addressed to him; it referred to him.

However swiftly the newcomer is coming for him, its hands are advancing faster still. Though the fire door is shut tight, it can't keep another set of elongated fingers out or, in a second, a further eager scrawny bunch. Maurice can only dash to the nearest classroom, where chalk dust hovers in the air like ash raised by a fire. The windows on the far side of the room are lower than those in the corridor—low enough to let him escape if he's as quick as he's desperate to be. He clutches at the handle of the door—

clutches at the bare wood and scrabbles at it, finding no handle of any kind. Shoving at the door with both hands simply bruises them. He backs away between the inhumanly extended fingers that are closing in from both sides and launches himself across the corridor. His shoulder thumps the door with all the force he can find, but the door refuses to yield, because it's an unbroken section of wall.

His lurch against it lets him realise that while he's in the school corridor, he's queuing outside the assembly hall. "God," his friend Len says, a word they aren't supposed to use like that. "Did you just doze off?"

"Don't think I slept much. Couldn't stop thinking what'll be in the exam."

"Thinking won't change it," says their friend Frank.

"I had a nightmare about our first day at St Morrie's."

"Let's hope today's not one," Frank says.

"Don't say that," Len protests.

As Maurice levers his eyes wide with fingers and thumbs to ensure he stays awake, the history master strides to the doors of the assembly hall. "Fine linen," he says, shouldering one door wide. "Note tall king."

When the boys start to file in Maurice sees that's what the men were told to do, and not to talk. The misperception leaves him more nervous than he cares to understand. In the hall the benches have been stacked against the walls almost up to the windows, and he wonders who could have performed the task. They've made way for desks set well apart, and he takes his place at the nearest empty one, next to Len and behind Frank.

A buff folder lies on it beside a stack of paper. Both are blank, so that Maurice has to remind himself that today's topic is Literature. As the last candidate finds a seat the invigilator makes for his desk on the stage. He bares his wrist and holds it in front of his face while he waits for a cue from his watch. "Penn's regimen," he seems to say, but Maurice is sufficiently alert to pick his pen up. "Sell lecture. Quest yon sand. Be gin."

The rustle of opened folders, a sound reminiscent of a wind in foliage, makes Maurice's response feel delayed by the need to piece the invigilator's syllables together. The first page in the folder warns him that he has two hours to complete the examination and tells him to choose one topic from each section. The first passage for analysis is familiar enough—

"Is *all* that we see or seem

But a dream within a dream?"

—and he feels confident until he sees the words that follow. *Disgusted poets in tension . . . This custard Poe testing ten shunning writing . . .* Is deciphering the language part of the test? The words won't even hold still. He tells himself he's caught the sense they're designed to obscure, but the sentence trails off into gibberish. The rest of the paper, including the quotations, is in a language he can't even name. "What is this?" he mutters, hoping at least one of his friends will confirm the problem. "Whose lingo is it meant to be?"

At once every boy in sight ducks lower. They're doing their utmost to go unnoticed. The stage is unoccupied, and the invigilator is at large in the hall. As Maurice strives to pretend he didn't speak, a chill breath stirs the hairs on his scalp. "You called me, Roston," a voice says at some indeterminate distance above him.

"Sir, no, I was talking to myself."

The invigilator plants his hands on either side of Maurice, resting them on the lowest joint of each finger. Maurice senses a bulk leaning down towards him, a presence that feels poised to settle on his back. He's crouching as low as the rest of the boys when the hands that flank him start to close in on him despite retaining their stance on the desk. The flattened sections of the fingers lengthen like grubs producing extra segments while the thumbs stretch towards him, lithe as snails emerging from their shells. He can't dodge aside or back away or leap up to escape. He can only wriggle out beneath the desk, but as panic makes him clumsy the base of his spine hits the floor while the edge of the wooden seat scrapes the back of his head. The impacts drive a cry out of him, and it's answered. "Maurice, what are you trying to do to yourself?"

The rescuer is Ruth. Concern gleams deep in her large brown eyes, and while her full pink lips present him with a puzzled smile, they look poised to deliver reassurance. He's tempted to give them a befuddled kiss as she helps him off the floor. He has slipped out of his padded wooden chair, one of the haphazardly unmatched items of furniture that surround the ageing television in the lounge he shares with Ruth and two more students. As she assists him onto the chair he feels as if she's tendering a glimpse of his old age. He thinks her action has brought them not just physically close, and he takes the chance to give her soft cool wrists a gentle squeeze as she lets go of him. "Were you dreaming?" she says.

"Must have been." Recapturing more language, he says "Was, of course."

"Anything you'd want to share?"

"I'd just fallen on the floor."

"You shared that all right. You made it shake and me as well."

"Sorry about that." He would risk taking her hand if she weren't out of reach in her chair by the dusty gas fire embedded in the cracked fake marble fireplace. "I don't know why I should dream about the past," he says. "I keep going back to how I used to be afraid I wouldn't understand what people said."

"Do you know what made you feel that way?"

"I'd rather not remember. I'd be scared of bringing it all back." In the hope of fending off the possibility Maurice says "I dreamed I couldn't do one of the exams I took to get here."

"Then you know it had to be a dream."

"It felt as if I don't want to be where I am."

As he regrets having put this into words Ruth says "Where would you rather be?"

"That's not what I'm saying. I can't think of anywhere else just now."

"Not even out for a drink?"

"There's always that." When her smile sketches expectancy it emboldens him to ask "Would you like to go for one sometime?"

"I have to do some research at the library but I should be free by nine."

"Shall we meet at the Timber House then?"

The name of the pub at the edge of the campus reminds him of a favourite childhood tale. This distracts him so much that he has to ask "Was that a yes?"

"It was," Ruth says with a look suggesting that she wonders where he went just then. "I thought you'd never ask."

Presumably she means his invitation. When she pushes herself out of her chair so forcefully it wobbles on its fractured stubby legs, he's afraid she has changed her mind until she says "I'll head out now so I'll be sure to see you later."

He can use the time for his own work. On the stairs the tattered carpet does its weary best to trip him. His room is so crowded with books—piled against the walls that look steeped in tea, heaped on the solitary chair, challenging him to read their spines in the dressing-table mirror—that it reminds him of his childhood. So does the desk the landlord has provided, but Maurice has grownup homework now. He's researching a thesis on alien invasion stories from the nineteenth century and earlier, not just those published as fiction, although he's certain that's all they are. The process feels like reaching for a past that never existed except in the popular consciousness. He makes notes about the last of the books he's managed to locate second-hand, which leaves him needing to order the rest from the library on the campus. He may see Ruth sooner than they planned, but hopes he won't seem aggressively eager.

Half a mile of the suburban street leads to the campus. Many of the houses have been divided into student flats. Along the pavements trees like props for the coalface of the sky sprout from squares of earth. They're as still as the posts of the streetlamps that bring bunches of foliage to golden life. The houses dwindle as Maurice jogs past them, and the trees grow more numerous. He isn't quite alone on the road. Although he hears no footsteps, a shadow is overtaking him.

A glance back shows him nobody, and a flagstone tipped up by a root nearly sends him sprawling. The follower must have dodged behind a tree, perhaps in the process of crossing the road, or into a garden. Maurice feels impelled to put on speed, though the uneven pavement is a hindrance; so many outstretched roots have undermined it that he could imagine the suburb is reverting to forest. The houses aren't much larger than cottages by now. Another rampant flagstone catches a shadow that extends past him. A streetlamp must be lengthening the shadow, and Maurice turns to find out who's there, but they've hidden again. "What are you playing at?" he demands, and instantly regrets speaking. A gangling silhouette has sidled out from behind a tree—from behind far too much of one.

A dislodged flagstone snags Maurice's feet as he backs away, and he barely recaptures his balance before stumbling in a helpless arc. As he flees towards the campus, stones seem to rear up to detain him. Beside him a shadow is growing far more swiftly than his own, while the prolongation of its fingers is faster still. He can see the campus now, across a main road beyond the trees, but all the concrete paths lit by globes on poles are deserted. He puts on a final desperate burst of speed that clogs his ears with his heartbeat. He doesn't know whether he's hearing a car until a police vehicle cruises into sight on the main road. "Police," he cries. "Help, police."

How much does this sound like "Please" and "Hell police"? He needn't care, since his shouts have halted the car. A policeman climbs out and rests his hands on the roof while a policewoman stays behind the wheel. "What's the trouble?" the man says.

"Thereafter." This is all Maurice can pronounce as he lurches at the car. "Me," he manages to add. "Thereafter me."

The officer extends a finger to tilt his peaked cap back. "I'm not understanding you."

"Summon it." Lack of breath isn't helping Maurice form his words. "Someone is," he tries again to say and twists around to see only the deserted treelined road. "Some bloody wuss," he protests and makes a desperate bid to get the words right. "Somebody was. Horse done thing."

"Still not getting you."

The policeman has risen to his full height. Maurice mustn't mind how tall the man is if it makes him equal to the pursuer. "Or something," Maurice struggles to hear himself say, "ice head."

The policeman hasn't reached his maximum height after all, and what's creeping across the car roof? It resembles a spillage of mercury, but the glistening tendrils are his fingers. His colleague doesn't bother lowering her window before she stretches an arm towards Maurice—really quite an arm. He's hardly started to back away when a shadow spreads past him as its owner rears higher behind him. "Getter wave rummy," he pleads, knowing that the words won't work unless he can articulate them. "Leave meal own."

"I will if you really want me to, Maurice."

Ruth is beside him, but she isn't on her feet, because the world has tilted. They've thrown themselves flat on the pavement in a desperate bid to go unnoticed. No, they're in bed, and as her concerned face looms above him in their apartment bedroom he remembers her helping him up off the floor in the student house, or was that a dream as well? "Another nightmare?" she murmurs.

"Not now. This isn't one."

"We won't let it be."

As if he's echoing a vow Maurice says "We won't let the rest of our life."

He recalls their exchange when he has to present his thesis and the day Ruth has to argue hers, and he could believe the vow is working. By the time they're interviewed for positions as lecturers he feels he can leave it behind, and at first he doesn't understand why it should come to mind on the day of their marriage. Ruth's parents don't like him much, but surely the occasion will keep them polite, and won't they be glad of the wedding? Just the same, he can't help experiencing some relief when he doesn't see them as he and Ruth parade down the aisle at the registry office. He's slipping the ring onto Ruth's small slim finger when her parents sneak into the room as if they don't care to be observed and sit on the back row. They look resolute, though he can't tell how. They stay seated while the guests converge to congratulate the newlyweds, but eventually saunter up the aisle to introduce themselves to Maurice's parents. "Sylvia," Ruth's mother says of herself, and her husband offers "Daniel."

"It's good to meet you," Maurice's mother says.

"Yes, at last," says his father.

"Mutual, I'm sure." As she deals them brief simultaneous handshakes Sylvia says "Though we might have wished for a happier occasion."

Maurice's mother gives this a blink. "How could it be happier?"

When Sylvia finds this unworthy of an answer Daniel says "Less enforced."

"Enforced," Maurice's father says as though the word is unfamiliar.

"Obligatory, if you prefer. Imperative. It rather makes a mockery of the event, would you not agree? At least it wasn't perpetrated in a church."

"When did you say the child is due, Ruth?" her mother affects not to know.

"It won't be for months."

"I suppose we should be thankful your condition isn't visible," Daniel says.

"I think it's rather sweet," Maurice's mother says, "getting married for the baby's sake."

"Not just sweet," his father says. "Admirable."

"Clearly we have different standards," Sylvia says, turning to Ruth. "And clearly you've abandoned them."

"Even if you won't consider us," Daniel says, "you might both reflect on the example you've set for your pupils."

"That isn't what they're teaching," Maurice's mother objects. "She's art and he's literature."

"We're aware of our daughter's achievements, but I understand your son's business is popular fiction." Daniel is already facing Ruth. "The best we can hope for," he says, "is that you'll keep your mistake to yourself."

"If that means what I think," Maurice's mother says, "I really don't believe there's any call to speak like that to her."

"Especially not today," says his father.

"We don't need strangers to advise us how to address our own child," Daniel says.

"You'd be more usefully employed," Sylvia says, "in dealing with your son."

Most of the guests have retreated, but a few are loitering within earshot. "You go ahead to the reception," Maurice tells them, suppressing most of his rage. "We'll be along soon."

"Let us leave you to enjoy your celebrations," Sylvia says.

With no apparent irony Daniel says "We trust we haven't spoiled your day."

"You haven't and you won't." Just the same, Ruth squeezes Maurice's hand so hard that it aches as she says "Thank you for coming."

She holds Maurice where they are until her parents are well along the corridor. By the time the four emerge from the town hall, Sylvia and Daniel are on the far side of the car park. Maurice can't help wishing them further away, out of sight at speed. As he and Ruth climb into his mother's car he sees another swerve into the treelined road. Daniel's car is receding into the distance when a shape leans between the trees and reaches through the open windows of the vehicle to lift two frantic puppets by their heads high into the air. "Maurice," Ruth cries as though she's expressing the shock he's unable to utter.

They're in bed, and her urgently concerned face is just visible above him. He feels as if he's tried to turn time back to elude some future terror until Ruth speaks again. "I think you'd better drive me to the hospital."

He sits up so violently the headboard scrapes his shoulders. "What's wrong?"

"Nothing yet, and we'll make sure nothing will be. I've started contracting, that's all."

She doesn't mean she's growing smaller. Her spasms have begun. Only the baby inside her is growing, which is natural. She insists that she and Maurice shower before they leave, and he wishes the cubicle were capacious enough to contain them both, as showers so often are in films. She doesn't want breakfast, and his shower has already delayed them enough. They're in the car, speeding towards a raw dawn and the hospital, when Ruth says "Were you dreaming again?"

"I expect I was." Not least for fear that she may ask for details, Maurice says "You did lose your parents, didn't you?"

"You know I did." After a long deep breath signifying a cramp Ruth gasps "On the road."

"It must have got mixed up in my dream."

"They were thrown out of their car the day we got married," Ruth says as though his confusion has forced her to speak. "I'd rather not go back there just now. Let's concentrate on our future, shall we?"

For a while this appears to consist of a dark deserted road. At least Maurice doesn't have to search for space in the hospital car park. On their way to the building, which stretches wide like a proposed embrace, Ruth digs her nails into the arm he's put around her. A nurse collects them from the lobby, where a receptionist is reading a countryside magazine with a sylvan cottage on the cover, and ushers them down a white-tiled corridor to a ward in which screens enclose most of the beds. When she wheels a screen around a bed so that Ruth can don a garment like a bag with arms and a gap at the back that a bow fails to close, Maurice has the unwelcome fancy that an intruder is about to peer over the seven-foot screen. Nothing shows itself, and he can't discern activity beyond any of the other screens as the nurse exposes Ruth's bed.

Maurice sits by it and takes Ruth's hand, and they reminisce to take her mind away from her insistent state. They remember their first awkward meeting in the student kitchen, and growing more than just acquainted over drinks at the Timber House, and moving in together before they left university, and buying their first house, a property so dilapidated it felt like an unsound fragment of the past, which they'd brought back to life in their own image . . . Once Ruth begins to squeeze Maurice's hand more forcefully she's less inclined to say much. He should have brought

a favourite book of hers to read to her, but instead at her behest he
tells her stories. Has she already heard the tale of the forest cottage
that's a refuge from the entities that tower among the trees? Surely
only Maurice has. "Perhaps we'll live somewhere like that one
day," Ruth says and frowns, presumably at a contraction. "Tell me
about it again."

He doesn't know how often he has repeated the tale—sufficiently
often to wish he could think of an ending—by the time a doctor
decides Ruth's progress warrants transferring her to the theatre.
As he follows the trolley Maurice catches sight of somebody, no
doubt a prospective father, pacing up and down a corridor. Doesn't
the man's partner want him with her? Ruth wants Maurice, and she
grips his hand while the maternity team prepare their equipment.
Her ferocious clutch reminds him how she held his hand while her
parents lectured her at the registry office. He mustn't think it feels
like fear made flesh. The words she gasps are mostly addressed to
the doctor and her assistants. "I think it's nearly here."

He's overwhelmed by helplessness until the doctor says "Keep
hold, Maurice."

As he matches Ruth's vigour he's distracted by movement at
the edge of his vision, and turns away from her. The impatient
pacer in the corridor has just passed the door. No doubt there's
a second theatre nearby, and whoever's in there is the subject of
his fretfulness. At least the man can't see Ruth, since the window
in the door is frosted, although is there another reason? When
Maurice came into the theatre the window was level with his head,
but was the silhouetted figure's head significantly higher? Maurice
is staring at the window, desperate for a glimpse to reassure him
he was mistaken, when Ruth's nails dig into the back of his hand
before a baby's wails recall him.

He turns his head in time to see a nurse cut the cord. She packs
its end into the squirming infant's navel while the doctor holds
the baby with both hands. Maurice will be glad to see the child
presented to its mother, given how the doctor is holding it, one
hand beneath its feet, the other at its hairless scalp. Surely nobody's

meant to support babies like that, and he's stepping forward to claim it when the doctor takes a different hold. One hand pins the feet together while the other closes around the head and then penetrates the cranium, the fingers streaming into it like rivulets into a pool. As the small body withers swiftly as a leaf in a bonfire, Ruth's hand jerks at Maurice, and so does her cry of despair.

They're in bed in their house, and she's clinging to his hand. Her cry has wakened her as well. She takes a breath like the ones she had to perform at the hospital. "I'm sorry, Maurice," it lets her say. "I've been dreaming too."

He has to believe she wants him to ask "What about?"

"Do you mind if I try to leave it there? I'd rather look ahead."

All the emotions he knows they're restraining make him say "Do you really want to go back to work so soon? Remember they'll give us as long as we need."

Ruth disposes of this by switching on the bedside light, and knuckles her eyes as though she's only clearing away sleep. "Work's what I need, and I think you do as well. It won't make us forget, but it may help to settle our minds."

Saying any more about it would be like probing a wound open wider. They don't talk much at breakfast, but find opportunities to touch each other, a contact more eloquent than language. Since Ruth needs to regain the will to drive, they take Maurice's car to work. As he parks it close to their departments they see the vice-chancellor bearing down on them. "Please allow me to offer my condolences once again," she says. "To you especially, Ruth."

"Why should I be special?"

"It was my understanding that it hasn't been too long since you lost your parents as well."

"It's been a while," Ruth says, not loud.

"Please forgive any intrusion. I simply wanted to convey my appreciation and the university's for your commitment to your work."

Maurice takes Ruth's hand, however unprofessional the gesture looks. "Thank you very much," he says, though each word feels yet more remote.

He lets go of Ruth's hand once they encounter students on the campus. He walks her to the Art block and then heads for his own department. The small auditorium is full of his pupils, and he wonders whether any of them have made a particular effort because of his loss. If this is true of Ruth's class, he can only hope it won't set her emotions too loose.

Today his class is talking science fiction. It feels like reaching back to the tales in which he used to lose himself, until Puthi objects that time travel makes no scientific sense. "It's fantasy," she says. "It could never work."

"You might hope fantasies can come true sometimes."

Nobody seems to hear Maurice, unless they find the comment unworthy of a lecturer. "The only way it could," Puthi says, "is in your mind."

"That's called remembering," Darshana says.

"I was thinking maybe you could travel back into your old selves."

"Why would you want to do that? You've already been there. Me, I want to find out what the future's like."

"If your future was some kind of nightmare you might want to go back instead."

"It won't be. It can't." Since this appears to go unheard, Maurice raises his voice. "I think we've exhausted the subject now."

Darshana hasn't finished. "If you could travel back like that," she says, "maybe whatever you were running away from could follow you."

"No, that's nonsense. It couldn't happen. There's no way on earth it could." Maurice's voice rises until the students acknowledge him at last, though they look unconvinced. "It's tripe," he's compelled to let them know. "It's balderdash. It's balls. Shit. Crap."

More of his life than he wants to remember has massed inside his skull, driving uncontrollable words out of his mouth. Before long he can't tell whether the noises he's emitting express thoughts of any kind or are even words as he understands them. Students are leaving the auditorium, but he needs to continue talking as long as there's anyone to hear. Somebody must have alerted the vice-chancellor, who arrives as Maurice starts to feel he's running out of breath, not to mention language. She looks as concerned as Ruth ever has, but he can't make out the face of her follower, even when its downcast head rises well above her. The head is a glistening grey bulb, featureless except for the round lipless version of a mouth that gapes in the domed crown, and he suspects its senses must be in the fingers it's reaching past her. Certainly their eager progress makes it plain that they're aware of him, and he backs away so fast he no longer knows where he is. When he topples backwards off the stage he has no idea how far he'll have to fall.

"Maurice, where are you falling to now? Won't you ever stop?"

He has sprawled half out of a bed, not quite touching the polished floorboards. Ruth is beside it, lifting him back in. As she draws the quilt over him he blinks at the small raftered room. Only Ruth is familiar, and he demands "Where are we?"

"At our cottage."

This sounds like a tale. "Which is that?"

"The one we rented for the summer."

"I think I've been dreaming about wanting to come here."

Beyond a window at her back he sees a greenish glow of foliage. Sitting up in bed shows him trees that tower above the cottage. "Well," Ruth murmurs, "now your dream's come true."

Why did she hesitate? Maurice thinks he remembers but has to ask "Did I have a breakdown?"

"If you did, you're leaving it behind."

"It was the first lecture I tried to give, wasn't it, after . . ." His reluctance to continue feels like losing language, and he makes himself add "After our loss."

"No need to remember anything you shouldn't, Maurice."

"Better to stay in the present, you're saying. I'll do my best."

When Ruth turns away he wonders what emotion she's hiding from him, though how can he have any doubts? "Anyway," he says, "it's past time I was out of bed."

"I'll make coffee," Ruth says but looks back as he follows her down the naked wooden stairs, above which a skylight frames an unusually greenish scrap of sky. "Aren't you getting dressed?"

"There's nobody but you to see, is there?"

"Nobody." This sounds oddly like a hope if not some other reference to the unspoken. "But we don't want you catching cold," Ruth says.

"Not much chance of that, surely, when as you say it's summer."

Does she falter before heading for the kitchen? Maurice is about to explore the cottage when a splinter of a floorboard pierces his heel. As he sits on a stair to extract the fragment, he's surprised how cold the wooden tread is. This and the twinges of his heel as he coaxes out the splinter demonstrate he isn't dreaming. His foot continues to smart while he pads along the short hall, glancing into rooms that look designed to evoke the past—a rustic dresser displaying plates patterned with blue leaves in the lounge, a table draped with tasselled lace in the dining-room, a black iron range and a vintage radio in the kitchen. "What can we get on the radio?" he asks Ruth.

She doesn't glance at it or him. "Nothing much just now."

"Shall we see what there is?"

"It's broken, Maurice. It can't be fixed."

She sounds determined not to be harassed. Is she still suffering their loss? He's about to hug her when the view from the window above the stone sink halts him. The kitchen faces an expanse of earth extensively gnawed by tyre tracks, which prompt him to ask "Where's the car?"

"It's just under the trees. Under the leaves as well."

It takes some peering to locate her car. Its russet colour is so nearly indistinguishable from its covering of fallen leaves that he could imagine it has been deliberately camouflaged. Now he sees that the odd greenish glow of the sky has lent the autumnal leaves in the treetops its hue. "How long have we been here?"

"A bit longer than we planned."

"Shouldn't we be back at work?"

"I don't think that's such a good idea just now."

Maurice takes their tragedy to be the reason, not least because she's averting her face. Rather than persist he says "Have we been in touch with whoever owns the cottage?"

"I think they've forgotten about us."

"Then shouldn't we remind them we're here?"

"No need to remind anybody." As he prepares to object she says "Anyway, they aren't answering."

This sounds oddly like a second thought. He senses her hoping he won't persist, and tries a neutral question. "How are we for food?"

"We filled the freezer on our last trip to the village. We meant to take some of it home."

"I expect we still can."

The percolator announces the completion of its task with an electronic note, an interruption Ruth appears to welcome. As she fills two of the blank white mugs provided with the cottage Maurice says "Any news?"

Ruth keeps her gaze on the mugs she places on the table. "Of what, Maurice?"

"Of whatever's going on in the world."

"There's no coverage here, if you remember."

If this includes their phones he has to point out "You said you'd been trying to contact whoever owns the cottage but they didn't answer."

"It works as a phone but it isn't picking up any data."

The lack frustrates Maurice so much he feels incomplete. "We'll have a television, won't we?"

"Yes." Ruth sounds unnecessarily pressured as she says "With the same problem."

"That surely isn't how it operates. It won't depend on going online."

"Don't ask so many questions, Maurice. Can't you just be here with me?"

Has she had a breakdown too? This might explain her desperation and his sense that she's withholding the unsaid. "You know I won't leave you," he says.

"Then don't go anywhere, even in your mind."

"I won't be far away." All the same, her demand seems excessive. "Nothing wrong with knowing what the world's up to as well," he says.

"We came here to leave it behind for a while."

"We've done that, haven't we?" Surely just her insistence is making him nervous. "We can switch it off whenever we want to," he says. "I'll just see if the television's working now."

As he stands up Ruth reaches for him. She looks determined to detain him, and he's about to give in to asking what's wrong when he glimpses activity beyond the window. Is someone interfering with the car? No, it isn't moving—just the leaves with which it's covered are. The wind that's shifting a couple of tall trees must have found the car. "What is it, Maurice?" Ruth whispers.

"Just a breeze clearing some leaves off your car."

"Sit down, then." When he doesn't instantly comply she urges "Sit down with me."

He drops into the chair and takes her hands, saying as gently as he can "Now you have to tell me what the problem is."

"If it's gone out of your head, maybe that's best." As he attempts to steady her hands, which are trembling uncontrollably, Ruth says "In fact I'm certain it must be."

"What is, for heaven's sake?"

"Don't say it. Don't even think of them." She sounds as though she wants to hide her voice. "Maybe thinking brings them."

He can hear the wind now. Its murmur isn't merely growing louder; it's multiplying. It must have found more trees with leaves to lend it a voice. Indeed, the sibilant chorus resembles a conversation in the treetops, even if it involves nothing Maurice would recognise as words. It occurs to him that this could be the source of his fear of losing language, an insight that feels like the threat of recalling far too much. As he struggles to rise to his feet Ruth clutches at his arms. "Stay down, Maurice."

This only makes him more anxious to see. By straining against her determined grasp he's just able to make out the car roof. It's entirely clear of leaves, and he glimpses several objects like elongated fingers shorn of nails slithering out of sight. "Something's found the car," he says so low it feels like a bid to deny what he's seen.

Ruth shuts her eyes as if this may fend off the intrusion, but they spring open at once. "I thought we'd managed to hide it," she whispers, and adds so hastily the words come close to running out of breath "Don't say any more. Come out of sight, quick."

She tries to hold him in a crouch as she manoeuvres them away from the table, but he catches sight of movement among the trees. He succeeds in believing a wind is at large until the thin shape leans down from the treetops. Despite its stature, it's no tree. "The tall ones," he mutters and immediately wishes he hadn't regained that scrap of language.

"Don't, Maurice," Ruth pleads and hustles him into the hall, where another splinter jabs his foot to remind him he isn't dreaming, however fervently he yearns to be. As they huddle in the space between the doorways, the nearest they can find to a hiding place, the glow through the skylight intensifies as though a searchlight has been trained on them. It leaves Ruth unable not to whisper "They brought their sky with them."

She claps both hands over her mouth, too late. A figure stoops to the skylight, and its fingers seep around the edges of the frame to grope for the latch. In a moment they spring it and throw the skylight open with such enthusiasm that the pane shatters on the roof. Before Ruth and Maurice can retreat, two arms descend like gouts of greyish water to the hall, splaying their numerous fingers as they plummet. One set seizes Ruth by her scalp and streams into it while the others close around her feet and swing her off the floor. As they twirl her like a spider's prize she cries out in more than terror. "They're finding stars in me, Maurice. They're making one of me."

Her last word rises to a shriek. He's overwhelmed by it and by a flare of incandescence so fierce it blinds him. When he blinks in dismay and from the need to see, his faded vision shows him flakes of ash sailing in a cloud down to the floor. He has barely enough will to back away, since he knows that won't save him even if he wanted to be saved. As he stumbles backwards like a puppet robbed of its strings, a pair of objects like a distorted inhuman notion of hands with fingers as lengthy as he is tall fumble out of the kitchen to find him. He can only close his eyes and wish with his entire being that however he's about to be transformed, he'll be with Ruth. Just the same, he's compelled to reassure himself with the last words that are left in his skull as the fingers grope deep into his brain. "Time you were up and gone, Maurice."

PAPA EYE
BY PRIYA SHARMA

It was on Papa Eye that I learnt to see. I'd only found it because of Dr Moore. I found *her* via the GP Support Service. It was for physicians who couldn't heal themselves. I discounted the first psychologist on the list because she dressed like Margaret Thatcher.

"You need to know I'm not a traditional therapist."

We sat in low chairs in her office, a cafetière between us.

"I've made a mistake, Dr Moore." She never told me her given name. *Good for you, Dr Moore. You earned the title too. Make your patients use it.* "I'm not sure why I'm here. I don't know how I feel."

"Then why make the appointment?"

"There must be something wrong with me. I should feel something about getting divorced, but I don't. I'm losing touch with friends because I'm avoiding them. Well, the ones who aren't avoiding me, because most of them are Amy's friends more than mine. People are expecting me to be sad or relieved, but I don't feel anything."

"Is that shock?"

"No. It's like it just doesn't matter. Nothing does. I mean, I care about doing my job well, but most of the time it feels pointless. I don't belong anywhere. I've taken antidepressants but they don't make a difference. I don't feel depressed. It's bigger than that." What I *was* feeling was embarrassment. I was self-indulging in some existential crisis. I put my mug down. I'd been using it as a shield. "I'm sorry. None of this makes sense. What's wrong with me?"

"What makes you think anything's wrong with *you*?"

The ferry only went as far as Little Isle, where I was met by Hector.

"Can I help?"

"Yes, grab that rope, son. Sorry, *Doctor*."

"Call me Ravi."

I turned my face into the wind once we were under way.

"This place is beautiful." It was a comment rather than a question, but the companionable silence had stretched out too long.

"These islands used to be mountains as high as the Himalayas."

"That's a sobering thought."

"Time's prerogative."

Hector. Ferryman and philosopher.

"Have you always lived on Papa Eye?"

Papa, papil, papale, meaning monk or priest. An island of stacks, rumps and heads, named for holiness.

"Mostly."

"Never wanted to leave?"

"I've been around the world on ships but there's nowhere like this. There's all kind of magic on these islands, but Papa Eye most of all. Look, there's the Iris."

The Iris made Papa Eye unique. It was half a mile from the island itself, a curved wall that went hundreds of feet up. It protected Papa Eye's most exposed flank, but was the shield that blocked communication with the other islands and the mainland.

Its jagged columns of rock teemed with birds. I recognised kittiwakes and razorbills as we got closer. Their lifted wings revealed the wind currents. Grey waves hit stone, sending up huge sheets of spray.

We rounded the curve of the Iris and there was Papa Eye itself. It was set in calm green waters. Yellow sand stretched away from the harbour wall. Houses rose up behind it in irregular tiers, painted pink, pale blue, yellow and lavender. A picture-book place.

The sun made it look Mediterranean despite its northern clime. Full of bright promise.

Hector guided the boat into the sheltered harbour at a chugging pace. A sign read Private: Report to the Harbourmaster.

A private island owned by its people, financed by clever investments, and with its own free healthcare and education system.

I recognised the giant man on the harbour wall. He stood and waved. His hair and beard were his signature, unruly and grey streaked. His smile broke his face open, revealing even teeth, white against black skin.

"How was your journey?"

"Good."

"Liar. You look tired. Let me take those bags. All your things have arrived. We moved the crates to your house."

"Thank you."

Truth was, I was suddenly shy of Samson, and in awe of him. I wanted to *be* him. Calm, with gentle authority, a benevolence clear in the smallest courtesies. I was relocating to join his practice on a chance discussion.

"Everyone wanted to throw a welcoming party but I didn't think you'd be up for that. The brass band were disappointed. They're terrible, to be honest," he turned back, "but don't tell them I said that."

Anna, Samson's wife, stood in the hall. The stained-glass panel over the door was of an eye. Rays burst from its pupil. The sun came through it, casting a hazy approximation of the design on the patch of carpet between our feet.

I'd seen the same symbol on all the other houses. Carved on lintels. On plaques beside doors. In the tiled mosaics on hearths. Eyes everywhere. Sometimes shooting out sunbursts or a series of stars.

"What's the eye story?"

"We've plenty of time for that. Here." She pulled something from her coat pocket. The keys jangled as she tossed them to me.

"Your Land Rover's been serviced. Samson's put a medical kit in there for you."

"You've thought of everything."

The house, the Land Rover, were all part of my relocation package. The house had been renovated and furnished for me in shades of heather and sage. Anna suggested I put my own stamp on it, but I liked her choices.

"You should go and explore."

Anna's vivacity invited intimacy, as though you were party to her adventures.

"I thought I'd join Samson at the medical centre."

"Samson and Fiona have it covered. Go and get your bearings."

She kissed my cheek. Anna had made me her conspirator in less than a week. "Think of it as reconnaissance for home visits. There's not a single house number on the island. Most have names. Or even worse are called by who lives there. Go for a drive and suss some of it out. You can't get lost. Head for the sea and you'll end up on the coastal road which leads back here eventually."

"Okay."

"And if you see someone on the road, stop and ask for directions. Not because you need them but because they'll wet themselves with excitement. Everyone's desperate to meet you."

A trail of people had already knocked on my door.

Welcome, here's a fish pie.

I live next door. Ask if you need anything.

I've just been baking. Here, have a cake.

"What time do you want us tonight?"

"About seven?"

"Grand."

I followed the grey road that swept down through the village and then along the coast. The right fork led towards the interior. The houses became more spread out, some painted, some pebble dashed, their panes glinting.

As I approached a humpbacked bridge there was a sign that read Otters Crossing. It made me look with a grin towards the tumbling river that ran alongside me, but I couldn't see any.

Papa Eye's landscape differed from the other islands. The Iris softened its hues and made the land more giving and forgiving.

"What shall we talk about today?"

"Tell me about an encounter with the dead. The first that springs to mind." Dr Moore leant back in her chair.

A memory came, unbidden. I was the junior doctor on call for Obstetrics. I'd been bleeped to Casualty.

There's something wrong, the patient said.

I'd read her notes. She had juvenile-onset rheumatoid disease and renal failure. The blue hospital gown swamped her and robbed her identity.

I'm going to need to examine you. Is that okay? Do you want your husband to stay?

I'm staying, he said.

No, Ben. She shook her head, her final word.

Pat, the nurse, helped her lie back.

May I?

I pulled the sheet aside when she nodded. She was twenty-two weeks gone from her notes. Her lower abdomen was hard.

Now, can you put your heels together and let your knees drop apart?

I glanced at Pat, who put a hand on the woman's forearm. The baby was partway out already. It slipped into my hands with a wet gush. Fast bleeping a paediatrician was pointless. It was long past revival, blue lipped, eyes closed to light and life.

Give me my baby.

It's a boy.

I wiped her son down, then laid him on a fresh sheet. I wrapped him with care but no matter how much I tried, he still looked shrouded rather than swaddled.

"What was the woman's name?"

Dr Moore's question startled me.

"Ruby Barker."

"Eye colour?"

"Brown."

"What was her husband called?"

I thought for a moment. "Ben. She called the baby Oliver."

"Your problem is memory."

"Problem?"

"Human beings need to forget."

"Ruby Barker won't forget."

"No, but hopefully she'll remember a truncated, filtered version of it. People would go insane if they recalled their most important moments vividly."

"Even our happiest ones?"

"Even the happiest ones. Think about it."

"My father used to say that we live on in memories of those whose lives we touched. When I tried to explain this to my ex-wife she called me maudlin. She told me that this was the function of children, the genetic code that lived on. It's not enough. I have all these moments inside me related to my parents, to strangers, all that's left of them. When I am gone, those will be gone too."

"Isn't life supposed to be transient?"

"I know but why do I find that so hard to bear?"

The children, varying in age from about six to ten, were by the road. They were dressed without concession to fashion. Practical outdoor gear and home-knit jumpers. I recognised Anna and Samson's granddaughter, Petra. Her black hair was a riot of corkscrew curls. They were huddled around something on the grass. I hesitated but felt responsible, so I pulled over and wound down the window.

"No school today?"

"It's half term." Petra looked over her shoulder at me.

"Is everything okay?"

"It's dead, Dr Ravi." Her face was fierce and pinched.

I got out, boots crunching in the road.

"We found it like this," said an older boy.

I knelt beside it. I'd never seen a real hare before. It was mightier than I imagined, not just a thinner version of the rabbit, but lithe and muscular. Its proportions different.

Its hindquarters were a miracle of construction. Such tensile strength, built for fight or flight. Its heart would've been a great engine. I wished I'd seen it with erect ears, the shine still on its eye.

There was blood on its mouth.

"Can you help us?" asked another boy. His blond hair curled down to his shoulder.

"Yes, Doctor, can we have some bandages?" Petra asked.

"I'll check if I have some."

I opened the kit that Samson had prepared, impressed by his organisation. I returned with a handful, uncertain of their needs. It was then that I noticed a child stood apart on the bank. She wore an oversized blue anorak, her hands lost in its deep pockets.

"Who's your friend?"

"Isla doesn't play with us. Or go to school. She prefers grown-ups." The blond boy looked familiar, but I couldn't place him.

Petra came first, followed by two others, each taking a roll of bandages as though I'd offered them a sacrament.

"Do you want me to help?"

They handled the corpse with the absolute intent of children, without revulsion, only tenderness. The eldest boy lifted the hare to let the others work.

"Are you going to bury it?"

"No." Petra elongated the word in response. "It's to help her."

"How?"

"So her skin isn't sore when she's in the deepest sleep."

I must've looked confused because the boy with the curls explained. "When she wakes up, she'll tell the other hares all the hare stories. Then she'll run again."

The hare didn't look swaddled. It looked shrouded.

"It won't work. The light has gone out of her." A girl in jeans and a thick flannel shirt kicked a stone with the toe of her boot. "I tried it with my cat."

When I looked up the girl in the blue anorak had gone.

Anna and Samson carried in wine and laughter.

"We didn't know what you were cooking, so we brought red, pink, and white."

"Fiona and Grace sent their apologies. Fiona's under the weather."

"Oh, right, okay." They'd spurned me.

"All the more for us." Samson was embarrassed.

"How can I help?" Anna clutched my elbow.

"Drink wine."

She filled the glasses with generous glugs as I brought out plates.

They wandered around the lounge-cum-dining room but it revealed little of my interior except for a few framed film posters and my favourite books. I'd moved the remaining boxes in the spare room. Full of things I didn't need enough to bother unpacking.

"Moussaka. Dig in."

Steam rose as it was portioned out.

"This is delicious." Samson spoke between forkfuls. "Anna can't cook for toffee."

"You didn't marry me for my cooking."

"No, but I'd marry Ravi right now."

Anna topped up my glass.

"Samson said you were both born here. When did your families arrive on the island?"

"The 1300s."

Anna enjoyed my incredulity. I expected her to say a generation or two at most.

"We're a cosmopolitan people. An island of immigrants. The original settlers were from Africa, Germany, Ireland, Spain, and England."

"Wow."

"Have you heard the story?"

"No."

"There was a ship sailing from Spain. It hit a storm and the crew put the passengers overboard and told them to row for their lives."

Anna took over. "They were a motley crew. There was a rich lady called Heloise and her servant Thora, a young Irish peasant girl. A stonemason who'd been working on Cologne's great cathedral and was in search of mightier spires to build. There was a Spanish poet, but no-one aboard could agree if they were man or woman. A widower and his child on pilgrimage. Una, the nun. And then our bloodlines, the Black Knight. He was a fearsome warrior who was protecting his sister, a great lady at court who was renowned for her intelligence and beauty. She was an emissary for England. Their forefathers were Nubian kings."

"That's quite a story. Shall I get dessert?"

"Tell me about one of the first dead bodies you encountered." Dr Moore settled back in her chair. "How did you feel?"

Coping with our feelings about mortality wasn't on the syllabus at medical school. As newly qualified doctors we learnt from our seniors and cultivated the blackest of humours. We thought it a clever defence. We grew out of that, accepting death with a shrug.

"We did dissection as students but the first post-mortem I went to sticks in my mind. We'd been allocated to a respiratory ward. The consultant had arranged for us to go to the mortuary. As a treat.

You're late, the pathologist said, *so Mrs Fry and I started without you.*

The naked figure of Mrs Fry wasn't an anonymous, shorn cadaver. I recognised her from the ward round the previous week. She'd been admitted with breathlessness.

Her head rested on a wooden block. Frizzy brown hair, streaked with grey, fanned out around her. Her cheeks were sharp, eyes sunken.

She lay on a metal dissection table, which was gently sloped to allow fluid to drain towards the hole at her feet.

Her ribs were cracked open at the sternum to reveal her chest cavity. It was the most indecent of exposures. An ugly, irregular mass covered the upper lobe of her left lung. The pathologist prodded the offending mass with the tip of his scalpel and then he pointed at me. "Diagnosis?"

"Mesothelioma."

"Excellent."

There it was, not pickled in a jar or micron-thick slices on a slide, my first killer *in situ*.

The health centre was in the village. Despite being newly built its pediment bore the same symbol as all the other buildings on the island. The eponymous eye.

"Hi Stephen."

The receptionist waved. He was young and efficient. Why did someone as capable as him stay here?

"Is Fiona in?" I hoped my smile didn't look like a grimace.

"Yes, she's free. Go on in."

I braced myself.

"Fiona, how was your morning?"

"Good. Yours?"

Her cordiality was a barrier I struggled to overcome. Perhaps she felt the same about me.

There were photos on the wall behind her. One of her and Grace at their wedding, both holding wildflowers. Another of them with a boy I recognised from his blond wavy hair.

I sat in the patient's chair beside her desk.

"How can I help you?"

I nearly said, *I've been getting this pain in my knee.*

"Are there any patients I need to know about?"

"What do you mean?"

I resented her briskness. When she spoke there were a myriad of meanings, none of which I could negotiate. I tried again.

"Are there any ill patients I need to be aware of?"

"Oh, I see. A few. Are you ready for a home visit? There's a lady who needs a review at the end of the week."

"Great."

"Kate Bonnard. She has a pineal gland tumour. They're rare. You might want to read up on them."

"Rare and tricky to treat. I've never seen one." The pineal gland was the size of a grain of rice, nestled between the hemispheres of the brain, where it was difficult to reach with a scalpel. "What's her treatment plan? Is stereotactic radiotherapy an option?"

Her mouth twitched with a suppressed smile.

"Very good, Dr Roshan. Sadly, it's pretty aggressive. Kate's declined treatment."

"I'll look at her notes."

I pressed my palms together. "Descartes believed the pineal gland was the seat of the soul."

Fiona's lips pinched together. It was the first time I'd seen her lost for words. *Let her stew,* I thought.

I carried on. "It's a photoreceptor that regulates Circadian rhythms, body temperature and hormones. Some people think it's a vestigial remnant of a much larger organ."

"Georges Bataille talked about the pineal gland in reference to the blind spot in Western rationality."

Fiona seemed disappointed when I didn't pick up this thread. I didn't understand where she was trying to lead me. She stood.

"I'll show you where the syringe drivers are for Kate, when she needs one. And the emergency drugs."

I followed her out and down the corridor to the stock room. Each basket and cupboard was clearly labelled. Sonicaids, assorted syringes and needles, specimen pots, IV kits, more dressings.

"You're very organised."

That seemed to please her.

She opened a drawer.

"Wow, Fiona, that's a lot of syringe drivers."

The drivers were a palliative tool to deliver a continuous infusion of drugs, not just for pain, but also nausea and agitation. There were twelve. A lot for such a small population.

"That was a mistake on the order. My fault. It caused such a fuss that we just kept them."

I couldn't imagine Fiona Banks, whose every word was chosen and delivered with precision, making mistakes. Or why she seemed so ruffled.

The light on Papa Eye is pure. I stuffed myself with it at every opportunity. Walking became meditation. It was the world unfiltered.

I drove to the eastern side of Papa Eye with a plan of seeing the Iris again and then exploring on foot. That end of the island was more dramatic. Instead of soft dunes shored up by marram grass there were cliffs plunging down to the angular rocks.

There was a building on the cliff overlooking the Iris that I hadn't noticed from Hector's boat. A church of sorts in plain stone. Faith at its simplest. I pulled on the heavy iron door ring. It was unlocked.

It was like stepping into a freezer. I turned up my collar and shoved my hands in my pockets. There were dry rushes on the floor. Niches in the walls held partially burnt candles. There were no pews for its congregation. Its congregation would stand.

A huge eye peered down from the ceiling. Its iris was blue-grey, the pupil flecked with gold speckles. There wasn't a cross anywhere.

A stone slab sat under the window, which I took for an altar. It was indented, the outline of a body in repose. It bore a rusty stain that the granite couldn't forget. I reached out.

"Don't touch that."

I thought I was alone. The man's long coat was open despite the chill. I put him in his sixties.

"I'm sorry." I wasn't sure for what.

"Dr Roshan. I've been meaning to introduce myself."

"Call me Ravi."

"I'm Michael. We should talk. My house is the first one along the lane. You can't miss it."

I was going to make an excuse about having to get back but he'd gone. By the time I got to my car he was taking a shortcut across a field.

His home differed from the others on the island in its modern design. Part clad in grey timber gone silver, with great sheets of glass to welcome the outside in.

The front door was open. The hall was double heighted, reaching up to a skylight. Display cabinets hung on one wall. They contained about forty skulls.

"They're prehistoric. I excavated them myself."

"Here?"

"Yes, in a mass grave."

"That's an odd place for trepanning." Each bore a hole in the centre of its forehead. "There must have been a lot of bad spirits that they needed to let out."

"Or they were trying to let something in." He didn't give me time to answer. "Come through."

He laid out a platter of cheeses, ham, slices of apple and dark bread. Coffee bubbled in a noisy percolator.

I followed him into the lounge. There was too much to look at for me to sit down and eat. There was a telescope by the panoramic window with a view of the Iris. A long, low bookshelf lined the opposite wall, on which photographs were laid out.

"These are remarkable. Are they yours?"

"Yes. They're for an exhibition."

There were whirling galaxies. Stars in transit. All those colours hidden in space.

"Were they all taken here?"

"Some of them. That's the joy of dark skies." He picked up one of the images. The sun wore a corona. "Everything's up there. All the answers."

"What are the questions?"

"It would help me immensely if I knew. Let's eat, I'm famished."

He poured the coffee. I bit into my snack. The cheese was smooth and tangy against the nutty bread.

"How old is the church?"

"Thirteen fifty-six. It's an interesting story. Anna said she'd told you about the boat of passengers."

Had all our conversations been recounted?

"A monk came here in 1355. He'd lived a full life with much to atone for. He took the path of green martyrdom."

"What's that?"

"Red martyrdom is the way to God through death. White is by castigation and ridicule. Green is by abstinence and labour."

"You sound like a believer."

"I don't believe but *he* did. He lived in a hut where the church stands. The wind was relentless, and he was always cold and hungry, but he worked every day because he thought his salvation depended on it.

"One day he saw a storm in the distance. There was a speck out on the water. As it got closer he saw it was a rowboat full of souls, one of them a child. He wondered how many children he'd fathered and abandoned out in the world.

"He prayed to God to bring them ashore safely. It was the first time he'd truly prayed for anyone other than himself. All the while there was a great wave building out to sea. It was getting larger and larger, blotting out the dark sky. God was deaf to his pleas.

"So the monk prayed to the Gods of his childhood, the ones older than Christ. He fell on his knees and begged. The wind screamed and the wall of water was getting higher behind the boat, but the pagan Gods were silent.

"There was nothing left to pray to. He called out to the sky itself. He promised it everything. And the universe answered. A wall thrust out of the ocean behind the boat and a hole opened in the black sky. A shower of light fell on them, passengers and monk both. It was so bright, he thought himself blinded. He collapsed, a worm writhing in time's eye.

"When he woke the storm had passed. He crawled to the cliff edge. His skin was burnt and raw, like he'd walked though fire. All his impurities had been burnt away, leaving only the essence of himself.

"He looked down. The immovable object that was the Iris had met the unstoppable force of the wave and the rowboat had settled safety on the shore."

With that, Michael leant over and plucked a grape from the plate and popped it in his mouth.

"Hello Kate. I'm Dr Roshan. We spoke on the phone earlier."

I put my bag down beside the bed.

"You caught me napping." She eased herself up on the pillows before I could help her. "Thanks for coming."

"How have things been?"

"That was delivered last night." She nodded to the commode in the corner. The harbinger of decline.

"How are your headaches?"

"Better with the pills Fiona gave me."

I asked her the stock questions about nausea, her memory, vision and co-ordination, all the time thinking how the body betrays us.

"I know you've spoken to Fiona about this already, but pineal tumours are unusual. Sometimes it's worth getting a second opinion. I'm not saying it would change anything, but I can do that for you."

"Bless you, no."

"Do you want me to arrange extra help? Ed might need a hand looking after you."

Ed stood by the door.

"The whole island will help. It's what we do."

"Is there anything that worries you?"

"The forgetting things. I'm scared of losing my most precious memories." She closed her eyes. "At least Ellen is coming home. She'll be here to remind me."

Ed leant over and kissed her forehead. "Have a nap."

We crept down the creaking stairs to the kitchen.

"Is Ellen your daughter?"

"No, we never had children." He filled the kettle. "She's a niece."

The kitchen door opened. It was the girl in the oversized anorak. Isla.

She doesn't play with us.

"How's Kate?" she asked.

"Isla." Ed's tone was slow and deliberate. As if Isla were about to step on an incendiary. "This is the new doctor."

"I know who he is." She flung her coat over the back of a chair. "How are you settling in, Ravi?"

I was so startled by her self-possession that I struggled to reply. She seemed aware of her effect on me. "I was by the road when you were helping the children with the dead hare."

"Yes. They said you don't go to school with them."

"Isla's home schooled. She's a bit of a prodigy. And very grown up for her age."

She seemed amused by that and Ed looked apologetic, as if chastened for speaking on her behalf.

"You're taught by your mum and dad?"

"No, they're dead. Michael. He's my—" She paused a fraction of a beat too long for comfort. "—uncle."

There were no signs of a child in what I'd seen of Michael's home. It was all skulls and stars.

"I'm sorry to hear about your parents."

"Thank you. It was a long time ago. How's Kate doing?"

"I've sent for Ellen."

Her expression softened, making her look younger. "I'm sorry, Ed. I'll stay with Kate until then. Let me do that at least."

She didn't wait for his permission and all we heard was the light creak of the stairs as she went up.

"I want to spend this session talking about life in general. You mentioned feeling out of step with the world last time. Give me an example."

It was a throwaway comment I'd made the last time I saw her. I never saw Dr Moore taking notes but she could quote our conversations verbatim weeks later.

"The speed of things, I find everything too fast."

"Like?"

"Everything. Instant communication without consideration. And I have all this stuff but no time to enjoy it. Plans I'll never complete. Nothing's explored to any depth."

She tilted her head, her way of saying *And?*

"Nothing feels important."

"Not even your job?"

"I visited an elderly man yesterday, to sort out his medication. Do you know what the most important thing I did for him was? I changed a lightbulb. He was ill but the thing he struggled with the most was not having purpose and a community that values him."

"Isn't that just modern life? Families grow up and move away."

"I'm not saying they shouldn't. It's just that he had all these memories and wisdom that nobody was interested in." I shrugged. "I know I'm not making sense. I just want to strip away everything that's not important."

"What *is* important?"

"Being connected to the world and each other. Not discarding people."

"So what's stopping you?"

"I want to live somewhere that doesn't exist anymore."

"What if it did?"

"I can't just leave."

"Why not? You've got no ties. What if I told you I knew about a job in a place that might suit you?"

Ed's car wasn't outside their house but I knew Kate wouldn't be alone. It had been a week since I'd last seen her and now she needed the final compassions, the simplest acts of bathing and changing the frail body, spooning in goodness while it could still take it.

I'd fallen into the islander's habits. The door was unlocked so I tapped and went straight in.

"Hello."

The house held its breath.

"Kate?"

There were sudden, light footsteps above me. Suitcases waited by the coatrack. A door closed upstairs somewhere.

The clock chimed the hour, startling me. The hammer struck the bell, deep within the wooden casing. I shook my head. I was being ridiculous.

"Kate, it's Ravi." I stood at the bottom of the narrow stairs. Its flanking walls were crowded with framed photos above the handrails. It was like being in a run or a trap.

"I'm coming up."

The doors to the bathroom and second bedroom were closed. The main bedroom door was wide open.

"Kate?"

A man sat beside the bed, his head close to hers. They stopped whispering.

"Hi." I blinked. Kate had an eye painted in the middle of her forehead.

"Hello." The man stood up and the room seemed small suddenly. He wasn't particularly tall, but he was powerfully built. His black jeans and sweater looked expensive and easy on him.

"We've not met." I extended a hand, trying to take the initiative, even though I felt like an intruder. "You are?"

His smile was that of an indulgent adult. He shook my hand. "I'm Morien."

Our hands made a knot, my brown skin, his black. His silver rings dug into my skin.

"Hello." Kate turned her head towards me. Everything was an effort for her. Concentration was a struggle. Her speech was slow. "Morien is a clever man. In business. Samson's so like him, isn't he?"

Kate was making more and more mistakes like that. She must have meant *He's so like Samson,* as Morien looked no more than thirty. She was right though. They were alike.

"Kate, I know you understand that the cancer's getting worse. We can't cure you, it's beyond that, but I wonder if we can help with some of the symptoms. It might be possible for you to have a shunt, a tube to drain some of the fluid that's building up in your brain. I can talk to a specialist about it."

She shook her head. "I don't want this to last longer than it has to. For Ed."

I nodded. She was right.

"Everything I need is here now."

"Tell me about this." I pointed to the eye on her forehead. Morien was motionless.

"It's a blessing. My eyes will close but this one will soon open." Her laugh became a spluttering cough.

"I'll top up your water." Morien grabbed her glass from the bedside. "Lie back and rest."

His feet thudded on the stairs, a different cadence from the one I'd heard walking above me when I came in. Kate stopped coughing. She shut her eyes.

I went to the landing. Water rushed through the pipes as Morien ran the tap downstairs.

The other bedroom door was ajar now. The seconds were heavy, the stillness full. I stood close to the gap, feeling every breath, every movement mirrored by someone on the other side. I touched the doorknob, poised to push it open.

Morien's footsteps were stealthier than before. He stood at the foot of the stairs, bearing a glass. My hand fell to my side. He said nothing, just came up, and I followed him back to Kate.

Dr Moore had a new picture of a body in her office. It was an androgynous outlined figure, hanging in black space. Its arms were held away from its body slightly, palms upwards and feet together as if crucified on a single nail. I could fall into it and be lost forever.

The outline contained a swirl of delicate colours that had been put down in layers on top of an inky blue. Pale seams of gold and orange, of turquoise, ran through it, all overlaid with speckled stars.

"Do you like it?"

"Very much."

"So do I. It was a gift from my friend. Well, she's a sister really."

It was the only time Dr Moore had disclosed anything close to personal. I leant down to read the words written at one corner. *Luciano by Thora Fahey.*

"Let's begin."

We settled in our respective chairs, the objects on the tray before us familiar now. I liked how the stoneware coffee cup sat in my hand.

"What does the picture say to you?"

"We are stellar and we are nothing."

"Do you believe in God?"

I shrugged.

"Were you raised with religion?"

"Father, liberal Hindu. Mother abandoned her Catholic background for an Indian guru. I went to a Church of England school. I accepted it all and believed none of it."

"So you're agnostic?"

"Atheist when I'm feeling brave." I didn't care if I seemed flippant. I was in a strange mood.

So was she. I couldn't decipher her smile.

"Has doctoring changed how you feel about it?"

"I struggle with the fact everything we are and all the love we have is gone afterwards."

"Is that why you don't commit to anything? Loss?"

I wanted to deny that, but all evidence was to the contrary. "I'm not stupid. I mean, I know loss is a natural part of life but it seems unfair, to make us all unique. Irreplaceable. And when we're gone, that's it."

"We've touched on this before. Snowflakes are unique. Transience is what makes them special. Who wants to live forever?"

The question was heartfelt and weary, but I ignored it in my sudden anger. "Why give us all this then? Why give us all these memories if none of it matters. When I go, they'll be lost forever."

"What memories?"

I told her about my father, who sat by the electric fire in the front room of the house on Acacia Drive, where I grew up. He clutched a letter in his hand, the blue airmail paper like dry blue petals crushed in his hand. Mum prised it from him and smoothed it out to read of his father's death. It was the first time I'd ever seen him cry.

Then I told her about the home visit to an old lady called Agnes Beswick. When she answered the door, she held up her hands to my face. She smelt of Christmas. She'd been studding oranges with cloves. She'd stacked them in an indigo blue bowl on the hall table.

I told her about Emily Taylor, who was thirteen years old and rushed to hospital in a diabetic coma. I stayed with her all night, taking blood samples every hour and readjusting her insulin pump. She was the youngest of three sisters and liked hockey. I wonder if she remembered me at all.

I told her about my first holiday with Amy, my ex-wife. How we sat on a rooftop terrace in Portugal, eating grilled prawns in garlic oil with our fingers, and I had loved her, but not as much she desired or deserved. Of her sense of fair play and the way she tied her shoelaces.

When I started to tell Dr Moore it was hard to stop.

I was driving back home from a visit to old Simon Gray a few days later. Isla's blue anorak lay in the road. I thought she must have dropped it. I found her about five hundred yards away. Her shirt had gone too, thrown aside.

Her narrow chest was blistered. There were raw areas that were wet and weeping, a stark contrast to remaining areas of white skin. Her left nipple was intact. There was a birthmark on her left shoulder that I took for a burn at first. Her trousers were stuck to her in charred patches. She still had her trainers on.

Her hair was burnt away, her tender scalp scorched. The skin of face had peeled, leaving it red and outraged.

She looked impossibly small, prodigy of Papa Eye, a place where children are free to roam.

I put my face close to hers. Air moved against my cheek. I ran back to the Land Rover and grabbed my radio and medical bag.

"Stephen, are you there?"

There was a crackle, followed by a burst of sound. I was relieved to hear his voice.

"Stephen, tell Hector to take the boat out beyond the Iris. We need an air ambulance and the police."

"What's happened?"

"It's Isla. She's badly burnt. Someone's set her on fire."

There was a long pause.

"Stephen? Did you hear that?"

"Roger that."

I picked her up. Heat seeped from her, searing my forearms. What remained of her skin stuck to my jacket as I tried to shift her weight.

Isla's eyelids snapped open. She stared through me. Her sclerae were bloodshot, livid against the pale blue of her irises.

"Who did this?"

She seemed to register me and then the gaze became blank. Her eyes rolled back in her head. I let out a yelp. It felt like she was on fire, even though there were no flames. I didn't mean to drop her. The ground beneath her started to smoulder.

A car pulled alongside me. I felt a surge of relief. It was Samson. He went straight to Isla and then opened the emergency bag beside her. Everything about him was direct and calm.

It was only then that I saw Michael was behind him. He wasn't shocked by the smoking body of a child. He didn't even look surprised.

"We'll take her from here."

"No."

"Samson and I will take her."

Samson put a hand on my shoulder. I pushed him off.

There was a roar as a motorbike rounded the bend. It slowed to a rumble before it stopped. I knew who it was before he removed his helmet.

"What's going on here?"

Morien, man of action. He got off the bike and unzipped his leather jacket. He pulled a gun from the holster beneath. I'd never seen one so close. It's a thing of gravitas and promise.

"You're all wasting time. We need to move her. Pick her up. Let's go."

The road to the old church was lined with cars. People came on foot, some across the field. Adults carried baskets and bottles. Children carried stars made from foil taped to sticks. Others wore tabards. A few of these were embroidered with gold thread but most were painted. All bore the stylised emblem of Papa Eye. Eyes everywhere. Third eyes painted on foreheads.

This procession fell in behind Hector, who carried a wooden shield and beat out a rhythm on it with a wooden sword. A heavy thwack that made my heart beat faster and my stomach lurch. The mood was of awe and worship, like the Spanish fiestas where saints' effigies were borne aloft and paraded through the streets.

I recognised some of the faces. Ordinary, everyday people who watched as Michael lifted Isla from the car. There were no gasps or questions. A boy hid his face in his father's side. The man stroked his son's head. "It's okay. You'll see."

A woman put her hand to her heart and murmured, "May she be bathed in the light of the eye."

"The light of the eye." Other voices repeated it in a gentle, melodic chant. I saw Stephen, mouth moving, eyes closed in prayer.

Help wasn't coming. Isla was going to die.

So was I.

Morien was beside me. He'd put the gun away. I could run but it wouldn't make any difference now. That moment was long gone.

"Ravi."

Anna. She pushed through the crowd. *Thank God,* I thought, when I saw her bright, familiar face.

"Anna, we have to help Isla."

"Yes. We've been struggling with how to explain it. Now you can see for yourself."

Petra elbowed her way through the crowd and ran to her grandmother and flung her arms around her waist.

"What do we say?" Anna looked down and raised an eyebrow at Petra.

"Hello Dr Ravi." Her bright face smiled into mine. "Grandma, can I come with you and watch?"

"Maybe when you're older. Now go back to Mummy."

Petra skipped away.

"You're all mad."

"After you." Morien motioned to the door.

The church's interior was even colder than I remembered. The elongated shafts of light through the slitted windows made the shadows even darker. Isla was on the stone altar. I thought of the indelible stains.

Samson had already started work, inserting a subcutaneous cannula into her arm. Anna joined him, using scissors from a dressing pack to cut away the remains of her clothes.

"Samson, it's not too late. We need to get her to the burns unit."

Anna hummed as she anointed the child with ointment from a plain white tub. Samson laid out medication on a plastic tray. He examined each vial, the routine of checking the drug name and expiry date entrenched.

"What are you giving her?"

"Morphine. Midazolam. Prochlorperazine."

"Samson, you can't just let her die."

A hand landed on my shoulder. It was Morien. He wore aviator goggles on his forehead. He passed me a pair and moved on, giving out more. They all had darkened glass. It was dreamlike. Events turned around me.

"Here, let me help."

Morien raised Isla's leg and Anna started to wind bandages around it. They finished at her hip, then started work on the other leg.

"Ravi, come here."

Samson connected up the syringe driver. I could hear the faint rattle of Isla's breath. I touched the stone beneath her. It had absorbed the heat she was radiating.

They were using it to cool her down.

"This has happened before, hasn't it? Who did this to her?"

"Nobody. It just happens. She'll pull through but the next twenty-four hours are going to be hard. She needs our help. When this is over, you'll understand. I'm sorry, I couldn't find a way to tell you." Samson looked contrite.

"Understand what?"

"The extraordinary. Now, put those goggles on."

It was too late. Isla opened her eyes. I turned away from the blinding light that shot out.

I'd no idea how long I'd been lying on the floor. When I opened my eyes the candles in the niches had been lit. Someone had rolled me onto a blanket and put another over me.

Everyone's attention was on Isla. They surrounded her. I crawled to the door. I didn't have a plan. I just didn't want to see what was happening.

It was night. Flares had been lit. People got up from camping chairs and out of cars when they saw me. I stumbled into the crowd. I swatted away the hands that reached for me. A murmur went through them as if they had one voice. I was flailing.

"Stop. You're going to hurt yourself."

A calm, authoritative voice marshalled me. Hands slid around mine.

"Ravi, look at me. It's Dr Moore. Dr Ellen Moore. I came to check on you. I need you to calm down. I don't have much time. I need to get back to Kate. She's dying."

My knees buckled. Ellen caught me and lowered me to the ground.

I woke up in a strange bed. My head was thudding and my mouth was tacky. The room was white walled and spartan. The blinds were partially drawn.

A small figure sat in a shadowed corner, folded up in the chair.

"Come forward. I want to see you."

Isla moved, coming to sit cross-legged at the end of the bed. She wore shorts and a plain T-shirt. Her skin was pink and peeling as though all she'd suffered was a case of bad sunburn. She put a hand to her hairless scalp, conscious of my scrutiny.

"It'll grow back."

"How long have I been out?"

"Only a few hours more than me. Ellen gave you something to sleep."

"She drugged me?"

"Don't be dramatic. You were hysterical. She was scared you'd hurt yourself. I'm here to show you I'm okay."

"I can see that but I don't understand how. Explain."

"You know some of our story already. From Michael and Anna."

"What? About the monk and the passengers in the boat?"

"Yes, Michael was the monk."

My laugh died under the weight of her gaze. Her eyes were so old.

"And you're the child."

"My father took me on a pilgrimage after my mother died. Since we got caught in the light we keep going through the same process. Every five years for the others, but for me it's more often. I think it was because I was so young when it happened. We never age. It took me a hundred years to forgive Michael for his *miracle* when I realised I'd be stuck in this body."

"Regenerating. It looks painful."

"It is."

"You can't die?"

"Only if the body is damaged beyond repair. My father was

killed in a motorcycle crash in Italy about sixty years ago."

"I'm sorry."

"I miss him. He saw me through the hardest years. He's always with me. If people are alive while we remember them, then he's always with us."

"Doesn't the past get heavy?"

I wasn't even sure what I meant but Isla seemed to understand.

"It's a privilege and a burden. Over time I've come to understand how to see it for what it is, not what I want it to be."

Morien nudged the door open and put down a tray. "Here. Sweet tea."

He handed us both a mug.

"Are you going to kill me?"

"You really mean that, don't you? Would I bother making you a drink first?" Morien snorted. "I'm sorry about the gun. You were all wasting time bickering."

He didn't sound sorry. He said it like a man who knew he should apologise but would do the same again. Morien would always do what was necessary, without hesitation.

"Sir Morien."

I could surprise him in that at least.

"I was on a mission for my king, protecting his best ambassador. My sister, Ellen."

"Ellen."

I was too tired to hide the venom in my voice.

"She wasn't trying to trick you. She's been a psychologist for decades. She thought you'd be right for us. And us for you. She said you were a kindred spirit and could fit in here."

"Why does she think that?"

"The light did different things to us all. She sees things in people. Auras. Chakras. Call it what you want."

"What was the light?"

"Heloise spent the 1950s convinced it was aliens. Una's still convinced it's God, whereas it robbed Michael of his faith. Luciano spent a decade on hallucinogenics but couldn't reproduce it."

"What do you both think?"

"I've no idea, but I think it blind luck saved us."

"Luck or curse." Isla's smile was rueful. "Michael studies the stars because he thinks it's happened before and will again."

"And what about Ellen? What does she believe?" After everything, her opinion still mattered.

"Ellen's theory is that the mind's eye has atrophied into the pineal gland. The light stimulated it, mimicking birth or death, which is when there's a surge of hormones from the gland. It changed us."

"That's a clever idea."

"It's more than a theory," Morien said. "We've all had MRI scans. Our pineal glands are four times bigger than they should be."

"Morien, how's Kate?"

He leant forward in his chair, mirroring me.

"I'm sorry to tell you that she died in the night."

"*I'm* sorry." I thought I had professional immunity from sadness. I was sad for myself and relieved for Kate.

"Ed, Ellen and Fiona were with her. She was comfortable."

A question occurred to me.

"How old was Kate?"

"Ninety-two." Her records had stated she was sixty-eight. That must have been an administrative challenge for them.

"They're all our children, well, those of us who could have children," Isla sniffed. "They live long, healthy lives."

"Isla, you're a mother to everyone, even me sometimes." Morien winked at her.

"Is it coincidence that she had a pineal cancer?"

"We don't think so. We have more of them than we should here. We hide the fact, to avoid too much scientific interest."

Morien clasped his hands together.

"We hold our children when they're born and again when they leave this world. It never gets any easier."

I followed the line of mourners. The same people who held vigil for

Isla were here for Kate's funeral.

I caught up with Ed. I'd not seen him since her death.

"I just wanted to say how sorry I am about Kate."

"Thank you. She liked you. You took good care of her."

How old was Ed? How many years had they woken up side by side?

I fell back to let others walk beside him. Fiona's wife, Grace, slipped her arm through mine.

"Thank God everything's out in the open. We can get to know each other properly now. Fiona's been furious with Samson. She wanted to tell you everything from the start."

"I thought she didn't like me."

"Far from it."

"To be fair to Samson, I wouldn't have believed it. And I'm not sure I'm even staying."

I waited for a telltale sign. The stiffening of her body or a change of expression. I still thought they might kill me.

"It's a lot to take on. We've been surrounded by it all our lives, so we forget. If you go, please know we'll always welcome you back. You're part of our story now and we're part of yours."

We went on in silence for a while.

"Grace, how old are you?"

"Sixty-eight."

"You don't look a day over forty."

She raised an eyebrow at me.

"Thirty-five."

"Better."

"And Samson?"

"In his eighties."

"No wonder he goes on about retiring."

We turned onto the path to the community centre.

"Have you ever lived away from Papa Eye?" The question had new resonance.

"When I was in my thirties, I lived in New York with a man. He wanted to have kids. There would have been too many questions."

"So you had to end it."

"Worse. I was a coward. I said I was going for bread and never went back. I owed him more than that." She took a deep breath. "We all end up back here. It's not a utopia but we have a lot of time to work out our problems."

The foyer was crowded. Grace drew an eye on my forehead in kohl and handed me the pencil to reciprocate. We filed into the hall, picking up drinks from a long table.

"I'm not one for speeches," Ed began. He paused, trying to compose himself. "My darling Kate's eyes have closed to the light for the last time. We've had a long and happy life together. We've been lucky enough to be part of this place. It's only being here with you all that makes a life without her bearable. Thank you. To Kate. May she reside in the eye's light."

We raised our glasses.

"May she reside in the light of the eye."

There was a buffet. People clustered in the hall, sat at tables or perched on windowsills. An old man came over to me, making slow progress on his walking stick. It was Simon Gray, the island's oldest resident. His notes said he was ninety-four. I went to meet him.

"Doctor." He clutched my arm to steady himself. Before Papa Eye I dreaded meeting patients outside the surgery, expecting them to ask me about their results or tell me about a new symptom.

"I'd like to introduce you to Thora."

He handed me over to her. It was like being presented to royalty. Her legacy was in the faces of the islanders who gathered around her. A heart-shaped face. Hazel eyes. They were comforted by her presence. It was in their expressions when she leant over to speak to them or touch them.

"Hello, Ravi. You've caused all kinds of excitement. We don't get enough newcomers here, as you can imagine."

"Thora Fahey. The artist."

"How do you know?"

"I saw your painting in Ellen's office. Are you the nun?"

"No, I was Heloise's servant, once upon a time."

She pointed to an older woman on the far side of the room. Someone handed her a baby and she laid it on her knee and peered into its face.

Petra slid under Thora's arm.

"Hello poppet."

Seeing Petra was an excuse for Samson to join us. He stood at my elbow.

"I'm sorry, Ravi. As the weeks went on, it got harder and harder to tell you."

"Just give me a bit of time." I wasn't sure whether that meant I was staying or not but he seemed satisfied.

Thora broke the awkwardness.

"We've all come back for the funeral. And to meet you."

They weren't hard to spot. They were lodestones to the people of Papa Eye.

I edged closer to a group and the circle opened to enfold me. Someone was telling a story. It could only be Luciano. They waved at me but didn't stop. Their diamond nose stud winked at me.

"Kate started walking at ten months. She never crawled. It was winter and there was a crowd of us at Lyndsey and Mark's. Kate pulled herself up on the settee and then was walking along. When she realised she was clinging to my knees she started to bawl and turned and staggered across the room to Lyndsey like a heartbroken drunk."

Luciano laughed at the memory.

"Ravi, here."

Morien handed me a tumbler of whisky and motioned with his head for me to follow him to a cluster of chairs by the fire. Ed and Ellen were there. I wouldn't hide from her. Nor she from me because she got up and kissed my cheek.

"Dr Moore." I sounded stiff.

"Ellen. You're not my patient anymore." She had her brother's unapologetic manner. Or maybe he had hers. "I'm an island resident so technically I'm yours now."

We sat down.

"I was there at her birth," Ellen began. Ed stared at the whisky in his hand. "It was the twelfth of October and a white mist clung to me as I walked over to the house. Kate was a solid baby, like her dad had been. Lyndsey was being stitched up. Mark knelt by her head, holding Kate like he was scared he'd break her. Something ignited in him as soon as he saw Kate. Something fierce but also the towering fear of fatherhood. Lyndsey saw it. She said, 'We can do this. Together. And we have all this help too. We're not alone.'"

Morien picked up the bottle from the floor beside him. It was unlabelled. He topped up our glasses. There were gold highlights in the amber liquid as I swirled it around. It was rich in my mouth, sweet and smoky on my tongue.

Ellen hadn't finished. "She was so nervous before your first date. She changed three times. Lyndsey pinned up her hair."

"She'd never worn it like that before. That's how she did it for our wedding."

"She borrowed my perfume."

"Gardenia." Ed closed his eyes. Smell, the greatest evoker of memory.

"She liked you so much that she wouldn't tell us anything about it afterwards. All she said was 'Tell Ed I had the best time. Tell him that from me, from this moment, if he ever needs to hear it.'"

Ed tipped back the glass and drained it. When he put it down he was smiling and crying all at once.

So it was that we went on remembering Kate, well into the night.

I go up to the church every night that I can, and light one of the candles in the niches. For favour. Or luck. Then I take a blanket out onto the clifftop and lie on my back, watching the sky darken. The Iris, out to sea, shelters me from inclement weather.

As blue becomes black I think about the colours that lie hidden beyond it, if only I could see them. I wait for the light, my eyes open.

VOLCANO
BY LIVIA LLEWELLYN

Have you ever been in danger?

Have you ever had to run as if your life depended on it, run as fast and as hard and with as much fearful feral animal instinct as your bones and flesh could withstand, have you ever run with such brutal purpose that it felt like your lungs were on fire, your heart pounding against your contorting ribs until you thought your entire body would explode like a dying sun?

And while running, did you ever pause ever so briefly, did you ever just take a quick and furtive look behind your back, just to make sure that whatever was barreling behind you with unforgiving, unstoppable speed and fury was real, was indeed still coming after you, was not giving up pursuit?

And in that moment when you looked, did you realize that the chase had been over long before you had sensed any danger in your life, long before you yourself set all the elements of your annihilation in motion, did you realize in that moment of looking back that you were dead long before you ever thought to run?

Every summer is the worst. I always forget that. The start of each school year is like being born again, with new classes and a new major, new rooms in new dorms, and autumn exploding across the campus and town and valley with such clarity and force; and

I say to myself, this is how life should be, it should be unlived and ahead of me, so I can always look forward to starting it.

I do try, you know. I try so hard.

But.

It's inevitable, what comes next. Like when the winter snow turns pocked and filthy, then bleeds away, leaving all that destruction behind, all the freshness and excitement disappears. All my choices gone wrong, classes that bored me, roommates turned into enemies, every aspect of my life revealed to be a rotting mistake. By the end of every school year, by every summer, it's all black. Black and barren like the scablands that surround us, scoured to the Pleistocene bone by the weight and rage of the Missoula floods, with nothing left of everything that came before. Empty black space, waiting for me to fill it up and stitch it up and, oh, for all the hot, sticky, bloody moments of creation I need to set in motion for that beautiful fresh beginning to return.

And now it's summer again.

I stand in the hallway outside the drama department costume shop, where I used to work until I decided to implode, as I always do. It is long past midnight, but light blazes from the open double doors as costumers, seamstresses, and actors swarm back and forth, the rev and whine of the sewing machines a floating constant under low voices and the constant droning thump of music from a massive boom box. I know the sound from that machine well, I know it as well as the sergers and the heavy hissing irons and everything else in the room, because it's mine, I brought it into the shop at the beginning of June when the university shut down and the summer theatre season began. In my mind I can see the open shoebox sitting next to it on the notions cabinet, filled with cassette and mix tapes, a communal offering from everyone who's been working sixteen-hour days for the past four weeks to finish all the costumes for a three-play repertory season that begins in five days. Well, I started off with good intentions, as always—I did the sixteen-hours-a-day, six-day-a-week thing for as long as I could stand it. It's just, I can never stand anything for very long.

"You can't come back in. You don't work here anymore." Jacqueline stands in front of the open door, blocking my access. She's the shop manager, my former boss, my boss until last week, when she caught me working on a dress I designed myself for myself instead of finishing a costume for the lead actress in *The School for Wives*. Now that costume is being finished by another little worker bee, a new Jacqueline's favorite who replaced me after I was escorted out with my dress and my fishing tackle case of personal sewing supplies. Everything except my boom box and cassette tapes. Which Jacqueline isn't going to let me take. Not much of a surprise, I'm slightly buzzed and bored and feeling a bit vindictive. I probably shouldn't have worn my new dress. Then again, it never occurred to me to not wear it.

"Fine, can you go into the shop and get it for me?" I over-enunciate each word, not just because of the buzz, but because I know it drives Jacqueline crazy. "I'll wait right here outside the door like a good little girl."

"Fuck you." Her breath is labored, as if she'd climbed one too many flights of stairs. "You stole supplies, you—"

"That's a lie and you know it, I did not steal a single fucking thing!"

"You stole time, you stole resources, you stole the trust of the actors, the directors, your coworkers, you stole *my* trust, after all I did for you! I invited you to my house, I fed you, you met my family and children, I confided in you—" Her voice rises, a familiar tinge of hysteria creeping into her speech—tears aren't far behind, followed by declarations of physical pain somewhere in the vicinity of her heart. Behind her, I see people slowing down and casually stopping just within viewing range. My young replacement smirks as she steps into full view, casually holding the dress I should have been working on before I was fired. What a cunt.

"Listen, I'm not here to stir things up," I lie. "But you said I could have it back, you said you'd call me and let me know when I could pick it up, and I waited, and I think I've waited long enough. I just want to take what's mine and leave, that's all."

"Do you understand the massive damage that you did?" Oh great, she's shouting now. "You don't get to decide when I should call you, you don't get to have anything to do with what goes on in this building anymore—"

"So you can just decide to keep my property and I don't get any say in the matter—?"

"You made that decision for me! You made your choice, you got paid to sew costumes for this company and instead you worked on your own wardrobe instead for god knows how long, so you don't get to just waltz back in like some little princess and demand—"

Everything turns black for a second, a blackness that is incandescent.

Not here. Not now.

"Oh Jesus fucking Christ—you know what? You know what?" I step back, hands up in that *keep your crazy off of me, bitch* gesture. "Just keep it, okay? Just keep it, it's not worth this bullshit. Keep my two-hundred-dollar cassette player and all my tapes and call it fucking even, okay? Call the bursar's office or the goddamn police if you have a problem with that, okay? You can calm down now, I'm done, I promise, I will never come back." I turn and walk down the darkened hallway, hands clenched as I try not to break into a run. Keep it cool, bitch, keep it light. Behind me I can feel everyone's stares boring holes into my head, I hear Jacqueline muttering my name and some obscenity or five as she shuffles back into the shop. A sharp burst of laughter bounces into the empty hall, and I seethe all the way downstairs and through the department I'm no longer a student of until I'm finally outside. I don't glance back, there's no lingering, sentimental last look at the drama department as I make my way through the dorms and off campus. I've done this before, with different departments. It's just easier to keep your focus on what's ahead.

The night air blankets me with soft warmth, and millions of stars pierce the cloudless sky. It's a long walk back to my apartment, but I don't mind. Ellensburg is mine at night, it belongs solely to me, the sprawling campus, the small wooden houses, the empty streets that shoot off into the desolate scablands. I walk uninterrupted and alone, unafraid, a light wind tugging at the hem of my dress. The fabric is silk, dark purple and navy flowers intertwined with emerald vines against a deep fuchsia background—very tropical, not at all practical or collegial. Was it worth my job? The design is a collarless slender column with a plunging V-front, and a thigh-high slit hidden under an extra layer of fabric that would reveal itself only if the wearer was reclining. A dress for a woman living in a different part of the world, a woman with a soft, elegant life. In the dark, under the sodium street lamps and swaying traffic lights of this dusty forgotten jumble of worn prairie brick and Brutalist concrete, it makes me feel connected to a creative life force that exists only outside the limits of this town, and now also within my heart.

Up ahead, in the middle of the block, squats a two-story house trying desperately to pass itself off as Victorian, the peeling white paint giving off a faint glow as if radioactive, or haunted. I never asked the landlord, who lives on the first floor, how long his family had owned it, or if they had been the original builders. He was cranky and somewhat menacing, and I toed the line for once and was polite and deferential right up to the moment I handed over the crumpled check for a set of keys. My apartment takes up the front half of the second floor, with a small unoccupied studio in the back. I look up at my window as I head up the small path along the left side of the house—the glass glows dark red as if a portal to Hell opened up in my living room. It's from a kitschy red-paned Moroccan-style lamp hanging in the corner—a leftover from decades ago, when the landlord was the son, living upstairs from his parents and carving out his college identity with shag carpeting and mandalas painted on the bathroom walls. I promised him I'd keep everything the way it was, just as all the other tenants had. I meant it, too. I sleep here, but this is not where I live. I haven't found that place yet.

Faint music from the radio and the metallic whomp of fan blades greet me when I brush away the new spiderwebs and open the front door. I slip off my sneakers, and by the time I'm in the living room, the dress is off as well. It served its purpose; I won't wear it again. Beads of sweat are running down the sides of my face, and pooling under my arms and breasts—it's stifling. Room by room I crack open the windows, knowing it won't help much until hours from now, for that short, livable time between late morning and noon. In the bedroom, I slip on an oversized T-shirt, one of the many crew shirts from productions I've worked on this past year, then pull a large jewelry box out of the closet. I open it up and stare at the tangled mass of diamond, ruby, emerald, pearl, and gold earrings, chokers, brooches, and rings. All vintage. All fake, of course— costume jewelry, a perfect name considering I pilfered them over the year from the costume shop. I run my fingers over the sharp and smooth edges, then snap the box shut and shove it back in the closet, next to some lovely, purloined stilettos. Fuck Jacqueline, and fuck that boom box. I always make sure I get paid.

Heading back to the living room, I stop to grab a beer from the fridge. This is my nightly calm-down beer, not to be confused with my earlier fuck-shit-up beers. The couch is littered with department catalogs, printouts of class schedules for the coming fall, degree requirement checklists, fat manila envelopes from other universities that don't yet know what kind of ruin of a student is sniffing around their programs. I'd call it ephemera but it's really detritus. I push it onto the floor and lie down—I recline—and listen to the DJ's voice as he introduces the next song. An old one, he says, and as it begins, I smile, my lips pulling back half in amusement, half in disgust. An old one. A song from my freshman year. That was seven years ago. Seven years and four abandoned majors. Old one. I drain the bottle and let it slip to the shaggy floor, then stare at the glowing red ceiling until, like the world, like my ambitions, like my life, it slips away. And all that remains is the sound of laughter, a pinprick of discomfort in the flat black landscape of sleep. A pinprick that some unnamed incandescent emotion threads in and out of, slowly and carefully widening the hole.

* * *

The next morning starts as it always does, around eleven, when the heat begins seeping back in through the aging plaster and wood, and the sun washes through the dusty windows, catching on stray spiderweb strands and bouncing off the wood-paneled walls.

"Fucking hell," I snarl to no one in particular. I sit at the edge of the couch, elbows on my knees, head bowed down. Little flashes of darkness and light explode as I rub my eyes hard, then leave my hands pressed against my forehead. Outside, the wind has picked up, that familiar wind that always thunders through Ellensburg regardless of the season, shredding leaves off the trees, tossing garbage cans into the air, and lashing your hair against your face until you want to scream. The house buckles and groans. I'm motionless, crouched over, eyes closed. Something is threading through me, a needle of hard emotion is piercing its way about the dark fabric of my heart, although whether it is stitching or unstitching, I cannot say. I do not want to say.

I'm out of the apartment by two, which is tragic, because the sun is relentless and I burn so easily. I've gotten good at finding the shadiest sidewalks and streets, but it doesn't stop the heat from making me a bit ill. And that fucking wind, again. By the time I get to the Student Union Building, I'm a combination of numbness and frothy rage over all the forces of nature and life I can't control. Inside, I pay a quick trip to the bathroom to wipe the speckles of grit off my face and neck before heading to the off-campus jobs board. The SUB is cavernous and quiet, and the sun pouring through the high windows feels benevolent instead of menacing. I wish it were like this all the time, everywhere: no people, no noise, just the faint drone of machinery making the world comfortable for me as I make my way through it. But that lovely feeling curdles into despair—even from a distance I can see so much empty corkboard. Of course. It's the middle of the summer, there are thirty thousand fewer people living here right now, what jobs would anyone have available, when there's no one to sell anything to? I stare at the few cards tacked up. Fruit picker. Nope, I'd drop like a fly after five minutes. Day care worker at the senior assisted living center. There's been a version of that card on the board ever since I started school here—I applied after my freshman year. Didn't even make it through the interview. A very professional and corporate poster advertising employment opportunities at the McDonald's out on Canyon Road. Already did that, two years ago. I lasted a whole month, walking a mile to work and back every day, reeking of onions and hamburger fat. I never did pick up my last paycheck. Room cleaner at the Motel 6 on East University Way. Ugh. Also, maybe. A last resort? I glance around, then rip the entire paper off the board and shove it in my backpack. Sorry, losers, that sweet used condom picker-upper job is all mine now.

I walk past the other bulletin boards, flicking the fringed edges of flyers advertising rooms and houses to rent, ride shares to Seattle and all other points west of the Cascades, furniture and dorm room junk for sale, going fast. Most of them dated from the end of spring. This place really is a ghost town in summer. The last board is the Have You Seen listings. In all the years I've been here, I've never once seen it empty. Photos and flyers cover its surface in, some stiff and yellow with age. Students who disappeared after class, left their dorms or a bar or party and slipped into the day or night never to be seen again. A few teachers and professors too, a couple of admin staff, some dogs. I run my hands across the curling edges, lift crackling paper to reveal faces I remember from long ago and not so long ago. Smiles frozen, breath halted, all possibilities stilled. Colleges are places of transience; people shouldn't stay here very long. There's a board like this in every building on the campus. Put all together, they are a single body, a single bulletin board of flesh that hangs from every corner of a black subterranean room lost to time and removed from history, a spiderweb of reworked bones and sinew, rotting away with the years even as more parts are stitched and nailed into it, a single shivering god-body of decay and death with a hollowed-out space in the middle for a heart yet to be found, a heart large enough and strong enough to bring it all into glorious life. Or a space large enough for a girl to slip into, to lose herself in, to never be seen again until some unnamable cosmic power in its eternal wandering stumbles upon her sleeping form, and with a fairytale touch turns her into the very heart she has always searched for, the very heart that will someday pump and funnel hot blood and fire through every bent and broken limb of her patchwork god, sending it soaring through the flimsy crust of earth out into the night and away, away from all of this, away to simply float forever throughout the universe with no purpose except to sublimely be.

Slipping my sunglasses back on, I push through the doors back into the dry furnace heat of afternoon and listlessly plod over to Mitchell Hall, crossing my fingers that they'll be open, that someone will be there, that maybe I'll find something in the campus job listings before having to apply for a job cleaning rooms that probably look like murder scenes.

The building doors are open, but it's as quiet inside as everywhere else. I make my way upstairs only to find a locked door, the long room with its multiple service windows dark and empty. How many times have I stood before each of those windows, picking up loan checks, paying tuition, sobbing over late fees? Hundreds of ghost me's are trapped in there, eternally negotiating for a little more leniency, a little more time. I head back downstairs and wander through the labyrinth of halls. A few offices are open on this floor, a few heads are illuminated by desk lamps as they tap away at word processors or talk softly on phones, but no one pays me any attention, and I don't stop to ask if the career center is open. I'm just enjoying the air-conditioning while I quietly meander and snoop. I stop and press my nose against a glass door, peering inside just because I can.

"Can I help you?"

"Shit!" I whirl around, my backpack slamming against the locked door. "Jesus, you scared me—I—I'm just looking for the career center. Sorry, I'm kind of lost, this is my first time here."

The older man standing in front of me isn't an office worker. He's dressed in worn jeans and a light blue work shirt, and a thick, worn utility belt loaded with tools hangs at his waist. A walkie-talkie is in his hand, raised to his face.

"Can I see your student ID?" He holds out his hand. His demeanor is pleasant, but firm. I will not be fucking around with him. Well, not that much. I slip my ID out of my backpack and hand it to him. He studies it, looks up at me, looks back.

"Calliope Juno Emerson. A senior?"

I give him a tight, polite smile.

"You look a bit young to be a senior."

My number one secret weapon—I still look like a teenager. "It's a blessing and a curse."

"The career center is closed today. How about I show you out so you don't get lost." He holds out his arm, that gesture that says start moving, that way, now. I do so, falling in step with his long strides.

"Sure. Thanks. Sorry to be such trouble."

"Oh, it's not trouble at all."

"Do you know when it'll be open again? The career center?"

"You have a directory? Call the number, they give the hours in their message. They're not open every day, they won't be until the start of September. They're not going to have much in the way of openings anyway, not until late August."

"Okay, thanks. I know, I just wanted to check here before going off-campus. I'd rather have a university job than, you know, McDonald's or something."

"Nothing wrong with manual labor."

"Oh, I know. I just spent the last year working on tech crews in the drama department." I point to his utility belt. "You're in facilities, right?"

He nods: his pace slows, just a bit. I fucking got him.

I slip my backpack off again, and pull out a file folder. "Listen, maybe this is a long shot, but if you could take my résumé—" I slip it out of the folder and into his free hand. "—and see if someone in facilities or operations has a job opening. I'd really prefer to stay on campus, it's just easier than rushing from classes to some place in town or out by the freeway."

We've stopped in the middle of the hallway, just a few feet from the doors I came through twenty minutes ago. As he glances at my résumé, I step back and grow quiet, in that thoughtful, respectful manner you assume during an interview. What he's reading, of course, is a very orderly reordering of the truth of my job history. Not so much lies as sanding the truth down to the more marketable accomplishments, accompanied of course by some very well-written and forged letters of recommendation. These are not the jobs that I can no longer speak about, disastrous situations that I have obscured so deeply in my palimpsest past that I have trouble remembering them, and am now somewhat skeptical that they ever occurred.

"So, Calliope."

"Callie."

"Callie. I'm Tom. So, it looks like you have some sewing experience. Are you any good?"

"Yes. I'm an excellent seamstress—I've been sewing and designing clothes since I was in grade school." This is an actual truth.

"Just clothes? Anything else?"

I shrug. "Sure. Pillow shams, I've done some quilting—machine and by hand. Table runners, placemats . . . Things like that?"

"What about curtains? Drawstring curtains?"

"Yes, of course." It's a half-lie, I once sewed up some flimsy half-curtains for my aunt's kitchen window.

"What about upholstery? Chairs, sofas, and not just the cushions, I mean the whole thing. Ever done that?"

I hesitate. He notices. "I've sewn a few pillows and cushion coverings, but not—not like tearing furniture apart and nailing it back together. I've never done that."

The man pulls a business card out of his shirt pocket and hands it to me. *Thomas Obermeijer, Facilities Supervisor,* followed by a long list of building names. I look up at him, a pleasant, expectant expression on my face.

"I have a job," he begins, and relief floods through me, almost orgasmic. "It's hard work, lots of sewing—do you know how to use industrial machines?"

"Yes, that's what my professors teach us on in the fashion design classes I've been taking—I've been using them all year." I don't mention the costume shop or drama department. Another area of my life that will sink into the black abyss.

He takes back the card, quickly scribbles on the back of it. "Meet me outside that building tomorrow morning—are you free?"

"Yes, absolutely, thank you!"

"I have someone else you'll be working with, another student— we'll visit the work site and go through the specifics, and then if you're still interested, you can fill out the paperwork to make it official. It's not going to be a fun job, but you'll get minimum wage. Forty hours a week until September, then we'll see how it goes with your class schedule. Sound good?"

"Yes, thank you!"

We've reached the doors, and he opens them. All the cold air rushes away in the blast of heat pouring over us, and it's like I'm being enveloped in fire. "Oh," I exclaim, "you think I'd be used to it by now."

"Does the heat bother you?" There's a look on Tom's face that makes me think I need to tread carefully. I slip my sunglasses back on, hiding my squinting eyes.

"Oh no, it's just that I'm usually never in air-conditioned buildings like Mitchell. Honestly, I never think about the heat. I love it."

Tom extends his hand, and we shake. "That's great to hear," he says. "I have a good feeling about you. I'm glad I ran into you."

I smile. I want to say, you didn't just run into me, someone told you there was a trespasser, that's why you were following me, but . . . "Me, too!" I hold up the card. "Again, thanks so much—I'll see you tomorrow!"

"Tomorrow!" We both wave, and he heads back inside as I walk quickly across the courtyard toward the south edge of the campus, and home, a massive smile breaking across my face. I can't believe it was that easy, it's usually never this easy. I mean, I'm done for the day—I'll stop at the store to stock up on beer and a few boxes of mac 'n' cheese, and spend the evening decorating the still-bare walls with my collection of art book prints. This was a good day. I deserved this.

Before I leave the campus, I stop at the SUB again, and furtively slip the flyer for the motel job back out of my backpack. Pressing it as flat as I can, I pin it back to the board. As I leave, I turn back. I don't know why. It hangs, limp and slightly wrinkled, in the middle of empty desert-brown cork. A sudden loneliness washes over me, and . . . is it trepidation that follows? Foreboding? The afternoon sun pours down in brilliant columns across the concrete floors, catching on millions of dust motes hanging in the empty space. For a giddy moment I'm one of them, lifeless and trapped in hot amber air, my fossilized bones catching the falling light of a sun I cannot see. I rub the sweat from my face, and continue out the doors to home, and eventually the strange familiarity of the moment melts away.

Usually the night before a new job, a new major, a new dorm or apartment, is spent the same way, with my beer or wine, with something terrible and unhealthy making its salty, greasy way down my throat, with the songs I love the most vibrating in the air as I dance in the shadows or lie back on the bed or couch, dreaming of triumph, of victory, of happiness. At last, happiness. I stand outside of Munson Hall, a few minutes early, in the warm and slightly windy air, and I can't for the life of me recall what I did last night. I got my six-pack and my groceries, I made my way up the rickety back steps and through the new spiderwebs into my apartment, and then . . . and then. It's all television snow, black-and-white static whispering things I can't quite make out. Images in a dreamy mist, too far off for me to fully see who or what beckons me. I woke up before the early alarm, without a hangover, without hunger or fear or apathy. The morning light caught the spiderwebs and they shone throughout the living room like tinsel, and it felt good to be alive. And now Tom is approaching, his hand raised in greeting as he crosses the street with a guy who looks around my age—not a freshman or sophomore, at the least—dressed like me in jeans, T-shirt, loose plaid work shirt, and sneakers. His cowboy hat gives him away, though—it's worn and fits him well. I'm willing to bet he's a local.

"Callie, meet Asher. Asher, Callie. You two will be working on this together. Come on, let me show you the job." We shake hands, giving each other a casual once-over as Tom leads us toward the entrance. I'm not used to working one-on-one, I don't like it, it most often gets intense, personal, messy. I let that happen with Jacqueline, thinking it would benefit me, and it did until it didn't. Well, we'll see. I've just got to behave this time and make this last until September. Eight weeks at the most. I can do that. I can do that.

"The seamstress?" Asher asks me.

"Indeed I am. And you are . . . ?"

"Upholsterer. I can sew. Not that fashion stuff, just, uhm, normal stuff."

Definitely not a drama major. "Industrial sewing, you mean. Factory sewing."

"Yeah, that's it."

"Here we are." Tom has led us into a massive room on the first floor, with two-story-tall windows overlooking a small parking lot lined with rhododendron bushes and small trees. Couches, tables, and chairs are scattered throughout the room—it's a lounge, larger than most dorm rooms, but this building is used for conferences and professional meetings and banquets. Asher has wandered over to the windows, staring up at the empty curtain brackets and hooks. It dawns on me what the job is. Holy fuck.

"As you can see," Tom says as he walks over to Asher, "we need curtains for this room. We have the fixtures and the fabric, but we need them sewn up and installed before the start of the school year. We've already got some events lined up for early arrivals and parents—mostly football related—but that's fine for now, the main thing is that we have the space done before September."

"Just the curtains?" Asher asks.

"Well." Tom gestures to the couches and upholstered chairs. They're covered in a rough dark orange material, that kind of fabric with the big weave, the kind that's easy to wash off if it gets covered in beer and vomit. All the dorm lounges and public spaces have furniture like this. "We need something nicer for this area. These will all need to be reupholstered, and there are a few more rooms in the building that will need the same—conference room furniture, private lounges."

"Will those rooms need new curtains?" I ask.

"Not for now, they have blinds and pull-down shades. But eventually, yes. And eventually—" He spreads his arms out. "—we'll need the same thing done for the rest of the campus."

Asher and I look at each other, and a small laugh, sort of a bark, escapes my lips. Tom's face is serious.

"The entire campus? All the dorms, all the public lounges, all the curtains and furniture—"

"Holy shit," Asher mutters.

"Holy shit indeed," Tom replies. "It's a big job. But we've needed this done for quite a while now. Some of those dorm lounges haven't had updates in decades. Listen, we can't afford a professional company to come in—it might take a quarter of the time, but it'd cost ten times as much. You know what this is about, why we're having students do this."

"This, all of this," I reply with the same sweeping gesture, "is going to be a very, very long job for just the two of us. It's going to take longer than a year to get everything finished, even if we didn't have classes."

"Right. But like I told you yesterday, like I told Asher, we can work out a schedule. The important thing is to get this room finished, to do a great job, and then figure out how we want to proceed after that. I know it'll be slow going to get it all done, but it's steady work, and after it's over—" He shrugs. "Who knows, you might like working here full time. Great benefits, free tuition. Not a bad life."

Asher and I glance at each other again, but I can see that we've already made up our minds, there's no need to confer or think about it. "We can do this," he says, and I add, "Sounds great, I'm in."

I fill out the tax form and sign all the usual school paperwork while Asher wanders the room, inspecting the stained cushions on the couches and the threadbare seams of the chairs. Outside, the trees and bushes toss and ripple in the constant wind, sending mottled shadows across the room in silent waves. I'm happy to have the job, but this room feels like a fishbowl, and the way out is so far above me that it's not worth the effort to struggle. It's not the job, and Asher seems pleasant enough—he's not the typical student I meet, the wedding ring on his finger tells me he's not going to be fucking around or enabling my chaotic side. I just feel . . .

It still bothers me that I can't remember last night.

After I finish the paperwork, Tom leads us out of the fishbowl. Kamola Hall sits right across the street, along with Sue Lombard— the two oldest dorms on campus, and the most typical buildings you expect to see on campuses, all red brick and small windows and strange Gothic angles everywhere. Genuine haunted piles; there've been actual ghost sightings over the decades. As we approach Kamola, Tom unhooks his crowded key ring again. "We're not going in the dorm," he says, anticipating our questions as he leads us around the building toward the back. "We've converted a space in the sub-basement for you—all the fabric and machines are down there."

My heart constricts and grows cold and quiet inside all my hot summer blood.

"Lots of space," Tom continues. "It's quiet, no one will bother you even when the dorm is full again come fall. I'll get keys made for you both, so you don't need me or each other to get in. The keys only work on the entry door and the sub-basement door, by the way. Oh, and there's a bathroom down there. The only problem is—" He stops at a plain metal service door with a series of black letters and numbers painted on it, utterly out of place in the beautiful ivy-covered brick. "—well, you'll see."

Asher mouths *oh shit what problem*. Swallowing hard, I shrug and roll my eyes as the rusting hinges screech in protest. "I'll get those oiled, come on."

We follow him down a narrow stairwell to two more doors. One has a small window in it, the thick glass threaded with wire—I press my face against it. My ears ring. A wide, well-lit hallway with multiple doors and rooms. "Laundry rooms and lounges are through there," Tom says. "You'll never need to go in there, you won't have the key anyway. This is our door." He taps the key against the second door before sliding the key into the first, then second lock. The door opens to pitch black, and the musty smell of spaces that should have been forgotten. "Light switch on the left. Hold the rail, watch your step." He flicks the light on and starts down.

Asher makes a face. "Well, I needed the paycheck," he whispers, then steps back. "Ladies first."

"Ha, thanks."

It's maybe twenty-five steps down. Old steps, old walls, with a tarnished brass railing coated with dust and cobwebs, and now streaked with Tom's handprints. At the end of the stairs, I stop. Asher comes up behind me, and I motion him to go ahead while I stand on the last step, barely able to breathe.

The room is large but crammed with industrial shelving against the walls and huge cardboard containers on wheels, each loaded with massive tubes of expensive blue curtain and upholstery fabric. There are maybe ten tables, and on each one sits an industrial sewing machine or serger. Tubes and wires are everywhere, cords snake across the floor and end in tangled bunches around electrical sockets set in the floor. Two massive, padded tables sit next to each other, with heavy irons resting on each. There's also a cork-lined cutting table, shoved next to a row of shelving. Across the room to the right, next to the restroom door, sits a table with an incredibly ancient coffee maker and several crumbling columns of Styrofoam cups. Everything looks old. Everything looks menacing. The air is hot and still down here, and I know by noon it'll be unbearable. It's like an abattoir for textiles. It's like an oubliette for creativity, dreams, ambition. I should loathe it, the way Asher clearly does, as he wanders the room in barely-concealed shock. Like Asher, like any normal person, I should feel rebellion against working down here in this hideous subterranean mouth with every fiber of my being.

Not a bad life, he had said. Life that goes on and on like mold, impossible to eradicate.

I don't know what I feel.

I do know what I feel, I just don't have the words for it yet. More like an image, a phosphene of something I've seen before, violent and deep glowing red and hot as the center of the sun, moving up through the darkness and back into my life.

"If there's not enough light, I can get someone in to string up a few more bulbs." Tom crosses the room and flicks another switch, and a second bank of lights turns on. They're long fluorescent tubes, flickering softly against the filthy ceiling.

"I think it's going to be just fine," I say, finally stepping into the room. Asher makes a beeline to one of the machines, flicking it on, checking the pedals, the foot and needle, the light. All those little movements of authority you make when you know the situation is bad. I inspect several boxes of sewing supplies—oversized cones of blue thread, scissors, boxes of long pins, packets of replacement needles, the usual things. But I'm not really inspecting. I'm staring at the far end of the room, at an open door, rusting hinges where a door used to hang. A large fan on a small wooden stool sits just inside the door, the blades whirling so slowly that I can see each one make its circular circuit inside its metal cage. Past the fan, there's a black so solid and beautifully complete that for one wild moment I think there's nothing there at all. And then I remember.

Everything is in there.

"Don't go past the fan." Tom has put a hand on my shoulder. I stop: I'm standing in front of the doorway. I didn't realize I had been walking.

"What's in there?"

"Just another hallway. More storage rooms, but—there's nothing down there, there's no electricity, you wouldn't want to hurt yourself. It's all part of the labyrinth." Tom laughs, but he's not really laughing. "Kamola and Sue Lombard have connected basements and sub-basements, there are so many rooms and hallways down here, we can't keep track. But I put the fan there, because it helps with the air situation down here. You can catch a breeze from outside every now and then, so there must be some window cracked open somewhere back in there."

"You've been through that door?" I ask. "You've been down that hallway?"

"Oh no, no one has, not for decades. I mean, security probably does sweeps every couple of years, just to make sure all the locked doors remain locked. None of the rooms are usable, and we especially don't want the students using them."

"So, past the fan is off-limits. Fine with me."

"Right, Asher?" Tom calls out.

"Got it," Asher says as he inspects a table covered in upholstery supplies. "We won't go near it."

The fan sputters and speeds up slightly, the clacking of the blades becoming a discontented metallic purr.

When I walk home, I feel the weight of the sun as it slides behind the Cascades, pulling all light and all sense of time with it, stripping away the falseness of our little lives and our little rituals, all the routines and rules and structures that have no meaning under the canopy of black space, space without end, space to fall into and tumble through until the flesh has been stripped from your body, your bones pulverized, until you're nothing more than a translucent wisp of a memory so old that you no longer remember who or what or why you are. I stop in front of the fake Victorian house, staring up at the red of my living room, noting how the light spills into the tiny second bedroom next to it so that it looks like the eyes of a colossus, slowly returning to hot life after the cold, mindless sleep of eons. Beneath them, the landlord's lights shine lemon yellow. I raise my hand and blot them out.

The days pass, but I don't see them. Rather, I see the edges of days, the crisp hem of dawn rippling in pastel waves overhead, the sun low at the horizon but bright enough to cause pain. The morning warmth is only the residual heat from the day before; by the time I can feel the air starts exploding in its full late summer glory, I'm already walking through that gray metal door, descending, descending, descending. Before it heats up, around noon, the room remains slightly cool for a while; when I stand in front of the open door and extend my hand ever so slightly past the frame, waving my fingers through the thin stream of air from the ancient fan, I do feel—not a chill, not the scent of the outdoors, but it's there. An opening, there in the darkness, far beyond the frame. A whiff of life, rich and loamy, like after a thunderstorm and the earth is all churned up and alive with insects and roots wriggling out of the chaotic aftermath. Sometimes Asher will place his hand on my shoulder like Tom did, and I'll laugh and say, it was a joke, I was trying to see how long it would be before you noticed. Sometimes Asher will stand in front of the door, too, hands slack at his sides, thin trickles of sweat staining the back of his shirt. Sometimes we stand there together.

Mostly, we sew. I think we sew. No, we sew, we pull nails and crack wood and rip fabric along the grain, we measure and press and cut, we stitch straight lines into eternity. We descend, and we turn on the lights and the machines and electricity thrums through the strange space, and we cut cushion shapes with long shears, we make piping out of white cord and bias-cut strips of fabric, we sew zippers into sides, we stuff foam cushions into pale blue envelopes and zip them up. This is what I remember us doing, day after day, all through July. Some days we descend only to collect supplies and lug them over to the giant fishbowl lounge, where Asher takes apart the couches and chairs, stripping them of the old fabric. I use those pieces as patterns, placing them on fabric spread across the floor like a river, cutting around them and handing them back to Asher, who nails and tacks them into place. Yard by yard we transform the colors from burnt tree bark to cool, elegant pool, and all while we work, we open up, slowly. There's no music, there's no television, there's nothing but the sound of the fabric and scissors, the sound of our labored breath, the crunch of nails slamming through wood, and our words. I find out that Asher has a two-year-old son, that he rents a trailer at the Shady Brook Mobile Village down the street from the campus, that both he and his wife have been students at Central on and off for almost as long as me, but really they just work here on and off, with no actual plans to get degrees. They drift. They're not happy. I could fix that. Pull them apart, pin them to a spot, stitch them together in entirely new ways. The sun moves across the sky, but we pay it no heed. At the end of the day we gather our things, slip back across the street, and head down again into our subterranean workspace, putting away tools, tidying up, noting on Tom's chart what we have and haven't completed, what we're running out of, what we desperately need.

And then the workday is over and we're outside. The door is locked, and the sun is descending. Asher is gone, home to his wife and son. I'm traveling through the liminal edges of day, breathing incoming night deep into my lungs as I pass neon-lit taverns, café windows radiating mellow warmth, cross parking lots filled with the tick-tick of cooling car engines, down cracked sidewalks and up the little walkway and through the shivering strands of webbing into my apartment, where I stand before my bathroom sink scrubbing dried brown flecks from beneath my fingernails, watching the colors perne in a gyre, disappear into the black hole beneath the faucet as I think of the black hallway, the black labyrinth beyond. The black hole beneath. The black hole. The black.

I said something to Asher this afternoon as we stood in front of the door, the words rustling like the yellowing edges of flyers on a forgotten bulletin board. I asked him all the questions, and he smiled and said no. But in front of us, in the dark, the answer was yes.

Our fingertips touched, dark and wet. The air smelled alive.

As I led him past it, the fan purred.

And down here, past abandoned rooms, past ancient machinery, past the flattened stratum of geological eras, epochs, supereons, here there is no sound, here there is no sun, here there is only the trapped heat of a billion years—and something more. And down here I've led them all, and down here they've remained, layered like flyers on a bulletin board, stitched together into a cyclopean reliquary for a nameless god. And down here it grows, pressing against my eyelids until I see galaxies of stars, pressing against my body until I relinquish all control, pressing into the void that used to house my soul. And down here I hold Asher's hand and feel him empty out, burn away in the centropic dark as the heat of creation transmutes him anew. And down here we rest, we drift, small sparks of life caught in the grip of a being that pours its primoradial desire into us until we are past the point of full. Until my dead heart is no longer so cold.

Curtains cascade down every window in waterfalls of soft blue, turning the fishbowl into a cenote. Tom stands before them, inspecting our handiwork. He runs his hands over the fabric, examines pleats and the seams, then tips several chairs forward to peer at their undersides. Asher and I stand to the side, awaiting the verdict. Asher has dark smudges under his eyes, he hasn't been sleeping very well, or so he thinks. He doesn't remember the nights anymore. I don't remember the nights anymore. I mean, I remember nightness, I remember passing through hours which hold the quality of nightness about them in that I'm not awake and it's not light and my body is no longer my own, but beyond that . . . Beyond that, I couldn't say what it was I passed through.

"Excellent job, just fantastic." Tom is beaming as he strides toward us. I almost flinch at the largeness of his energy but manage to suppress it. "Now, you're going to start on the curtains this week, right?"

"We've already started," Asher says, and I continue his sentence. "Yeah, we started taking apart the old curtains last week—we've been bringing them in and laying the fabric out here, so we can use them as patterns."

"Oh." Tom looks around at his feet. "It's not too dirty to do that, is it?"

"No, it's fine, they're completely clean—"

"It's better than laying them out in the workroom," I cut in. "There's more light, and we need to make sure they're the right length and width, and that the pattern is in the same direction on every panel. You don't want any mismatches, it'll look weird."

"We just want them to look professional," Asher chimes in. He knows that's the word that gets Tom in a lather. "They need to be perfect, especially this room. So . . ."

"Of course, of course. Well, everything here is amazing, just amazing. You both clearly know what you're doing, so—keep it up. I've got a meeting in—" He squints at his watch. "—okay, gotta run, I can't miss this. I'll check in with you next week, alright?"

We say our goodbyes and watch him leave. The entire room seems to relax at his absence.

Asher places a hand on my arm. "It's almost noon, do you want lunch?"

I place my hand over his. I can feel the heaviness drift through me, dragging my eyelids down, softening my muscles to the point of collapse. "You know what I want."

He smiles.

We walk quickly through the heat back to Kamola. It's August now, and summer isn't fucking around. It feels like we're broiling in a microwave, and the wind we cursed last month has disappeared, leaving us to crisp and burn with no relief. The door to the stairwell burns at the touch, but I know how to insert the key and turn the knob without touching the sizzling metal. I've always known, and now Asher knows. And we descend, and descend, and descend, into an incinerator. Asher turns one of the banks of light on, leaving most of the room in a twilight gloom. Mountains of pale blue fabric lie on the sewing machine tables, each in various stages of completion. Asher sits at his machine, and I settle in at mine. All the fans in the room are off—when Tom visits, they're on of course, but when it's just us, it's better without all that noise. Only the fan in the open doorway clicks and flutters away. We need it to be on, because when it shuts off, that's when we know it's happening.

The room goes quiet. We can't even hear the sound of our breath, it's nothing compared to the sound of nothingness pouring over us, the un-sound of the earth, the ur-sound of geological time flattening everything alive in its path. Sweat pours from our skin, our clothes are wet with it, we weep like statues. We've never felt heat like this before. This is cremation.

Asher goes first. Arms crossed, head nodding several times, and then he slips away. It's not sleep. His body is completely still, but attentive; his eyes are open, but what he's looking at isn't in this room, this planet, this universe. Maybe I'm always a few minutes behind him because I'm stubborn or defective, there are more cracks and wounds to fill inside of me, more putrefaction to abrade. Maybe it's because I'm always looking at the door, watching the blades of the fan slow to full stop, waiting to see what it is that comes pouring through, familiar and hideous and sweet. It almost feels like sleep, and then when it happens it's like I'm being burned alive, it's like I'm being fucked by a cosmic ocean of pure vomit and even as I'm silently screaming so hard that I feel parts of my brain implode, I can't help but orgasm because this is what I have always wanted and my body is nothing but meat anyway, it's just a little jewelry box of stolen things that vastation roots through and rearranges and dumps out and refills with things I can't possibly understand, equations that span galaxies and star nurseries churning with impossible life and corpses of long-dead gods whose bodies begin in one universe and end in another and the place that occurs after time itself has ended, the place where no one has gone or everyone has gone but we just don't have the words for it yet, we just don't have the ability to understand where we've been taken and what we've been shown because we're single-cell specks writhing and dying on the obsidian sands of an eternally collapsing shore. Because we are fabric, buttons, thread, all mere piles of raw materials waiting to be reworked into a higher being. Reworked not with love or balance or wisdom, but with death and terror and pain— all the things we run from, that we cannot understand.

And whatever it is that flows out of the door and into us and through us and uses us eventually recedes, back down through rooms and hallways and into the heavy folds of scabland basalt and crystalline lava that lie in wait beneath us, back into the sculpted mass of the dying and the dead, fluttering against each other like layers of old flyers on a bulletin board. And slowly Asher and I are unpressed and unfolded and softened back into life, our heads nodding slightly as we begin to blink and stretch in the semblance of people who have simply fallen asleep for a short while. We have no sense of time once it starts, it's always a shock to look at our watches and realize how many hours have passed, and then another shock to remember that we can't touch our faces or the fabric or anything else until we've stumbled to the tiny bathroom sink and washed the clotted blood from our hands, blood that has come from no part of our bodies. Under the single bulb in the porcelain tile-lined room, we study our ghostly reflections for stray flecks of red, squirt toothpaste in our mouths and spit it out, watching it swirl in green and red ribbons around the sink and disappear.

Upstairs, the door locked behind us, we part as usual, polite in our good-nights. The sun is as always just above the shimmering summits of the Cascades, the trees are always glossy green and swaying in the early evening breeze, there's always that faint putrid smell of death in the air from the local rendering plant, as if we've lived this day a hundred thousand times. I feel bad for Asher, knowing that someday, soon, he'll be going home to an trailer empty of his own doing, and of mine. Change is good, though. He's been chugging along for years, spinning in his own tracks longer than me. I had to help him. It was for the best. Now he can see things in a new light, now he can see all the roads ahead, and know that there's only one road to take. Like me, walking down this ill-lit street I never walked down before until this summer, me with a lovely apartment where I could store all the lovely things I'd collected over the years. And who knows what the future will bring? It's so long, life is so horribly long, it just fucking drags on and on and with what purpose? For what reason? You just become an uglier and more useless version of yourself, and there are *too many goddamn choices,* and even getting old doesn't make it simpler, there are just more choices that are as ugly and infuriating as you've become, and even after you die it's should we throw this away, did she want her money to go to that, what kind of coffin, where should we send these old clothes, the choices reverberate out and out and out like an infection, and it's like your life never fucking ends, everyone absorbs your choices like cancer, like a virus, always jumping to the next person, all the way through the future to the very last human. I'll be there, in that person, poisoning their life. And when they ask themselves, what is this strangeness haunting my life, befouling my every decision, when they turn to look back at all the terrible choices barreling down toward them, the last rotting wisps of me will pour into their brain and whisper what I whisper to every one of you I've ever met: *you were dead long before you ever thought to run.*

Now, in the blink of an eye, I don't remember the walk home, it's not quite midnight and I'm standing in the middle of my living room, sweat pouring down my breasts as I nurse on my calm-down beer, the lava red light of the Moroccan lamp turning the room into a caldera. Little flecks of blood cover my forearms, commingling with my freckles. A few have smeared into comets against my pale skin. I didn't do a very good job washing up. I never do, deliberately so. I like the look of it. I wish I could always keep it on me. I'm so tired of washing it off. It makes it all so distant, like when you dream about a place you've always known was the place for you, the perfect phantasmagoric country that the memory of fills you with rage when you wake up, because you know you will never find the way back. And I want to belong to it, to belong to something greater than myself, to be filled with it. I want to remember, to be awake and remember and be crammed full of everything that leaves me when I scream.

The beer bottle drops to the shag carpet, empty and spent. But I am full. I raise my arms out as if enveloping the world, and the red light pours into me and ignites, erupts from my head, a column of triumphant rage that plumes up into the star-studded night. Would that it live there forever, blocking out the sun until no one ever remembered anything but night. But that's not where it's destined to live. I close my eyes, pretend I'm in the sub-basement, walking past the fan, walking down the hallway into other hallways into other rooms and rooms within rooms that become crevices that become caverns that become the cavern to end all caverns, the place that holds a darkness so complete that the darkness inside me becomes incandescent by comparison, a darkness I pretend is whispering to me in a patchwork charnel god's command, *sotto voce,* like Asher and I whispered to each other: *soon, soon, soon.*

ALL THE THINGS HE CALLED MEMORIES
BY STEPHEN GRAHAM JONES

Bo had learned early on in his relationship with Marcy that test-driving her studies or experiments or head games or whatever they were nearly always ended with her explaining to him that this was her fault, she shouldn't have brought her work home, it was nothing he could be interested in, she was just looking for someone to bounce ideas off of. So, in the kitchen, when she started easing into some of that talk, he knew he should have drifted down to the basement to lose himself in work, wait this out, hope she would call one of her lab partners and run it by *them* instead. But, at the same time, with campus shut down from the pandemic and none of the grant money flowing and all of her colleagues probably checked out of the profession, homeschooling their kids and nursing their parents, trying to stay off a breathing machine, who else did Marcy have, really? *Me*, Bo knew. It had just been the two of them locked in their remodeled Victorian for the last six weeks, no kids, no parents. He was her main and only subject.

To make it fair, show him she was game, she went first.

What they were doing now that breakfast was over and cleaned up was telling each other the scariest thing they had balled up inside them, walled up in brick, pushed into a corner—that's how Marcy explained it to him. Something they'd seen, heard tell of, dreamed up. It wasn't about if it was stupid or childish or unbelievable or any of that. It was about that actual dark kernel festering inside each of them, and its composition, its origin.

They hadn't set up flickering candles, no deep shadows were pooling around their respective wingback chairs. It was an hour before lunch, still. All the windows were open. Outside the viral winds were blowing, people made up like train robbers were scurrying up and down the sidewalk singly and in pairs, hunched around groceries, and in the kitchen the radio was burbling some talk show or another. Just another Tuesday, or Wednesday—Thursday?

Bo's upholstery van was parked in the driveway. The passenger side rear tire had been low for the last week, he could see it from the window, but getting it fixed would mean talking to someone across a counter, which is to say, being in the blast zone for their aerosolized droplets of maybe-infected saliva, and . . . it's not like the jobs were rolling in this month anyway.

Marcy's checks kept right on coming, though, even though her lab was shuttered. Which was Bo's excuse to himself for playing this particular head game with her: she was still getting paid. So, if she needed to feel like she was working, not stealing money, then he kind of owed it to her to help with that, didn't he? It's not like the undergraduates were lining up to let Marcy's team attach electrodes to their arms or stage questionnaires for them to work through.

Bo's favorite way to rib her about her work was to say all her experiments and studies were just a glorified series of Pepsi or Coke challenges. Marcy's usual comeback would be to tip her glass of red wine over and over, threatening the thirsty cream fabric of the kitchen chairs Bo had re-covered.

Anyway, the scariest thing Marcy had lodged in her chest, in her head, in her life.

Her setup for it—her excuse, after she'd said there would be no excuses—was that she was pretty sure she'd nabbed this from a homeless man she'd been confronted with in first or second grade.

"*Confronted*?" Bo asked.

"Surprised by," Marcy clarified.

"In the city," Bo clarified back.

"This was different." She studied the kitchen doorway, maybe tuning in to that talk show she despised for a sentence or two. "My dad was . . . he was on the phone, I was trailing behind, and then, just suddenly, there was this dirty man lying by the building, right there on the sidewalk. His eyes were closed but he was saying something."

"Sounds homeless," Bo said, not sure what his contribution was supposed to be, here.

"I was just standing there," Marcy went on, not seeming to have heard him, "and then suddenly my dad was jerking me away by the arm, dragging me behind him. That was it, nothing big."

"But it scared you."

"It stayed with me, yeah," Marcy said, flashing her eyes to him for a moment to be sure he was taking this seriously—that he was digging deep, to find what scared him the most.

To keep the experiment as close to honest as possible, she wasn't laying out the parameters, her hypothesis, any of that. But Bo had an idea: she was trying to figure out if people's scariest things were outliers to their identity, pulling their lives this way or that, or if those fears were at the core—were the thing everything else was built around. Basically, he imagined, she was probing around in the dark, secret places, to see what identity or selfhood was made of.

The reason he could bull's-eye in on that was because, at some point in the process, she usually broke down and talked her experiments through with him, to see if he could punch holes in her thinking before she presented it to her group. Usually Bo couldn't, but, too, by the end of their back-and-forth, she'd have a stack of question marks in the margins of her notepad, assuring him that his pragmatic approach was helpful, where "pragmatic" was code for "unscientific," "layperson"—"unedumacated," as Bo liked to frame it, claiming it so Marcy wouldn't have to dance around its edges.

He insisted it didn't get to him, didn't bug him. He was happy to help, to offer her a perspective nobody from her lab could. In similar fashion, he'd sometimes ask her opinion on this or that bolt of fabric, though he'd already made his decision. It's how marriage works, he figured. Wheels within wheels, games within games.

"So this homeless dude," Bo prompted, being a good and caring husband *and* a proper sounding board, "he became your boogeyman, what?"

"Well . . ." Marcy said, leaning back, tapping the hinge of her jaw with her middle finger like she always did when thinking. "I had a dream, I guess. But it stuck with me."

"That's what I'm here for," he told her, faking an Austrian accent and crossing his legs as if making himself more receptive for these problems she needed to talk through with him.

She threw her balled-up napkin at him, said, "It wasn't the same—I mean, it wasn't him, I don't think. Not exactly. I was older, like now, I guess. I was walking down a hall and when I rounded the corner there was a dead person lying there in a doorway."

"You know he was dead?"

"He was dead. There was a fly crawling across his eyeball? It wasn't making him blink, though. And for some reason I couldn't call to anyone about this. But I wanted to tell someone about him all the same. So I needed to know who he was. I squatted down, held my breath—I don't know why I was holding my breath—"

"Homeless guy."

"Probably. But this wasn't him. Anyway, I steeled my nerves and pushed my hand into the pocket of the jacket he was wearing, to try to find his wallet, learn his name. And . . . I don't know. I could feel his wallet right there at the tips of my fingers, but it's like it kept nuzzling deeper into the pocket, away, keeping me from catching it."

"'Nuzzling'?"

"Shut up. But I was reaching for it, grasping for it, and that's when I realized what was happening."

Bo didn't say anything now, could sense this was where she'd been headed, and didn't want to push her off-course.

"The man's mouth," she said. "It was moving."

"He *wasn't* dead."

"He was. But his mouth was moving all the same. And—this is a dream, okay? So, that kind of logic. But I figured out, I could tell . . . his mouth was moving with the opening and closing of my hand, if that makes sense."

Bo narrowed his eyes, trying to see this as she had.

Marcy went on: "Of course I pulled my hand out, his jaw went slack, and—awake. But after that, everyone I passed on the street or the hall or wherever with their hands in their pockets, I would always look away from their mouths, because I didn't want the movement of their hands in their pockets to match up with whatever they were saying, right?"

"Shit," Bo said. "All your gloves."

Marcy had gloves for every day of the week, pretty much. Every day of the *month*. Every cranny and crevice in her life had a pair of gloves stuffed in it, should she need them.

"I keep things in my purse, don't I?" she said—which is to say, *not* her pockets—and Bo had to nod. He'd always assumed it was because of the uselessness of girl pockets. But . . . he could kind of dimly feel where her hypothesis for all this came from, now: this kernel of fear had deviated her life this way instead of that, hadn't it? First for a week of school, when that dream was still fresh, but then for the month after that dream, when this pocket-phobia was becoming a habit, and then for the year, and all the years after, when it wasn't even a habit anymore, was just a fact of life, a way to navigate the day that she didn't even know to question anymore, because to do so would be to become someone else altogether.

"Shit," Bo said again. It was all he could seem to muster. You can be married to someone for fifteen years and still be finding new things out about them, evidently. It made him clock back through all the times his hands had been in his pockets, and how she must have been looking away from his mouth, even though she knew engaging that fear—keeping that dream alive—was irrational.

"I'm sorry," he told her, and completely meant it, one hundred percent.

"It's not about that," Marcy said back, shaking her memory off. "We all have something, that's what I'm saying, Doctor Freud." She leaned back, settled her penetrating gaze on Bo, then. It made him feel like a butterfly, the pin descending from the sky for his abdomen. "Your turn."

"Anything I can say can be used against me, I take it?" he asked with a halfway smile, readjusting in the wingback chair.

"All participants will be anonymized," she repeated, grinning as well, but not letting him weasel out of this, either.

Bo came back from the kitchen with a glass of water for each of them.

"It's okay if it's stupid?" he said, settling back into his chair.

"Like mine wasn't?"

"Generic, I mean."

"Drowning, burning, buried, spiders, what? That would mean you're . . . wait for it, wait for it . . . *human*?"

"It's just not as specific as yours."

"I've had longer to think about it."

"Meaning mine's more honest?"

"How much preamble you need here?" Marcy asked, making a show of checking the watch she wasn't wearing. "Want me to keep this going? Must be something really scary, if you're having to do all this stalling."

Bo took a long drink, said, "I'm not gonna get tumors from your X-ray vision, am I?"

"Anytime, Stally McStallpants."

Thing was, Marcy was right, as usual: Bo *was* stalling. Waiting for a werewolf to stand up from his childhood, for a vampire to creak a casket open in his memory. He'd seen dead people, sure, and not just at funerals, and once he'd seen a motorcyclist go under a semi. But there were no homeless dudes with puppet mouths, he was pretty sure. Just zombie and chainsaw movies he'd smuggled into his dreams and then couldn't cry to his mom about, since he'd had to sneak around to watch that movie in the first place.

"You forgot being abandoned," he said, circling his fingers towards himself to rewind their conversation. "Drowning, burning, spiders . . . and being abandoned."

"The time your uncle left you at the water park?"

Bo shrugged. "That's there, sure," he told her, shrugging it off all the same. "I'm not scared of waterslides now, though. It's not . . . what's the word? 'Formative'?"

"Then what is?"

"There's got to be something?"

"Fear isn't something you pass through. It's what you tell yourself is over. But . . . it's like that popular conception of how allergies work? Like, you eat an apple with a tinge of leftover pesticide. Your system doesn't know to key on 'pesticide,' but it knows it's dangerous, and all it's got to associate that danger with, now, based on this one incident, this one bite, is an apple. So you become allergic to apples."

"How you're . . . not comfortable with pockets, now."

Marcy shrugged sure to that, her shrug that meant Bo was oversimplifying, but she wanted to move on.

"It's not abandonment, okay," Bo said. "But it is kind of related to that, I guess you could say. It's being alone."

"Explain."

"Said the robot. Anyway, when I was kid, I don't know, third grade, fourth grade maybe, when I got home from school, Mom wouldn't be off work yet, right? I mean, *right*. She wouldn't be, that's what I'm saying. And we were living in that house my uncle had been renovating since forever. It was way bigger than the amount of junk we had, and there were all these, like, hardwood floors everywhere."

"This a family house I don't know about? Your family *owns* it?"

"It won't be in any wills. My uncle finally finished it, sold it. Never mind. I'd be home on my own for sometimes nearly two hours. My orders were to not leave the house, not answer the door, not mess with anything in the kitchen, and to do my homework. So I mostly watched TV, yeah? Just for the sound and the distraction, I mean."

Bo got up, went to the window to watch the train robbers straggle back and forth through the pandemic, their eyes furtive, none of them taking a full, lung-expanding breath. Not thinking, he buried his hands in his pockets, then, remembering, he faked a stretch, freed his hands up. Then didn't know what exactly to do with them.

Marcy, ever the patient research scientist, was just waiting through what he knew she considered his theatrics. People had always been just interesting mechanisms to her. Even on an outing to the office supply store, she could never help noting a preponderance of, say, brunette women working the registers, the copy department, the aisles. What this meant to her was that whoever ran the job interviews here was, first, male, and, second, probably had a non-brunette in his life, either as mother or significant other. She'd even go so far as to steal business cards, look that assistant manager up on social media, then search for blondes in the people he was linked with—this counted as fun to her.

Bo just bought staples, paper, whatever. Let her dissect the world with the scalpel her mind was. He just needed an accordion file to organize his work orders in.

"But sometimes, you know how it is," he finally went on, "sometimes you have to go upstairs, or into the utility, wherever. And—this is the stupid part, okay? From that first week until we moved, I never felt actually . . . alone, I guess. As long as I was sitting still, and had a good enough field of view of the room, I could be safe. *Feel* safe, I mean."

"Where 'unsafe' would mean not-alone," Marcy added, ever the clarifier.

Bo nodded, found his chair again.

He was pretty sure his hands were trembling.

If they were in his pockets, his teeth would be chattering, he thought, and, going off Marcy's reaction, he evidently grinned the littlest bit as well.

"What?" she asked.

"It was when I was moving that the feeling came the hardest," Bo said. "Or, the softest, really. I could make it about three steps up the stairs before I would feel a sort of . . . I guess you'd call it a presence? I'd feel it behind me, right in my steps, like, walking its right leg ahead right when I walked mine."

"A shadow."

"But not. And, I mean, I wasn't a kid scientist or anything, but I always knew where the light sources were, and I knew where my own shadow was beside me, or on the wall. And it was always just me. That was just the thing, though. These—these imaginary whatevers—"

"*Plural.*"

"I don't know. But they were such that they couldn't be seen straight on. Which I guess applied to shadows, and reflections. No matter how fast you spun around, they would always be gone."

"Or right behind you."

"*Still* behind me, yeah. That didn't mean they weren't one hundred percent there, though, right? I had to remind myself to breathe, going up the stairs. But I couldn't go too slow either, because then that would give them time and space to lean forward, get their mouth right to my ear, and, like, whisper something I didn't want to know."

"Like what?"

"Like—okay, I'm just gonna tell you, cool? Later, like, high school, I guess, I could do this thing with dice, where I could guess them a lot of the time. Not cards, just dice. And I could always tell when the wall phone was about to ring. I'd hear a buzzing in my head. I got the idea that I was some, like, I had some hidden telepathy or clairvoyance or something. And then I went back to my old terror of walking up the stairs alone, and I told myself that that presence I'd been sensing, it had been this mental ability coming on, right? Since it didn't make sense, though, I had to dress it up in the supernatural. I didn't want it, either. Because it might tell me something I didn't want to know. About my mom. About something happening to her, I guess. It was just me and her, right? I didn't know what would happen to me if something happened to her. But if I didn't see, or get it whispered to me, what might happen to her, then that was like protecting her, keeping her safe."

"So . . . prognostication, then?"

"Like Nostradamus."

"And the dice?"

"It went away. Phones too. And not because of cellular. Remember when we were getting all the utilities turned on here, and you left it to me if we needed a landline or not?"

"You didn't want one."

"You didn't know why, though. I think it's because every time one of them rings, it feels like—it feels like I should have *known* it was going to ring, right? And then I think that maybe the phone will jar something loose in my head, and suddenly I'll be able to guess dice again. But if that door opens, then what else might come through? What if I see something—something happening to you, right?"

"Or yourself, alone at the water park."

"You said this wouldn't be analysis."

"I'm sorry. Really. I shouldn't have—forget it. I'm just scratching open wounds, aren't I? Picking at scabs."

"It's all good, no worries. It's kind of . . . it's a weight off me, right? I've always felt sort of like I was lying to you, about no landlines. And I'll try to keep my hands out of my pockets if I can, too."

"That's not—I guess I'm trying to shape how to ask the question, right? How to phrase it. If I ask a test group to tell me the scariest thing from their lives, then I'll get near-misses, 'the time we almost wrecked,' 'that time there was a bear on the trail.' But what I want are the dreams of homeless men who don't control their own mouths. What I want is an aversion to phones, and the mechanism behind that."

"Why?"

"Because our minds are puzzle boxes," Marcy said, obviously. "You can twist them this way, that way, and, if you're really lucky, maybe once in a while you unlock one of them."

"I like mine how it is, I think."

"It's called gaze detection, you know?"

"What is?"

"Your feeling, that someone was watching you. It's a biological phenomenon, a survival thing, kind of an aggregate of senses. A soldier comes back especially jumpy from a tour of duty, it can be because their gaze detection has been jacked up to eleven for the last four months, and it's hard to acclimate back to non-battlefield conditions. Especially when they feel they owe that gaze detection for having kept them alive."

"You never know when you're in someone's crosshairs."

"You kind of do, though. Just, you learn to tamp it down."

"Like Daredevil?"

"Who?"

"That movie. His senses—he has to learn to dial them way down, or he'll go crazy."

"Gaze detection uses some of the same neural pathways as pareidolia. That's our conditioning to recognize faces in stuff where there's maybe not a face."

"You should go on the History Channel," Bo said. "You'd be a great ghost debunker."

"Oh, no, ghosts are real. But they're in our *perception*, they're afterimages and projections, our fears made manifest."

Bo worked his phone up from his front pocket, said, "You want me to call them, tell them about you?"

"Just like your knowing when the phone was about to ring," Marcy rolled on, not amused. "You were probably cueing into a pre-buzz, the line kind of sighing open with the coming connection. You thought you were having illegal and potentially dangerous access to future events, but really your adolescent senses were just overclocking, and your mind was making connections between that input and the ringing sound that always followed. Voilà—Bo, the Nostradamus of 2020!"

"This would be more like 1988," Bo said, kind of sullenly. "And, if I were Nostradamus, I would have seen this coming, and been a computer programmer or something—I could work from home."

"And, pockets, that's my thing, I don't mean to foist it off on you. If you start ducking landlines and dice and pockets, then you'll be carrying too much for—"

"But if I can—"

Marcy waved him off, and ten minutes later she was on the back porch with her leather notebook, thinking-on-paper as she called it, leaving Bo to fiddle around the empty house. Listen to his own footsteps.

In the dining room, after being sure Marcy was still in her place on the back porch, he shrugged into a windbreaker from the coatrack, put his right hand into the right pocket, and moved it open and closed as if his pocket were a sock, and, in the mirror, he moved his mouth with his hand, and then he closed his eyes to his reflection, on the idea that would make it more real in some way.

The next morning, Marcy announced that she was terminating the fear study at the germ line, as it wasn't an experiment that could be run either remotely, through resources and data available online, or with her limited set of participants: her and Bo.

"So it was a trick," Bo said, bumping her hip with his. "You just wanted me to reveal something about myself, so you could push my buttons better."

"You cracked it," Marcy said, playing along drolly. "Your on-off switches are so hidden that I could never find them without my devious tactics . . ."

"That's me," Bo said, grinning. "A mystery wrapped in an *X-Files* episode."

"That doesn't even make sense," Marcy said, but it made her smile all the same.

By lunch, Bo had reorganized the pantry according not to color this time, which let pasta and cans of corn share a shelf, but by perishability, which meant the beans he loved were on the lowest shelf, with the extra ketchup Marcy insisted on keeping at-hand.

At least it had been something to do, he figured.

Tomorrow . . . maybe he would stack it all by food group. Or maybe he'd mask up, sneak into the dangerous outdoors, run a plumbing snake up the rain gutters affixed to the side of the house, just to see that segmented metal tentacle flop up at roof level like a small, desperate monster.

The days were stacking up against him.

Marcy, too.

That evening after dinner, she had a new study in mind. This time she wanted to run the numbers such that she could see if people afflicted with OCD were more resistant to the various age-related dementias. She explained that it was proving the old "use it or lose it" maxim, just, it was allowing that maybe the OCD crowd's brains were always clocking, counting, cooking—always busy, like Tetris'ing a crossword puzzle into a Rubik's Cube. What Marcy was wondering was if that kind of constant background calculating insulated them to some degree from mental atrophy.

This was exciting to her because she was pretty sure she could piggyback on existing studies, could come at their public data from a different angle, with different eyes, which was Marcy-code for "I'm going to be pouring my soul into my laptop screen for the next eight hours or so, until I run this down, cool?"

Cool with Bo.

For a while he watched the street in front of their house.

On the far sidewalk, a woman in a paper mask was carrying a candle carefully along. Bo watched her until she was gone, trying to imagine what vigil could be happening, or what pilot light she was aiming for the next block over, and then he tiptoed past Marcy's office to the junk room, where he'd connected his old video-game console to the junky monitor he'd bought at a garage sale last year. The monitor was just 720p, but his old console only pushed its signal through RCA, so: match made in sort-of heaven.

The hours melted away, and by the end of the session, his neck hurt, since the monitor was just on a nineteenth-century vanity he'd had plans to restore, and he had just been sitting on the edge of the guest bed.

He blew on his controller before putting it away, a stupid thing he'd used to do in high school, like breathing the smoke away from a hot pistol. Maybe if this pandemic went long enough, Marcy would come up with an experiment that got him to tell her that, too. At which point she'd surely divorce him.

He chuckled, holstered the controller in the brass loop of a drawer pull, and imagined that it might be bedtime again, right? If that could even be said to matter anymore.

Marcy's office door was half-shut now, meaning she'd been to the kitchen, the bathroom, maybe to check on him, but the keys were clacking in there, meaning she was on the trail of something sea-changing, something paradigm-shifting. Good for her.

Would the analogue for Bo be flipping the pages of his fabric catalogue faster and faster, like the truth was going to be on the next page, if he could just get there fast enough to catch it before it scurried away?

Who cares?

His eyes were shot, his fingers were twitchy, and his neck was both creaky and hot at the same time. Because Marcy wouldn't think of it, he cruised downstairs, checked the front and back door, pulled the window in that he'd opened in the heat of the day, for breeze.

Out in the world, he knew, people were coughing their lungs up, people were gasping oxygen in ICUs, and their loved ones were making whatever deals they could in the hospital parking lots, which were probably the new waiting rooms.

He didn't have it so bad, he meant.

So he was locked in with his scientist wife. If he had to have a cellmate, though, then of course her, right? They were in this for the long haul. And now, thanks to Marcy's aborted experiment, they each knew one more thing about the other, which he had to admit was probably for the good, somehow.

He followed the banister upstairs, trying to get his head properly dial-toned for sleep, and he was two steps up from the landing when . . .

What?

He looked behind him, but of course there was no one. No *thing*.

He laughed quietly to himself, about how stupid he was being, here. Of course going into all that with Marcy would reawaken the old fears, the old certainties. But he'd always been all right, all those afternoons and evenings before his mom got home, hadn't he? The only thing consuming him, finally, had been his own dread.

He was twelve, though. When you're twelve, you think stupid stuff.

He wasn't twelve anymore.

Still, at the top of the stairs, Bo stopped again, and looked back down the steps. Where he was really looking, though, was to when he'd been *on* them: What, already?

"You're getting spooky again," he told himself, thinking that saying it aloud would make it go away.

What he was remembering, or half-remembering, or allowing into possibility, was that, in the thin glass over the engagement photo Marcy's friend had interior-designed onto the wall right above the landing, on the right . . . had there been, just for a moment, a reflection? A slight motion of some sort?

Bo steeled himself and walked back down, moved the engagement photo back and forth on its nail to see what light it might catch, and from what angle.

This time when he walked up, trying his best to approximate his same place on the stairs but moving much more slowly now, just for the thinnest slice of an instant, he caught a tall shadowy rectangle, which of course, once he spun around, was just the doorway on the first floor that opened onto the formal dining room they never much used, that they used rarely enough that the carpet in there, once vacuumed, would show the footprints if either of them crossed it.

Had the motion he'd either sensed or made up not been in the reflection caught in that glass, then, but in the *dining* room?

Bo held on to the railing, studied that tall empty doorway, and the black space beyond, that, because of that blackness, could be two feet deep, or fifty, even though the dining room itself was maybe two tables wide.

For a moment Bo felt unmoored, like there was the distinct possibility that he could fall into that doorway, and just keep falling.

He clamped his hands on to the rail tightly enough that it creaked.

"About to bless the masses?" Marcy said from the hallway above him, her laptop clutched to her chest, her glasses hitched on her forehead. Bo looked down to his hands, remembered—how could he have even forgotten?—that when they first moved into this house, he'd said standing on the landing and looking down on the first floor must be what it's like to be a preacher in a pulpit.

Bo waved his hands over the imagined congregation, told them all to take their seats, yes, yes, and, almost to the top, and purely a kindness, to save him the trouble, Marcy clicked the overhead light off.

The excuse Bo gave Marcy for hiding in his basement workshop the next morning was that his sewing machine needed maintenance, that, once this whole shut-in thing was over, his work phone was going to be ringing off the hook: with everybody's orbit suddenly reduced to the walls of their houses, their apartments, that had to mean more spills on precious chairs and couches, didn't it?

Upholsterer Man to the rescue!

At least the way Bo framed it for Marcy.

The sewing machine was industrial, was honestly kind of overkill for the kind of . . . *non*-volume he carried. He'd bought it at auction four years ago, from a seed research outfit's leftovers. Originally, it had been for sewing the tops of bags of sorghum and corn shut. The smallest needle was the size of a coffee straw.

The drive belt, once he got the side panel off, was actually a bit dry, it turned out—did need some maintenance. Bo ran the pads of his fingers along the crackling edge, liking the way it grabbed at his skin, and then he doused a rag with belt treatment, lovingly rubbed it into the rubber and then detailed out everything he could reach with a different rag. Just cobwebs and dust.

He was just putting it all back together when he heard Marcy's footsteps in the kitchen above him. He ran the last bolt in, patted the machine like it had been a good boy to endure all this idle fiddling, and padded upstairs, coming out of the closet the basement was hidden in and running straight upstairs, to wash his hands with the good soap—the belt treatment had left him greasy.

"Turkey?" Marcy called up after him.

"Sure, sure," Bo said, even though he was pretty sure it was his day to make lunch. But, if Marcy was pulling sandwiches together, that had to mean her data-dive was producing promising results—maybe OCD *was* insulation against dementia.

Lathering up in the sink, forearms too because some of those crevices had been a reach, and who knew what kind of old pesticide had been in the air for this sewing machine back in the day, Bo found his back . . . not stiffening, but—coming awake?

It was like when his big sister and her friends used to run their fingers lightly over his back, to give him the shivers.

Bo didn't turn the water off to hear better, didn't *want* to hear anything, but he couldn't help looking up into his reflection, to see was anything standing right behind him, its chin just over his shoulder.

"It's the middle of the day," he said aloud, like a defense against anything this stupid actually really happening.

And it wasn't happening: he was alone in the bathroom. Of course.

Just before he focused back on his hands in the sink, though, he saw it.

A sort of face in the closet, in the reflection.

He looked deeper into the sink, re-set his feet, turned the water off, and turned around toweling off, as if insisting that this normal activity of drying his hands would ripple out, make everything around him normal as well.

From his new angle, the closet was just dark. The sleeves and shoulders of jackets and shirts, blouses and dresses.

"Coming?" Marcy called.

Bo nodded yes, but it was more about her being downstairs. That meant it wasn't her, hiding back against the wall in the closet, to jump out, boo his heart to a standstill.

Because he had no choice but to beat this, to face it down before it metastasized, Bo made himself flick the closet light on, stand in that doorway.

He chuckled at how stupid he was being.

The mannequin-head wig-holder thing Marcy had inherited from her mom, that she'd been keeping on the top shelf of the closet, he guessed, had just gotten jostled, was facing *out* now.

Marcy must have needed something up there, not noticed she was turning that head around with whatever she'd dragged out.

Bo breathed in, held it, then reached up, rotated that blank face back around.

"End of *that*," he told himself, and went downstairs to hear about Marcy's new study.

When the router went down, and after they'd contacted their ISP, been told to expect service again by seven, promise, the bingo Bo and Marcy played in the living room wasn't license plates of cars driving by or even sidewalk people being masked up or not. It was animals.

You could either be the first to see a bird, a squirrel, a cat, a dog, and any kind of insect that the other could confirm was really there, or you could Yahtzee out, see—somehow—five squirrels at once, or five cats. You couldn't Yahtzee on birds, though, since they swept by in flocks.

"These are the doldrums, aren't they?" Marcy said.

"Dol-what?" Bo asked.

They'd moved the wingback chairs to the two windows that faced front, were each sitting the same distance back, so they had the same field of view.

"When sailors don't have any wind in their sails," Marcy explained. "They're just sitting there, waiting, trying to pass the time."

"Swab the deck!" Bo said. It was pretty much the only nautical thing he knew, and, if he had to admit, he mostly knew it from *SpongeBob.*

"Squirrel!" Marcy called out, and Bo looked in time to see a flash of brown zipping up a tree, as if the tree had been something else a moment before, and now it was suiting up for the heat of the day.

The prize for completing your card first was having dinner made for you. Whatever you wanted.

When Bo lost, as he knew he would—Marcy was forever quicker on every draw—he ended up making the ramen he'd have been going to ask for anyway. So it all worked out, he figured.

"Making it all make sense up there?" he said when they were done, sitting there with their bowls still on the table, the wine bottle down to dregs.

Marcy shrugged, said, "I didn't realize the hazard involved with looking this all up."

"Headache?"

"Contact OCD," she said with a sort of guilty grin. "For the last five minutes, I've been counting every handle of all the cabinets on that side."

Bo considered those cabinets, told himself not to count the handles, even though he was already ticking them off in his head.

"That head in the closet upstairs," he said.

Marcy leveled her gaze on him.

The question was in her eyes.

"I don't know," Bo said, collecting the bowls and glasses, rattling them sinkward. "I think all this . . . all this being inside. It's, like—I don't know."

"Perfectly natural," Marcy said, but the way she was watching him, the way he could feel her watching him, Bo realized she was scrutinizing him with science-eyes, not wife-eyes. Like, trying to crack into his head, see the mechanisms.

"Just—" Bo started, but Marcy was suddenly behind him, her chin on his shoulder.

"We all go a little crazy in a situation like this," she whispered, her fingertips light on his side, on his other shoulder, and—he jerked, a kind of inner flinch—on his *hip* as well?

And then he heard it, felt it for the first time in years and years: a sort of humming buzz.

An instant later, Marcy's phone on the table rang, but not with her usual ringtone, but an old-style bell clapper.

Bo dropped the bowl he was holding, it shattered against his shins, and Marcy declined the call, shushed him out of the kitchen, told him to fix them both a drink, she'd sit with him as long as he needed, cool? Right after she cleaned this up.

His heart spasming in his chest, Bo paced the living room, was two drinks ahead by the time Marcy stepped in, sat down.

"You don't need to," he said, handing her drink across. Well, the replacement for the drink of hers he'd already drunk.

"Like I have anywhere to be?" she said back, watching him again, he wasn't sure with which kind of eyes.

Bo woke alone in their bed. What he vaguely remembered through the vodka was Marcy helping him upstairs, and what he brought with him out of sleep, that didn't feel like a dream but had to be, was the distinct sensation that, years ago, his mom at work, him home alone, it had been *Marcy* on the stairs with him all those times. That the presence he'd been feeling was the future, was last night, just it was out of joint, timewise, was how his mind was processing these flashes ahead, this precognition or whatever it was.

Which he'd never wanted, never asked for, didn't need, please.

Bo grabbed on to the sheets, balled them in his hands.

Where was Marcy?

Instead of sitting up, which would leave room behind him for—for *some*thing to be—he just stared straight up until the ceiling took dim shape.

He didn't fall back asleep like he wanted to, though.

What he couldn't stop thinking about was someone lying under the bed, perfectly in line with him. And before he could chase that away, bury it in the shadows, he realized that the mannequin head he'd rotated back around in the closet was now positioned perfectly to be watching him through the wall with her never-blinking eyes.

Wonderful.

Bo grinned in the darkness, his eyes heating up with tears.

He couldn't help wondering if this is what has to happen when there's no work to keep his hands busy. The mind starts feeding on itself. It's like—it's like the whole house was a sensory-deprivation tank or something: in this great yawning darkness with no new input, just the days stacking on top of themselves, tottering higher and higher, burying him under them, he was starting to see flashes of neurons in the blackness, little flits of energy flicking across the dendritic spaces or whatever that Marcy would go on and on about, if he let her.

To calm himself, Bo re-covered a chair in his head, first cleaning and polishing all the antique, hand-carved wood, then measuring the pad, then selecting the fabric, then using his dummy fabric to mock the cover up, make sure the corners all tucked like he wanted, and using that dummy fabric as a pattern on the good fabric but cutting wide too, so he could use his smaller sewing machine to double it under in a hem no one would ever see, but that, to Bo, meant quality, meant "craftsmanship."

Only, while he was bent over his small sewing machine in his head, the big one behind him fired up, that huge needle cycling up and down with that distinctive *whumpf, whumpf,* and Bo wasn't asleep for this, was completely awake, which was when the basement he was trapped in in his head suddenly flashed bright white.

Marcy was in the doorway of the bedroom, her hand to the light switch, her open laptop to her chest.

"You were knocking on the wall?" she said.

Bo checked his hands, still clutching the sheets.

He breathed in, knew he had to be sweating, that it had to be obvious he was losing it.

"The internet's back," he said, about the work she was obviously doing at last.

Marcy sat on the edge of the bed, closed her laptop, found his knee with her palm, but instead of looking at him, she was . . . she was watching the doorway to the hall?

Why? Had she heard a floorboard creak? Seen a shadow?

Bo swallowed, the sound loud in his ears, and for a moment was sure that when she looked back around to him, her eyes were going to be painted on, lidless, and he was going to fall into the hole in his life opening up under him.

For lunch the next day, Bo made grilled cheeses. It was his specialty. He could brown them to the perfect point, then would wait to serve them until the cheese had dialed back from melty to just sticky, so as to avoid strings stretching out and out.

"My brother used to make omelettes," Marcy said, studying her grilled cheese.

"Non-sequitur much?" Bo said back about this, smiling.

Marcy shrugged it off, didn't explain. She'd been lost in her head all morning, was probably working through some snag in her data, her models, her whatever.

"Your new ringtone," he said, trying to drag that into the discussion they weren't exactly having.

Marcy picked her phone up, scrolling through her settings, said, "I was trying to latch on to the Wilbanks' Wi-Fi, and got bored, started playing with—there."

She played her new ringtone: a horse, neighing.

"Better?" she asked.

"Long as it doesn't ring at night," Bo said with a smile. "Literal night-*mare*."

"Too early for that kind of humor," Marcy informed him.

"It's lunch," Bo countered, holding his grilled cheese up as proof.

"In life, I mean," Marcy said.

"Thinking about going into the face mask business," Bo told her then, partly for her reaction, partly because he'd really been considering it.

"Halloween already?" Marcy asked back.

"For this—the virus stuff," Bo explained when he could. "Nobody needs their chairs covered right now, but everybody needs their mouth covered."

"Everybody *needs* to just not go anywhere," Marcy said.

"Then maybe I'll go in the tether business instead," Bo said back to her. "Tie your loved ones to the newel post."

"I'm sorry," Marcy said, lost in her phone again. "Yes, masks. Booming business. You'd order the fabric in, though?"

"If they're shipping."

"Is there some . . . how small does the weave need to be? How big is the virus?"

Bo nodded with this. She was right: he needed to do more research. Or, rather, *some* research.

Marcy looked at him over her phone, said, "You just want to use your sewing machine."

Bo looked down, caught.

"If you want to, go for it," she said, collecting their plates, leaving a whole triangle of her grilled cheese for the compost, "but—you know my checks are still coming, right? You don't have to. We'll be fine."

Bo sat at the table for probably twenty minutes after she'd retreated upstairs to her work. When he was sure she was lost in her laptop, he tiptoed up the stairs, went the long way around her office, angling through the junk room for their bedroom, for their closet, to check which way that mannequin head was looking. The reason he was skulking was that he had no explanation for checking that closet.

He didn't make it that far, though.

Instead, stepping through the doorway of the junk room, a flicker of motion at the other end of the hallway stopped him.

It was that smoky mirror he'd picked up at an estate sale last summer. Just a wide oval on a chain, meant to hang over an umbrella stand, probably. But it was just leaning against the wall, even though . . . had he left it there?

He must have. He hadn't thought about it for months.

The motion he'd seen had been in its reflection, though.

It was angled up into the doorway of the attic stairs.

It was angled up onto a face, a woman's face, looking down *into* that glass.

"Brown dress, short hair," Bo heard himself muttering, like taking a mental photograph, and then the mirror was empty.

Bo didn't know what to do. He didn't know what he *should* do.

To get his thoughts together, he stepped back into the junk room, his back to the wall, his breaths deep and not as calming as he wanted them to be, but—but it was *daytime,* this was *his* house, and whatever he thought was happening here couldn't actually be happening, could it?

Still?

That was definitely a floorboard he heard creaking.

"Marce?" he said, not really loud enough.

No answer.

He stepped back around, into the doorway.

The mirror was still empty. Or, was empty again. But that just meant the woman with the short hair and the brown dress had stepped twenty inches to the side. Or up the stairs she had to have been standing on.

As to who she could have been, who Bo could be conjuring . . . shit: no idea. His mom had always had long hair, his sisters too, and Marcy's hair was mostly blond, meaning . . . meaning what?

It didn't make sense.

Was she some future woman, someone Bo would see in two years, in twenty years? If so, what could she be trying to tell him, to warn him about?

Bo shook his head no, no, this was stupid, he was making it all up, he was seeing things. "Ghosts are projections," he recited. Insisted.

Bolstered by that, he strode down the hall, his heels thumping on the hardwood, and when he stepped into the doorway of the attic stairs, they were just stairs. The same as ever.

He pulled the light cord. Nothing much changed.

"Hello?" he called up there anyway.

"I'm over here," Marcy said from where Bo had just been, in front of the junk room. "What are you doing, Bo?"

The way she said his name, the way she pointed it at him, it made Bo see himself in a way he didn't like.

"Nothing," he said, and pulled the light off, spent lunch in the basement, his hands shaking too much to sew any of the fabric scraps into masks.

Instead he just fired the big machine up, sewed stitches into nearly a whole bolt of light green velvet, ruining it past all hope, that big needle coming closer and closer to his fingers, its warm smooth metal sometimes even brushing his skin on its dip down, that contact keeping Bo's mind focused like he needed it, so it wouldn't wonder, so it wouldn't turn on him.

By late afternoon, Marcy was on the back porch, was to the stage of her research where she needed to talk it through with some non-layperson, it didn't matter. Whoever'd been calling at lunch yesterday, probably. It didn't matter.

She was in the wicker chair, her feet tucked under her for the long haul, her laptop open in her lap, strands of her hair falling from its bun.

It was good she was still getting paid. She was still working. She couldn't stop working, couldn't stop trying to solve the puzzle box of the human mind.

Bo ate a piece of wheat bread straight from the bag, then another. It wasn't the brand they liked, but it was the brand the market down the street had delivered, and wrong bread was better than no bread.

He washed the second slice down with half a beer, but poured the rest of it down the sink. He didn't need to start day-drinking now. Who knew how long they were going to be shut in, right? He dropped the empty bottle into recycling and shook the bin so the bottle's weight would sink it, hide it.

What was he doing?

Starving people's bodies start to eat their own mass, he knew. That's what he was doing, he imagined.

Unless he stayed busy.

There was no upholstery work, but there's always chores.

Bo went upstairs, nothing spooky about that walk even though he was waiting for it, and collected and divided the laundry, staged it on the landing to carry down to the utility, and then, his legs suddenly mechanical, he made himself walk down the long hall to the attic doorway, pulled it shut and tested to make sure it had caught. And he turned the mirror around too. It still had the estate-sale sticker on the back. He peeled it in ragged strips, balled that gumminess between his fingers all the way back up the hall, not letting himself look behind him, even though every follicle on the back of his neck was open, was listening.

Next he went to the bedroom closet, piled Marcy's scarves on top of the mannequin head then reeled them off, wound that foam head in layers of them instead, only realizing at the last moment that that fly crawling on the eyeball of that homeless dude in Marcy's dream, it wasn't a fly anymore, but the silk of the inner scarf.

Still, "Take that," Bo said, sort of satisfied, which was pretty much all he could ask for, he knew.

He started to make the bed but then realized he'd probably sweated the sheets all up with his juvenile night terrors, so he stripped it, snowballed the sheets down the stairs with the rest.

Because it was always a thing with Marcy and him, about how carrying the trash out meant not only delivering the bag to the dumpster but *also* putting another liner in the can—complete process, complete process—he followed through on the bed version of that, and went to the linen closet for replacement sheets.

When he pulled them out, though, going for the ones on the bottom of the stack instead of the top, because he liked the all-over way the flannel felt, even if it was hot, something else came out with those sheets. Something that had been tucked in under that stack.

No, something that had been *shoved* there.

A . . . a brown dress?

Bo rubbed the fabric between his fingers, considering this.

The woman *had* been real? If the dress was real, then that meant the woman wearing it had been real, too, didn't it?

Only—only she hadn't actually had short brown hair, had she?

That mannequin head in the closet, it had come with a brown wig, he was pretty sure. What had become of that wig over the years?

More important, it had been in what Bo had always thought of as a syndicated television hairstyle: short, a bob, curled under at the bottom like all the idealized moms of yesteryear.

"Marce," he said, staring down into the weave of this fabric.

It had been *her* standing on the attic stairs? And—and when he'd ducked back into the junk room to collect himself, she'd hustled down the hallway, stuffing her disguise where she could along the way, because getting caught with it in her hand would . . . would give up the game?

No, he realized, his face going cold and numb: it would wreck the *experiment*.

Shit.

She hadn't moved on to OCD and dementia. She was still doing her fear study. What she'd done—what she'd done was plant the seed with her out-loud questionnaire about the scariest thing in Bo's life, and now, now . . .

Bo tucked the dress back in its hidey-hole, stepped out of his shoes so he could drift soundlessly down the hall, into Marcy's office.

Just like his workshop, it was optimized for the person at the center of this swirling mass: it was Marcy's mind, arrayed in concentric circles out from her chair.

Bo listened hard to confirm the burble of her conversation on the back porch, then he stepped across the threshold into her space, settled into her chair.

It spun a bit, adjusting to his weight, the momentum of his careful sit, and he catalogued all the items paper by paper, book by book, until . . .

Her leather notebook. Her "thoughtpad," as she called it, usually while hugging it to her chest.

Bo swallowed, listened downstairs again, and didn't so much impel his hand down to that leather binding as watch his fingers grasp onto it, pull it into his orbit.

He unsnapped it, and—no. No no no. Please.

A pair of dice rolled into his lap.

"I gave you everything you need," he said.

That new ringtone on her phone, he knew that if he looked into it, it would have been customized by someone from her lab, customized so there was a low humming buzz right *before* the clapper went off against that bell.

And, next, now, it was going to be dice.

To what purpose, though.

Instead of paging through her notebook—that felt like the same kind of invasion she was staging against him—Bo cast around again, for what she was reading.

Three of the five books at hand had something to do with gaze detection. One was a soldier's memoir, even.

"Shit," Bo said, the feeling finally coming to his cheeks, his eyes heating up.

Marcy, she was—she was making do with what she had at hand, wasn't she? Locked in with a potential subject for weeks on end, she was . . . she was testing and probing, feeling around for what mechanism might heighten someone's gaze detection. Only, of course, she couldn't let that unwitting subject, Bo, know about this, could she? Of course not. That would wreck this ad-hoc study.

And what harm could it really do, right?

Granted, it wasn't near-scientific enough for publication, but it might inform the setup she would use when she could finally do this for real, with fifty or a hundred participants.

"I'm not losing it," Bo said, and, the final capper, on the way downstairs to collect the laundry, go on with this charade, he stopped at their engagement photo, took it down gently. On the back was just the right amount of modeling clay on one side. Just the right amount to angle the glass over at the dining room, where she'd probably had . . . had that mannequin face on the table, maybe, because face-completion or whatever it was called was a part of all this, wasn't it?

Bo hung the photo back up, careful to straighten it.

After starting the laundry, he made two turkey sandwiches, using both heels for his, and delivered the other out to the back porch.

Marcy took it, nodded thanks, and switched her phone to the other ear.

In the basement an hour later, then, not completely on purpose, kind of just running his own experiment, Bo let the needle from the big sewing machine stab down through the flesh of his index finger, then shush back out, just missing the bone.

He took his foot off the pedal, looked at the thick green thread trailing from his finger.

When the blood came, he wrapped that green thread tight just under the puncture, trying to stanch it, but the harder he pulled, the wider the puncture tore, until finally he had to bite the thread, drag it out from inside him.

Instead of a Band-Aid, he put a latex glove on, and a leather one on top of that, and then buried that hand in the pocket of the winter jacket he found he was wearing, and he was standing like that in the doorway of the kitchen when Marcy closed the refrigerator.

She dropped the pickle jar she'd been eating from, and while she was looking down at that spill, Bo pivoted away, into the rest of the house.

Breakfast and lunch the next day were exceedingly normal. Bo made sure of it. He was responsive and willing to participate, but he felt like he was on stage, like he was reciting lines.

"What happened to your hand?" Marcy asked, about the gauze.

"Basement," Bo told her, waving it off as beneath talking about.

The hole was seeping a thin yellow fluid, though. He was having to sneak off, change the gauze every hour.

After dinner, then, he suggested a board game instead of sidewalk bingo.

"Like college," Marcy said. "I'll get the wine."

Bo came to the kitchen table with all four games they had, and had to open three of the boxes before finding which one Marcy had harvested the dice from.

"Wow, where could they have gone, you think?" he asked, going for the Oscar.

Marcy stole two from the other game, and they played two rounds—two rounds of wine, too—and then she claimed inspiration, her eyes already looking upstairs to her office.

Bo told her go, go, he'd wrap the boxes and glasses up.

He watched her up the stairs, though.

He'd intentionally left their engagement photo just out of square.

Marcy straightened it, looked down to the dark dining room Bo had stepped into.

Did she see him there?

He couldn't tell, but didn't move.

She continued on to her work.

After cleaning the glasses—red wine goes instantly sticky—Bo realized that, attentive to details as Marcy was, he might be outing himself: the formal dining room carpet.

Of course he would have left footsteps.

He stood in the doorway of it, clicked the chandelier on.

Sure enough, there were his dark footprints.

Only, just behind them there were . . . smaller, lighter prints?

"Hunh," he said, impressed.

From when Marcy had placed the mannequin head. Had to be.

They'd each walked in nearly the same steps, too.

Bo got the vacuum cleaner out, didn't plug it in, just ran it over all the steps, more or less erasing them.

Next he stood in Marcy's window in the living room, watching the dark street.

He was sucking on his hurt finger, that yellow fluid warm and slight in his throat.

Soon enough a flame at chest height wavered up the sidewalk—the woman in the paper mask, returning from whatever journey she'd been on? Whatever pilot light she'd been tasked with carrying a flame to?

Maybe.

Maybe not.

Bo reached over, turned the porch light on, but she was already gone.

To get this over with once and for all, not string it out and out, maybe mess everything up, Bo finally just decided to have it out with Marcy. To explain to her that he knew what she was doing, and he understood why, and it even made a sort of sense. But still, he didn't want his old fears reactivated, right? Who would? At what cost progress, all that.

He went through it on the slow way up the stairs, and—of course, of course: three or four steps up, the old feeling came back, right on schedule.

Someone behind him, walking in his footsteps.

Bo closed his eyes, shook it off, and pressed on, even—as he never would have as a kid—stabbing a hand out for the banister, not allowing the possibility of another hand moving there with his own.

That had been stupid.

He stood in Marcy's doorway for a full ten seconds before she looked up to him over her reading glasses.

"Yes, what?" she said, on alert, it seemed.

Bo breathed in, had it all worked out in his head, but when he opened his mouth to explain to her that he was her husband, not her subject, not her lab rat, something different was coming out. He could hear the burble of his words, could feel their vibrations in his jawbone, was even aware of his mouth moving, but—

Had Nostradamus gone into a trance when he'd scry into the future? Would he come out of it, find all these verses or whatever on the page, and then read them for the first time?

Probably, Bo figured.

Almost definitely.

At least judging by what was happening to him now.

Finally, on some sort of delay, like what he was saying had to make the circuit of the room before coming back to him, Bo started to register what some part of him was telling Marcy: she's driving on a thick stretch of highway and there's a bag with milk in it on the seat beside her, and in slow motion a bright silver tanker truck is rolling across the median, cartwheeling over into her lane, and she slows, she slides, she screams, and the milk is floating beside her now but it's not spilled yet, but it will spill, and the man who pries the door open not to save Marcy's life but to free what's left of her body will stop for a moment to appreciate the way her blood is marbled with that milk, red and white ribbons laced together, and if the Marcy who's going to take that route home someday thinks she can avoid it by never drinking milk again, then she's right, only, ten years later, her bones brittle from lack of calcium, she'll fall down the stairs of her department's building late on a Friday afternoon, and many of those fragile bones will burst inside her, crumble into her muscle tissue, and she'll lie like that until Monday morning, when she's found, not saved, because who she spends the weekend with is a family of raccoons, who nibble and pull at her flesh, their black eyes hungry and merciless, their hands so human, and if she tries to avoid this by quitting her profession altogether, then—

Bo tried to stop, to reel these futures back in, because Marcy was shrinking back, drawing her feet up into her chair, her eyebrows climbing her forehead.

The coffee cup she drank water from was spilling into the old rug she had in here, that her chair pretty much refused to roll on but that she insisted upon anyway. She was shaking her head no about what Bo was saying, no no no, which was when Bo became aware of another sensation, this one at his right side, just under the ribs.

The fabric of his shirt was moving against his skin?

Then he remembered: of course, of course—his hurt finger, his throbbing hand. Of course he would be hiding it in his pocket, not getting Marcy worried about it.

Only, now that he'd stopped telling Marcy about what was coming, about what he never wanted to have to see, his pocket was still again. He held his hands up to her like wait, wait, he can explain this, which was when he realized what he was seeing now, between him and her.

Both his hands. The left one *and* the hurt right one, in the double gloves.

He opened his mouth to tell her not to worry, but the fabric moved against his side again, and he realized there *was* a hand in his pocket, moving his mouth like a sock it was shoved into, and Marcy climbing over the back of her chair now, was it—was it not from these eventualities he was laying out for her, but something else?

With his real voice, being as calming as he could be, Bo told Marcy that it didn't have to be this way, that he'd tamped it down once before, in elementary, he'd rationalized it away, and he could again, he knew, with her help, if she'd just stop trying to solve the puzzle box of the human mind, or at least stop trying to use him to do it?

She wasn't listening, though. She was opening and closing her mouth like a fish pulled up onto shore, gasping for the world it used to know.

Bo slowed his thinking down, burrowed into the moment, considered the mechanics of it all, and, slowly, bit by painful bit, it started to register with him: If there's a hand in my pocket, then that means someone's standing directly behind me, doesn't it?

Someone who had been there all along.

That's what Marcy was crawling away from. She wasn't even really listening, was she? She was that little girl in the city she'd been once upon a time, only there was no father to take her by the hand, lead her away.

There was only Bo.

Who, evidently, wasn't alone, and never had been.

With his real hands, the ones that were still his, he reached forward, pulled her door shut to keep her safe, to keep her out of this, away from him, and on legs that didn't feel like his, that felt like there were legs pressing against them from the back, walking with him, in his footsteps, he went downstairs once and then again, to the basement, that hand moving in his pocket the whole while, making his mouth mutter about how it's going to be Marcy who finds him, Marcy who will have to live with this for the rest of her life, but that's fair, isn't it? Because she's the one who had unlocked him after all these years, and because he had already said it, because he was saying it now, that meant it was really going to happen, so there was nothing he could do to stop it anymore, really.

It made it easier.

Bo set a brick on the big sewing machine's pedal, its heavy wheel gathering speed, that dry belt limbering up. He set the dial over, sat up on the runway, as he'd come to call it, and—it was the only rational thing to do—he scooched over, lay down beside the pumping needle, and began stitching.

All he wanted to do, all he needed to do in order to stop all these futures from spilling through, was keep that third hand out of his pocket, so his mouth couldn't follow it anymore, but he had two pockets, right, so, after the needle had closed his right pocket, plunging into his organs and guts and bringing up little bits, he turned for the other side to finish the job but there was thread everywhere, and it was strong, it was for upholstery, it was meant to last for decades if not longer, and Bo knew his plans had gone awry when the needle, bent now, thrust through his upper lip, scraping up his right canine into his gums and running down along the roots of his teeth, breaking them all free in turn.

He tried to turn over for the other pocket but was too wrapped, had too many holes, and because this next dip of the needle was coming for his tear duct on the right side, was going to come back up with all the things he called memories, the presence who had been walking behind him his whole life finally reached ahead to embrace him in its arms, to hold him there long enough that the young girl walking behind her father in the city can stop, see him, see his mouth moving, but not understand that what he's telling her is to run, run, to never tell anybody about this, but of course it's already too late for that, this is where they are, where they've always been, and it's already starting again.

TRINITY RIVER'S BLUES
BY CHESYA BURKE

Trini saw dead people. It's somewhat of a cliché, but she was the real thing. Since she was a kid, they appeared to her, talked to her, were called to her for some reason she could never quite understand.

The dead were not sad as they were depicted on TV and in the movies. They were content, just in another time and place, sometimes not-living their lives—going through the motions—like most living people. No. They weren't evil or sinister or insidious.

She had seen her first ghost as a kid. Her grandmother's favorite blues musician was T-Bone Walker. He had a hit song titled "Trinity River Blues." The old woman had the chance to meet him once, and he was a magnificent performer; he worked the crowd with the best of them. "That dirty Trinity River . . . sure has done me wrong . . . it came to my window and doors and now all my things are gone . . ." or something like that, the song goes.

The Trinity River floods all the time, but on the night Trinity was born it was storming and the damn thing was threatening to flood once again. That was why her grandmother had insisted on calling her Trinity. It was about power, the old woman said. Anything that powerful should be respected and honored and so they called her Trinity. First name Trinity. Middle name River. That was nearly twenty-two years ago. The way her grandmother told it, her momma was screaming so loud the whole hospital could hear and she was ripped from "stem to stern" but her mother never did give up on her, until baby Trinity popped out into the world.

That was how her grandmother put it: "She never did give up on you, baby girl," the old woman always said. Her mother pushed and pushed until she couldn't anymore. Even after the doctor told her there was no use, that the baby was dead, she yelled at him and told him that she wasn't giving up. Least that's how her grandmother tells it. She said she was standing there telling the doctor to listen to my momma, when my momma whispered a prayer.

"The whole world stood still for that prayer. The winds stopped, the rain, and the doc," the old woman would laugh.

"My life for hers." Her mother said, "My life for hers."

She died. Trinity didn't.

So, her grandmother named her after that dark night, Trinity River, so she'd never forget her momma, she said. So she'd never forget that night. That fateful night her mother died. Unspoken, of course, was that the Trinity River was deadly. It killed things, like she'd killed her mother.

Trinity knew it wasn't just a coincidence that she had been born on a night like that described in her grandmother's favorite song.

The dead were always there to remind her.

From the time that she could remember, Trinity had always been full of that stupid childhood ignorance that all kids have—except she talked to a dead man.

T-Bone Walker—and he talked back.

Along the years, she realized that her ability wasn't limited to T-Bone and that others—many others—would soon come to her. But she wasn't quite ready for them as a kid and T-Bone did everything he could to prepare her.

She could never say why they chose her. Her grandmother had her own special abilities and rootwork was simply a part of her history, but there was something different about the way they gathered around her that scared even her grandmother: "Careful child, always. They summon them." Who was *them*? It took a long time for her to understand what the old woman meant.

When she got older, she realized that talking to dead people was not normal and so she hid it. She learned not to talk about it. Eventually she figured that T-Bone had chosen her because of her name and that made her feel special. But she knew now it wasn't true. And by the time she found herself in that tiny little hole-in-the-wall club, she knew dead things when she saw them.

What she didn't know was why everyone else in the club had seen him, too.

She had arrived at the Grand Sixes, a club at the corner of Wheeler and Broadway, early that evening. It was Jazz Night and she always made sure to come to hear the acts and to keep her feet on the pulse of what was new. Many people thought that the art and genre was dead—much like the man who was on stage in that moment—but it wasn't. Jazz would never die. It was as alive and well as Charlie Parker himself, she mused. In the club, Trinity turned to look at T-Bone. He didn't look back at her. Something was very wrong. She could feel it. Bone knew it. She sipped her drink, two, three times.

The performer, the Master, was wearing a nineteen-thirties-style, perfectly manicured, pin-striped suit with a wide-tail tie in the design of a piano. The sax player moved diligently, in a particularly limber way. The keys of the music tie seemed to dance along with its owner, in a perfect unison. His dark skin hung loosely around his bones—as if he had none. It was unnatural. His bushy eyebrows and full head of wavy hair swayed and bounced as he shook, as if playing to a rhythm all their own.

Trinity's mind was whirling, and she felt she was seeing things that could not possibly be there. Then she heard the one thing that made her know that this was no ordinary sax player. The four-chord change.

It was *him*. She knew it.

Charlie "Bird" Parker. One of the greatest musicians who had ever walked the face of the earth.

Charlie Parker was dead.

When the performer was done, he walked off stage without even waiting for applause.

"Let's go." Bone nodded and followed her. He had a habit of not talking to her when she was in public because he didn't want people to think she was crazy.

The Master was waiting for her outside.

It was nearly one in the morning, and the moon had barely broken free. It had been raining all that day and the dark night clouds were smothering its radiance.

It was dark.

He was darker.

"Good evening." His voice, as soft as a whisper, came from behind her.

She jumped, fell against her car door and spun around. It took her a moment to gather herself. This close he looked thinner somehow. If that were possible, frailer. His eyes were yellow. They almost seemed to glow in the darkness. He hid within the shadows. Seemed to melt into them, as if he were part of the darkness surrounding him. He was wrong. Very wrong.

He said it again. "Good evening." Then he added, "Trinity River."

"How do you know my name?" Her voice cracked and she instantly regretted responding.

"You called me."

"I didn't."

A coy smile spread across his face. "But you did."

"What do you want?"

That smile again. It scared her.

"And now they know."

"I . . . I don't know what you're . . . Are you him? Are you him, are you the Bird?"

"Shhh," he whispered, looking around as if he were searching for something. Or as if someone were searching for him. "Don't call me that."

"What? The Bird?"

"Don't!" he snapped, startling a flock of crows nearby, sending them into a frenzy.

She took a step back; this thing scared her. She had talked to dead people her whole life, yet this was different. She looked to T-Bone, who had positioned himself nearly between the two.

"What do you want?" T-Bone asked.

The thing squinted his yellow eyes at Bone and smiled. She hadn't noticed before that his teeth were gone. "Now the dead man wants to speak? The parasite?"

"There's only one parasite here," T-Bone replied.

There was silence. That strange kind of silence that is only heard in a graveyard. With the dead.

"Look. I don't know what the fuck you are. If you're a ghost of the Bird or . . ." The name came out of her mouth before she could stop it.

The Master lunged toward her, as the crows fluttered in the distance and landed in trees only yards away. T-Bone stopped him, using his incorporeal body to block the thing from getting to her. His spirit melted into and through T-Bone and ended up right in front of Trinity. She stepped back, putting space between herself and the Master. Her shoulders were drooped, so she straightened them, standing tall, trying not to show fear but failing miserably.

Face-to-face he looked down on her. His breath smelled hollow, big, empty. "Remember." Then he was gone. Within the shadows. Melted into the darkness.

Trinity had known about T-Bone all her life—or really, she had known *of* T-Bone all her life. The things her grandmother didn't tell her, she researched herself. She had been obsessed with him as a child, with his life and his talents. Her grandmother would play his records all day long, and the pair would stand in the kitchen of her giant house and dance to his music. The old woman would sing, "That Trinity River . . . That Trinity River," as if it were written just for her ears. Trinity loved it and in turn she began to love him.

He was a ghost, but she knew him, loved him as if he were alive—in all his vibrance and bubbliness. But she always wondered if that was because of how he looked in all the pictures she had ever seen of him. She related to T-Bone so well because he, too, had a longing inside him that he couldn't quite fill, and she felt that same way. Like there was somewhere she needed to go but couldn't, or something she needed to do. Something was missing and that thing had been jazz. She wanted so badly to be on a stage, everyone in the audience rocking out to music that she created, but she never had the talent—so she'd called out to T-Bone, her childhood love, and he came.

But he was *there,* more than mere imagination. She only questioned it when she was young enough to not understand what was happening to her. Before the other entities showed themselves to her. T-Bone had made himself known in a lot of ways, though. And he had helped her on more than one occasion get her ass—and others—out of trouble. Like when she was eight years old and her friends were playing hide-and-seek, and one of them had hidden in an abandoned refrigerator. Everyone else had all but given up on looking for him—who in their right mind would hide in a fridge with a broken handle? But the boy had.

And just as she had given up, T-Bone was there. "You can't leave that boy out here," he said to her.

"He's gone. He probably got bored and went home," she replied while everyone else had left.

T walked about twenty feet away and pointed to the refrigerator. "Check in there."

She swung the door open and saw Andre, sweating like a pig, screaming how he'd won. "You idiot, you could have died," Trinity had said to him.

"You found me, didn't you?"

No stupid, T-Bone did, she had thought. But didn't say it. You don't tell people—not even children—when you talk to the dead.

T-Bone Walker was a good man. He was a good man when he was alive, and he's a good man while dead—at least if you asked

Trinity River. So what she talked to a dead man? Who hasn't at some point in their life? What person hasn't lost someone and told them how much they loved them and known in their heart that not only could they hear every word, but that the dead spoke back, saying how much they loved them, too. Who hasn't missed someone so much that they sat next to their grave and cried, just to feel better seconds later? And you just know it was that dead family member comforting you.

"You've got to feel the blues to make them right," the dead man would say to her, and bang his guitar one time for good measure.

You've got to feel the blues to make them right. She guessed that could be said about everything, especially life, she supposed.

"Keep on shufflin', Trinity River," he'd say to her and smile.

"I plan to, T," she'd answer, louder than she should.

The next morning, she awoke to a bird singing at her windowsill. A large black bird. A crow. A singing crow.

She sat up. Crows don't sing.

Its song, although beautiful, was sad. It was almost as if it were crying a tune of pure pain. She had never heard a bird do that before. Or since. It was a beautiful song, however, that was matched only by the luster of its black coat, which seemed to change colors as she watched; from black to darkish purple, then to shimmery blue and then back to black.

It brought her mind back to the dead thing she had seen the night before, the Master. She didn't want to call it a ghost because it wasn't. It was something more than that, something connected to her in a way that made her hurt deep inside and she didn't know why.

T-Bone wasn't around, so she couldn't talk to him. She never knew what he did when he left her, and she didn't ask. She never thought it was proper to talk to the dead about them being dead—or where they went or what they saw. It was not only rude, but it always felt wrong and forbidden. Besides, the dead didn't talk much, they didn't have much to say. Trinity guessed that they had said everything they needed in life and there wasn't anything left. Some talked more than others, some never said a word in their whole afterlives.

That thing, the Master, was stuck in her head and she couldn't get him out. She had gone to sleep thinking about him, she had dreamed about him and now she had woken up with him on her mind. She thought back to his toothless grin, the way the flesh hung from his bones as if he had none at all. She thought about the way his presence was empty, hollow, like a void.

In that moment, with that thing on her mind, she felt strange. Something within her made her climb out of bed and grab her old sax. She hadn't played it in years. Never even took it out of the case. She attached a fresh reed from the unopened box and blew. The sound was magical. She stared at the sax for a moment and everything in her wanted to put it down, didn't want to do what she eventually did.

She played.

The notes were light and effortless. The rhythm came to her as if she had practiced all her life. She was, for a short time, the Master. Or something that was so much like him that they were indistinguishable. She was the player that she had longed to be but never had enough talent. She got high off the feeling; it was amazing.

Power surged through her body. It felt so good. She wanted more of it. It was deep and overwhelming, but pure. Powerful. She could barely contain the feeling of adrenaline coursing through her veins. Her fingers moved ferociously but it was because her brain no longer belonged to her—instead yielding to this power that she could barely contain. He wanted her to succumb to him, she could feel it. He whispered things just out of reach of her understanding. Things she wanted so badly to know, things that were forbidden to her. There were promises in that whisper. Secrets. But it was wrong. All wrong.

She knew it wasn't right. She refused to give up herself to become something that she didn't understand. That's not what she wanted. She understood that in those moments he worked to take over her essence.

She threw the sax across the room, as her nerves got the best of her, and she felt sick. Something was bubbling up inside. She rushed to the bathroom just in time as she began to retch over the toilet, the bile splashing everywhere. She dry-heaved until her abs ached and pain shot through her stomach. The vomit came up into her throat and then she swallowed it again. This made her sicker, and she began to gag.

This time it was more productive as she felt the tickle of something in the back of her throat. Something sharp and hard. She coughed, hoping to bring it out, but it was stuck there, just sitting between her tonsils. Coughing was not helping, and her breath became impeded. She reached into the back of her mouth and felt something there. She grasped for it, but pushed it back down her throat, causing more pain. Her fingers slipped on it again, and the thing scratched her tongue as pain shot through her mouth. Finally, she gripped it. It was narrow and slick. Slowly, steadily, she pulled it out of her mouth. It felt soggy and wet on her tongue.

A feather.

A black feather, from a crow or a blackbird.

She stared at it for a long time, then at her reflection in the mirror.

Her reflection revealed one of her eyes had become black opal. It was clear and glistening like glass. She touched it softly and it gave a little under her fingers. It didn't feel like it was solid, it only seemed that way. And the vision from that eye was blurry and tinted dark, as if she were wearing blackout shades.

As she looked into the mirror, one eye almost blind, she saw T-Bone staring back at her. "What's happening to me, T?" Tears came to her good eye, but the other remained unfazed by her emotion.

He looked sad. "You don't remember?"

She shook her head.

"You need to go to Grann. Now."

Trinity River had heard once that "crows don't fly to music;

they whistle to a black beat. March to a dead melody. Sing to a tuneless song." She has since learned that these things, of course, are not true. She has since heard the song of crows—they sing to hopelessness.

Her grandmother was the type of person that everyone respected. The woman in the neighborhood that people went to when they had "troubles." Those kinds of things that you don't talk about, but that need to be solved. She was a rootworker, a healer, a hoodoo woman. She was everything that Trinity feared. Not that she was particularly scared of the woman or what she did, but because she was afraid that she would become her. She didn't think that she could ever have what it took to fill such great shoes. She respected the woman in a way that she could never respect herself. And that, she knew, scared her. That was power, that was talent. Trinity did not have either.

The woman lived in a big house on the southside. It had been gifted to her before Trinity had been born by a man who owed her something. Her grandmother never told her what he owed, but whatever it was paid for this house and most of the things Trinity got when she was growing up.

Old people keep secrets in ways that younger generations will never understand. They hold on to things, keep the confidences of people so that one day they will keep theirs. Trinity knew that her generation did not understand this; they were built different. It was not that younger generations could not keep secrets; it was that secrets hit harder when you have to fear for your life within a system that wants you dead. Trinity understood this more than many.

The girl did not have to knock on the door. Before she could get to the top stairs, her grandmother opened it. The woman looked at her, but through her. The way she always did when she wanted to know things that her granddaughter would never tell her grandmother from her own lips.

"What have you done, yon ti kras?" Her little one. She always called Trinity that when she was disappointed with the girl. Her people were from Haiti once upon a time. The woman opened the door wider and Trini walked past her, into the dimly lit foyer. As the woman shut the door, Trinity fell into her arms, holding on to Grann for dear life. She didn't want to let go, didn't want to stop holding the woman who had always been such a comfort to her, but mostly she didn't want to have to tell her what was happening.

Her grandmother had always protected her, kept her safe. She did not want to have to disappoint the woman. As a kid that had been her biggest fear. Now, she realized, she was still that little kid who was scared to upset her parent, the one who had put so much time and energy into her.

Grandmother peeled the girl away from her, stared into her opal eye. "The world is a very big place, yon ti kras. You have no business in it, messing with it in these ways. Very big things happen to very small little ones. Everyone and everything is small to a world that is so big. And we, yon ti kras, are never big enough to stop the blese." That "hurt" her grandmother had always tried to protect her from had finally found her, and Trinity indeed had been too small and insignificant to stop it.

"I don't know, Grann. I don't know." The tears were streaming down now, that one eye still suspiciously dry.

The woman touched her child's head. "You don't remember? It's lost to you? Was it a spell?"

Trinity shook her head; she really didn't know. She wasn't hiding anything, and she didn't think that she had any kind of memory loss or a loss of time. She just simply had no idea what the hell had happened, especially if she had done something. She looked over at T-Bone, who nodded that she had *done* something. He had followed her in and watched as the women held each other.

She took Trinity to the one room in the house that the girl had never been allowed to play in. It was her grandmother's special place. She talked to things in that space, she did things that she never talked about and for which Trinity always knew better than to ask.

Grann was wearing a long bright dress that swayed when she walked, colorful and lovely on her. The woman said she wore it to defy expectation and make people comfortable when they came to see her. People who came to Grann were in trouble and seeking her assistance, but they were also scared and didn't know where else to go. She gave them that help in a package that was comfortable.

As she entered the room, T-Bone slid in just as the door shut. He could not enter this space without permission and since her grandmother had already willed it to her, Trinity gave him unspoken permission. That was a small bit of power that the girl had in this place.

The older woman stopped, turned to look at her granddaughter. She closed her eyes for a moment, but Trinity knew she saw everything she needed even when they weren't opened. When she opened them, though, she squinted as if she could not quite see what she needed. Or she did not like what she saw. Trinity did not know which and did not like the idea of either. After a moment Grann cocked her head, walking to her little one. She put her hand on Trini's head again, but this time more forcefully.

Trinity wanted nothing more than to fall into the woman's arms again, but she did not dare move, not one inch. She knew to let her grandmother do whatever she needed, not to speak, and most importantly, not to interrupt the process.

After what seemed like forever, Grann stopped. "When did this happen to you? Your eye?"

Trinity shrugged. "This morning. Maybe while I slept last night. I don't know."

"While you were sleeping? Not yourself."

That was not a question and Trinity did not try to answer. She stood, quietly. Unblinking and emotionless. The opal eye was rough under the skin of her lid, so she tried not to blink too often. She could tell that it was getting worse, beginning to harden. She could feel the ligaments within slowly toughen and get stiff. Blinking was becoming a chore, so she was happy not to do it.

Her Grann smiled but there was no humor in her face. "You always wanted to please. Always longed for the talents you didn't have, for the gifts that were out of reach. That was you, yon ti kras. Never content with your own abilities, never happy." She let her go and turned her back, walked a few steps away.

"Grann, what is wrong? What's happening to me? Did someone put roots on me?"

The woman did not speak for a long while, as she often did when she was lost somewhere that was not on the plane with the rest of them. She spoke slowly, and Trinity knew she was trying to think of the words. "No. No one put roots on you. You did this."

"What do you mean? I haven't done anything," and as soon as she said it, she knew it wasn't true. Not because she remembered anything that she had done, but because she could feel it wasn't the truth.

"I'm sure you didn't mean to do this. No one would do this to themselves on purpose. But it's you." She paused a moment. "This here . . . this is longing. Its power manifested. You don't understand who you are and so you let your fears and insecurities control you."

She cried again, "What did I do, Grann?"

"This thing is eternal, and it's attached itself to you because you invited it."

Trinity closed her eyes. *Invited it?* Then she knew, absolutely, what she had done. She had been studying and researching jazz at the college and had become obsessed with Charlie Parker. She had, somewhat jokingly, asked the universe for that kind of talent a little over a week before. Somewhat because she really meant it, she knew it as sure as she was standing there with this thing, whatever it was, attached to her.

She had called out to it.

"This is . . . he's big and overwhelming."

"Can you get him out of me, kill him?"

For the first time her grandmother could not meet her eyes. T-Bone sat quietly in the corner, in a chair that was usually reserved for a guest. Trinity felt like he had always known what her grandmother was telling her, but he couldn't say. The dead are bound by rules the living never understand. She stared at the floor, seeming to think about what to say next, contemplating her words carefully. "You can't kill him. He's in you. That would kill you, too."

"Then what, Grann?"

"I can try to temporarily unbind you from it, but then you will have to find a way to destroy it, send it back to where it came from. But if it binds with you again, you will not be able to get free."

"How long will I have?"

"A day, maybe two until he can find your soul again."

Her grandmother moved back to her, grabbing her head, one hand positioned in front and the other cradling the back of her skull. She was strong. Trinity knew the process. She had never seen it with her own eyes—her grandmother had told her that one day she would be ready, but that day had not come before then—but her grandmother had told her some things: Listen, obey and believe. So, she closed her eyes; believed in her grandmother. T stood up and inched a bit closer, standing by in case something went wrong. She saw him in the murky shadow of her black eye. He was dead and he had more sway in the afterlife than she did, she figured. That comforted her when it shouldn't have.

As her grandmother's hand steadied the back of her head, she rubbed her hand down the girl's body, caressing her abdomen. Her fingers paused, drawing a circle over the girl's ribs. Slowly at first and then faster and faster as if she herself were possessed. No one would ever believe that her grandmother was so agile and in control of all her faculties, if they did not see her in this way, in her best form. She normally looked frail and thin; however, when she surrendered to her powers, letting them take over, she became freer, less encumbered.

Her grandmother continued creating a circle around her child's midsection. From her periphery Trinity saw something move within the flesh of her stomach, jump as if a baby kicking its mother. At first, she believed that she had imagined it, but as she watched it happened again. This time it was unmistakable. Something lived within her.

Her first reaction was to startle, moving slightly. She couldn't help it.

"Do not move," the woman warned.

Grann gripped her stomach tightly and closed her eyes and held her hands there, unmoving. With strength twice that of an ordinary woman her age, she pulled Trinity to the ground and laid her on the rug. From somewhere within her big dress, the woman whipped out a pair of scissors and cut the girl's blouse open, exposing her belly.

Trinity's upper body was completely bare. She hadn't been naked like this in front of her grandmother since she was a small child and she didn't even care. Her skin was smooth and inconspicuous, no hint of what lay beneath the flesh, deep inside her.

Her grandmother grabbed her, holding tight, sending a shock through her body. Trinity jumped from the bolt of electricity. Again. And again. As the last bolt shot through her, a face emerged within the flesh of her stomach, its mouth spreading slowly into a smile. The eyes opened, exposing her own brown skin as its eyeballs.

Trinity was terrified, but her grandmother was calm, controlled. "It's powerful. Called to it, but it could only come to you because of your own power. It used your power to manipulate the dead to attach itself to you. This is no ghost, but it's not alive in any way that we understand. It has never lived in this world, and it wants to desperately. You have no idea what you have done, little one."

Without warning, the woman sent another shock through Trinity and she began to convulse, her body shaking violently. It stopped after a moment, the younger woman tired and unable to speak on the floor. "Is . . . is . . ."

"No. It's not over. It's coming. . . ."

The greatest pain that Trinity had ever felt attacked her body. She could not think and wanted desperately to just fade away so that she wouldn't have to feel it anymore. Like many Black people, Trini had been taught not to show pain. Not because it didn't matter, but because to let go was to lose control, and to lose control of one's emotions was to show weakness to people who wanted to harm you. It gave them an excuse when they already saw you as less than human. This way of responding to one's pain was toxic and harmful, but it was how Black people had survived. Instead, you take that pain and you push it deep down inside. Trini, like she was conditioned, swallowed the agony; went somewhere else, mentally. And now, to give in to the pain would be to relinquish her own soul to this thing. She knew, could *feel* that. What Grann had taught her to survive in the real world, she hoped would keep her safe in the underworld. Instead she suffered, feeling as if this thing were ripping right out of her essence. The bones and flesh of her body felt as if they were being torn from her.

She escaped to the mental place and endured the pain because she had caused it.

The Master ripped out of her with such force, peeling itself from within her. She was dizzy, hazy and her eye was burning. She was doing everything she could to keep from passing out. As her eyes began to find their equilibrium again, she realized there was a presence in the room that had not been there before.

Sitting up slowly, but as fast as she could, she saw it, tall and dark. The Master that had worn her like a bad fitted suit, now stood there wearing Charlie Parker's skin, as if it belonged to him. As if the Master deserved it.

"Are you okay, yon ti kras?" She looked at her granddaughter briefly, but then back in the direction of the fake Charlie Parker. Grann didn't see the dead, though she felt the universe and knew something was wrong. "What is it? What came out of you?"

"I . . . I don't know. It looks like a man, but it's not. It's wearing the skin of someone dead."

"Ak Bagay Ki Mal." T-Bone stared at the thing, not moving his eyes as he spoke.

She told her grandmother what Bone said. "Aha. The Evil One."

"Trinity River, lovely to see you again," said the Master. His voice was smooth, slick. Like a jazz player, he was playing a role. Nothing was real with this thing, everything could be manipulated, controlled. "I see you figured it out. Good. I look forward to sharing you again soon. I have so much to teach you, you just need to stop resisting me." The thing was taunting her.

"What do you want?"

"You. Your power."

"No."

"But you know you want to. You're missing me already, aren't you? You wanted the talent instead of the power. I want the power and can offer you the talent. I can feel you longing for me."

She shook her head, but even as he spoke, she knew it was true. She wanted it, she needed it. That thing . . . He had felt so good. Ak Bagay Ki Mal smiled, knowing her emotions and feelings without her saying them. "Why don't you come to my last performance tomorrow night? You can see all of the fame and fortune that awaits you if you just let me do what you asked."

He turned to walk away. Then he was gone, through the door, out of the house, not a care in the world. He didn't fear her, he *knew* her. That was worse.

Her grandmother couldn't see him, but she felt him leave just as she had felt him come from within her. "Ak Bagay Ki Mal is very strong. He's very powerful. He attached his incorporeal self to you because he was powerful enough to do so, and you aren't powerful enough to stop him from doing so next time. He's tasted you now. He will be able to find you anywhere."

Trinity tried to stand, but she couldn't without her grandmother's help.

"I'm scared that you want it, though, my little one."

Trinity did not answer because she couldn't.

"It'll consume you completely eventually. You won't be yourself anymore. You won't be in that body."

"I don't know what to do, Grann. I can feel him. He's so . . . delicious." The word fell from her mouth before she could stop it. But once it had, she knew it was right. Ak Bagay Ki Mal felt good, he felt right.

"I know."

She pulled over on the way home, not wanting to be in that

apartment alone. She and T-Bone got out of the car and stared at the stars. There was such a big world out there. It was hard to believe how much human beings don't know, how much was so scary and unhindered. She sat in a soft patch of grass on the side of the road near a park, the sun setting in the sky. She looked up, twirling her finger around a blade of the greenest grass, and T-Bone sat on a rock stringing his guitar. The way the sun bounced off his greased-up hair made her smile. He was such a cliché, he behaved in all the ways she always needed. She could join him if she still had the Ak Bagay Ki Mal, she thought, but stopped herself. The thought came from nowhere; he was in her head, controlling her thoughts. No, that wasn't completely true. She longed for him because that was always who she wanted to be, but not because the thing forced her. She had to reconcile that she was a person who had brought Ak Bagay Ki Mal into the world. She was powerful and stupid, her Grann said. Those would never be two things that would mix well.

T, probably reading her thoughts, sang to her, his Trinity River, of things that once were and of things that would be. She closed her eyes and listened, thinking. He looked down on her, not smiling, but lovingly just the same. She wished at that moment he had been her father. Actually, she kind of felt he was her dad. She never had one but needed one.

He stopped playing. "I would have loved to be your father, Trinity River."

Somehow, he always knew what she was thinking, "You are."

"You have a father, Trinity. And I ain't him."

"You're the only father I ever knew, T."

"But you made me up."

This was the first time he had ever said this. To be honest, it hurt like hell to hear it. And it wasn't true, she knew it. He was real; and he was the closest thing she had to a father. She needed him, needed to believe in him.

She said simply, "I didn't make you up. You're T-Bone Walker. I called to you because I could, and you came because you wanted to."

He looked at me, smiled and nodded. "Remember that power,

because it's the only thing we have to beat it."

* * *

She woke the following morning not to one crow serenading her with its sour melody, but to many cawing the song of despair. They sat on her windowsill and stared into the apartment with their almost sightless eyes. She experienced an eerie recognition as she realized that her own eye had looked exactly like those the day before.

There were more than a dozen of them now. Their song was terrifying. Lonely. Desperate.

They wanted in.

They thought she was him; that thing that had taken her over.

She stared at them for a moment longer than she should have, getting lost in the thoughts of surrendering to the Ak Bagay Ki Mal and finding joy in the power she had felt when the two were merged. But she put those thoughts away; they were toxic specifically because they were so inviting.

After breakfast, she sat and wrote down everything she knew. Her last will and testament. Someone might need to know her story to keep it from happening again. She kept thinking back to how people keep secrets. She didn't know so many things and she had gotten into this mess because of the secrets of the underworld that she had always been afraid to ask and never really wanted to know. It was time for her generation to do better—stop running from those secrets that the older generation held so powerfully. Embrace them, own them.

She was responsible for it now, and she needed to own that. T-Bone didn't show his face until toward the middle of the day. That was fine by her. She wasn't particularly excited about what the two had planned. But she didn't want to remain attached to this thing forever, no matter how amazing he felt.

While T was gone, Trinity called Sam, the owner of the Grand Sixes, to ask a huge favor. She needed him to run some wires and cables to set up a loudspeaker outside. Sam respected her grandmother—and if she were to be honest, most people in the area were afraid of the old woman. Because of this, she'd had Grann contact the man first, calling in any favors he might owe her. When Trinity spoke with him, he was pleasant and did not seem upset that he was being forced to help her. Grann had probably paid him too.

Of course, plans of this magnitude never quite work out as expected. Something always goes wrong, and she had a sinking feeling that this was the end of everything she loved.

When they arrived at the club, preparations had already begun. Outside, Sam was standing on a ladder and he waved as they walked up.

"Hey. What's up?" he said.

"Absolutely everything. How's it going, Sam?"

"Pretty good. I'm almost finished with these wires. Hiding them like you wanted. Mostly just putting them up high and outta sight. That cool?"

"Yeah, that's good. Where's the speakers?"

"Right there, I used a few posters from the club to cover this, so they're not conspicuous. We've done that a few times in the past, so nothing unusual."

Inside, she and Sam—T quiet and invisible in the corner—went over the plans again. She was nervous and even though she tried to hide it, she knew Bone and Sam could see her hands trembling and hear it in her voice.

At eight when the club opened, the Master hadn't shown up yet. Sam said that that wasn't unusual; performers often didn't show until it was time for them to go on. She thought it would be best for that thing not to find her in Sam's office, so she went out into the club and found a table—in the back. She waited.

The room was almost empty, except for her and T there were only three other people, and she found herself oddly comfortable with the familiar surroundings. The lights were dimmed and the track lights were lit. Beautiful blue light rained down on the stage. The first act had already taken the stage and they played surprisingly well. Perhaps the fear of death had overtaken Trinity, and she was less critical of people more talented than her. A week before she would have been very judgmental about this group on stage doing what she could only dream of. Now that she had finally wielded the talent she'd craved for so long, she didn't want it. Not anymore.

She watched with anticipation in an unusually detached way. She clapped when she was supposed to and showed the appropriate enthusiasm, but she didn't actually feel any emotion that she could put her finger on in that moment. By now, the club was full.

She felt him before she saw him. He was standing right above her when she turned around. The blue light, from the track above, made his eyes look almost mystical and she could not see their pupils within the darkness.

"I knew you'd come. I knew you couldn't resist."

She couldn't move.

He pulled her chin toward him, staring into her eyes. "It healed nicely; I see." He looked to T-Bone. "You will lose her, you know. When I have her completely, I will make her forget you ever existed."

T said simply, "You will try."

She glanced behind him and saw Sam staring. He looked more afraid than Trinity. Her grandmother must have told him more than she realized. Before that moment, she hadn't doubted that he would help them and go along with the plan. But now she could see it in his eyes. He had changed his mind. If her grandmother had indeed told him, then he might not want to get involved. She thought about giving him some sort of thumbs-up, but that would've looked suspicious. She had to just hope that he would help, when the time came.

"What do you want from me?" She had to say something; she was about to shit herself.

"Everything. You were a woman who could have had anything she wanted, everything at your fingertips, but you were scared. I can have anything, and I want more. I want to feed on your soul."

"What have I done to you?"

"You called me, remember?"

The Master must have tired of the conversation because he vanished into the shadows. Sam stood in the doorway, still watching. Neither of them dared to look at the other for too long. Sam walked back into his office and closed the door.

The next two acts had played the week before and even they sounded better to her that night. The waiting was the hard part. She was ready to get whatever would happen over with. Whether Sam changed his mind, she didn't know. He, after all, had nothing to lose. If he had decided not to go along with it, he could get away unnoticed.

The Master took the stage about ten p.m. He brought his sax with him and didn't bother waiting for his cue to begin. His song was even more mesmerizing than it had been the first time she had heard him. He blew with expert precision, his jaw muscles tight and airless.

He stared at her. His eyes flared brightly with each note almost as though they were the notes themselves. He was consumed with the music, fused with the rhythm as he played. Harmony danced in his eyes and he seemed to leave the stage and float on the melody alone. High on the song he danced across the stage in musical delight.

She almost enjoyed the show, as much as he seemed to enjoy putting it on for her. But she stood and walked to the door, her knees wobbling with every step. T-Bone followed behind. Outside Sam was waiting. He held some kind of remote in his hand. It was smaller than a TV remote control and it had several little buttons on it. He handed it to her.

"Hope this works," he said, forcing a smile.

"Me, too." She took the controller and thought for a moment—almost stopping herself, afraid—then she pushed the red button.

The overhead speakers, which Sam had installed earlier, crackled and burst to life. They rang loudly and she recognized the tune immediately. It was another track from *The Master Takes*, one of the real Charlie Parker's songs. Of course, the Master played flawlessly. She cranked it up as loud as it could go. The windowpanes in the building shook. Beside her, Sam covered his ears. He grabbed her arm. She couldn't hear him, but she read his lips: "It's too loud."

She pulled away from him and T-Bone shook his head. "No it's not."

Above them, the speakers rattled on their hinges and the paper covering them flapped wildly and then flew off. One of the posters floated to the ground and landed at their feet. She reached to pick it up.

In the distance, she saw movement in the trees above several of the buildings. She smiled. They were coming. Darkness surrounded them, but in the sky, large black clouds overtook the moon. Her ears began to ache from the noise, but she was already beginning to rejoice. A mistake. Nothing comes this easy.

Sam nudged her arm and pointed to the parking lot. There was a large blue-and-white pulling into the lot. Her heart fell into her knees. She watched two officers get out. She glanced up and the birds were nowhere in sight.

Sam nodded to her and walked back into the club. She knew what he was doing; he was evading the cops for as long as possible. Good man.

The police walked up to her, since she was the only person standing there as far as they could see. Trinity still couldn't hear what they said, but this time she pretended not to be able to read their mouths. She shook her head and shrugged her shoulders, as if to suggest that she had no idea what they were there for.

One of the police officers leaned in close to her and she smelled the coffee on his breath. "Is this your club?" he screamed. She still hadn't quite heard him but guessed that excuse would only fly once.

She shook her head. "No!"

"Where is he?"

"Don't know!" She screamed as loud as she could, but the sound was carried away by the music. She guessed he'd heard her or he'd read her lips well enough to know what she'd said. He looked up at the building.

His partner handed her a handwritten note. It read: "Get the owner of this club out here, or we'll have someone cut those wires."

"Shit. Shit. Shit." They could not see T's lips, which was probably a good thing. She and T had not planned for this.

Trinity nodded to the police, checked the sky one more time and slow-walked back into the club. T-Bone did not follow her. He stayed back to keep an eye on the cops.

Inside the noise was only slightly louder than it had been before—unnoticeable. She walked over to Sam and nodded her head toward the door, trying not to look obvious. Sam walked outside. Trinity didn't follow.

She took her seat and waited, prayed.

Nothing happened.

She wondered what Sam was saying to the officers or if they could even hear him. This had not been part of her plan. They hadn't even thought about it. How could she have missed this obvious flaw?

She kept her eye on the door for any sign of Sam. After only a few minutes, he walked into the club and whispered something to Frankie, his bouncer, and they both headed back out the door.

They were going to shut it off.

She had no words. None. Not one. Her mind wouldn't allow her to think anything, nothing good, nothing bad. She had nothing.

She thought about going back outside to see what was happening, but if she did that, Ak Bagay Ki Mal would know something was wrong and might stop playing altogether, which would have defeated everything. If she stayed, then Sam might not be able to stall the cops and the music wouldn't play to bring the crows. What to do?

She didn't go. Didn't feel in control of her own destiny anymore at that point, so she put it in the hands of whatever force was watching over her.

The Master looked at her, and she thought she saw him smile through a mouthful of sax. His notes hung heavy in the air, and as on the previous Wednesday night, the patrons were captivated. So was she, but for different reasons.

That's when she heard them. The flock of crows descended on the building in massive numbers. She could hear the roar of the wings even louder than that of the music and its player. A fluttering of wings enveloped the club.

She looked to the ceiling. As she did, she saw Sam and T-Bone run back inside with Frankie and the two officers. They were ducking and covering their heads. T-Bone looked at her and winked. She nodded.

Suddenly the music from the stage stopped.

She jumped to her feet and looked to the stage. The Master was staring at the ceiling, too. Everyone in the building had begun to do so. Save for only Sam, T and her; they all stared at the Master.

Slowly he lowered his eyes to them, then turned to her.

Indicative of its name, Ak Bagay Ki Mal, evil glared into her eyes. He knew what they had done. His face contorted into a snarl that was far more inhuman than she could have imagined. He dropped his sax, threw back his head and roared.

Everyone in the club lost interest in the birds and turned to watch him.

Outside, the sound of a tornado blew against the building, which creaked and sighed with the pressure. Loud squawks of angry birds filled the room. But not a sound came from any of the customers inside. Even the officers were silent.

The Parker thing growled again and dropped down on all fours. Foam ran from his lips, as though that of a wild dog. She thought for the first time she was seeing his true form. Suddenly he sprang across the room like a large, agile beast, leaping from tabletop to tabletop. People jumped out of his way and stumbled to the floor.

He was coming for her. She looked around for somewhere to go, but the Master was fast, and he leaped up on the table in front of her before she could run. He howled, like a wolf to the moon, and stared at her.

Beside her, someone screamed, "Oh shit."

Then both officers pulled their guns.

The evil-thing looked at them and smiled. He crouched on all four legs, the back ones bent only slightly, and lunged at them. They got one shot off before he reached them a full twenty feet away. He grabbed one of the cops' guns and held it in his hand as he squeezed. The man screamed in pain. Almost at the same moment, he slapped the gun out of the other's hand, and it clanked as it slid across the floor.

Everyone began screaming, fighting to get away. Above, the vicious birds still swirled.

The monster used the officer's own hand and spun him around, grabbed the back of his neck and twisted it. Trinity heard his neck snap as his body fell to the floor. The Master had taken the gun from the man before he fell, and he used it now to put two bullets into the chest of the other officer. Sam was next.

The cries in the room had almost surpassed those from the screaming crows outside, and Trinity got an idea. She ran for the stage and got there just as the Master wrapped his massive hand around Sam's neck and lifted him off the floor.

She picked up the sax, put the piece in her mouth, and began playing. "Yardbird Suite." She had never really been very good, but that night, like the previous day, she played expertly. She still had the spirit of that thing in her. Notes came into her mouth that she had never been able to play before or since. She tipped her head and pulled the song from her lungs into that sax.

Outside the fury was solid, wild. The building began to shake with force. Still she blew. In that moment the windows burst inward, a strange bright light exploding into the room, shadowing the thousands and thousands of black birds.

She kept playing.

In the back of the club, T-Bone expelled a dark blue light from his fingers. It pulsed and breathed. In a swift action, he threw the light toward the Master. The light seized him, and his body began to jerk, uncontrollably, causing him to drop Sam to the floor. The man scrambled away, holding his neck.

From the corner of her eye, the first of them appeared through the window. First only a few entered, but then a murder of crows flooded the room. Black silken wings fluttered in the blue neon lights. They moved, as if with one brain, toward the thing that was once Charlie Parker. In a swirling line of black fury, they raced for him.

Just as he bounded to attack her, they caught him midair. There were thousands upon thousands of them. They carried his body as though it were weightless.

The birds pecked at his flesh while still carrying his body across the club. Hundreds of holes began to emerge as bright lights seeped from his exposed wounds. The Master screamed in pain. Round punctures opened in the Master's body, and he exploded with light. As each bird pecked his body, he jerked in spasms of flightless despair. His arms and legs hung limply in the air. He struggled, but there was no point. The birds tore away chunks, exposing more and more light, the body fading right before their eyes. As the birds fed, loud raspy calls filled the night. The Master was suspended in the air, his body almost completely subsumed by light. Eventually he was consumed into nothingness, the final piece of light exploding, blinding the room in brilliant white. When Trini's eyes cleared, the crows had disappeared with the Master.

T-Bone was gone too.

A few weeks later and the official word was that there was a cop killer on the loose. No one had seen him before. He was white with blue eyes. It was safer that way.

Behind her, T-Bone touched Trinity's shoulders. She hadn't seen him since that night. Not once. He was leaving her, she knew it. She didn't think she could make it without him. He'd been there her whole life. How would she survive without him? She closed her eyes, just feeling his presence there with her for the moment.

"How are you?" he asked.

"Okay, I think. You know, it is what it is, T."

He nodded. "Well, I knew you could let it go. I just had this feeling." She didn't say anything. She didn't have to; she knew what was coming. "I have to go, Stormy."

"Go?"

"You know I can't stay."

She cried, "I need you. I can't . . ." He stared at her. But the truth was, she knew he was right.

He smiled, and it was as bright as the light he had conjured. "Goodbye, my Trinity River."

"Goodbye, my T-Bone Walker."

She wrote this down, like she had everything else.

It was her new passion.

Grann had worked too hard. And Trinity River realized that the old woman never kept secrets, as she had always thought, but that Trinity had been afraid to learn the mysteries that sustained her community. She had fought it until now, but it was her turn to keep those confidences of the people that others had forgotten.

THE FAMILIAR'S ASSISTANT
BY ALMA KATSU

I'm standing on the doorstep to the vampire's house.

It's been a couple minutes since my last knock. I've been standing here for twenty minutes, total, been outside this door every night for a week, waiting for hours at a time. It's taken me days to work up the courage to get this far. For weeks, I stood on the other side of the gate, staring at the seemingly lifeless house. Praying for courage. Knowing I had nothing to lose.

There's movement on the other side of the door. It's the vampire's familiar. I can feel her anxiety through the wood. "Go away," she says in a voice taut with anger. "You don't want to be here. It's dangerous."

This is the third time she's spoken. Each time, she'd said the same thing.

Tonight, it's raining. The canopy over the door is tiny and provides no protection. My hair is plastered to my head, my clothes soaked through to the skin. Nonetheless, I continue to stand, unflinching, in the downpour, as pitiful as a puppy in a shelter.

The old town house is somber and foreboding. It's one in a row, all abandoned, each more decrepit than the one before. Once grand, they're the domain of city rats and the homeless now. You'd notice if you watched, however, that someone lives in this one. Lights come on at night from deep within. This woman, the familiar, slips in and out as unobtrusively as a mouse.

My ploy works. The door opens. The familiar is about thirty, maybe younger. She doesn't weigh a hundred pounds soaking wet, so not much of a gatekeeper: I could knock her over and rush inside if I wanted to. What's more shocking, now that I can see her up close, is her appearance. Her clothes are ratty, her hair unkempt.

She appraises me with wary eyes. Once she's determined that I'm not a threat, she asks, "Do you have any idea what you're doing?"

I try to appear humble, sincere. She has to believe me. "I do. I want this."

"That's all I need to hear." She turns, obviously expecting me to follow. "It's your funeral."

She leads me through the house to a little room at the back. It's furnished with two mismatched chairs and a small table, all obviously salvaged on trash day. Heavy drapes are furred with dust. A weak bulb burns overhead. She gives me a rag to dry myself with. "Don't leave this room."

Once she departs, I listen for noises elsewhere in the house. Sunset was a half-hour ago. Is he up? Where is he? My skull buzzes with anticipation. I imagine I can feel his presence lurking in the background, omnipresent. But I only hear one person's movements in the house. Tiptoeing up and down stairs, opening and closing doors. Timid, mousy movements. Hers.

I take off my drenched coat and drape it over the stone-cold radiator, then pull my messenger bag over my head and let it drop to the floor, where it quickly forms a puddle. Next, I tousle my hair and mop my face. As I start to feel more human, the magnitude of what I'm doing hits me like a wave. *I'm going to meet a vampire. The* vampire.

The thought is so overwhelming that I have to distract myself. I turn my thoughts to this ramshackle old house instead . . . How did he get here, why did he choose to live here? From what I can see, the house has been abandoned for some time. It's old and out of fashion. The wallpaper is streaked with water stains, the plaster crumbling. Light fixtures flicker on and off. It's a miracle there's power; I can't imagine someone is paying the electric bill. It's more like an animal's den than a place where humans would choose to live. Is this state of disrepair the familiar's fault? I imagine it would be her job to take care of things, and I immediately like her even less.

After about an hour, the familiar returns. She stands with her arms crossed, saying nothing, giving me a long look of pity and scorn. Assessing me. It's an opportunity for me to get a better look at her, too, and I can see she's not healthy. Her hair is brittle, her skin sallow, her nails chipped and torn.

I see, too, that while she may be small, she's wiry. She's tougher than she looks. I imagine you'd have to be, to be a vampire's familiar. There's got to be a lot of abuse—and yet she stays. She's spotted with hideous bruises on her neck, her wrists, wherever she's not covered by clothing. Purple and that sickly shade of chartreuse. Hidden somewhere within those bruises are little wounds. I wouldn't put up with such abuse—not unless I felt I deserved it, like I do now. But I've walked away from abusers before, so I know I can do it again if I need to.

She fixes me with a glare. "Before we go any further, I want some answers. How did you find out about him?"

She has to cover their tracks, I get it, but I don't think I can tell her the truth. It happened when people I knew began disappearing. Disappearing more than usual, to be honest—we're a pretty transient bunch—and under mysterious circumstances. Then someone started this rumor that a vampire was to blame. I didn't believe it, of course. I figured it was just user talk. Addicts disappear all the time for a variety of reasons—we overdose, yes, but we're also arrested, or kidnapped by family members who want to stage an intervention, or we slink out of town because we owe money. We are notorious for making our own problems, so why invent a story about a monster? That's what we do, don't we? We rationalize our addiction. We're always the victim.

But the whispers got more specific. Then, I finally met a guy who claimed to have seen this vampire and there was something about the way he described the encounter that made me believe him. The vampire was impossible to describe, he'd said. Your memory of him faded as soon as you were no longer in his presence. The feeling, though—that had been tattooed into his memory. He thrummed with a million volts of electricity, recalling it.

The experience had been transformative and now all he wanted was to be with the vampire again. Only, he didn't know how: he'd wandered into an alley when the vampire had appeared to him like a vision, then disappeared. And now, this chance encounter had wrecked him. All he had to reassure him that it actually had happened were two neat wounds on the inside crook of his elbow.

This guy said he tried to find the vampire for six months with no luck, but that didn't stop me because, frankly, I knew I'm smarter than him. I made a pest of myself in all the usual haunts, asking if anyone knew of him. There were dozens of false starts (addicts being notorious liars): following people who claimed to know where the vampire was hiding, the delusional who claimed to be the familiar themselves. Finally, however, someone pointed out the vampire's familiar to me. She was good at disappearing in plain sight, though. I had to follow her for three weeks before she led me to this townhouse. And all that time, during the weeks of tailing her, I worked on a way to get inside the door. To meet him.

And now I'm here. It's all going to plan. I can scarcely believe it.

I can hardly admit this to her, though.

I claim to have met someone who told me about the townhouse. Pure dumb luck.

"Have you *seen* him?" I shake my head vigorously. "Then how did you know he was here?"

"I didn't. I just had a feeling."

She rolls her eyes; it's hard to tell if she believes me. "Why are you here? What are you looking to accomplish?"

"I want to meet him."

"No shit. But what do you think will happen if you do?"

This is the important part. The $100,000 question. I've got to sell it. She's got to believe that I'm sincere. "I don't care. He can do whatever he wants to me." I toss my head, maybe a little too dramatically. "I'm ready to die. I want my life to be over."

She snickers, though she seems relieved. "Death by vampire. Don't think you'd be the first. One last question: it's not painless. Are you prepared for that? It's going to hurt—a lot." She watches but I stay stoic. I won't give her any excuse to deny me.

"I've already felt pain. I live in pain."

"Stop right there. Not another word. I don't care what happened to bring you to this point, what put this stupid idea into your head"—she looks right, then left, like she thinks someone might be listening—"but there's still time to leave."

She wants to sound tough but there is a hint of sadness in her voice. Did someone say the same thing to her once? Where is that person now? Does she wish she had listened?

"I've been standing outside your door for a week—and I've wanted to do this for a lot longer. I'm not going to change my mind now."

She chews this over for a minute. "What's your name?"

I consider giving her a fake one, but what the hell. "Eric."

"You're not bringing trouble to our doorstep, are you, Eric? You seem like trouble. Is somebody going to come looking for you? The police?"

Must I respond? In this day and age, it's a rare bird who doesn't have something to hide, who hasn't had a scrape with the law or made a bad decision or two. We're all entitled to our secrets, that's how I see things. It's not like I'm hiding anything terrible, just a few lapses of judgment. One recent lapse in particular.

For the most part, though, those days are behind me.

When I don't answer and try to look repentant, she tries another tack. "What about your family? They're not going to show up to drag you home?"

"No. I burned those bridges a long time ago." Burned them to ash, if you must know. "The reason I'm here is . . . I'm not a good person. I've done a lot of bad things. Whatever happens to me tonight, you needn't feel responsible. I deserve to die."

If I expected that to melt her stony heart, I am to be disappointed. Her laugh is mean and sharp, like a punch to the face. "Everybody who comes here has a story like yours. Everyone feels sorry for themselves." She's happy enough to help me die.

She pauses, hand on the doorknob. "Just so we're clear, I don't give a shit what you've done and why you're here. I'm here to protect *him,* you got it?"

Where have I heard that before? Never mind. As I listen to her footsteps recede on the other side of the door, I break out in a sweat, my heart accelerating like a jet. *I've passed. She believes me. This is really going to happen. I'm going to meet him.*

Another hour passes before the familiar returns. By now, I reckon, it's deep into the evening and the sky outside must be like indigo velvet, closed around us like a tent. "If you still want to do this, you can follow me." We go up two flights via a narrow, claustrophobic staircase at the back of the house. The servants' stairs, once upon a time, but today they threaten to collapse with each step. I can't really be afraid to die on the steps, can I, considering that I am on my way to my probable demise? This buzzy, fizzy feeling is familiar, however. It's what you feel as you approach the first big drop on a roller coaster or pay your ticket to see a horror film. I want to be afraid. I want to be thrilled.

We pass through a door into a huge space—most likely the attic. It's cavernous and dark, with the only light coming from two candles at the back of the room. As she continues toward those candles, she seems to shrink with each step, collapsing into something smaller.

At the other end of the room, there is a presence. He's hidden in darkness but I can feel him. This feeling is heavy and pulls me forward like a gravitational force. I couldn't run away even if I wanted to.

"Here he is, master," she says or rather, it's what I imagine she says because I can barely hear her. She signals me to stop and goes the rest of the way alone, nothing more than a vague white figure flickering in the gloom. I know that I am not to move. No matter what happens, I must not speak or react in any way.

She takes off her clothes, her body glowing in the darkness. Even from a distance, however, I can isolate clusters of bruises all over her body: buttocks, calves, groin, breasts.

An indistinct figure moves toward her. My heart seizes and I hold my breath. I'm trying to get a good look at him but it's impossible, not just because it's dark but because—just like the other guy told me—he is impossible to take in whole. My vision jumps around, like the ground is shaking. The best I can do is to snatch glimpses of him. How I really know he is there is by *feeling* him. There is terror, yes, but also something more, something thrilling and exciting. His presence triggers something strange and animalistic in me. I want to throw myself at him, and I struggle to remain where I'm standing.

He steps behind her, towering over her like a tree. Eyes closed, she offers him her neck. He blocks my view as he bends his head low, but I know he's bitten her by the sound she makes, more a surrender to pain than pleasure. Then there's a sucking noise, so raw and feral that it turns my stomach.

This goes on for fifteen minutes, maybe more. The entire time, his eyes are fastened on me as surely as the mouth on her throat. The only way to keep from screaming or throwing myself at him is to cast my gaze to the floor, so the two of them are barely in my peripheral vision. When he stops feeding on her, I'm disappointed that it's over—and excited for what comes next.

I wait for it to be my turn, but no. Instead, he positions her on all fours and mounts her. I've had strangers fuck in front of me before (sadly, it's been a recurring theme in my life) but there's something unsettling about this time. Maybe it's her complete joylessness or the sad noises she makes, but there is obviously nothing pleasurable about it. The two of them grind on and on and I'm afraid I'm going to bolt from the room, unable to take any more, when he finally releases her.

She slumps to the floor but she's not unconscious. After a minute she stirs and starts to dress. Meanwhile, the vampire has drifted back to the darkness. I can no longer see him nor feel his presence.

That's it? I've merely been brought in to witness this—admittedly—thrilling act? I did not expect to be a bystander. My blood starts to roil but I manage to contain my fury until she's leading me down the stairs. "What was that? What just happened?"

Over her shoulder, she shoots me a look of disgust. "Did you think he would take you the first time, just like that? It doesn't work like that. He always does the choosing. You have to be patient. If you can't be patient, don't bother coming back."

If she thought I'd be so insulted that I'd storm out and vow never to darken the doorway with my presence again, she's wrong. Or that their sadomasochistic performance would frighten me away. There's no question that I'm going to come back. His absence has already left me a wreck. As I am pushed out the front door, in the rain, I'm sweating and trembling.

I used to chase a supreme but elusive high, until I did something terrible and lost it. That's when I tumbled, thinking I'd lost it forever.

Is that why I've come here? To try to find it again?

I won't experience the vampire's teeth until my third visit.

The second visit goes exactly like the first, except that sex goes on for much longer. She cries, she whimpers, and once or twice she even begs. She passes out and I carry her to one of the bedrooms, leaving her to wake up on her own, figuring she wouldn't want to be reminded that I am witnessing her humiliation. It's while I'm lugging her downstairs that I realize she reminds me a little of my mother. Something about the eyes, or the way she carries herself.

It's been a long time since I've seen her, my mother, but once I see the resemblance, I can't unsee it.

The third time, however, she escorts me to the attic but stops at the door. Gesturing that I should continue alone, she gives me a look of warning—*are you sure you want this?* Hell yes; I'm so excited that it feels like I'm about to orgasm. Whereas earlier I'd been afraid he was going to kill me, now I know that's not going to happen, so there is no dread—well, maybe not *zero* dread. There's always the possibility. I know that about monsters.

None of that matters. My petty desires, my fears . . . None of that matters anymore. In a few minutes, I'll only exist to please him. I'm going to freely give myself completely to someone else. I'd given myself to someone before, but it wasn't freely. I was taken. I had no say in the matter, I was young. I didn't understand.

I understand now.

He pulls me toward him through sheer will, his command—not words exactly—booming in my skull. I'm to take off my clothes. I fumble with the zippers and buttons like I've suddenly forgotten how to dress but finally it all falls to the floor in a puddle. He's closer to me than ever before, standing directly behind. His pull is so strong that it feels like I'm going to be crushed. I can barely think and could slip into unconsciousness at any second.

His hand falls on my shoulder. It reminds me of when I was eight or nine and my father ordered me to hold my palm over an open flame to see how long I could last. My older sister hadn't lasted a minute, earning our father's ridicule. I tried to hold out, tears blooming in my eyes as the heat became unbearable. But this is different. The burning is instantaneous and fierce. It rages all over like I've been set on fire.

I don't think about this for long, however, because he immediately sinks his teeth into my neck. He tears muscle and suddenly everything is red-hot pain, like I've been opened up and lava poured inside. I can't feel where my body ends anymore. I am afloat in an ocean of hurt. I think I'm going to pass out but somehow remain standing. My knees start to buckle as he sucks hard at my throat. I can feel blood sluice through my veins. *This is what it feels like to be consumed.* It's glorious and horrible at the same time. And vaguely familiar.

I struggle for consciousness, willing the rush of pain and panic to pass, but only grow weaker and weaker by the second. Suddenly, it occurs to me that this might end differently from the previous two times. He might very well intend to kill me.

And why not? That's why I came here, wasn't it? That's what he thinks I want.

He shows no sign of letting up. His mouth is wetly noisy at my throat, the force of his feeding strong. With his every draw, I feel I'm being depleted. He holds me up, pressing me against his body, a promise of what I know will come next whether or not I'm awake to experience it.

And yet his touch is the most sublime experience in the world. I thought I'd never feel its like again.

If I die like this, it will have been worth it.

I am surprised to wake up.

I recognize the bed: it's the same one I carried the familiar to a few days earlier. To call this a bedroom would be a high compliment. I've seen tidier crack houses.

She sits on the edge of the bed watching me. Is that concern I see on her face or is she just worried about getting rid of the body? There is so much déjà vu in this moment. By the time I'm fully conscious, however, she's her usual scornful self. "I thought we were going to lose you."

I struggle to my elbows. "Did you pass out the first time?"

She smirks. "Do I look like that much of a wuss?"

Her name is Sarah. She has been with him for two years. Like me, her journey started with rumors. Also like me, she was sick of what her life had become. She tracked him down hoping he would end it for her, but instead she became his familiar.

"Do you hope he'll make you a vampire, too, so you can live forever?" I ask her, once.

"At which point in my story did you stop listening?" She doesn't want eternal life any more than I do. I don't need to ask her why she's stayed: once you've had it, all you want is to keep feeling his touch. You dread it, but you can't live without it, either.

By the end of the first week of nightly visits, Sarah tells me I'm to move into the town house. I'm to quit my job. I'm not to tell anyone where I'm going or what I'm doing, not even my family (like that was even a possibility). I'm given a room on the first floor, close to the anteroom where she made me wait the first day, as far from the master's chamber as possible. I'm to earn my way up. Like my older sister, Sarah is the favorite. The master's familiar. I'm only here to assist her.

I'm carrying my possessions to the Uber when I feel eyes on me, but it's a busy city street and there's no telling who's doing the watching. There are a lot of people who would be interested in knowing where I'm going and very few are what you might call friends. I brush the concern away. Trouble always follows me, the way mysterious fires follow an arsonist. I've learned not to obsess over it.

She begins to tell me about herself in odd moments during the day. She was a lonely child in a large family who acted out for attention. She stole trinkets at the corner shop, pilfered her mother's purse for cigarettes. She graduated to setting things on fire. She was convinced she was unlovable and the notion stuck. We misfits, we're not so different.

By the time she was in her mid-twenties, she had zero friends and her family refused to have anything to do with her. Every time she made a new acquaintance or started a new job, she'd fall into old patterns: stealing from them, lying to them, disappointing them until they left.

I listen—I have no choice, trapped together as we are—but I don't want to hear this. I want her to remain a mystery. Now she's too human. Too much like me. I fight the urge to tell her about myself. It's only natural: everyone wants to be seen, for others to understand how we became the person we are. But I know that in my case, telling Sarah anything would be a mistake. There is no chance for understanding, only revulsion. I destroyed my family, didn't it? Had my father sent to jail even if he was, undeniably, a monster. Left my mother with nothing, with nobody to hide behind. Even my sister hates me for what I did because now everyone knows what she did. What we did.

So, Sarah, reminding me so much of my ungrateful mother—it's no surprise that I start to lose respect for her, that I protest, inwardly, when she gives me orders. I start to question whether she deserves to be the familiar. She is certainly no more deserving than me.

I ask Sarah about the master. I want to know everything about him I possibly can. I'm curious, it's only natural. What's his name? How old is he? Where has he lived, before? And how did he become a vampire? Is he the only one?

She gives me a sour frown. "It's not my place to tell you these things. If he wants you to know, he'll tell you himself" is her answer. After a few days of suspicious and frightened glances when she thinks I'm not looking, I come to the conclusion that she doesn't tell me because she doesn't know. Just like Mom.

This dearth of information only fans my curiosity. I try to imagine what he was like as a human. What could his life have possibly been like before, what unfortunate incident put him on this path? It's hard to picture him human, though, because he is so fundamentally different from us. But if he didn't start out as human, where did he come from? The man he was before this transformation, was he filled with self-loathing, the way I am? Did self-loathing drive a wedge between him and the rest of humanity, turning him into something apart?

The more time I spend with Sarah, the more I see how careless she is. I'd thought at first that she was eagle-eyed, but on closer inspection, I see nothing could be further from the truth. She is slatternly. She is his primary feeding vessel and yet she doesn't take care of herself. She lets her wounds fester and doesn't bathe as frequently as she should. I wouldn't be surprised if she has indiscriminate sex on the outside, or started using drugs again. The house is a sty but when I make the effort to tidy up, it meets with open scorn.

One of our most important jobs as familiars is to find food for the master. This entails enticing strangers to follow us to a desolate area for the master to join us. I quickly see that Sarah is not discerning in her choices. Her victims are obviously unwell or disease-ridden, often weak and half-dead. Surely the master doesn't want to be served dregs, I wonder aloud. "We take what we can get," she snaps when I bring it up. I understand, then, that she wasn't doing me a favor the night she let me come in out of the rain. I was merely an easy meal. She thought he'd drain me dry and that would be the end of me. She didn't expect me to stay on and on.

I don't owe her anything.

She continues to talk about herself. Why not, she has a captive audience. Now, whenever we are together, it's non-stop: memories from childhood, years of regrets, how much she misses her family. She wants to see them—surely all is forgiven by now? She worries they assume she's dead. It's cruel to let them labor under that misconception, don't you think? There is a new gleam in her eye, almost wholesome, as she prattles on all day, every day.

All this prattle annoys me, of course. Her talk of families reminds me of mine, something I've worked so hard to leave behind.

How can she want to go back to all that? I'm afraid she's lost her mind. It's a cry for help.

Sarah and I are sifting through the debris field that is the dining room, looking for a pair of her earrings that she has allegedly lost, when she tells me a man came to the house looking for me.

"He said you owe his employer money." Her demeanor has changed entirely: one minute she's friendly Sarah who needs my help, and the next she is the familiar. My superior.

I try to blow it off. "Don't worry. It's nothing."

"It doesn't sound like nothing. I asked you about this kind of thing, didn't I? I told you we didn't need you bringing problems to our doorstep." Her voice is shrill, using the tone that makes men's testicles shrivel, as my father used to say. A tone you'd do anything to get away from.

To stop.

But it won't get to that. I have it under control. "I said don't worry. I'll handle it," I say through gritted teeth.

* * *

A few days later, I'm returning from the corner market with cigarettes when I see a car idling in front of the town house.

I walk to the driver's side and squint at the glass. It's probably the same guy who spoke to Sarah. I recognize him: he works for Vincent Smalls, an acquaintance of mine for many years, and by acquaintance, I mean someone I've bought drugs from. He is slightly smaller than your average refrigerator and looks like he's gone face-first through plate glass. I think his name is Dan.

It's an overcast day, so dark that it might lead you to think it's later than it actually is. I glance reflexively toward the attic. It's not nightfall, so there's no chance that Dan will serve as tonight's main course. Not that the prospect bothers me; he undoubtedly has blood on his hands and fully deserves a violent end, no matter how that might happen.

I motion for him to lower the window. "Whatcha doing here?" I ask, feigning ignorance.

He looks me up and down with the undisguised amusement he reserves for men he finds totally unthreatening. "Vincent got worried when you disappeared, considering how much you owe him."

Only a fool would advance a lot of drugs to a junkie and expect to be repaid. "You shouldn't show up here unannounced. In the future, call first. It's for your own safety." He's been warned.

Dan answers my obviously genuine concern with a big patronizing smirk. "Refusing to take care of your obligations to Vincent . . . that's suicide, Eric. Is that what you want? Are you looking to die?"

If I'm honest—yes. Sometimes.

But not today.

I shrug. "I'll have it tonight."

He frowns. "If you have the money, just give it to me now."

"I don't have it at the moment, but I can get it." I give him a location and tell him to meet me there around midnight. "I'll have it then, I promise. And we can put this sordid mess behind us."

"You talk funny, Eric." He starts the car, still wearing his patronizing smile. "It don't bother me but you should know, some people say you're not right in the head."

I know this, of course. It's been said about me my whole life, but by people who had no idea what I'd been through. If he thinks this hurts me or will make me weaker, he's in for a surprise. I've used this pain to make me stronger.

I smile at him as I turn to leave. "See you at midnight."

Dan is to meet me at an abandoned industrial park outside of town. You can't take an Uber to this kind of rendezvous, so I borrowed the keys to Sarah's old sedan. I hope to be back before she realizes the car is missing, but frankly it's a gamble I have to take.

I lean against the hood, chain smoking, while waiting for Dan to show up. We've used this location about six or seven times for our little operations, Sarah and me, and it's worked like a charm. It's dead deserted. No one comes out here. There's no road traffic and it doesn't overlook a highway. Oh, it might play host to drug deals or other nefarious activity (and I can feel their presence on the periphery like rats, those junkies and prostitutes, curious about Sarah and me but keeping their distance) but they're not the kind to go to the police.

It's half past midnight when a shiny muscle car comes around the corner of a building. I recognize Dan's bald head but don't recognize the guy at the steering wheel. Of course; Dan wouldn't come alone, even if it's just little ole harmless me. Sweat blooms under my arms; we've never brought two victims for the master at the same time. Will he do it? Can he overpower two men? My mind races, picturing the many ways things could go awry, and it goes badly for me in every one of them, shot by whichever one the master doesn't overpower immediately.

The car brakes about eighty feet away and, after a minute, Dan emerges. He seems to sprout taller, taller, taller, like some kind of origami monster folded up to fit inside that car.

He takes his time walking toward me. "Let's get this over with," he says brusquely.

The other man, however, doesn't get out. He remains stolidly behind the steering wheel. This is not good. It will be too easy for him to escape.

I dawdle with my cigarette to buy time. Dan is now twenty feet away from me. I say, "How about asking your friend to come out where I can see him? He's making me nervous."

Dan jerks his head in surprise. "Nobody cares if you're nervous. Stop playing around—I got places to be—"

Then a plan—a possibility—occurs to me. Dan is next to me now, intimately close. I drop my voice to a whisper. "Here's the thing . . ."

He groans. "I don't like the sound of this, Eric. Don't jerk me around. No excuses . . ."

"I have the money." I don't have the money. "The thing is I don't have *all* of it. Not quite. I'm shy a hundred. So . . . how about if I work off the difference in trade?" I give him a simpering look.

He tips his head back, like he's pleading with the heavens. "I'm not into boys, Eric."

The fact is, I couldn't care less what he's into. Boys, girls, or inanimate objects. I'll use anything at my disposal to get him out of sight of the man in the car.

"Is that what you think I'm offering? You should be so lucky. No, no, I'm talking about something else. Could make you some real money. But I don't want to discuss it in front of him"—I nod in the direction of the car, even though there's no way the second guy could hear us. I don't wait for an answer and start walking toward the empty warehouse, looking back at him with my best come-hither smile—and damn me if he isn't following. Though it might be out of frustration, chasing me for the money he thinks I have.

Please, please, master, be out there.

Once around the corner of the building, hidden from the man in the car, I halt and turn to face Dan. He's right behind me, over two hundred pounds of muscle coming right at me like a bull. His face is dangerously red. He's angry. He's not interested in my little offer at all, and if he finds out that I do not, in fact, have Vincent's money, he's probably going to beat me to death right here. "This better not be bullshit, Eric. I don't appreciate having my chain yanked, not by the likes of you . . ."

He is five strides away from me. I'm trapped. There's nowhere to run. I have finally overplayed my hand and am going to get what I've long deserved. I close my eyes and ready myself for one of Dan's meaty hands to grab the front of my shirt and . . .

But there's no meaty hand.

Instead, I feel the rush of something go by fast. The force buffets me, the way a truck knocks you around as it passes. The hairs on my arms stand up and the wind quickly drops and then I have the sense—of absence.

I open my eyes. Dan is gone, as completely as though he was never there.

My empty innards fill with happiness. Hallelujah. This is exactly what I'd hoped would happen: the master saved me. *He. Saved. Me.* Dan is strong, a brute and a bully, but the master is stronger. I have been at the mercy of bullies my whole life with no one to protect me. He is exactly what I needed, having been born to a monster, with no uncles to take an interest in me. I had to save myself and look where it got me. But now I have a protector. I never dreamed it was possible, but here he is.

After Dan, the man behind the steering wheel is no problem. When I come around the corner alone, he leaps out of the car like he's spring-loaded. He's pissed and confused and starts coming toward me, getting more worked up with each step. "Hey, where's—" is all he manages to say before he, too, is gone in a blur, whisked aside by nothing more than a ripple in the darkness. I don't know how the master is able to move so quickly, or if he bends matter to his will, but it's just like this when we bring outsiders for him to feed on. Breathtakingly fast, brutally efficient.

He is the perfect protector.

I have seen him feed and it is not pleasant. Not in the least. Tonight, I don't get to witness what he will do with them. He has taken them away. I will never have to see Dan again. Never fear Vincent again.

Never have to fear anyone.

I am grateful for a second chance. I was ungrateful the last time, an ungrateful child, but this time around, I will be the loyalest of servants. I will keep his secrets. I will be grateful, even when he inflicts pain.

After all, there can be no pleasure without pain, my father always said. No reward without punishment.

I get into Sarah's sedan and drive home.

I didn't think Sarah would find out about what I'd done. It was a private matter between the master and me. But the next day, she pounds furiously on the door to my room, forcing me awake. She doesn't wait for me to answer but throws the door back and barges in. "What the hell did you do last night?" she demands, standing at the foot of the bed.

I pull a tatty old blanket over my head but she rips it aside. "I don't know what you're talking about," I say.

"Bullshit. You can't hide anything from me. I know everything he does—everything. You had him take care of the guy who came looking for you." I say nothing, unable to think quickly of a way to clear myself. She fills the awkward silence with another roar. "Are you insane? That guy worked for some criminal, didn't he?"

I roll my eyes and fall back onto the mattress. "Don't be so dramatic. These guys come and go all the time . . . He won't be missed."

"You're delusional, you know that?" She has grabbed my shirt and shakes me. "You're bringing trouble right to our door—*big* trouble, things we can't explain. I warned you . . . We don't need this . . . What the fuck is *wrong* with you?"

There's nothing wrong with me. I'm perfect.

It happens quickly. I strangle her right there on the bed. I'm so much taller and stronger than her that it's over in no time. She stares at me with bulging eyes and I swear I see acceptance there, if not gratitude. She had to know it would end like this once she'd taken up with the master. You can't accept a monster in your life and think that you're safe. That you'll be able to control him.

I don't feel bad for killing her. At this point, eliminating her is completely logical. She's pathetic. She doesn't deserve to be the master's familiar; she doesn't even enjoy her position anymore. In the few months I've been in this household, she has changed, probably becoming more like the person she was before the master chose her. He wouldn't want that.

Just to be on the safe side—and because I'm feeling a bit squeamish—I put a plastic bag over her head and tape it tight. I wait outside the door, one eye on the darkening sky, and at the end of an hour, I go back inside to make sure the deed is done. I nudge her foot, lift an arm and let it drop to the mattress. There is no reaction.

I take the plastic bag off her head. Her eyes are riddled with burst blood vessels. A thin rivulet of red trickles from her nose. Does the smell of blood wake him, I wonder? She said she knows everything that the master does, like there's some connection between them. Up in the rafters, he lies in wait for the night to welcome him. What I did to Sarah—was he jolted awake by her last, dying thoughts? Is he just waiting until it is safe to emerge before I get my reckoning?

The glistening red line running down her face hypnotizes me. It beckons me. What does blood taste like, I wonder. If I taste her blood, will it bring us closer, the master and me?

I dip a finger tentatively, only the very tip wet with red, and then press it to my tongue.

It tastes like family.

The sun set an hour ago. I stand outside the door to the attic the same as I did the first time, tremulous as a little girl. There are stirrings behind the door, so I know that the master has risen, but I haven't yet felt the familiar tug that lets me know to enter.

He must know that Sarah is dead. He must've felt her consciousness ebb away, even as he was trapped in the box that keeps him safe from day.

How strange it feels to kill another person. I was horrified by what I'd been driven to do, of course, because I am not a monster, but at the same time, there is no denying that it is thrilling. Is this how *he* feels when he kills, I wondered in the immediate aftermath, as I looked at my hands with new wonder. I couldn't help but hope it will bring us closer, make me more worthy of his favor. That it will make me more like him in some small way.

I feel his presence grow stronger, and there's an emotional note I've not felt before and is impossible to interpret. There's nothing to do but wait for his judgment. I'm prepared to accept whatever comes: I'll suffer his wrath, if he's displeased with what I've done, or accept his gratitude, for ridding him of the sulky harridan. I came here that first night to let him kill me, after all, so if he were to kill me now it would be no more than what I expected. The end I'd been expecting, come to me at last.

Or he can spare me and—dare I hope—elevate me to Sarah's position? He's going to need a familiar and it's a safe assumption that he intended for that to be me one day, or else why would he have invited me to live here in the first place? That's why I don't think he's going to kill me. Why I don't think this is my last hour on earth.

There is nothing I can do but wait for his judgment.

And so, I continue to stand outside his door.

Waiting.

SWIM IN THE BLOOD OF A CURIOUS DREAM
BY JOHN F.D. TAFF

In the end, it was for Gus.

Not for Hildy, not for myself.

I did it because to not do it would deprive Gus of the love and experiences of his mother.

I did it because what if the shoe had been on the other foot, and *I* was cut off from Gus?

I did it because Gus loves us both, no matter the circumstances, no matter the living arrangements.

Because, as I've learned, separation doesn't diminish the love a child has for their parent.

Nor does death.

I was exhausted, just wanting to arc into peace and quiet, a crumpled can tossed into the recycling bin; emptied, its purpose fulfilled.

Nothingness.

But my whole reason for life sat behind me, slumped within his harness, his jacket rumpled and snarled between his sleeping body and the belts that were there to hold him tight, protect him. A Captain America action figure drooped from one limp hand, as if caught in the motion of throwing his shield out into the void of night.

Highway lights rippled orange over the car as I drove farther and farther from St. Louis toward our new home deep in the agricultural flatness of southern Illinois. Far from where I'd grown up, where he'd grown up, at least until this point.

No one in the passenger seat.

No one had sat there for a long time, not since his mother, and she wasn't sitting anywhere anymore. The dust of her remains had been carried on a gentle wind off the banks of the Mississippi River months ago in a simple ceremony attended by Gus and me and Hildegard's parents. It was a quiet affair, for the obvious reasons, but also because I spoke broken German and Gus spoke exactly four words—*ja, nein* and *Guten tag!* His favorite—how could it not be?—was *nein.*

His grandparents spoke almost no English, being from a very rural burg in Germany. As little effort as I made to learn German, and it was definitely little, they did zilch to learn English.

While I had armed myself with enough German to make sexy pillow-time talk with Hildy, it wasn't enough to bridge the gap between me and her parents.

Hildy had been that, but it had been a bridge little used from the start. They resented me, an *Ami,* for stealing their daughter away to our chaotic, turbulent country, for turning *Hildegard* into *Hildy,* but mostly for keeping their only grandchild a world away.

I half suspected they thought America and I had given Hildy the cancer that killed her. Or I was at least a willing accomplice.

And me?

I can't say I resented them for anything in particular. Sure, they skipped our wedding, but because of their dour disapproval, I saw that as a positive. Once we were back in America, we saw them infrequently. I waved at them or said a few broken words in German during Hildy's frequent FaceTime sessions. But when Gus came along, well, they didn't even bother to feign wondering if I were still in the picture.

They always seemed angry and alien to me, as foreigners mostly seem to Americans these days. I never wondered why it was, just uncomfortable shouldering that burden with them, I suppose. Until Hildy, I'd never been *the American* in the equation.

Her parents and I parted months ago at the airport in St. Louis, in a terminal filled with soaring, arched ceilings and windows looking up into grey, swirling skies. There were awkward hugs for me, over jubilant kisses for Gus. He and his grandparents clung to each other as the last parts of Hildegard, not eager to separate that connection, make her absence a finality.

I doubted very much I'd ever see them again, and I believe they hoped the same. I doubted they'd ever fly back to America, and lord knew I wouldn't be booking any extended vacations to Germany. But I'd also never keep Gus from them, from that country, for he was the last part of Hildegard all of us had left. He had her eyes, her focused yet buoyant attitude, her honey-blond hair. They saw those parts, I'm sure, just as they overlooked whatever parts of me showed in him.

When they were shuffling down the concourse to their gate, two generic old travelers lost in a sea of others, Gus gazed up at me with huge, solemn eyes. His grandmother's too-red lipstick blotched his cheeks like a heat rash.

"Do you even *like* them?"

I stared down at him, nonplussed.

"Who?" I asked, honestly thinking he must mean the Teenage Mutant Ninja Turtles or Paw Patrol or Cap'n Crunch. He was pretty good at random, non-sequential questions.

"Oma and Opa."

That threw me for a loop. I wanted to say to him *Have you met them? Of course I don't like them.*

But, again, they were his grandparents. He loved them, so of course I couldn't say that.

Not knowing precisely what to say, though, I blinked, squeezed his tiny, sticky hand in mine. We headed home to what had become a structure that felt more concerned with what it had lost than what it still had, whose only remaining purpose was to keep the elements at bay.

Or was that just me?

* * *

Grief has a weight, even a specific gravity, doesn't it? Sorry, I'm a chemical engineer, so it's hard for me to tamp down that side of myself sometimes.

But . . . it *does,* doesn't it?

Even on the nothingness around it, grief exerts weight, like a black hole on the fabric of space, pulling everything in with it.

From nothingness into nothingness, right?

Sorry, I guess that's more physics.

But that's what happened. Our grief was a collapsed star, pulling our entire lives into it, crushing it down to its constituent atoms, reducing it to nothing.

What was I without her? I honestly couldn't say. When I looked back to my time before Hildy, all I could see was a young man who seldom cared about how he looked or what was in his refrigerator, if his socks were clean or even his apartment. The most responsible thing I did then was make semi-regular payments on my student loan.

Was I back to that guy now? Was that who I was without Hildy?

And Gus? What was Gus without her? I'm not sure he knew either, because before Hildy, he was truly nothing. She had literally been his entire reason for existing.

So, there we were, Gus and I, orbiting the remains of our family, staring into that singularity and seeing absolutely nothing reflected back at us.

Wrapped in ourselves, we missed the question that mattered most. What we should have been wondering was simple.

What was *she* now without us?

Without him?

The McDonald's I'd put into him at Mile Marker 125 made its presence known at around Mile Marker 214.

"I haveta pee. Really bad," he said, and his voice from the dark backseat made me jump and swerve the car a bit. It was sleep-croaky, but still so adult.

So much like . . .

"I'm hungry."

"You just ate, But, sure, okay. We can do that, too," I said, then thought better. "How bad is the pee?"

"PeeCon One," he said. It was our sliding code for the severity of toilet events, one that had been carefully honed through trial and error, so I knew he wasn't joking. I could hear the rustle of his coat as he fidgeted in his car seat.

"Okay, kiddo," I said, stabbing at the screen of my phone, mounted on the dashboard so I could see the GPS. "Let me find the closest place. Can you hang on?"

"Sure, Daddy."

I kept one eye on the road as I scrolled through Google screens to find something. But we were evidently right in the middle of a giant nothing, no turnoffs, no restaurants, no gas stations for at least thirty miles. And it was already after midnight, so it could be longer until we found something open.

I looked up just as a blue road sign flashed by.

REST STOP EXIT 217, 2 MILES

"How about a rest stop, huh? Stretch our legs, take a gentlemanly pee, maybe grab a few things from the vending machines?"

"Soon?" he asked, his voice ratcheting up at the end of what he'd turned into a three-syllable word.

"Just a quick two minutes until you can let 'er rip," I said, goosing the accelerator a bit.

The exit appeared, bathed in pools of melon-colored light. A single building wrapped in a parking lot on a little island of its own, whiter illumination. Even in my haste to park, I noticed there was no one else there. No car stuffed with teens crashing on their way to somewhere distant, no weary family of five spilling out to use the restrooms. Not even the truck parking lot, usually filled with idling over-the-roaders, was occupied.

But I had a kid who had to pee, and none of that mattered.

I grabbed our masks just to be safe. Place probably would get a few people, even at this hour.

"Where are we?" he asked as I wrestled with his clasps. "I gotta wear a mask?"

"Yep. We might be in the middle of nowhere, kiddo. But you had to pee, and Daddy delivered." I flipped Captain America back in after Gus lost his grip on him.

"But Cap . . . ?"

"Trust me, the Avengers aren't going to call while you're peeing."

We walked hand in hand to the shelter. It was a cool, Midwestern autumn night. A crisp wind, lots of skittering leaves, and the rasping of tree limbs like cricket skeletons. The air smelled of that spicy, leafy deadness, the damp of some recent rain, the faint mold of neglect. Missouri wasn't a state that paid particular attention to its rest stops, and it showed in this one.

The building was an ugly, squat cinder-block affair, painted some bureaucratic, dirty yellow green, screened with walls of open, concrete circles, lit by an autopsical tone of light. I pushed through the full-glass doors that led inside the structure. A bank of vending machines in the closed-in space between the women's and men's restrooms all lit and shiny and ready to go, evidently the only things really maintained here. A display of tourist brochures lined one wall, shiny advertisements for Onondaga Cave, Branson, and the Gateway Arch. Dog-eared, probably pulled out, glanced at, stuffed back. I briefly wondered who even read brochures anymore. A small ATM and a few trash cans kitted out the rest of the place.

I hustled his mask on, then frog-walked him to the men's room, thinking that he must be pretty near full deployment. The ambiance of that room was one or two whole steps down from the rest of the place. The cinder block here was plastered over in yellowed tile, the half-walled stalls covered in graffiti, painted, then covered in graffiti again. The entire place smelled of piss, old farts, and some caustic, antiseptic cleanser.

Gus, who demanded privacy for his *toilette* now, wriggled from his coat and pushed the door shut behind him.

"You can undo your pants?"

"Yeah . . ."

"Get them down all the way, your underwear, too."

"Daddy," he cautioned.

"Be sure to leave your mask on. Are you gonna sit or stand?"

This was greeted by a peal of little farts and the sound of a stream of urine striking porcelain.

"Everything okay?"

"Leave me alone," he groaned, muffled a bit by the mask. "I'm going."

I drifted to the wall of sinks, looked at myself. The scratched metal mirror, the horror-video lighting, showed the haggard, drained face of someone I barely recognized. I undid my mask to get a better look. The lights accentuated the hollows of my eyes; my unshaven whiskers accentuated the hollows of my cheeks.

Is this what he saw? Is this the face Gus looked up into these days? His one remaining parent.

As I heard a door behind me open and close, I bent to the sink and splashed cold water over my face.

When I looked into the mirror, I didn't see Gus.

Instead, a large, unmasked man in a down coat barged into the bathroom, made his way right to the sink two down from mine. He lurched to a stop, let loose a torrent of vomit that splashed against the battered porcelain, up onto the mirror, and onto the sink between us.

I stepped away. The bathroom stall door had swung open and I saw Gus framed in the act of zipping his pants up. His eyes were huge as he took in the barfing intruder.

Not knowing what was up in these pandemic days, I snatched Gus, pulled him all the way to the end of the row of sinks to wash his hands, somewhat proud he'd kept the mask on. I helped, but he couldn't focus on this simple task while there was a large man in the room retching and gasping for breath between continued splats of puke.

"Is he okay, Daddy?"

"I don't know. Let's wash your hands and get out of here. You hungry? Want a soda or something from the machines?"

I wanted to get him fed, get back to the car so we could get out of there. I didn't want to know what Mr. Puke's problem was. I didn't care. Who knew what kind of germs he was off-gassing into the bathroom air? The acrid smell of his vomit already filled the room.

"I want a fruit punch," he said, as I practically dragged him to the wall of hand dryers, where he rubbed his hands together under the air. I straightened his mask, then took his hands, and stuffed his arms back into the coat.

The guy was still hunkered over the sink panting as we hustled back into the lobby. Gus darted to the three enormous vending machines, displaying their goodies wedged into corkscrew dispensers behind plexiglass.

I glanced back at the closed restroom door to ensure Mr. Puke didn't make an unwanted reappearance. Then, I squinted through the glass doors to the parking lot.

It was snowing. *Hard.*

It's trite to talk about being angry at the person who's dying. Angry at the young man leaving his spouse, the mother leaving her family, the child skipping out on her parents.

How could they? How dare they?

As if the dying have any say in the matter. Still, it's pretty normal to feel that way. I went through it myself. So did Gus.

We seldom talk about how *they* feel. How the dying feel about dying, about being torn away from loved ones, from family and friends.

How they feel about leaving things they wanted to do, to complete.

How they feel about losing their homes, their possessions.

How they feel about not *being* anymore.

As if to comfort ourselves—because aren't all our American coping mechanisms about death really just to comfort ourselves?—we tell each other the dying feel melancholy, dismay, sadness. But we're just projecting, really, burying what they must be feeling, wrapping it in our own overwhelming grief.

How could we not? It's just too much to process. I guess it sanitizes it, makes it easier to digest if we're all sitting around—the dying and those left behind—feeling various degrees of *sad*.

Sad. *Sure*.

I can tell you that most of the time, they're not sad. Not really.

I can tell you, at the end, when we sat around Hildy's bed, clutching her hands, only ours were tears of grief.

Hers were *rage*.

In the five minutes or so we'd been inside the rest stop, a thick mat of snow already covered the grounds, the parking lot.

Where in the hell did this come from?

I didn't remember seeing anything on my phone about snow.

Fuck.

What would this do to our plans to get down to Carbondale tonight, be there for the movers bright and early? Shit, what would this mean for the movers arriving at all?

I imagined a few days sleeping on the floor of our new house, no pillows or blankets, no television. Just a bag of clothes, my phone and its charger, and Captain America to see us through. Gus might be convinced of the adventure of it all, but thinking about what it meant, I was not. Until the snow cleared, and we could wrap ourselves in the comforting blanket of the rest of our stuff, it would be annoying.

Gus had apparently decided which curated mixture of sugar and salt he'd have: the gigantic, iced honey bun and a bottle of Hawaiian Punch so red it made my eyes hurt.

"Can I get this, Daddy?" he asked, his eyes meme-wide and pleading. "And look! Fruit punch, just like I wanted."

My inner parent wanted to say no, but I also wanted to get out of there with a minimum of effort. And that included not arguing with a tired, strung-out five-year-old who needed a fix.

So . . .

Sugar and sugar. Mwah! Fantastic choice, monsieur! And here past midnight no less. Magnifique!

Well, it would be nice to have someone awake in the car for what was looking to be a long, stressful drive.

Hildy might have filled that role, though probably not. She'd have curled up with a pillow in the passenger seat, asleep with her head pressed against the window, the vibrations of the car tickling into her sleeping skull.

But no.

Her sleeping skull was truly, deeply asleep now.

All we are is dust in the wind, one of those seventies bands sang.

"Sure, let's get moving, kiddo. Looks like snow outside."

The word *snow* is a talisman to a child, one of the most powerful of words. My uttering it momentarily derailed his junky fascination with the sugar on display before him. He turned to the windows, his eyes practically rolling cartoonlike back in his head.

"Snow." He endowed the word with several long, drawn-out syllables. "Can we play in it before we leave?"

"We need to get on the road before it's too bad. Don't want to miss getting to our new house on time, right?"

He regarded me suspiciously, as if the trade of getting to our new place for playing in the snow was a sucker's deal.

"I guess." His tone said he didn't really agree.

"Okay, just pick your stuff and let's get out of here," I said, pressing a few dollar bills in his hands, knowing that the next fight would be not letting him make the transaction, just doing it myself to speed things up.

As I urged him on, I felt more than saw the door behind me swing open and Mr. Puke stepped out.

"Whew!" he shouted to no one in particular. "I feel a million bucks better after that, I can tell you!"

I spared him a look back—he was mask-free, of course—then steadied Gus's hand on the limp dollar bill he was trying to force into the machine. It whirred, spit it out, whirred again. I gave Gus another dollar as Mr. Puke strode to the drink machine looking for something appropriate to wash the vomit from his uncovered mouth. He looked a little green around the gills, skin a little grey, eyes sunken in dark circles.

I began to feel the vaccine I'd gotten earlier in the year was in for a workout.

"Honey bun, huh?" he snorted. "I don't think my stomach could stand one just now. But they are *dee-lish-us*. Particularly the iced ones, little man."

He fed a few bucks into his machine, cracked a neon-green bottle, and drained almost half of it. He was a big guy, maybe six four or five, well past three hundred pounds, balding with a scruff of beard around his blunt thumbprint of a face. No visible tats, but I was sure there were some under that down jacket.

"Wow," he muttered, stepping toward the door. "Where the hell'd that come from?"

"Yeah, looks like it's getting bad out there," I said, helping Gus with the money to get his fruit punch.

"Bad? Looks like a fucking blizzard," he said, then looked at Gus. "Oh, sorry. Excuse my language."

It did look like a fucking blizzard. Like the weather had gone from zero to sixty in less than a minute. The air was choked thick with snowflakes that didn't just sway softly to the ground but were pounded there by the closed fist of an angry sky.

It had already piled what looked to be at least two inches on the ground, an unbelievable amount in such a short time.

I could barely make out the white lump of my car there in the lot. The dense curtain of snow blotted out even the tall dusk-to-dawns, leaving just smears of salmon-colored light.

Gus had uncapped the fruit drink on his own. He guzzled it, belched, then asked, "Why can't we go outside and play, Daddy? Mama would've."

Okay, *that* hurt. In the months since Hildy's death, in all his dealings with his one remaining parent, he hadn't once used that tactic with me.

Now when it came, he slipped it in easily, casually, like an ice knife between the ribs and right into my heart.

"You're probably right, kiddo," I said, looking down on the sleep-curls of his hair. She would have pulled us both out there, lobbing snowballs, making snow angels. Laughing that infectious laugh of hers.

But I didn't feel like playing in the snow just then. I didn't feel like laughing. I wanted to finish this trip, get to our new home, begin a new life by finally ending the shitshow that was our life . . . or had been since, well, since . . .

Someone came from the other side of the lobby, out of the door to the women's restroom. Her head lowered and covered, hoodie cinched tight.

She must have come in while we were all in the men's room. Perhaps she was with Mr. Puke, though that seemed unlikely. She looked up, unsheathed a mass of braids from the lowered hood.

A young woman, perhaps twenty-five, perhaps younger, masked.

"You been out in this?" she gasped behind her mask. "It's bad. Real bad."

"Yeah, we can see that from here," said Mr. Puke.

"It's already buried the cars out there. *Buried*," said the woman, lifting her mask to blow into her cupped hands.

"Well, not my truck," Mr. Puke said.

"Wouldn't lay money on that, mister," she said.

I bent close to the fogged doors, drew my hand across the glass. It did little to improve the view. I could just distinguish the lump of my car there in the parking lot, the halos of the streetlights. The whine of the wind was something out of a sea disaster movie. I half expected the floor of the rest stop to tilt and lurch like the deck of a masted ship caught in a storm.

"Where'd this come from?" I asked, mostly to myself. "I mean, there was nothing, absolutely nothing fifteen minutes ago, and I don't remember any weather report mentioning even the possibility of anything like this."

"Global warming," said the young lady, nodding resolutely. "Climate change. We should have done something decades ago. Now, well . . ."

Mr. Puke turned to me, rolled his eyes.

"Yeah," I said, moving back from the doors into the center of the room. "But this?"

Gus had opened his honey bun and was chomping it thoughtfully, staring up at us, following the conversation. I patted his head, hopefully to show him there was nothing wrong, nothing at all. I desperately wanted someone to pat my head.

"Well, we really need to get going," I said, tightening my grip on Gus's shoulders.

"Going?" the young woman said. "Mister, do you see what's happening? I was barely able to get off the highway and slide into the parking space out there."

"Yeah, buddy, come on," said Mr. Puke. "You don't want to take your kid out into that. Wouldn't be sensible. It ain't safe."

Outside, the wind screeched like a banshee. I could hear the snow gusting against the sides and roof of the building as if they were being sandblasted. I began to imagine getting sideswiped by an eighteen-wheeler or skidding off the road, rolling over into a drainage culvert.

"Well, then, I guess we're stuck," I said, smiling down at my son's worried face. "At least the heat's on, and we have plenty to eat and drink."

Just as I finished, the lights flickered, flashed, then died.

"Well, shit," laughed Mr. Puke.

"Sir," said the young lady. "There's a little kid, remember?"

"Hey, sorry, man," he said to me, then to her. "Sorry, ma'am."

"Name's Maya."

"I'm Peter, this is Gus."

Maya waved to him, smiled sweetly. Adopting a shyness he didn't really possess, Gus buried his face in my coat.

It wasn't completely dark, even with the main fluorescents off. The vending machines lit the room like a casino.

"What the hell?" I asked.

"Different circuit maybe," muttered Mr. Puke.

"The streetlights are off, too," said Maya.

The lights were definitely off. Now, the outside took on that blank look of winter darkness, somehow brighter, whiter.

"Luckily, heat's still on," Mr. Puke said, holding his hands over the floor grate near the bathroom entrance.

"Just the lights. That's odd," I said.

"Daddy, I'm tired. Can I lay down in the car?" Gus said, passing me the sticky plastic honey bun wrapper and his half-finished bottle of punch.

"No, kiddo, we're gonna have to stay inside. Snow's pretty bad. Why don't you lay down over there in the corner? Take off your coat and use it as a pillow."

"But I'll be cold," he argued. I knelt beside him, taking his coat off.

"I'll cover you with mine. You'll be nice and warm."

"But *you'll* be cold."

"Don't worry, I'll be fine," I said, shrugging out of mine.

"Can I take off my mask?"

I considered that, let it go. "Sure, kiddo."

He curled on the floor, drew up his knees to keep himself warm. I wadded his coat into a ball, tucked it under his head. He smiled at me, lips and cheeks glistening with sticky honey bun icing. I kissed his head, tucked my coat around him.

"Take a quick nap, and when you wake, we should be able to hit the road again."

He closed his eyes and by the time I stood, he was out.

Kids.

At the very end, they'd disconnected her from the tubes and wires that pumped the stuff keeping her alive, made the pings and alarms verifying that life. Because they knew, the hospice workers we'd paid to come to our home, they knew that soon these machines and their fluids and noises would be as unnecessary as the breath she drew in, the blood running sluggishly through her veins.

You want me to say that she was beautiful right before she died, that she was an angel, serenely awaiting some golden ray of light from heaven to carry her up into eternal peace and harmony? Wings and robes and haloes and the choir invisible and all that?

Well, you wouldn't be the only person.

But it wasn't like that, no. I doubt it ever is.

She weighed less than a hundred pounds; most of her hair was gone. Her eyes had receded deep in their sockets, animals cornered in their dens. Her teeth were discolored, her hair was discolored, her skin was discolored.

And the smell. She exuded a sour, metallic tang, like onions and copper pennies.

At the very end, I sat with her on her deathbed, my arm around her frail shoulders, held her gently, feeling as if I were embracing something as insubstantial as an angry cloud. Gus sat on a chair nearby, aware of what was happening but, because of his age, not able to really process it. What child could? I'm surprised that adults can, myself included.

Or maybe we all just *can't,* we're equally ignorant.

Anyway, he sat there watching, eyes wide. He came over a few times to hold her hand, gently stroke the paper-thin skin of her arm with his delicate, pudgy little-boy fingers.

I rose from the bed, sat on the chair with Gus, still holding her hand, listening to the raspy rhythm of her labored breathing seesawing up and down, rising less each time, drifting lower each time.

At the very end, her eyes snapped open, sharp and distraught, as if she realized that this was it, there wasn't much time left. Her hand wriggled free of mine, and she reached out with arms that had become winter tree branches, thin and grasping, reached out to us.

Before we could react, she fell back on her pillow, eyes still wide, flooded with tears. Her arms flopped to the bed, hands clenched.

It took me a long time to realize that she hadn't been reaching for me.

At the very end, she'd been reaching for Gus.

When I rose, I saw Maya huddled near the door. Mr. Puke surveyed the vending machines.

"Kinda wished they had coffee or something hot," he muttered. "Not exactly in the mood for Fritos and a Pepsi."

"You okay?" I asked.

"What? Back there?" He waved in the direction of the bathroom. "Nah, that was nothing. Just hard, you know?"

I didn't.

He went back to scanning the products on offer.

"Cute kid." He nodded. "Probably had the right idea."

"About sleeping?"

"Honey buns," he said, sliding some bills into the machine, which replied with a satisfied whir and the *kerplunk* of one of the substantial pastries into the dispensing window.

He grabbed it, unwrapped it, and took a huge bite.

"God, I miss these. *This,*" he said around his mouthful of honey bun. "Guess we're stuck. Where you headed?"

Watching him eat, I grew hungry. I saw a Zero bar in one of the machines. Hard to find these days, reminded me of my mom. She'd loved them, always gave me a bite. I got myself one, gnawed off the end.

"Southern Illinois. Moving."

"Ahh, divorce?"

"No, not that," I said, even though what he'd said hadn't been a question. *We're really going to have this discussion?* "His mom . . . my wife . . . died."

He frowned. "Sorry to hear. Didn't mean to bring that up."

"No, no, it's okay," I said, chomping off another wad of the candy bar.

"Still, death is kind of the ultimate divorce. I mean, I know plenty of people who got divorced and wished the ex *were* dead."

"No, it wasn't like that at all."

"How long?"

"A few months. We've dealt with it."

He looked as if he wanted to say something about that revelation, instead jammed a piece of the honey bun into his mouth and chewed.

"How's the little man handling it? Being without his mom and all?"

It seemed we're going to have that *conversation, too.*

I looked to Gus, barely a lump under the spread of my coat. Just a tiny face, relaxed in sleep under a tousle of hair. He really needed a haircut, something his mother would have admonished me about.

"Well, he's only five," I said. "He's doing about as well as can be expected, I guess."

"Helluva thing for a kid to lose a parent. But a mom in particular. How'd she die, if you don't mind me asking?"

I did but most people asked anyway, and I'd grown as cold to the question as she was now.

"Uterine cancer. Nasty and aggressive. Six months from start to finish."

"Damn."

"Yeah."

"Sorry."

Tired of that, too. But . . . "Thanks."

He shook his head. "Still, damn. Kid should really be with his mom. Even in a divorce, kids spend half of their time with the other parent. Doesn't seem fair, right?"

I blinked at him. That was literally all I had.

Be with her? She was dead, Mr. Puke. *Dead.*

A comical image of Gus sitting on his bed next to his mother's urn came into my head. Well, it was comical at first.

"There's nothing . . . just nothing," he said.

Nothing to say? No words?

Or . . .

He looked at me, his eyes strange and piercing. So odd, in fact, that I found myself almost leaning in toward him, as if I might fall into them. His irises . . . they seemed to spin, pulse slowly swirling around the black hole of his pupil, which was so black it seemed a negative space. His gaze held me fixed, as if his eyes exerted gravity.

And I saw myself reflected back in his eyes, my image bent and warped, as if caught there, circling that flat, black disc.

When he broke contact, I stumbled forward as though released, caught myself on the bulwark of his shoulder.

"Sorry, I . . ."

"Not a thing, buddy. Not a thing," he said, drifting from my hand as contemptuously as if he'd lifted it from his shoulder, dropped it like a piece of trash.

He took the last bite of his honey bun, wadding the plastic wrap into a tight ball and flicking it into the open trash can near the vending machines. From there, he drifted away, back into the restroom.

After a moment, I heard the echoes of violent retching.

I stared at the bathroom door, wondering what had just happened, until I was interrupted.

"There's something out there," said Maya, looking over her shoulder to me, her body crouched at the front windows. "In the snow."

"What do you mean? What's out there?" I said, leaning into the glass, cupping my hands to block out the reflected light from the vending machines.

"I don't see anything but white," I said, my breath fogging the window.

"Yeah, it's like a rally out there," Maya said, turning to me and smiling.

"Hey, I resemble that remark," Mr. Puke grumbled, coming behind us, glowering.

Maya smirked, turned back to the utter blankness outside the glass.

"I bet you do," she said.

He breathed out, and it was like a bull snorting. He flashed me a look that spoke volumes.

These people. Am I right?

I ignored it, looked past him to make sure that Gus was still sleeping soundly.

My coat lay on the speckled linoleum floor like a discarded snake skin.

I jerked away from the window, pushed past Mr. Puke.

Yanking open the bathroom door, I was assaulted by an almost impenetrable wall of stench, something so thick and foul it seemed to congeal on the air. My eyes watered, and I raised the crook of my arm, buried my nose and mouth in it.

"Gus! Gus, you in here?"

He was in there, he *had* to be. Where else could he have gone?

There's something out there. In the snow.

Nope. No no no no no.

Even though my nose and mouth were buried behind my mask and arm, the stench was dizzying. I pushed open each stall door, totally assured that he would be in there, squatting on a toilet, kicking his feet back and forth, flashing me a surly look.

Daaaad.

But he wasn't.

He wasn't in the restroom at all.

I crouched and looked under the stall doors, as if that would help, under the sinks. I looked at the frosted glass transom windows on the far wall. They didn't open. He couldn't have gone that way.

He wasn't *here*.

I spun, caught a glimpse of my haggard, panicked face in the warped metal mirrors over the rows of sinks. I looked somehow worse than just a few minutes ago.

Behind me, one of the stall doors creaked open slowly.

Inside the stall, seated on the toilet, was Hildy.

I gasped behind my mask, stood motionless.

She wore a colorless grey shift made of some rough material. It draped listlessly, fell in bunches around her. Her bare shoulders were smooth as marble, pale and lovely as the drifting snow outside.

One shoulder of her dress was pulled low, baring one swollen, gleaming breast.

Gus lay across her lap, his head turned from me, suckling.

Her attention was focused on him. But as I took all this in, her head jerked up, eyes as colorless as her gown, frosted.

Hildy opened her mouth, and I winced before she spoke any words, anxious to hear the voice I hadn't heard for so long.

But no words came, just a spill of thick, curdled grey liquid that flooded over her chin, spattered the front of her shift. Steam rose from it, temporarily clouding her face.

A wave of that same unbelievably foul odor washed over me. I felt my gorge rising, and I pressed my ass back against the lip of the porcelain sink.

As the flow of that spilth subsided, Gus slowly turned his head, his eyes popping open. They fixed me with the same force his mother's had. And they, too, were bleached white.

He'd uncorked the nipple he'd clamped tightly, and more of that clotted, grey liquid drooled from his mouth.

"Gus? Gussie?" I whispered behind my shaking hand. "Why don't you come to Dad now? Okay? Come on, we've got to go."

I held my other hand out to him, saw the muscles there quivering.

Gus considered my words, my outstretched hand with an indolent, almost contemptuous look.

"Don't want to," he said, his voice a kind of sleepy mewl. "I'm staying with Mama."

He wrapped his arms tightly around Hildy, turned back to feed at her breast. I thought of that putrid, grey liquid going into him, and I dry-heaved behind my arm.

"Gus, please."

"He's mine," she said, her words stunning me. It was definitely Hildy, her voice, but the words keened like tinkling crystals, hard-edged and as cold as her eyes. There was need behind that voice, *want*.

"He wants to be with me, not you."

She stroked his hair with fingers that looked to be made of

polished granite. Her words brought more of that rancidity, and I was starting to lose the battle with the vomit I desperately held back.

Not knowing what else to do, I staggered to the door, pushed through into the lobby. I bumped into the trash can next to the door, yanked off my mask, and barfed extravagantly. I lowered my face until my forehead pressed against the cold, metal ring encircling the can's mouth. I heard nothing but my retching and the sounds of vomit dripping down the length of the black plastic bag lining the can.

It went on for a while, until I felt a hand on my back.

"Peter," said Maya. "Are you all right?"

I took a deep breath, wiped my face with the sleeve of my shirt. I unbent, saw Maya and Mr. Puke nearby.

"Yeah," I sighed. "Better now."

"Where's the kid?" asked Mr. Puke, looking around, his arms thrown wide.

He moved toward the door, and I clutched his arm, stopping him. He flashed a look at me that said not too many people grabbed him that way.

"I wouldn't go in there," I said.

He offered a disgusted twist of his lips, yanking from me, pushing to the bathroom. When he opened the door, more of that noxious odor spilled out. He didn't recoil, though, didn't pause or shake his head to clear it. He went in as if that was oxygen he breathed now.

He stepped into the bathroom, the door slowly closing behind him.

Maya went to one of the vending machines, pushing bills into it. A bottle of water clomped down, and she snatched it up, passed it to me.

"You need to wash your beard," she said, gesturing to her own chin and cheeks. "You're a mess."

Leaning forward a bit, I upended the bottle over my beard, let the water wash away the clumps and strands tangled there. It smelled vaguely of McDonald's.

"What happened, Peter?"

I thought of Gus, still in there.

With his mother.

"I don't know," I muttered. "I don't know . . ."

"What did she say to you?" Maya asked.

She . . . say?

"I don't know," I shouted. "I don't fucking *know*."

"Where's Gus, Pete?" she said.

"He's in there," I said, panting the words out like a dog on a hot day. "But I can't . . . I just can't."

"Why did you leave him there alone with her?"

Then, a worried look crossed her face, and she darted toward the glass doors looking out onto the parking lot.

"He's not in there anymore," she said, crouching and peering through the condensation she'd wiped away. "He's out *there*."

I went to stand near Maya, peered through the fogged glass. The snow had piled nearly a foot or so deep now, but was still coming down in large flakes, crazy fast. The wind was ferocious. I could feel it rattle the glass, see it swirl the snow as if it were a kid frantically shaking a snow globe.

There.

He stood near our car, clad only in his street clothes. He was turned away, facing out past the parking lot and into the tree line beyond a chain link fence.

He seemed achingly small, innocent and fragile. Alone. I could see his breath briefly steam the air around his head before being whipped away by the ferocious wind.

Rearing over him like a tidal wave was . . . was . . .

I'm not sure what it was.

It was a towering swirl of wind and snow, an ice tornado. It seemed stable against the wind, a cylinder of twisting air apart from the rest of the storm. And it glowed at its center, blue-white, hot or cold.

I was sure what it was.

Her.

Hildy.

My dead wife.

His dead mother.

"You want your kid, I'd go out and speak with her," came Mr. Puke's voice near my ear. I winced as much from the surprise as I did the vileness of his breath.

"Speak with her," I repeated. "You . . . you *saw* her?"

"Yeah, I did."

"Speak with her about *what*?"

"Him."

I turned slowly to him, my face a mask of disbelief.

"Wouldn't wait too long," he said. "She'll take him. She *is* his mother. She has rights, too, you know."

I was too dumbfounded to process what he was saying, what he meant.

"She's *dead*."

"You better go talk with her. But not alone." It was Maya who said this.

"She's my wife," I said. "I don't need help to talk with her."

"She's not your wife anymore," said Maya. "You need to remember that."

I grabbed my coat from the floor where Gus had lain, thrust my arms into it.

"You sure you don't want me to come with you?" Maya said, grabbing my arm. "There's a storm outside."

How could I ask this woman I barely knew to accompany me out in all that, to save my son from his dead mother?

"No, Maya. I have to go because that's where he is. *Outside*. And because he's *my* son. More so than hers right now."

"And how's that?" Mr. Puke said.

"Because we're both alive."

I had never experienced cold like that. Ever. And I grew up in Chicago, where the winter winds whipping across the lake can peel the skin off your face. This was worse.

Instantly, my cheeks and forehead began to sting. Before I took four or five steps toward the parking lot, they went numb. The wind blew so hard, the snowflakes were so dense, that I had to squint to see my way.

The blown snow was now more than a foot deep, wet and packed. It was hard to get through, each step a slog to drag my feet forward. I didn't have any gloves—the weather reports hadn't mentioned weather this cold or any possibility of snow—and my coat was much thinner than it needed to be.

But I pushed forward.

Gus.

The parking lot cupped the rest stop like the hump of a snake that had just eaten. The service road that wound from the highway into the lot then back was bordered by a thin strip of ground set off by a chain link fence.

When we'd driven in earlier that evening, the ground was covered mostly by scrub grass and dead weeds. The fence had been clotted with leaves and wet trash—McDonald's bags and chip and candy bar wrappers from the vending machines inside.

Now it was draped in an unbroken sheet of snow, a layer of fondant laid over a cake, all smooth and sugary.

Except for the line of tiny footprints leading off into the swirling darkness just past the parking lot.

I could just see him there, a small figure alone in all this snow, his bare face upturned. I could just see his smile, his lips moving as if speaking.

I pushed ahead. I felt spittle running from my mouth, freezing in a growing, bristly clump in my beard. My eyes watered, and my fingers were frozen sausages, too numb to feel or even move.

I trudged forward, keeping my head down, until I stood just behind Gus.

Lifting my head, fighting against the relentless wind, I looked up to what he stared raptly at.

She was beautiful, terrifying.

Held aloft by the tornadic air, Hildy floated just above Gus's head. Her body was rigid, her legs together, toes pointed down. A blue aura clung to her, the snow on the ground, in the air focusing the reflection of that light, giving the scene the hint of a Bierstadt painting.

The grey robe that had artlessly draped her body in the restroom stall now flowed around her marble form, billowed in a current much calmer than the frenetic snowstorm. Her hair spilled out into that serene stream, too, looking as it did when it had fallen across her pillow, sleeping next to me.

But that was all that was peaceful or placid about her.

Her eyes were cold, fleckless white, as if holes through which a vast, featureless plain of snow shone. Her face was severe, her jaw set. Her whole attitude screamed "Do Not Fuck With Me."

I realized that she was no longer looking at Gus, but at me.

Fury.

There was no love there, no warmth or feelings, no memory of the handholding or the lovemaking or the butterflies in our stomachs when we saw each other after an absence, brief or otherwise.

No recognition, no fond recall.

Nothing.

She was a force of nature now, entirely focused on one thing and one thing only.

Gus.

I was nothing to her, just someone who stood in the way of her child. I wondered if she even knew my name anymore.

I thought then, and know now, that the answer is no.

This was no longer Hildy, at least not the Hildy I knew.

This was *longing.* This was *want.* This was *need.*

But not for me, not any longer. That part of who she was had burned off in the fire set by cancer and banked by death.

The only thing that motivated this form of Hildy now, that gave it animus, was the aching, raw yearning for her child.

But that yearning had soured, curdled, had become covetousness.

As I realized all this, she held her arms out, beckoning him.

"*Meine mama,*" Gus said in his sweet, clear little boy voice.

My frozen heart lurched in my chest, and I felt a hand drop onto my shoulder.

"You'd better speak up or she'll take him." It was Maya, her face so close to mine I could hear her over the howl of the wind. Her hoodie was down, and her braided hair whipped in the wind.

Her calm face swam into view, cheeks flecked with snow that didn't seem to melt. I noticed a few specks of something thicker than snow at the corners of her mouth.

Greyer.

"Take him? *Where?*"

"Does it matter? Once she's got him, you won't ever be able to get him back."

"How do I . . . how do I stop this then?"

"You work it out *now.*"

"Work it out?"

I could feel the cold burn through my woefully inadequate coat. The wind scorched the breath from my lungs. My hands were bent into claws.

Hildy's apparition beckoned our son to her, to go with her, away into . . .

"Share him," Maya shouted. "Split the time."

"Share him?" All I could seem to do was repeat words thrown at me. They were losing their meaning, their weight. They seemed to condense on the air, whipped away by the wind.

Maya's breath didn't. In fact, she didn't seem to breathe at all.

And she wore only the hoodie she'd worn when she had appeared at the rest stop.

"She *will* take him. She *will* keep him."

"Maya, I don't understand."

"Agree. That's it. Just agree. You can work out the details later."

I looked back and saw Gus moving slowly toward his mother, as if in a trance. He held his arms out to her as he'd done when he was smaller and wanted to be lifted from the bathtub.

And I knew, I knew definitely, I knew intimately, that if her arms enfolded him, if they closed around him, he was gone from me, gone with her. Forever.

I couldn't allow that.

"I agree."

* * *

I awoke on the floor inside the rest stop, disoriented at first. There was no transition, no segue from the raging storm outside to the quiet inside. The lights were back on, and the vending machines glowered over us.

Us.

I looked at Gus, asleep in the crook of my arm.

I eased him over to prop myself up on my elbows. Gus made a whimper, but otherwise kept sleeping. The rest stop seemed deserted. There was no trace of either Mr. Puke or Maya.

Climbing to my feet, I went to the glass front of the place to look out onto the parking lot.

There was no snow.

Not a trace of it. Just the autumn night we'd pulled in on. No wild windblown snow, no drifts, nothing on the car. Not a flake.

It was as if it had never happened at all, none of it.

As I went back to check on Gus, the door opened, and I heard a gaggle of voices. It came from a group of four college-age kids, excitedly talking. They slowed as they caught sight of me crouching over Gus sleeping on the floor in a tangle of coats.

"Everything okay, mister?" one of them asked.

"Sure," I said, putting on my best fake smile. "Weird weather we're having, huh?"

They all frowned back at me. One of the girls burst into soft, nervous laughter, then ducked into the restroom. The guys hung back a bit, watched me as I lifted Gus into my arms, grabbed our coats.

When I got to the door, one of them opened it for me, and I thanked him. My car was as I left it, untouched by any hint of snow. It was cool outside, but nothing I couldn't handle in shirtsleeves. I slid Gus into his car seat, covered him with my coat, belted him safely in.

As I went to close the door, Captain America tumbled out. I picked him up, put him into Gus's arms.

"I had a curious dream," he muttered, not quite awake. "About Mama."

Curious dream? That was what Hildy called the dreams that confused or scared him. It was her term. *Their* term.

She'd say, *There, there* liebchen, *you've just had a curious dream, that's all.*

"About your mama, huh?"

"Yeah. It was nice. You were there, too. And some lady and a big guy who smelled funny."

I flinched at that. He did remember. Something evidently did really happen. I'd been salving my emotions by telling myself it had all just been a dream. But the two of us sharing the same dream?

"Did it scare you?" I asked, frightened myself of his reply.

After a second, "No. It was nice. I wish I could see Mama more."

I buckled him in and drove to our new home.

All the way afraid he was going to get his wish.

We have a routine now.

Every other Friday evening, I lean against the door as he brushes his teeth, drinks some water. He changes into his pj's, and I tuck him into bed. I read him a story. Maybe we talk a little about what happened that day, things he wants to do or see.

We don't talk about his mother or where he's going. We never do. He never mentions it beforehand, and I never ask afterward. He talked about it a few times at first, but only in the sense he'd dreamed about Mama.

I'm sure he knows now it's not a dream.

I kiss his forehead and tell him I love him.

I linger in the doorway for a while after turning out the lights, watching his little face with the covers tucked below his chin.

Sometime during the night, she will come. Dead Hildy will come to take our living child for her visitation.

Late on Sunday afternoon, I will go into his room. She brings him back early enough for me to prepare him for school the next morning. I guess she's conscientious like that, but I assume it's just part of the agreement.

He will wake up, groggy, confused, and I will wipe the foul-smelling grey vomitus from his lips, clean him up as best I can. I will escort him to the warm bubble bath I've already drawn for him. I'll help him out of his soiled pajamas, get them right into the laundry with his sheets and pillowcase. While he bathes, I'll strip the mattress protector, replace it with a new one. They're cheap, and it's just easier that way. I'll disinfect the room, spray everything down with Lysol and deodorizers to mask the smell of that grey stuff.

I hate that most, that odor. It takes me right back to the rest stop, back to that bathroom where Hildy made her demands.

All the time, every time I do this, I think *What do they do? What do they say? What things has he seen?*

Does she ask about me at all?

I genuinely have no idea. Gus doesn't talk about it at all with me.

I understand Gus's position. You don't discuss the mom with the dad, nor the dad with the mom.

There is one thing I do know, though. This will all get harder the older he gets. Of that I'm sure.

That's what keeps me up at night, what keeps me hovering at the closed door of his bedroom, my forehead pressed against the cool grain of the wood.

I'm not sure what I'm afraid of more.

What I'll have to tell him.

Or what he'll have to tell me.

THE SANGUINTALIST
BY GEMMA FILES

And the Name said unto Cain, Thy brother's blood cries out to me from the ground.

I wake up covered in blood, but it's not mine; I wake up covered in blood, and it *is* mine. Six of one, half-dozen of the other—take your pick. This is the world I live in, and always has been.

I am a forensic necromancer for hire, of a very specific kind. Some of us work with flesh, some with bone, some with what flesh and bone leave behind. I once knew a woman who chased memories along their neural pathways, those electrochemical ghosts that can live on for days inside a corpse, even when its human topsoil is already being furrowed by insects looking for somewhere warm(ish) and easily permeable to lay their eggs, a field their children can eat their way free of. Her gift was a hard one, easy to mangle and misconstrue, like braiding tissue paper. Eventually, she ended up with a headful of other people's voices and a datebook full of the sort of types fragile people really should best avoid, for fear of getting the pixie-dust rubbed off their little wings. I'm not entirely sure what happened to her, in the end, but I do keep my eye out for any trace of her, lit or fig.

For myself, I work with the red stuff. It's my calling. And easier by far than so many other things, given the relatively short window of its particular half-life. Accidents and murders, that's my meat: a short stop, a sudden drop, a spatter or a pool. By the time it's dry, it locks me back out, mostly. Or so I tell my customers.

They don't need to know everything about you, after all, not when your relationship's purely business.

So I'm out picking up dinner, and my phone buzzes: arsehole number ten, it says, because you need to be specific. Number Ten's name is Satyamurthy. Murder Squad when he's at home, and even when he's not.

I sigh, thumb working. *What you want?* the blinking text asks him. Another buzz. *You, obviously. Here.* And an address.

I'm eating.

Do it fast, then. The cursor rests, then: *You might regret it.*

You might be surprised.

Inhale my curry, then I'm off. The site's not exactly walkable, but I grab a cab pretty easy. They don't send cars for you, more's the pity; don't want your name on the record.

Satyamurthy's outside, impatient, waiting to wave me in. His partner, Colville, turns around quick-time as I enter, hand almost twitching in the direction of that gun they're neither of them supposed to have.

"Don't step on the evidence," she barks.

"Try my best," I reply. It's a challenge, all right—stuff is everywhere you look, splashed up high, probably from carotid *and* jugular at once, given how wide the corpse's second mouth gapes. But she knows that.

The body's nude, and basically faceless. Looks like someone did it with a brick? Everything's all mushed up, red stuck with shards, shattered bone-bristles, the occasional tooth; hands are gone at the wrists, possibly for time's sake, dumped somewhere they'll end up similarly deconstructed. If it wasn't for the dick, lying snug and slack up against one gore-smeared thigh . . . ah, but that doesn't always mean much, does it? Or less than it used to, anyhow, as I should know.

"You want a name, I take it?" I ask Satyamurthy, not looking up to watch him nod. Because my gaze is all on this one, now—that blank ruin, equally dented all over, only a rough geographic idea left to tell you where the eye sockets should go. Yet there's a pull to it nevertheless, a sort of gravity; I can feel it, even from here. It's telling me bend down, get closer, ask my questions. It's telling me it *wants* to tell me, so come meet it halfway, before its time runs out. Before the blood it's still trying to shed finally goes cold.

You damn well wait your turn, I warn it, as I do.

So: Down on my haunches, a deep squat, arse to heels. I rummage through my pockets, slipping on my thumb-rings—antique bone, fossilized, worn so thin with use my skin tints them from the inside. Iron reinforcements so they don't break under pressure, with sharpened horn set in a deep groove across my knuckles: right, left, curved like beaks, points extending well past my nails. Set them to the pads of my forefingers and they dent the skin; no scar tissue, see? I don't have to break the skin to draw blood, never have.

Not when it comes when I call it.

Cruentation, that's the old term—blood evidence. Bring a corpse with traces of violence into the presence of its suspected murderer and watch to see if it starts to bleed. Root of the word comes from the Latin, *cruentāre,* to make bloody, and they really did use to not only pull that whole rigamarole but bring it up in court afterwards, way back before proper forensics. Back when the intersection of maths, physics and biology, alchemy, religion and magic was a sight more slippery than it is today, and the same people who'd just learned you could see little bugs swimming around in a drop of water under a microscope's lens still thought women's wombs wandered around their bodies, getting all clogged with rotten sperm and producing fumes that made them go hysterical.

My blood to yours, then, and your blood to mine—cry out, make your plea, your last appeal. I'll help you, if I can; justice isn't always possible, but I'll try my best. Hear you and remember from now on, either way.

This promise is an old one, older than old. My mother taught it to me, like hers taught her. It goes back forever.

We were priests and kings once, Lala, my little one, my nani used to tell me, and still does, even when I don't want to listen. *Long before Kukkutarma became Mohenjo-daro, for all its name reflects our former glory. Before the glaciers grew and retreated, even, in the very morning of the world, when everything was equally unstable. When all our cities were graves, and all our graves cities.*

(Yes, yes. But this ain't then, is it? And I'm on the clock and time is money, theoretical square root of this whole bloody late-stage capitalism barter system. I scratch Satya's back, he scratches mine . . .)

That's how it should go, anyway; almost always does. Even if we don't often itch in *quite* the same places, him and me.

I close my eyes, feeling my fingertips pink and bruise as the drops start forming: All that tiny life, forever swimming and fighting, eating and dividing, without rest, or pity. Each globule a secret universe caught in the moment of creation, utterly unaware of its own precariousness, dim and scarlet and salt.

There's a thrum in the air when the corpse's blood recognizes mine, sparking, a struck string. A red mist rises from the body's pores, sending out feelers, and I can already hear Colville draw breath behind me, give out a disgusted little grunt. It doesn't break my concentration. I know my business better than that.

Now, I say, silent, tongue moving against my teeth, the roof of my shut mouth. *Tell me now. Show me, if you can't form the words. Let me see it.*

Let me see it all.

Turns out, Satya takes notes on his phone, same as every other wanker working on a screenplay down at the local coffee shop. Probably helps to be able to send them to himself via email later on, though I doubt whoever manages Murder Squad IT security likes it much.

"*Eithne* Morden?" Colville repeats, reading over his shoulder, to which I don't bother nodding.

"En-ya," I correct her pronunciation. "Used to be Eustace, 'til she had it legally changed. You really did miss Diversity Training day, didn't you, Detective? It's all right; lots of Old Girls on the job these days, I'll bet, now the Old Boys Network's finally dying out. You'll all have to catch up, eventually."

She opens her mouth, but Satyamurthy waves her silent. "Skip the vinegar, Ms. Mirwani. Anything else we need to know?"

"She was down from the North, couch-surfing, staying with pals in Stepney. Came out to have a good time and mainly did, 'til she didn't. The last place she remembers being is the Five-Pointed Star—dropped her phone in the washroom, but the person she left with stepped on it, 'by accident.' They said they'd pay to get it fixed, then dropped it down a drain, after. She was drunk enough by the time they got here she can't recall exactly how it happened, which I suppose is just as well. Last clear thing in her head is a really nice kiss, then getting spun 'round and rammed into the wall, face-first."

"And her clothes?"

"Like I said, she doesn't know. I'd assume whoever did it burnt them, maybe in one of those cans over there." Adding, as he raises a brow: "That's what *I'd* do."

"Hm. I'll keep that in mind."

Behind him, Colville sighs, crossing her arms. "Don't reckon you caught a look at the bugger's face, after all that."

"Not how it works," I tell her. "I see what they see, how they see it. You've watched me work before."

"Ah yeah, cert. 'Cause that'd be *far* too easy."

Now it's my turn to shrug, stone-faced, even as the red ghost of Eithne's memories hangs heavy in the air around me, refusing to dissipate just yet—a heady mixture of thwarted desire and terrible surprise, disappointment, familiarity: This was always a possibility in her life, one she'd accepted early on, same way I had to. Though I do like to think I'd fight harder at the end, if and when I find myself here. I *like* to think I've lived long enough not to walk into it with my eyes wide open anymore, glitter-encrusted and high on hope, led on like a lamb to slaughter by some toxic combination of dumb youth, drugs and alcohol.

"It was a woman, I know that much," I tell Colville. "Eithne wouldn't've gone with her, it hadn't been. And not some straight woman putting on a show to pull a bit of the new, either, or a lady who goes both ways—girls don't hang 'round the Five-Pointed Star unless they're queer through and through, no matter their accoutrements. It's a biphobic bloody dive, that one."

"Been there a lot, have you?"

"Enough to know."

"And why does this not surprise me?"

"Well, you do look a bit hard to surprise, Colville, sad to say. Rather a disappointing way to live, I'd think."

And here the banter ends, thank fuck. Satya puts his hand up, reins her in, gives me the nod; they both of them sod off, leaving me with Eithne. Not really a place to hang around much longer if I don't want the hangover I'm courting already to last into tomorrow, but there's still a few loose ends to clear up—you have to be polite, always, when dealing with the dead, especially those killed traumatically. They appreciate gentleness.

Need to go now, love, I tell her, slipping my finger-rings back off again. *It's a cold place, this, and there's nothing much left worth the seeing. I'll do my best to make sure things go right, from here on in.*

From her blood's dimming tide, eddying ever downwards, I can still hear the last few rags of her voice issue, so small and sad. Asking me: *But why, sis? She really did seem like she liked me.*

They all do, darling, in the moment—that's the hard bloody fact of it. But it isn't your fault, you have to know that. Or hers either, if you can believe it.

. . . why not?

I shut my eyes and take a breath before I answer, long enough to settle myself so I can be dispassionate about what I have to tell her, circumstances notwithstanding. Seeing, as I do, one more awful flash of Colville's face seen through Eithne's cunt-struck eyes, caught in that split micro-second of transformation: desire to calculation, lips reshaping in a wolfish sort of half-grin that doesn't quite reach her gaze, because someone else's has just . . . dropped over it, like a filter. Two phantom fingers hooked through her medulla and poised to twist, turn down the empathy, turn *up* the all-too-human atavistic urge to rip and rend and tear. That crossover point where kiss becomes bruise becomes bite, adding a vile cannibal savour to the sauce; *lustmord,* that was the term, back when old Sigmund Freud was first slapping his dick-centred psychological worldview together before inflicting it on the rest of us poor sods, no matter how nature, nurture, gender and anatomy might admix.

Colville, completely unaware of how exactly she woke up feeling so sore this morning, but still with that tiny little bit of a shine about her, the after-trace of someone else's magic. Hadn't known if I was right until Eithne showed me, but here it is in all its former glory, a sigil set to flame between her brows like a tiara's centre-stone—something roughly triangular, point down to signal malign intention, a signpost to the Left-Hand Path. And inside it, shimmering, a filigree made from lines and loops crossing over each other at odd angles, impossibly compact. I study it 'til I've got it down, then file it away for tracing in my memo book, once I'm done with the immediate; think I know the right person to take it to, difficult though that'll be. But one way or the other, it's nothing I'd ever bother Satyamurthy with, even if it *didn't* point directly to the bitch who plays his back-up.

She's just a tool, after all; innocent, at least of this. And maybe she really did find her target beautiful for those few flirtatious minutes, if only because whoever turned her on poor Eithne told her to. Maybe the something new she's learned about herself will even keep on resonating away under the hood, albeit subconsciously, formal lack of gender identity jargon aside—I mean, I don't ever expect apologies, or anything like that. But considering how she and Satya come linked at the hip, be nice to get through a few of these meet-ups without her constantly trying to point out how I should feel shite about the way I'm made, even by implication.

Because she was used, that's all, I tell Eithne, finally. *Used and thrown away, just like you but worse, 'cause she's forgotten all about it.*

"But worse"? I'm *the one who's dead, sis.*

I know, love. I'm sorry. But . . . you're the one who's free now, too, free of it all. And her, until she knows the sin she's committed . . . she never will be.

Does that help, though? Probably not; wouldn't for me, if our places were reversed. Still, Eithne seems like she's a better person—*was* a better person. Better than I'll ever be, by far.

I'll make it right, I promise again, rage washing up over me from my deepest parts, poisoning myself from the inside out with it, against everything my nani ever taught me: Need to be hard and sharp, from now on, considering who I'm going to be dealing with. Because *We stay away from each other, Lakshmi-child,* she always used to tell me, even back when my mum still insisted my name was Latif. *Especially those who deal with the living, not the dead . . . stay clear, let them damn themselves in their own ways, and meet their own punishments. When magic calls you take note, but do not answer. It will call you to your doom, if you let it.*

And god knows she had the right of it, too, as I well know myself, from almost every time my path's crossed another magician's—but who else can we trust to police each other, if not ourselves? Who else is qualified?

(*No one can say, Lala; no one knows, or ever has. Not even me, or you.*)

Exactly, Granny. And since I'm gonna die either way, just like everyone else . . .

Eithne gives one last sigh and leaves me. I stand there alone in the dark, trying not to shiver; above me, there's a skittering from the rooftop, the unseen rafters. Birds, or rats, or bats.

You do what you must, my nani whispers inside my skull, the curl where ear meets cartilage meets bone, making my jawbone thrum in sympathy. *Only be careful, Lala, when you do. There are so few of us now, and you . . . you are one of the last.*

"Not dead as yet, though," I say out loud, like I'm making another promise. And turn to go.

When you're born something people don't expect, you learn to value being valued, and pretty damn quickly. That's the core of what attracted me to Caelia Asperdyne, in the first place—I mean, besides her being beautiful, and sexy, and posh. Besides her being at least as outstanding in her chosen field as I ever was in mine, if not more so. There's a tradition of *hijra* in my family, spoken or not; if you're born to the blood, no one much cares how your bits dangle or don't, unless there's literally no one left to breed more little necromancers. But there's not a lot of women, cis or otherwise, who choose the path of *Haute Magie;* plain truth is, the High Hermetic Arts appeal mostly to detail-obsessed system junkies who get off on getting all the bells, whistles, flourishes and correspondences right for their own sake, and that almost always means blokes. The women I've met who took up a Path did it either 'cause they wanted something right away, too badly to bother with a learning curve, or 'cause the magic wanted *them* too badly to leave them alone.

I never asked Caelia what made her different, that way—that's just etiquette. A worker wants to tell you their story, they will; they don't, you don't ask. We had plenty of stuff to do with each other in the meantime, anyway.

Caelia and I met when her lawyer, who works for one of these five-name third-generation family firms whose hourly rates start at three digits, approached me on behalf of his client—he'd found me through Satyamurthy, pursuant to some questions Caelia needed answered. *About what?* I asked; *Blood,* he said, unsurprisingly. Turned out, she needed to know whether a particular sample had come from an honest-to-God virgin or not (it hadn't), and whether the donor was still alive when it was taken (she was, and still is). And since there's basically no one who'd want to know this sort of detail aside from someone else working the magical side of the street . . . well, I got interested. All the more so, once I actually met her.

Not that the alive-or-not part had anything to do with scruples, mind you, as Caelia herself later told me; *I can use it either way,* she'd murmured in my ear, trapping me between her black steel wine cabinet and her tall, lush body. *Just need its correspondences, so I can know* how *to use it. That's all.*

Really don't think that matters as much as you think it does, I remember gasping.

It does, to me. Those are the rules we play by.

You play by.

Exactly so.

Which is magic in a nutshell, right there. Doesn't matter *why* it works, or how, so long as it does. It's surprising how far you can get, in fact, without asking those sorts of questions at all. Certainly explains why Caelia and I got on as well as we did, for as long as we did.

For people, though, the *why* of it very much does matter. Which is why we don't get on anymore, her and me.

Still, I can't pretend I don't like having an excuse to see her again, no matter poor Eithne had to die to make it happen. Can't pretend I haven't missed brushing up against Caelia's whole world, really . . . that lovely place where bills were a joke, the fridge was always full and you could say *fuck you* to anyone looked at you sideways. Can barely keep from jumping her, in fact, when the doors to her condo's private lift roll open for the first time in two years just to show her already standing there waiting for me, arms folded over a red satin dressing robe with nothing much on underneath, and smiling her old familiar half-smile as she watches my eyes widen at the sight.

"Lala Mirwani," she says, upper-class drawl touched with just a hint of Welsh music you could feel against your skin, like being stroked with fur. "Fancy a drink? Or is this just business?"

Only Caelia could make a word as dry as "business" sound that dirty.

Have to make myself look down where her shadow meets the imported marble tile, to remind myself what dangers lie hid inside that gorgeous package of hers. Because yeah, there it is—harder to spot when she isn't moving, but if you squint just the right way it becomes obvious, even when you don't know exactly what you're looking at: A second layer of darkness fitted almost-but-not-quite over the first, lapping it less like water than like flame. Her angel's black halo, edged in corner-of-the-eye UV flares like static, telling you whatever you'd just caught a sidelong glimpse of was inherently . . . *wrong,* neither good nor evil, simply far too much and definitely not right. Nothing that should exist, at least not here, not now, not yet.

I mean, we're all a bit more than baseline normal, those like Caelia and me . . . but the thing that distinguishes *Haute Magie* from almost every other type of working lies in its practitioners' willingness to call on pretty much anything that'll get the job done, no matter what that entails. Some stick themselves inside circles, or stick what they called down/up inside there; some ink wards on themselves and conjure spirits into objects or other people (dead, alive, whatever), assured they're far too well-protected to worry about possession if the item in use suddenly goes boom. What Caelia's done, though . . . that was the opposite, basically. She's invited something in and let it live there rent-free; didn't even ward herself after, to keep it from leaving. And by allying herself with this *thing,* she's made herself over into something almost as powerful, as improbable; by taking it inside herself, she's signed a bargain whose after-effects shed contagion, a radiance no one but her could live alongside, without starting to change in ways they might find troubling.

Never did figure out whether it was an actual big-A angel or just some poor elemental brainwashed John Dee–style to think it was, but either way, being with Caelia was always a package deal. I think I was just the first one she'd ever stayed with long enough for that to get to be a problem.

So: "Business," I force out. Then adding, not quite too low for her to hear, "Business first, anyway." Which gets me an even wider smile and a step forwards, 'til I hold up my memo book: "No, not yet—safe room, then we'll discuss it. Please."

That shuts the charm off. "Of course," she replies, coolly. And leads the way.

Caelia's safe room used to be her penthouse's smallest guest bedroom, before she remodelled it into a hermetic workspace: long tables along all three back walls, floor retiled in slate that would take chalk markings easily, oil lamps to back up the ceiling fixtures, extra ventilation ducts laid in, and—most importantly— the door remounted with hinges on the outside, plus an extra layer of warding runes round it. *So if worse comes to worst, I can seal whatever I can't deal with in behind me with one slam,* she'd explained. *Until someone opens the door, anyway; but by then I'll be at least three cities away, living under a completely new identity.*

It wasn't a joke, so I hadn't laughed, and she'd noticed. That might've been the moment things started to change between us, now I come to think.

Still, it's a comfort to feel her wards go up all 'round us both, as the door closes behind us. Caelia listens, attentively, then takes my memo book and pores over the sigil I've drawn, her finger tracing its lines. The movement stirs memories.

"Not your classic alchemy, I'd guess," I note, to distract myself. "But you're the expert, so . . . what is it, *Transitus Fluvii*?"

Caelia shakes her head. "Looks to me like a recursive acrostic— you write the spell down as an acronym, laying all the letters on top of one another; maybe do it in Enochian or Hebrew and then translate it numerologically first, for extra oomph. Almost impossible to decipher, unless you already know what it's meant to do, and why."

"I know the *what*," I tell her. "Not sure about the *why*, yet. Though I have an idea." She raises an eyebrow, waiting for me to elaborate. "This is too much effort for something isn't personal, and no way a sweet little girl like Eithne made this kind of enemy. So my guess is, it's about Colville—ruining her life, turning her into what she hates, every way you can. And timing it so she'd be the one to catch the call, after? That's twisting it, right in the soul. Exactly what a bastard like this'd laugh about."

(A bastard like this, a bitch like you—or me, under the right circumstances.)

It isn't anything we've had to say to each other, not out loud. And one good thing about Caelia? Even if I did, she wouldn't be too insulted.

Caelia nods slowly. "Given she and her partner are familiar with—our community—they may well have made enemies in it, or one who at least knows who to hire."

"You, for example."

"Or *you*." She gives me a meaningful look. "You do realize, the people most able to answer that question are going to be those least interested in doing so."

"Yeah, yeah, I know," I mutter. "Thin blue line, etcetera."

"Quite. And still . . ." Caelia taps the glyph. "If your reproduction here is accurate enough, I should be able to follow its traces to its maker, for at least a little while longer." She pauses, then takes my hand. My insides lurch. "But Lala, listen to me here, love— anyone who could do *this* is as good as I am, maybe better. They'd be dangerous even if all you wanted was information. If you want to make them answer for this, however . . . be aware going in, you may not be able to."

It rings true, or true enough—worry, on my behalf. Gets under my skin in a way I can't guard against. But I make myself remember Eithne—how bewildered she'd looked, even at the last— and Colville, who doesn't even know to be. This is worth the risk.

"Never mind me," I say. "Just do it, or don't, whichever. Let me make my own call, after that."

"Lala, please. Of course, I'll do it." She lets go of my hand, and I sigh—then freeze as she cups my cheek. Her voice is soft; her eyes hold mine. "You *know* you were the only person I couldn't say no to."

I clear my throat but can't hide the rasp. ". . . that's flattering . . ."

"Yes, I'm sure."

". . . but since you said we had a narrow window, we, um— ought to get started soon, I'd think."

She leans into me, then, and the movement of her lips against mine lights up my body from scalp to groin. Whispering: "Not *that* soon."

Oh, Lakshmi-child, my nani's voice groans a few hours later, the second I cross the threshold of my shitty little no-bedroom apartment. *What's this smell about you now? What've you done?*

I roll my eyes in the direction of my bed, where a carved wooden box sits atop a set of bookshelves made from plastic milk crates, remembering now how much I've always hated coming back from Caelia's place to mine—it feels like falling from a luxury hotel room window straight into a garbage skip. "Nani, enough. This is not like before, and not your business, anyway."

That girl again, isn't it? Nani replies, not at all put off. *She's no good for you, Lala.*

"Fwah. Like I don't know *that.*"

Do you, though? Ah, well. Children.

"Just doing what I have to, like always. You were the one always told me to, remember? If it was up to Mum . . ."

No answer. I sigh, go to the bookshelves, take down the box and open it. "Nani," I repeat, addressing the object within, tone gone all conciliatory and respectful, "I made a *promise, hai?* To one dead, and to myself; to Her, beyond us all. Please don't make me break it."

From inside, cradled on a nest of scarves, my grandmother's shrunken, mummified head seems to squint up at me through the wrinkled slits that are all that's left of its eyes—and though it doesn't move, memory alone supplies the wry, toothless smile. *Hum, I see; fair enough. But none of us ever knows as much as we think we do, and it's what we don't know kills us, Lala. Don't forget.*

I swallow, nod—then shut the box back up on her and go to take a shower. The hot water's actually working, for a change. I step under the spray, close my eyes and try to stop myself from overthinking things so much.

* * *

"This's him," Caelia tells me, a few days later, scrolling her phone to show me a snap of some semi-handsome bloke, bald and bearded, a haematite stud in either ear—pure Guy Ritchie hipster-gangster, aged about twenty years past his sell-by date. "Don't let the smile fool you, he's a dangerous, powerful man, and a lot older than he looks, for all he knows not to look *too* young. Goes by the name of Dominic Traeger, these days."

"Sounds like you know him."

"*Knew* him, yes; he's . . . my type. My *other* type."

"Oh, ta."

Caelia shrugs, beautifully, and rolls off of me; I lie there tangled in her ridiculously high-fibre-count sheets, buzzing everywhere we've touched thus far, though my groin's obviously got the brunt of it. *Stand down now, fool,* I tell myself, harshly; *fun-time's over, back to business.* Can't quite keep myself from admiring as she pads glory-naked to her dresser, though, with both shadows following like a live-action blackwork tattoo designed to highlight her effortless desirability, never quite in sync. Plucks a parchment scroll from the top drawer's secret inner compartment and unrolls it, holding it up: I recognize the calligraphy even from here, though not the glyph itself.

"This is what tipped me off," she says. "His style's . . . memorable, if not that particular sigil. And no, I still don't know what the other one says, aside from 'find a complete stranger and fuck yourself over, Detective,' presumably. This, though—he had it *everywhere* at what used to be his place, back when I went to him for a short course in hard-won life-hacks *vis à vis* our mutual hobby. Probably has it somewhere on his body, too, just for good measure."

Like you don't know, I think, but don't say; just sit up, instead, immediately interested enough to not bother taking the sheets with me. "Ah. So what are they, wards?"

"The *ultimate* ward, or so he thinks—an anagram designed to protect him from everything, living, dead or otherwise. Nothing gets past it. *I* certainly can't, and I was there when he wrote it."

"This doesn't exactly sound promising, Caelia."

"Doesn't it, darling? Ah, but think about it just a little harder, for half a mo'; a working like that only has one limitation, the same inherent weakness *every* magician has, by nature. And definitely every man."

As she glances southwards with a knowing smirk, I feel my brows half-rise, not sure if I'm meant to feel insulted—then pause, considering it further. "You're talking about imagination," I say, finally.

"Oh, I very much am. It's the Achilles heel of all hierarchical magic, you see; a sadly heteronormative tendency to separate everything in the universe by nature and degree, even those things which share qualities that make them far more inherently liminal, not to mention interstitial. Much like your own sweet self, Lala . . . you, and your little trick. The one you don't tell most people about, unless you really, *really* like them."

And here it comes, fast and hard, a slap in the mental face made from equal parts memory and embarrassment; me and Caelia swapping stories in the dark, me all lax and happy enough to be far more post-coitally stupider than usual, while she used every charm she had to pry from me the secret even my mum made sure to warn me should *never* be told out loud, ever, especially to outsiders. The most primal use of blood-based necromancy, which only we Mirwani—supposedly—have ever been able to master; that much-lauded skill which set us apart from every other dead-worker in a whole city of the same, a whole nation. The thing pilgrims would travel thousands of miles for, paying us in prayer and dread and riches untold to perform it upon their behalves, so long ago that the very fortunes we'd reaped from them had all long since crumbled to ash and dust, just as surely as the pilgrims, their justice-seeking dead and the necromantic city-state, which once gave birth to my family itself.

So: ". . . ah yeah," I say, at last, without much emphasis at all. "*That* trick."

* * *

The blood cries out, and we answer, taking on their grief, their anger, their hunger for revenge. Their blood sinks deep inside us, becoming ours. We gather it together and send it out, seeking justice. It isn't easy; it costs, a lot. But it can be done, and—so far as we've been able to tell, after yea these many millennia (two, maybe three at the most)—only by us.

Like a tulpa, or a golem? Caelia had asked me, there in the dark; *Sort of,* I'd replied, like the fool for her I've always been. Because a *tulpa* is a thought given flesh and sent out, half fantasy, half detritus; because people are dirt and blood is dust, you only wait long enough, and a golem is dust brought to life by magic, by the literal application of God's own Word. But no, it's not really like that at all, like either of those things, except metaphorically.

We call it *Peccai-ji Madam,* this thing only we can treat with— Queen Blood, That Lovely Red One, Justice's Price. Her titles built around one catch-all word for many different things, but always with an affectionate diminutive applied as though it's just one more member of our family, a female one: a sister, a cousin, an auntie. Or perhaps someone even further out, a person whose kinship is entirely more difficult to define—a good neighbour, a respected elder, someone we know we can turn to when all other avenues are blocked or lost; something that will always answer *our* prayers, if no one else's. A literal court of last resort.

Does it come from inside you, or outside?

Both . . . maybe.

Do you control it, or does it control you?

Both. Neither. I don't know, *Caelia.*

Then who does?

Nobody, Cee. Doesn't work like that.

I remember her lying back, eyes on the ceiling, studying the lack of cracks. Saying, eventually: *It'd drive me bloody mad, that sort of magic—no language, no control, no rules. How do you stand it?*

I shrugged. *Because it's mine,* I told her.

(Mine. Ours. Its own.)

You accept what you're born with, I might have said—but that's not exactly true, is it? Or it is, but it's complicated: I was born knowing I shouldn't be male, after all, and eventually I was able to make everyone else accept it, without even having to resort to surgery (thank you, modern medicine). Which is a sort of magic on its own, I suppose . . . and like every other kind, you do still have to pay for it, once you've figured out the cost. That's why Caelia's arts and mine remain truly antithetical, in the end, no matter how much we enjoy one another's company; on some fundamental level, the *Haute Magie* crowd think so long as they find the right middleman, they'll never have to pay for anything. It's just contract work to them, everything done at a safe remove, all neat and tidy. No crossed lines, no *mess.* Sex magick aside, even their sacrifices usually involve something else's precious bodily fluids.

Not how I was raised, let alone what I've learned from personal experience. Because what does the price matter, so long as the right thing gets done? There has to be balance in this bloody world of ours, or nothing's worth a good goddamn.

You'd really think the people who made up the phrase "As Above, So Below" would have already figured that part out, wouldn't you? And yet.

So here I am now outside Mr. Calls-Himself-Traeger's office tower, waiting. Or not *me,* rather: Her. The version of Her She lets me be, once all the necessaries have been done.

Real me still lies at home inside a ring made from rings, corpse-posture assumed, naked. Covered in blood—all mine, this time, up to a very tiny yet important point. The biological grit cocooned around a single red liquid pearl of Eithne's blood-memory, hidden away inside me somewhere . . . left resonating, one more note in an endless scale, a raga that never quite stops skittering beneath the beat of my own pulse.

I can't ever completely let go of any of these people, that's the truth. Their cries keep on resounding, thin though they might dim, with time; that's only as it should be, considering their grievances. So we absorb their hurts, let them sink deep and scar over ... which is why, much like the dead, the *Mirwani* never forget. And why, in turn, when you learn how to fuel your magic with pain, it becomes that much harder to hurt you enough to make you stop what you're doing, once the judgement's been agreed upon between all three of you at last—by which I mean you, the client (the corpse whose final pain you share, whose inconsolable cry you ride), and *Her.*

Never let yourself believe the gods can't be bargained with, my Lala, my nani says, *both ours or theirs, or anyone's. But again, remember:* Bargained *with, only. Not* cheated.

So yeah: It's a tricky dance, the blood-walk, even with all six theoretical feet going in tandem, tracing a chart that changes with each fresh client's complaint. Summon the blood, theirs and yours, then slip it like a skin, stepping disembodied into the psychic shell held in every erythrocyte's genetic memory; feel it rise up and swirl around you in a glinting red torrent, forming a new self only held together by will, power, grief and loss, the four hands (or so Nani always said) of Kali Herself. Thus becoming something both real and unreal, neither ghost nor living, neither golem nor undead: indestructible, untouchable, unstoppable ... as long as you can keep the balance.

To walk with *Peccai-ji Madam* is a gift, and it bears a price. It has to. When you do it, your flesh is made of blood and fire and anguish, and it burns. Oh, you can push it down if you want, let the power numb you; have to, really, at least a little bit, or you lose your grip. Then it all falls apart and you wind up slamming back into your true flesh like some ham-fisted stunt wrestler's clotheslined you. *Not* fun. But push the pain too far down, you forget you have flesh at all, and you'll wander blissed-out and blind until your heart gives out from dehydration. Every journey with Queen Blood is a fresh test. Just how much pain can you bear, and for how long? And most importantly of all—is what you're doing it for really worth it?

That part, at least, you usually know the answer to, by the end. One way or another.

By itself the blood-shell looks exactly like you'd expect: a wet, shiny, scarlet image of its worker's body, like you've stripped down, plunged into an abattoir's catch-tank and come up streaming crimson. But it doesn't take much practice before you can make it look like what you want, or even nothing at all if you don't feel like being seen, though that takes effort. I'm playing it simple; I'm huddling in the mouth of an alley across from the skyscraper, unglamorously glamoured up to look like your average out-of-their-head hobo, mumbling and shivering and cursing in filthy rags. If Traeger's the sort of person Caelia says he is, he won't even notice me . . .

. . . and I guess she really *wasn't* lying, after all, 'cause he doesn't; comes strutting down the street like bloody Willy Moon, swiping a bright gold keycard to let himself in without even a glance in my direction. *Owns the top three floors*, Caelia told me, *with his workspace in the penthouse; means home's at a safe remove, but it also means he has to go there regularly, after dark, to renew the wards that need that kind of working. So he'll be there tonight.*

Suppose his schedule changes? I'd asked.

It won't have. A very thin smile. *It can't.*

Don't know why it bothered me she was so certain. Jealousy, I thought, at the time—not that I have any claim on her, really, any more than she does, over me. And not that that's in any way what tonight's about, either.

If I needed to breathe, I'd take one, deep. But I don't, so I just rise instead, hobo-guise shucked off on the instant for a no-filter selfie-image, nearly forgetting to remember to make myself walk after him rather than simply glide a half-inch above the asphalt street, smooth as if I'm skating. No keycard needed, on my part; with a mere flick of the will, I pass myself through the glass, reach the elevators, slip between steel doors and pop the ceiling hatch, leap up. Spark up the cable like a charge along a fuse, right to the top, a fizzing (in)human bomb. Then I pour myself out through the crack those still-shut outer doors slide along and eddy back to "normal" height, following the fading heat-ghosts of Traeger's footsteps through empty corridors 'til they disappear beyond a set of double doors carved from what looks like whole slabs of black oak, each rimmed with half of some mediaeval Satan's gaping mouth: lips and teeth, concentric rings of fire spiralling inwards and downwards to those great bronze half-tongue braces in the middle, worked all over with bas-relief images of sinners in hell that'd make Hieronymus Bosch puke.

Stuck together, both doors lock fast into one huge rune, same as the one Caelia sketched for me. Its power seems immense, blazing, threads linking out through every brick in the workshop wall, hot against my lack of face like hatches thrown open into a furnace at full roar. If she's wrong, trying to pass through will tear me apart, so fast and hard the backlash might reach all the way to my real body; landlord won't like that, considering how it'll make it nigh impossible for him to ever rent my place again. Be a good way to kill me, she only wanted to—so I'll just have to trust she doesn't, as yet. That I'm still right in that assumption, now I'm out of her lovely warm bed and back into the World Invisible, where everything I do (or don't) brings a hundred unsung dangers, at the very least . . .

Sod it, though; Eithne needs avenging, not just grieving. Colville too, for that matter.

I think about closing my eyes, for all I can't. *Think* about stepping forward. And—

—there I am on the other side, all of a sudden, no safer than before but none the bloody less, either. With that giant ward still quite intact behind me, and barely a flicker to mark my etheric wake.

Never been quite so happy to be made to feel like I don't exist, before, I think. *Not in the flesh, nor out.*

Inside is what rings like a repurposed boardroom, with three whole walls of windows facing east, west, north. Doesn't even have

the drapes closed, though I can see the gold tracks of their runners
framing each bank of panes and each gold-shot red carpet-weight
mass drawn back to either side of the door, heavy as a Doric column:
Ooh la, look at *him,* quite literally. 'Cause there's the man himself
once more, just like I figured—Traeger, tracing his chalk from
point to point of a massive pentagram on the tiled floor, kneeling
stiffly down at each juncture to murmur incantations. Not sure if
he's spotted me yet, since I probably register most as a vague blur
against the tiny screaming faces carved underneath his All-Ward,
but I already know how things will change once I move further
inside. How the air all 'round me will start to smear, colours gone
prismatic and deformed, caught on the blood-shell's aura. How
Eithne's almost-gone Kirlian signature will tangle with my own
astral body's silvery trail, both of them snagging and scattering
in polluted shards around Queen Blood's incandescent, inverted
halo. Quite an effect, 'specially when it takes you off-guard.

But none of us have time for all *that,* really. Do we?

Nah.

I flare all the way up, therefore, glamour whipped aside fast
as a shed cloak, Jean Rollin sex-vampire sudden entrance–style:
CrackaBOOM, you naff wanker! See him jolt a bit right where
he's squatted, halfway up and halfway down, knees cracking like
twigs; his voice rises, incantation-pace doubling but not pausing,
let alone stopping—it *can't,* like Caelia said. There's far too much
at stake for him to get thrown off-course, after all, what with all
those para-dimensional mind-worms and what-have-you nosing
hungrily all along the edges of his personal defences, blindly
seeking for a crack to stick their toothy tongues through. One
second's inattention, or distraction, and he's gone—devoured.
Consumed beyond recall.

Time it right, Lala, you won't even have to fight him, Caelia'd
told me, her eyes glittering. *Just . . . interfere.*

I can't lie: It's a rush, seeing that realization of helplessness shoot
through him—helplessness, confusion . . . fear. Things he probably
hasn't felt for years, if ever. Even more of a rush, knowing it's me

causing it. I slide up to him, moving as he moves, red hand lifting to cup his throat, red fingers poised to clamp shut and choke off the binding words; his eyes bulge wide and white. Around us, the aether crackles like bacon frying, twisting as forces both mindless and sentient nuzzle hungrily at this world.

I think about saying something like *This is for Eithne,* but that's pointless; he won't know who she is. And I can't really get angry enough about Colville to posture on her behalf. Maybe it's the best karma of all, now I think about it, that he won't even know *why* this is the moment when he ends. . . .

Karma.

Shit.

Nani's voice comes back to me, her first lesson, and her last. *We hear the dead, my girl; we help finish what they've left undone, to send them on. Lay them down, when they won't rest. But one thing we don't do? We don't decide who's fit to join them. We don't pass judgement on the living, no matter how deserved it seems. That's not what the Gift is for. Forget that, and we'll answer for it.*

I hear Caelia laugh, short and sharp. The way she's always laughed when this sort of talk comes up. *Childishness,* she called it, in the last and bitterest of our fights. *There's what you want, and what you don't want. If you don't know the difference, Lala, you've got no business with the Art.*

There's a different anger in me, now.

I ease my hand back from Traeger's throat. Not all the way—close enough to still be dangerous—but enough to make it clear what I've decided. His fear recedes; the panicked babble slows, his voice firms. The queasy-making shimmer in the air subsides. When at last he finishes, standing from the pentagram's final point, he turns and looks at me. Sigils of poisonous violet light ripple through his skin, jellyfish current-eddying.

When he speaks, his voice is hoarse enough an accent leaks through, more like mine than I'd've guessed; one he worked a long time to lose, I'll bet. "Dunno which t'ask first: How the hell you did this, or *why.*"

"Haven't done anything just yet, have I?"

I've blurred my face and form to vagueness, made my voice a sexless croak. But his eyes narrow nonetheless as he looks me over, all too sharp. "You spent power to get here; more'n a little, I'd say. Means you want *something*." He takes a breath, forces his tones back into learned poshness. "Want it bad enough to need me at your mercy, but not enough to kill me—not right away. Which means you need to know something only I can answer or need me to do something you can't." He smiles, the sort of thing a foolish, hopeful little snip like Eithne would've probably found charming. "Either way, I'm perfectly willing to talk terms."

I don't move, but flick my red right hand into claws and thrust them to prick his throat, five scab-black scalpels cupping his larynx, freezing him where he stands. The smile collapses; he holds very still. I shudder in a breath.

"Fuck your terms," I growl. "Just tell me why."

"Care t' be more specific, luv?"

The words are insouciant; the look in his eyes isn't. I like—*She* likes—that.

"Blood cries out," I tell him. "From the ground, where Eithne Morden fell. And off of Colville's hands, after."

He swallows. "Still . . . not quite getting the reference, darlin'. I mean, I'd *like* to be helpful, but—"

"Petra . . . Colville," I say, very clear. "Detective Inspector. Same one as you geased into murder, so I fucking *know* you know the name. And workers like you don't believe in karma, mate, but right now? Only thing between you and permanent payback is whether or not I buy your reasons, so spill it."

His eyes narrow. "'Workers like me,'" he repeats, softly. "Meaning—you're not, or you couldn't have gotten in here. But you know someone who is, someone who had to untangle this spell for you, this geas you say I laid. . . ." His mouth twitches like he's about to smile again, before he visibly stifles it; so earnest, I almost want to laugh. "Now I think on it, p'raps you're right. It *is* about reasons. Just not mine."

"What—" I cut myself off an instant too late; he's heard it, and the doubt behind it. He relaxes, as I kick myself.

"Just think it through," he says, and I still want to gut him, just for the condescension in his voice. "Eithne Whassername, this cop who killed 'er—cat's-paws, all the way down. And now you, playing judge-jury-hangman on a stranger, just on someone else's word? You telling me it never occurred to you, even once, how maybe I'm not the mage you're lookin' for?"

I want to scream, but I don't. Just point out: "The sigil, though. It's yours."

"I'm hardly the only bloke in my craft uses sigils, for all we're *mostly* blokes; Magick-with-a-K 101, that is. But there's at least one who isn't, so ask yourself—"

I want to tear off Traeger's head and wallow in the gush. I want to smash this pentagram and let in every invisible horror it's keeping out. But however good that rage tastes, I know—*She* knows—its target isn't here. Which sets Madam and I all a-tremble, both: Called Her up for retribution, so that's what I owe her; the punishments for abusing our links to Her made for some of Nani's most horrific bedtime stories, back when. But if I'm wrong and he's right, the mistake I've made, not to mention why I've made it . . . oh, hell.

"—who was it identified that particular work as *mine*, exactly?"

The dead don't lie, though it's not like they can't, more like they don't want to. Why would they? *People* lie. Bloody people, like Traeger, though he's not lying now—not when I can see inside him, through Madam's eyes.

No, he's not the liar here. Neither of us are. The liar . . .

. . . she's somewhere else, entirely; in her own studio, probably, bent over a bloody black mirror, eagerly scrying to see what I do next. While already having metaphorically washed even the faintest trace of the blood she sent me to shed from her beautiful, long-fingered white hands.

And meanwhile, Traeger, too blithe now to be anything but innocent—of this, at least. He keeps nattering on, obliviously.

"Don't think I'm not grateful, mind. Never averse to knowing about a gap in my work, even if you're like to be the only one I ever heard of could fit through it—" He brightens, suddenly. "Wait a bit: bloody *karma,* yeah, which makes you that Paki corpse-fiddler Caelia's taken up with. Venus over Mars, Scorpio rising . . . the last *Mirwani* in London, as I live and breathe." His grin is wide and malicious. "*Thought* I smelled curry."

All that steadies us is Eithne's soundless whisper, somewhere deep within: *Not finished yet.* So I master the blood-golem with a final tremor of will, letting myself float backwards, towards the door. "Got my eye on you, arsehole," I tell him, no longer bothering to cloak my voice. "Remember that."

He shrugs. "You and a hundred others, luv."

Bastard.

Peccai-ji Madam allows me one tiny indulgence, for the disrespect. I spit at him. The blood sizzles on his cheek like eggs hitting a smoking pan; he bellows in shock and fury, and I take with me the immensely satisfying sight of him slapping at his face and dancing like a circus monkey, before I snap back out to the street in a flickering whirlwind of power.

I almost lose my shape in the process, spiralling over the city in a crimson cloud, but rage is still holding me together. I know where I have to go.

The Five-Pointed Star is still open, and I barely have to wait at all—like magic (ha)—before I see who it is I'm here to find, stumbling out, piss-drunk: Colville, alone this time, looking torn between laughter and nausea. I swirl 'round her, nudging her into an alley mouth, where she finally gives in to the latter. Only when the spasms are finished does she realize there's a figure standing over her. Give her credit, though; once she knows she's not alone, her gun comes out and up with *amazing* speed.

"*Back* off, assho—"

But then her eyes rise further, meet the gaze of the Red Madam, and her jaw drops. The gun wavers in unsteady hands. *Peccai-ji* and I take it from her, almost gently, tossing it aside. Then we spread our arms, as if to embrace her.

Threads of blood fine as spider-silk whip out from the Madam's face, lash across the air between us and sink into Colville: her eyes, her nose, her lips, her temples, her ears. She tries to shriek and can't; her head goes back in spasm, and her arms fly out and lock stiff. Memory kicks awake the buried echo within, turning over a folded layer, and we all three watch together as Colville stares slackly into the mirror of a ladies' bog while *someone* reaches over her shoulder from behind, traces the sigil on her forehead. Can't really see the face under that blur of moving light Caelia's angel's halo makes when she's wearing it instead of it wearing her, but it's a mere instant's work to substitute Traeger's self-satisfied mug before showing Colville how the rest plays out, in full surround sound and Technicolor.

Give anything to avert my eyes from Eithne's suffering again, but the Queen makes me stay steady; I'm here to be a witness for Colville, this time, and pay the price for my own blind trust at the same time. Briefly, I wonder what's more awful for a copper—the realization of what she was made to do, or just how easy it was to make her do it. By the end, Colville's on the filthy ground hunched up, bawling like a baby, and I'm feeling sick at myself for wishing I could still hate her.

"*They will come for you,*" *Peccai-ji Madam* tells her, with my voice. "*Stay or run, as you choose. But now you see how it was done, and might be done yet once more.*"

('Cause who's to say Traeger's never run this game on anyone, after all? And better yet . . . now I see why Caelia sent me this way, at him. He deserves *some* sort of justice for the part he's played in all this ruin, even if it's only the kind Colville dishes out when she's mad enough.)

Oh Lala, Nani would sigh, disappointed, if she saw how easy it is for me to point any human being at another, like a gun. But not our Madam.

She simply licks her teeth and laughs.

Without warning, then, Her power disintegrates around me in a burst of blind dark. There's a sickening plummeting sensation in my guts, horribly familiar, right before I slam back into my circle-bound body, the hot slick blood covering me gone instantly to cold, dry powder. And all the strength goes out of me at once, a blown-out candle-flame, as I topple over, with barely time enough to close my eyes. When I wake, hours later, my hair is matted redly to the floor by that ghastly bruise-slash-scrape 'cross the back of my head, throbbing like a hangover times twenty. Even my teeth hurt.

I failed, Nani, I think, through the pounding ache. *I failed Her. And you.*

(But: *No, child,* comes her sweet, dry voice, full of awful understanding. *No, never. You were failed, is all. As so often happens, amongst humans.*)

And: *Yeah,* I think, lying there, beyond exhausted. *True enough. Fuck if I wasn't.*

Caelia's waiting for me again when her penthouse lift doors roll open, but fully dressed this time, and not smiling: No surprise, there. What hurts more than I expect is that she's carrying her walking stick with her, polished oak carved with charcoaled runes—whimsical fashion accessory to the normies, deadly weapon to anyone with the Sight to see it for what it is. I look at it, then her.

"Bloody really?"

"Had to be sure," she says, without a flicker of shame.

She steps back, gesturing me to the living room. Two glasses of wine are already poured, waiting. I sink down on the couch and pick up one, but only moisten my lips with it, wondering how far it'd go if thrown. Caelia sits beside me, carefully, the stick still close enough to reach. She's studying me like she's never seen me before, or not quite *this* clearly. And all the while her angel-shadow ripples back and forth over the carpet beneath us, a cat's tail twitching, if that cat was made from power; turns its black outline of a head towards me now, though Caelia's gaze has shifted to my glass instead.

"Not in the mood for red, for once, I see," she notes, so coolly the joke barely registers. Which makes the shadow tilt its head even further, same way some people do when they're smiling, if it only had a mouth to smile with.

"Not sure if you knew it was a possibility, Cee, when you first set this thing in motion," I tell her, still looking at my wine, "but you almost got me killed, last night. Very badly."

"That was never my intention, Lala."

"Yeah, well; even so."

I really do take a sip, this time, just for luck, before setting the glass down, gingerly; delicious, of course. Expensive, too, probably.

Too bad it tastes like blood.

"Not to mention how Eithne *is* dead, still," I point out, meanwhile. "Always will be."

"Yet Traeger's still alive."

"Was when I left, yeah—still is, far as I know." I angle myself to face her, letting the rage inside me show, if only just a bit; enough to sting, but only if she ever really gave a damn. Suggesting, as I do: "Maybe *you* should do something about that, this time, it bothers you so bloody much."

She doesn't flinch, not quite. "Maybe I would, if I could."

"Oh, I'll bet *that* would, if you asked it," I snap back, pointing down. "But then . . . there'd be a price, yeah? One *you*'d have to pay, personally."

"Yes," she agrees, and looks away, voice very small. "There would be."

"So. Better to geas some mundy into murder and set up some poor bitch to get killed; would've happened sooner or later, anyhow, the way they were both going. Better to lie to a . . . *friend,* make her almost break the only bloody law that *matters,* aside from gravity . . ."

"Lala, for Christ's sake, I never meant—to hurt you. Not *you.*"

"But you did hurt me, Cee; quite a lot, as it turns out. More than I expected, if I'm honest. And all that stops now."

I get up, and Caelia follows, stepping back. The cane's in her hand. Around her high heels, the angel-shadow coils and puffs itself, trembling with anticipation: *Use me, oh use me, let me go.*

Let me fly at this creature who dares to question us and teach her a lesson that will burn her to the soul.

All it would take is a twitch of those skillful fingers, but she doesn't do it. Just dips her head a bit and replies, without preamble: "Would it help, if I told you what he did to me, as part of my apprenticeship? How he . . . broke me, as payment for teaching me?" Here she stops and swallows, wincing in what looks like actual pain, something I've never seen her register before. "I can't remember the person I used to be, Lala—and no, I'm not overstating it; that's just the truth, plain and simple. I'm *owed* vengeance for that, surely."

I surprise myself with my own calmness. "Absolutely. But so's Colville, and Eithne—so'm *I,* for fuck's sake. You fucked us all to collect on your debts when you could've just done it yourself, you'd really believed it was worth the risk."

"If I could have attacked him directly, don't you think I would have? He made sure never to teach me anything he couldn't already ward against. I've spent fifteen years trying to find something he didn't know, and nothing ever worked. Until . . . until you."

"Then why didn't you just *ask* me? I'd've done it for you, myself, you just *asked*. If you'd told me the truth."

At this, she gets up and starts pacing, cane still clasped, now for comfort. "I was afraid," she finally says. "That you'd be angry, at first—that you'd think all I wanted you for was the trick. And then . . . then I was afraid you'd say no; tell me I'd survived, so I should be grateful, and move on. I couldn't've borne that."

"That's someone else you're thinking of, Cee."

"Is it?" She turns on me. "You walked away! Left him upright even though he'll come after me next, now he knows I set you on him . . ."

"Because it would have damned my soul, I hadn't!" The spark burns hot, but it fades fast: All I feel now is tired. Numb. "I have *laws* I follow, Cee, just like you; magic's no different than the rest of the world, that way. You don't get what you want, ever, if you're not prepared to pay. So again, if you want him dead so badly, why don't you just run him down, like a normal bloody person? Buy a gun, a knife—buy a man *with* a gun, or knife?" Caelia clenches her teeth, aggravating me further. "Or is that too messy, too personal? Too up-close-and-risky?"

"I'd end up in gaol."

"With *that* following you 'round? Seems unlikely." The angel-shadow punches up even higher, fawning on her, lapping at her calves: *Let me, oh let ME*. But she just shivers, eyes tight on mine, 'til just looking at her is enough to make me tired. "Okay, then," I say, quieter. "Then I guess you'll just have to do what the rest of us do, when somebody kicks us in the teeth for fun and pisses off, laughing . . . learn to *bloody live with it*."

For a second, I almost think I see what might be a flicker of shame cross her face, but it's gone long before she looks away. Then her voice goes cool and light once more as she shrugs, blond hair swinging. Asking, as she does—

"Very well. So . . . what are you going to do about it?"

"Not much I can do, can I? I mean, take away the whole magic angle and the whole thing sounds like I lost my mind—you're still white, still cis, still rich; my word against yours won't mean much, 'specially when they search my flat and find my nani's head. I'm just a grimy little foreign fortune-teller from a long line of such, buggering idiots out of their dosh with tricks—exotic, but untrustworthy. Must've been what you liked about me."

"Oh, Lala. It was so much more than that."

I almost believe her.

And: *You know nothing*—something—says suddenly, inside my head: a voice that's nothing like one, plucked and tingling like a harp-strung nerve. I barely manage to control my start, glancing back at Caelia, who hasn't moved; can she really not hear it, even with the thing it's coming from rising to darken her thighs, sending reversed wing-pinions up to graze her shoulder-blades and shrug themselves around her like a wrap, a not-quite-living clasp, pumping power into her through her pores? *You who ask no questions except of raw meat, of dripping juice, opening*

*your flesh wide to the Queen of all Decay. How dare you touch my
vessel, whether or not she allows it?* Half childish sneer and half
echoing roar, a fleshless waterfall of contempt. *At least this one
knew the terms of her bargain when she made it, well enough to
not make more.*

You're welcome to her, is what I want to tell it, in return. But
even now . . . even now, I don't believe that. If Caelia ever asked me
to help her shuck this awful thing from her, I would.

But: *Be grateful she has never thought to,* the thing whispers
back, growing even further, eclipsing Caelia's outline 'til she
narrows all over, an air-starved flame. *You would . . . you will . . .
die trying.* And she doesn't even seem to notice, that's the truly
terrifying thing; just leans forward, smile returning, sadder than
it's ever been. And tells me: "I know you don't believe me, but it's
true. And I did miss you, too, Lala. I still do."

I lean forward as well, kiss her slowly, let my tongue taste hers
and suck her breath deep inside me one last time, drunk on it in
an instant. But when she finally lifts her hands to pull me against
her, I just back away.

"Good," I say. "Keep on missing me, then."

And turn, punch the elevator's button, never looking back. It's
harder than I expected.

Maybe she watches me, maybe she doesn't; the angel-shadow
stays where it is, folding around her like a cloak, humming its
satisfaction at my departure. But already, inside Caelia's mouth,
the drop of blood I worried from the inside of my cheek which
holds Eithne Morden's last memory will have already vanished
through the mucous membranes underneath her tongue, its transit
powered by the heat of our kiss. Within days, its colonization of
her cells will be too advanced to stop. It will spread and spread,
reproducing as it goes, turning the insane complexity of Caelia's
microcosmic interior universe against her; slow but steady,
impossible to alter.

Because here's what I know, the wisdom of mere meat and
juice, the Fleshly mantra: How we're all one vast intersection, a

decay-bent machine that runs on balance, a series of interlocking systems, chaos theory in action; so incredibly easy to disrupt catastrophically, with so little effort. So maybe it'll be cancer, or a thickening of the blood, an aneurysm, a heart attack; maybe her immune system will detonate in a cytokine storm. By the time she understands what's happening, it'll be too late; her angel will desert her, flee the sinking ship like a mutiny.

This is the problem with a separation of magics, all drawing what must surely be the same basic power, but for very different things.

Very, very different.

The next text I answer from arsehole number ten, Satya comes to get me himself, gesturing me into the passenger seat of his car. Colville isn't with him. When I get in, he doesn't pull the car out right away. Doesn't seem able to look at me, either.

"Did you know?" he asks me, eventually.

"Wasn't her idea, mate," I tell him, already knowing it won't help. "I can't prove it, but . . ."

"Whereas forensics *could* prove she did it, no matter why. And did." He sits there a second, considering whether or not to tell me the rest, as I just wait. "She wasn't there when they came to arrest her, so they tracked her phone to some office building and found her just sitting there on the steps outside, another corpse at her feet. Some knob named Traeger—a 'consultant,' that's all his cards said. I asked her why she did it, when they brought her in. 'Didn't like his face,' was all she said."

"I'm sorry, for what it's worth." A pause. "Don't guess I'll be seeing you again, hm?"

No reply. But—he just keeps on. Sitting there. Until I suggest, delicately:

"Unless . . . you have something for me."

A long moment crawls by, before he finally meets my eyes, and I can see his answer. A lot of corpses in this city. A lot of dead people with no name, and no one else to ask them for it. Their blood, crying out from the ground.

"Please," he says.

I sigh. "My pleasure," I reply.

By which I mean my duty.

MRS. ADDISON'S NEST
BY JOSH MALERMAN

Jonathan sits at a large round table, facing three people who have played major roles in his life, three he's never seen together in the same room. There's Dad to his right. Wearing a flannel shirt rolled up to the elbows, his hair still mostly brown, his smile as inhibited, but genuine, as ever. There's Melky to his right. Jonathan played baseball with Melky after high school. They failed to stay in shape, but they tried. Across the table is Darla, a woman Jonathan hasn't seen in ten years. Her hair looks less blond than he remembers. Her roots are showing. Gray.

The three are laughing. As if Jonathan's caught them mid-joke. That's how it feels. Like he's just, suddenly, shown up.

Dad. Melky. Darla.

Where are they?

In the center of the table is a gaping hole. As though a hole in the ground, but up here on the table. Its serrated lip is frayed, lined with gray dirt.

Jonathan begins to lean forward. It seems, from this angle, the hole goes deeper than the floor of the room they occupy.

"Cheers," Dad says. He's got flinty eyes. Thick eyebrows. He nods and tips his beer Jonathan's way. Jonathan looks down and sees he has a beer, too.

"Dad . . ."

Dad drinks.

"Jonathan!" Darla says. Her eyes are bright beneath blue

makeup. She looks cool, Jonathan thinks. But why is she here? There are no pictures hanging behind her, no walls at all in the darkness beyond her face. "Let's get fucked up!"

Jonathan smiles. Sort of. It sounds good. Maybe. If he could only remember how they all got here. Darla sips from what looks like a gin and tonic and when Jonathan sips from his beer, he discovers it's the same. Gin.

He feels hot. He shifts in his seat.

"Guys . . ." he starts. But it's embarrassing, not easy, asking questions like these.

"We could hit some balls," Melky says.

Jonathan nods. Okay. This sounds good. Sounds like something Melky and he used to do. But was he dating Darla when he hung out with Melky? And did Dad look the way he does now back then?

Jonathan looks to his dad, but the old man is talking to Darla. The blackness beyond both makes Jonathan uneasy. Is it the same behind himself?

Something moves inside the hole in the middle of the table.

"We could hit some balls," Melky says again. Jonathan looks to his old friend.

"That sounds good," Jonathan says. "But, Melky. . . ."

He almost says, *What the fuck is going on?*

"Darla says you're scared of spiders," Dad says. "Is it true? She removes the spiders from the house?"

Jonathan is married now to a woman named Anderson. Has been for four years. He and Darla ended a decade ago.

"Spiders?" Jonathan asks. Then he blushes. Because sure, that's how it used to be. Is this some sort of reunion? Is Jonathan's head okay? He brings a hand to his head. It feels okay.

"Oh, go on!" Darla says. "Tell them how scared you get around the house!" Wide-eyed, she looks to Jonathan's dad. "We watch a movie, a scary movie, and he asks me to go to the bathroom with him at four in the morning. He hears a sound and I have to go investigate!"

"Really?" Melky says. "But you're good with a bat."

"Jonathan," Dad says, "that's not how I raised you to be."

"Oh, it's not quite like that," Jonathan says. He worries. Will Anderson be upset he's here with Darla? Will she ask why Darla was laughing so hard with Jonathan's dad?

"I raised him to be a man," Dad says, with pride.

Something breathes in the hole in the middle of the table.

Jonathan looks to Dad. To Darla. To Melky. To his hand as he raises the drink to his lips. To his forearm, exposed.

There is a tattoo there. It says:

REMEMBER WHERE YOU ARE

Jonathan drops his drink.

"Easy," Melky says.

Remember where you are . . .

Jonathan remembers getting the words printed on his skin. Remembers the drunk night he and three others (not these three) spent in a parlor on Division Street. There was a seriousness to their being there. A purpose.

What?

Jonathan looks up, sees Dad, Darla, and Melky are staring at him. Watching him.

Something breathes in the hole.

Jonathan leans forward to see what's breathing. A fourth voice comes from the darkness over his shoulder:

"Don't get any closer to it."

Larry is gambling. Feels good. Hasn't gambled in years. And, really, why not? He loves doing it. Always has. It's never for much money. It's not for much money right now. Forty dollars a hand, tops. He's missed it. Glad he decided to go to the casino in Milton, Michigan. Aubrey is probably upset about it, but hey, it's not like she doesn't have her own nights out, dancing to country music with her friends at Saddles. In *fact,* Aubrey went out last night. Two nights ago. What night was it? What night is it?

And how long has Larry been here?

By the looks of the stacks of chips in front of him, he's been here all night.

"Rolling," he says. Because he must be. Though he has no memory of rolling. No memory of coming here or even making the plans to do so. His cards look good. He feels good. Or mostly. Feels a little nervous, truth be told. He looks to his right to remind himself who he came here with and it's like worrying about losing his mind. Shouldn't he remember who he came here with?

"Keep it up," Blake says.

Blake? Jesus. Maybe Aubrey would have reason to be upset. The last time Larry hung out with Blake they did so much coke Larry came home naked. Whether that was a good night or a bad night, Larry doesn't remember. What he does remember, or *thinks* he remembers, is that he hasn't hung out with Blake Willis in twelve months. At least. Probably more like eighteen.

"I'm doing well?" Larry asks. He didn't mean to ask it. Meant to say it.

"Well?" A voice says to Larry's left. Larry looks. Two more old friends. Howie and Loop. Howie says, "The room tonight is on you!"

"If you can keep what you got," Loop says.

"And why couldn't you?" Blake says. "Who says luck ever really runs out?"

Larry smiles. Okay. Looks to his cards. Says, "I'll stay."

He looks to the dealer but there is no dealer. Only a big hole where the dealer should be. Larry lifts his elbows fast. It's not the green felt of a casino table but grass. Some green, but mostly gray.

Something breathes inside the hole.

"What the fuck?" Larry says.

"Easy," Blake says. "You won."

Larry looks down. More chips. He looks to the hole. Looks to Howie and Loop. They both examine their cards. Beyond them is darkness. Why did Larry think there were lights in here? Slot machines? Waiters and waitresses?

Wasn't there music a moment ago?

He looks to the hole.

Only breathing now. Far down.

"How far does that—"

"Fuggetaboutit," Howie says. "You're rolling."

Larry nods. Okay. Looks to the table. Or the grass. Whatever this is. Does the Milton Casino have themed tables? And if so . . . what's the theme of *this* one?

The hairs on his arm are at attention. He's nervous. Okay. He looks to his cards. Still good. Looks to his arm. Sees a tattoo there:

REMEMBER WHERE YOU ARE

Larry remembers getting this tattoo. He and Jonathan and David and Duncan. They got real drunk on purpose. Larry remembers the talk they had before opening the fifths of whiskey:

We never drink to wallow, hide, or drown, David said. *We drink to celebrate. But tonight? We drink because we're scared.*

The tattoos mean it's real, Duncan said. Duncan looked about ten years old, his eyes so wide. Like when the four of them went to see *Aliens* at Chaps Movies. *The tattoos mean we're no longer just talking about it. We're doing it.*

"Snap out of it," Blake says. He holds a card flat out to Larry. Larry sees white powder in a small pile upon it. "Do a bump."

Larry leans forward, hears that breathing. Feels like it's coming from his own chest, it's so loud. He brings his nose to the line.

It wiggles.

"What the *fuck*!" Larry says. He leans back in his chair, begins to fall into the darkness behind him, reaches out for the table, for the grass.

Strong arms catch him from behind.

"Remember where you are," someone says.

David?

But before Larry can ask, husky, slow coughing comes from the hole where the dealer should be.

* * *

Duncan stares at the words on his arm. He wants to understand them. Wants so badly to know what they mean. He knows they're important, knows that much. But just like the tests he failed in high school, he doesn't feel up to the task of deciphering them.

Remember where you are . . .

Okay. Where?

He thinks. Hard. He won't look at the hole again because of what he saw the last time he did. Nope. Won't do it. Instead, he stares at his arm. He tries to understand. But thinking has never come easy to Duncan, the group fool, the willing butt of endless jokes, the first to leap from the top of the sauna into the lake, the one who tried buying beer when they were twelve. Still, he must be as intellectually sound as the three people facing him in foldout chairs, the four of them constituting the lot of this AA meeting, his penance for getting caught urinating in public. It's driving Duncan nuts, being here. He thought he'd long moved on from this stuff. Hadn't he shook everyone's hand the day his hours were up? Hadn't he made a funny exit of it? And hadn't he seen concern in the eye of the very man, the bearded counselor, the very man who sits across from Duncan now, across from the huge gaping gray hole in the gymnasium floor?

"What's on your mind, Duncan?" Mr. Addison asks. "It's okay to talk about it. That's what we're here for."

"That's what *you're* here for, Duncan," a redhead named Kay says. She winks.

Duncan scratches at his arm. Not to rid himself of the letters that are apparently tattooed, but to remember what the fuck they mean.

He thinks of David, Jonathan, Larry.

Something to do with them.

"I just wanna see my friends," Duncan tells Mr. Addison.

His voice echoes off the high gymnasium ceiling and seems to fall directly into that hole.

Duncan won't look at it again.

"Great," Mr. Addison says. He has a way of saying things. "Because we are your friends. Possibly your best friends in the world."

Duncan looks from Kay to Mr. Addison to the third. A man, Duncan thinks, slouched, his face covered by long, gray hair.

"Well, I meant my buddies," Duncan says. "And if I'm gonna be honest—"

"Please," Mr. Addison says. "Honesty."

"Right. Thanks. Well, yeah. If I'm honest, I was with them last night. We got ripped and went and got tattoos."

Duncan holds up his arm.

"We got the same tattoo, each of us. But I can't remember what it means for the life of me."

Kay looks to her fingernails. Mr. Addison doesn't have to say a word to express how he feels. But he does:

"Did you say you . . . got ripped?"

"Well, yeah," Duncan says, scratching at those words. "But that's not really the point."

"But I think that it is," Mr. Addison says. "I absolutely do."

"What does it say?" Kay asks. She squints at Duncan's arm.

A slapping sound rises from inside the hole.

"Remember where you are," he says.

"Ah," Kay says.

"And where are you?" It's a woman's voice. But not Kay. Duncan looks to the man with his face hidden behind his hair. Did he just speak?

He looks to the hole. He doesn't mean to. He just does.

"I think that's absolutely the point of this," Mr. Addison says.

But Duncan can't respond. He's shaking his head no.

Then he's up. He's turning. He hears the unmistakable sound of David's voice beside him.

"*Werther Woods*," David says.

Duncan looks down at his arm. His *other* arm.

Right.

There's a tattoo there, too. It says:

WERTHER WOODS

* * *

David remembers where he is. He's always been the most responsible of the quartet, but he's never felt the pressure of that as much as he does right now. Duncan and Larry are messes. He expected more out of Jonathan, but Jonathan is the sensitive one. For all his smarts, he gets rattled. Still, the way they all spoke back in David's living room, it sounded like they were ready.

Were they?

Could they ever be?

"Werther Woods."

David says the name and thinks he hears a hissing from deep in the hole in the forest floor. He holds the rifle like he would the handlebars of a bike; he reads the tattoos.

Why aren't the others doing this? David wants to position them so they're looking at their arms, both arms, but he can't leave his post. That's big. And so far, the others remain at theirs. Despite the spacey looks, the seemingly random things his best friends say, the four of them form a wide square around the gray, smoking hole. But the longer David looks away from his arms, the looser his hold on this truth becomes.

The thing in the hole can do that.

"Werther Woods!" he yells. They could leave. They could come back and try another time. They can't be expected to succeed on their first trip out, can they?

His eyes locked on his bare forearms, David thinks of the events that led him and his three best friends to this spot. A lifetime, it seems, though it's really only been fifteen years. Not for the first time he wonders what binds him to these three men. Are they tied, forever, to what they saw Mrs. Addison do in the Chaps High library when they were only sixteen?

They'd always got in trouble, each in his own way, but especially together. Like when Larry pulled a beer from his backpack in history class, flashed the label David's way, coughed as he popped it open. Not loud enough, it seemed, to block Mr. Carrington from hearing it. David remembers stealing *Cracked* magazine with Jonathan at the local drugstore, believing they got away with it, until the police knocked on the door of David's home. And Duncan, well, Duncan was a walking juvenile delinquency. Always had been.

Trouble. Most of it fun. Most of it funny. You didn't have to be a bad kid to get into trouble. David didn't consider himself a bad kid. And while he understood he was the least wild of the bunch, he knew his friends were good people, too. Trouble didn't have to be mean, didn't have to be cruel. Trouble, when seen through the right eyes, could mean freedom. Lust. Creativity. A lack of stimulation. Or forget all that; sometimes it was just fun to break things.

Still, good or bad, trouble usually ended in some sort of detention. The friends weren't surprised by this. It was only a matter of time before they shared the Chaps High library after school, as the sun pressed flat against the windows, as everybody else they knew was out tossing a ball, driving up and down Haley Street, trying to buy beer at Hobo Joe's. Way David saw it, you did the crime, you did the time, no big deal. Could be worse scenarios than an hour after school with your best friends, nice weather or not.

Yet, this one particular time *became* worse. This seemingly routine moment *became* the touchstone by which each would endure their own unique phases of obsession; from initial denial, to, as they aged, questions, ones David recognized as becoming more philosophical over time, until the four of them took very seriously what they'd seen that day in the Chaps High library.

"Werther Woods," David says. He doesn't want to take his eyes off his forearms. But who's watching over his friends? The four of them are armed, have to be. The four of them block the four semi-paths through the unfathomable brush. The four of them are prepared to kill the thing in the hole. But the way Larry's talking . . .

"Larry," David says, sweat forming under his stocking cap. "We're in the woods. We're here to kill her."

He doesn't have to look at Larry to know his friend makes the confused face he always makes before comprehension sets in.

"The woods?" Larry asks. "Is that true, Blake?"

"There's no Blake here," David says. "Wake up."

Yes, David is sweating. He can't tell how much daylight is left in here. The way the trees bunch, the walls they make. Does it get darker in Werther Woods than it does in other places?

He looks to his arms. He reads the words. He's shaking. Fucking *shaking*. How can he shoot a gun like this? And did they really think they were prepared?

How could they think they were prepared?

"Dad," Jonathan says. "Why are you here?"

David stares at the letters on his arms. He remembers where he is. But is he the only one? Jonathan sounds just as bad as Larry. And Duncan . . .

"Werther Woods," Duncan says.

Ah, good.

"*Yes*," David says. "Keep reading your arms, Duncan."

"I am."

They are far from the hole. About as far as they were from Mrs. Addison when they saw what they saw in the Chaps High library fifteen years ago. Jonathan pissed himself that day.

David hears a stick crack. He points the gun at the hole without looking at it. He's shaking. He looks to his right. Sees it's Jonathan, walking toward the hole.

"*Stay away from it*," David says. Jonathan looks to him, squints. Like Jonathan isn't sure who spoke.

"David?" he asks. Like calling into a dark hallway. Like he forgot he was in the woods.

Mrs. Addison can do that to a person.

"Yes," David says. "It's me. Get back. Step back."

Jonathan does. David feels his own grip slipping.

"David, I saw my dad. Darla . . ."

"Read your arms. Like we talked about."

"Both arms," Duncan calls.

David nods. Watches Jonathan inch his way back. Wants him to move faster.

"*Fuck!*" Duncan calls.

David almost fires at the hole without looking at it. Can't do that. Larry's somewhere on the other side. Won't look that way. No way. Not again.

"*What's going on?*" David calls.

Duncan doesn't answer. David turns to look at him, has to see the hole as he does. It's a blur of gray. Thinks maybe he saw Larry pointing the gun at the hole on the other side. Looks to Duncan. Looks ahead.

Sees Lois staring back at him.

How long has Lois been here? And where exactly are they?

"David," she says, her vivid artist eyes locked on his. "You are *sweating*."

David is embarrassed. Didn't mean to sweat in front of Lois.

"Wait," he says.

Why is Lois here? Why does he feel this way?

He looks right, sees Greg and Carrie. Wearing matching turtlenecks. Gray slacks.

David doesn't remember coming here. When's the last time he saw Lois?

"Is it really so effective?" Lois asks.

"I guess it is," Carrie says. "Success, Lois."

"It's truly fantastic," Greg says.

David knows what they're talking about now. He even knows where they are. 2222 Haley Street. Lois Peters's art studio. Is David still dating Lois?

"Cheers," Carrie says.

They all raise champagne glasses. Gray liquid bubbles.

David has never been big on hunches, but something is telling him not to look at the floor at their feet. To where the others look. To Lois's latest work of art.

"To me, it's a face," Greg says. "Barely peeking out of a cluster of snakes."

"Really? A face?" Lois asks.

"Totally," Carrie says.

"People see snakes and faces in everything," Lois says. She sounds disappointed. "David?"

David looks to his arms. Sees words there. Isn't sure what they mean.

"David?" Lois asks again. "Can you see a face?"

David looks.

"It's right there," Carrie says. "Peering over the rim."

"The rim," Greg echoes.

"David?" Lois asks. "Do you see a face?"

David leans forward. Closer. Doesn't see what they're seeing. Wants to see it. Wants to say yes, there it is, I see it, too. Wants to feel included. Always feels just a little outside Lois's world. Like her and her friends are from—

Someone slaps David's face.

Hard.

Duncan has left his post. He knows he shouldn't have. He's left the path through the brush open. But he had to slap David. Had to bring him back. He hurries back, his eyes on his arms.

REMEMBER WHERE YOU ARE
WERTHER WOODS

He remembers. He's got it. He's good. But David was so close to the fucking hole and he wasn't listening to Duncan. Duncan had to stop him.

They shouldn't have guns.

"Guys," Duncan says, taking the role of the responsible one for the first time in their lives, "we gotta get the fuck home."

"Aubrey's gonna kill me," Larry says. "But I'm rolling."

"Larry," Duncan says. "You're in Werther Woods."

Duncan, feeling confident, feeling like he's completely in control, certainly compared to his friends, looks across the hole, over the hole, and sees Jonathan is staring down at his arms.

"Jonathan," Duncan says. "You with us?"

Jonathan looks up. He looks like a kid. Scared out of his mind.

"We need to grab these two and get the fuck home," Duncan says.

"We can't," David says.

Okay. Does this mean David is with him, too? Does David remember where they are?

"Come on," Duncan asks.

"We went over this."

"Remind me."

"She'll catch us in the woods."

"Jesus, David. Fine." Because it has to be fine. They have no choice now but to do what they've come to do. Then, "Where'd you go?"

David is looking at his arms.

"I don't think we should talk about that stuff."

"Maybe we should."

"Go?" Jonathan asks. "You guys went somewhere, too?"

"Larry," Duncan says. "We all remember where we are. Do you?"

Silence. Duncan looks to Larry. Sees he's reading his arms.

Okay.

Are they all good, then?

"Lois's art space," David says.

"Ah," Duncan says. "Yeah, maybe we shouldn't talk about that stuff."

"I was at the casino," Larry says.

"She plays with memories like cats knock shit off tables," Jonathan says.

It's supposed to be funny.

From the hole, silence.

"Listen," David says. "I'm worried. I'm thinking of something we overlooked."

"Come on," Jonathan says. "Why would you say that?"

"Because if she doesn't come out, eventually we're gonna have to go to sleep."

"Not a fuckin' chance," Duncan says.

"But we're in a spot," David says.

"Not a fuckin' chance."

"Jesus," Larry says. "We can't fall asleep out here."

"What are you guys saying?" Jonathan asks. But it sounds like he knows.

They can't leave their posts. But they can't stand where they are forever.

"We need to coax her out," Duncan says.

Jonathan turns to leave.

"No, no, no," David says. "Stay right there."

David actually considers raising his gun, pointing it at his friend. Forcing him back.

But Jonathan pauses before the path. Turns back. Reads his arms as he walks slow to his post.

"If she doesn't come out," David says, "we're gonna have to go in."

Chaps High library. The four best friends are in detention. They're fuckups. Not because they're dumb. Not because they're mean. But because they're fun. They met the way birds of a feather do, recognizing in each other a similar song. David and Duncan grew up on the same street. Friends since birth. Even Duncan's mom recognized a guide for her son in David. Larry's parents saw something similar in Jonathan, the two having met playing soccer. Chaps isn't big enough for the paths of young boys to never cross, and so both duos were present when David and Duncan blew up the teeter-totter in Blankenship Park. Larry stood the closest, got a splinter in his leg. Police arrived. The four were detained in the back of the same pickup truck. They weren't allowed to leave until all their parents were informed. They were inseparable from then on.

Even in trouble.

"A little gang," Mrs. Addison says. She's plump. Blond hair that looks like a wig. She leans against a table facing the individual tables the four friends sit at. Her blue and white floral-patterned dress looks particularly small-town.

"Do you know who my husband is?" she asks. The boys have never seen Mrs. Addison before. "If you don't by now, soon you will. Each of you. He's the guidance counselor at the Edsel House. Do you know what goes on in that house?"

The teens do. Duncan says it:

"It's where the drunks and druggies have to dry out."

Larry laughs.

"Yes," Mrs. Addison says. "Yes. Dry out." She taps a fingernail on the table behind her. It's uncomfortable when her eyes alight on each in turn. They expect to laugh at her. To glare back. But none want to. They'd rather not look at her at all. "Do you have any idea what it's like . . . drying out?"

The quartet is in detention for different, but the same, reasons. Duncan and Larry were caught smoking a joint behind Chaps High. David and Jonathan were caught with acid. The latter pair were worried about jail. Some rumors suggested a certain amount indicated intent to sell, others said LSD meant intent to overthrow a government through mind control. None of that turned out to be true. But detention did.

"You there," Mrs. Addison says, pointing a blue nail at David. "Tell your friends what it's like."

David shifts uncomfortably in his chair. Turns a little red. How the hell should he know?

"I don't . . . I have no idea."

"No?"

Mrs. Addison holds David's gaze. He can feel his friends' uneasiness. He's suddenly, surprisingly, embarrassed. Here he thought he'd laugh her off.

But he can't look away.

Instead, he begins shaking.

Something foul turns in his stomach. He feels hungry. No. Something bigger than that. He feels empty. Sick. Angry. It's all so sudden, every joint in his sixteen-year-old body begins to pine for something, something he can't pinpoint.

David turns his head and throws up.

It comes fast, and it scares him, and he can't stop it.

His lunch splatters on the library's patterned carpet.

The room goes silent.

"It seems you *do* know what it's like," Mrs. Addison says.

She looks different to David through teary eyes. No longer just the woman who was tasked with watching over them.

"You okay, David?" Jonathan asks.

"You," Mrs. Addison says, ignoring the puke on the floor.

Jonathan looks up to see she means him.

"I don't know anything," Jonathan says. There is fear in his voice. Why? It's not like Mrs. Addison just *made* David throw up.

Is it?

Jonathan begins to groan, sweat, he leans forward, grips the table—

"Stop it!" Duncan says.

Mrs. Addison looks to Duncan.

"What's going on here?" Larry asks.

Jonathan gasps and sits up straight again.

Is it over? Whatever just happened to Jonathan? Is it done?

Mrs. Addison speaks:

"I have you for an hour. You will remain seated and quiet."

She steps behind her table like she's going to sit in the chair there, like she's going to sit and stare at each in turn for that full hour. But she doesn't. She continues into the aisle of books beyond the table instead.

The teens watch her slip into the darkness like she would black water.

They don't speak. Jonathan is red faced, flushed. David threw up! The library clock ticks. Mrs. Addison makes no noise in the aisle.

Where did she go? How far back does it go?

David looks to Duncan. There is fear in their eyes, then . . . it's quickly replaced with smiles. Because . . . because . . . no way. There's simply no way the small woman who just vanished into the far side of the aisle had anything to do with David's sudden puking or Jonathan's spasm.

"That was messed up," Larry whispers.

David wishes he wouldn't speak at all. Despite the smiles, he'd rather not see Mrs. Addison again.

He looks to the clock. They still have fifty minutes in here.

Is he supposed to clean up the bile beside him?

Duncan lifts his bag onto his table. He unzips it. David supposes he should do the same. Vanish into a book for the duration. Fuck it. If Mrs. Addison isn't worried about the mess, David surely doesn't need to be. Outside, teens their age laugh loud, their voices muffled by the distance and the glass.

"Hey," Duncan whispers.

David looks to see a firecracker resting on his friend's palm. They've blown these up before. The parking lot at the TGIF. In Blankenship Park. David looks to the dark aisle. The shelves of books like solid black walls. He shakes his head no. No, it isn't worth it. What's one hour?

"Read," David says.

"Naw, do it," Larry says. Because of course he does. They will one day call Larry "the Egg." Because he always eggs the others on.

David and Jonathan look to the aisle. Pitch black. Is there a door at the other end? Did Mrs. Addison leave the room?

"Come on," David says, eyeing Duncan again. But Duncan is smiling.

They're sixteen years old. There is a disciplinarian exerting authority over them.

What does David expect Duncan to do?

Jonathan, of all people, pulls a lighter from his jeans.

David eyes the aisle.

Duncan slides his chair back. It's easy to be quiet on the carpet. He stands and David's heart picks up speed. It would be impossible to explain to his friends the want, the *need*, he felt when Mrs. Addison was talking about people drying out at the Edsel House. It was as if, for a second, David was *there*.

And did he actually see it? The inside of that place? Has he ever been there? What is this memory he has . . . ?

Duncan tiptoes to Jonathan's table. David grasps for a fleeting image of himself and a few others (strangers?) in the lounge area of that drunk house.

He smelled it. He *felt* it.

"Duncan . . ."

But Duncan is already crouched by Jonathan. They whisper.

David sees a spot of silver high up in the darkness of the aisle just as Jonathan flicks his lighter. David turns to his friends, to warn them, to say hey, maybe not, just as Larry joins the other two.

"Guys," David starts. But he can't get up. Not because somebody won't let him, but because, for the first time in his life, he's scared of making trouble.

Why?

He hears the wick burning first, then sees it. There's going to be an explosion. Here in the Chaps High library.

David looks to the aisle. Sees that sparkle of silver up high.

Duncan tosses the firecracker toward the head of the aisle.

He and Larry rush back to their tables. They're sixteen. They could've either been quiet like the woman told them to be or said fuck you instead.

They've said fuck you instead.

David eyes the burning wick.

The firecracker explodes.

Jonathan cries out. He pisses himself. Not because he's hurt, but because he sees the same thing the others do.

By the violent flash, the library aisle is revealed, and with it, Mrs. Addison crouched upon the top shelf, her face without expression, her eyes like silver, reflecting the light before it goes dark again.

"I'm not going down there," Jonathan says. "No way, David."

"I understand," David says. He does. They all do. But the horrifying realization that they are required to carry this out today while being wholly unprepared isn't fading.

They have to do what they came to do.

"We may have no choice," David says.

"She's making you do it," Larry says.

Larry. Back from whatever false reality she'd given him.

The huge hole in the forest floor is silent.

"No," David says. "She wants us to wait. She wants us to wait until we fall asleep. Until we make a mistake."

"We need to go home," Jonathan says again.

The fear is driving David insane. Could Jonathan please act strong?

"We already went over that," David says. "If we leave—"

A sound from the hole. A deep intake of breath.

David thinks of Barb. Knows they all do.

The four friends inch back.

"How would we get down there anyway?" Duncan asks.

They are each aware that whatever Mrs. Addison was doing to them moments ago, she's not doing it now.

Is she resting? Does she *need* rest? Was that intake of breath . . . sleep?

"She gets in and out somehow," David says.

As if this means anything. As if, because a witch can get down there, so can they.

"Rope?" Duncan asks.

At least he's talking progress.

It gives David a sliver of hope.

Yet . . .

"We don't have any."

"Shoulda brought some," Larry says.

"Yes, we should've."

"Why didn't we, David?"

Panic in his friend's voice. The heat of hysteria on the horizon.

"We didn't know what we were doing."

"Do we now?"

David breathes deep. It should all be so much simpler than this. He needs a good shot. A straight sight line. He needs to *see* Mrs. Addison like he's seen a deer. Just one sure moment. One look. One—

Is Mrs. Addison peering out of the hole right now?

Do you see a face, David?

David raises his rifle and fires it at the rim.

The sound explodes through all of Werther Woods. Sticks crack. Wings take flight.

And through the rising smoke of the barrel, David sees Barb.

"Oh, Jesus," he says. "Oh, no."

"David," Jonathan says. "Do you see her, too?"

"Barb . . ." Larry says.

Duncan falls to his knees.

Yes, David sees her, too.

Barb is half out of the hole, half in. Her face is obscured by her hair.

There is blood in that hair.

As if shot. Yes. Shot by David.

Just as she was escaping Mrs. Addison's nest.

David first starts thinking of frequencies when the boys meet Barb. It's not that she's "lower" than they are, David doesn't look at life that way, but the events in Chaps High library have sent each of the teens into decided confusion, denial, fear, all these rotating counterclockwise, bringing the friends something resembling depression. How to fight it? They're too young to either accept or not accept what they saw with their own eyes. It's easiest not to talk about it. To distract themselves with meaningless activities. To get into more trouble, bigger trouble, even if it means never going back to that school at all.

That's what they do. They stop going to school. They drop out. It'll be weeks before their parents are notified of this, and truthfully, none of their parents care. And would it matter if they did? What they saw in that library . . .

They'd rather not face it. And in turning away, an entire *other* world is revealed. A world in which people their age don't go to school. A world in which the futures of these people are different than the futures of the people they passed in the high school halls only days before. If you blow up a teeter-totter out here? So what. If you get caught? So what. Go see a judge. Go see a counselor.

So long as it isn't Mrs. Addison in the library.

"Girl," Duncan says, like a hunter might say "deer." It's as little description as possible. Yet, profound. A girl? Out here on the streets of Chaps? In the middle of the day?

Girl is not yet *woman.* What is a girl their age doing out here?

The boys are congregated at the head of the alley next to the Million Dollar Shot, Chaps's only bar with a pool table. They haven't cajoled the man Brian to let them inside yet. But he certainly lets them lurk. And there's a feeling that, with time, and charm, they'll make their way in. They'll become regulars. They'll get so good at pool people will make movies about them. *The Four Chaps from Chaps.* They'll get good at drinking. They'll wear sweet jackets. Boots. They'll learn how to talk with women. They'll be respected, desired. They'll win games. Money. Reputations. Brian will wink at them from across the bar and say, *Glad I finally let you in.*

Brian won't let them in. Not yet. So, outside they stay. In plain sight, yes, but also barely. The deeper shadows of the alley like a cloak. If a cop comes up Wanda Street? One step back into the shadows does the trick.

Just like when Mrs. Addison stepped into the shadows of that aisle of books.

The boys don't talk about this.

"Who's she?" Larry asks.

But they don't know. How could they? The Million Dollar Shot is a million miles from Chaps High. They're not seeing any part of the world with the same eyes.

Frequencies . . .

David thinks of it. Theory at first sight. He and this girl, he knows, would never have crossed paths, not in any way, if he and his friends weren't hiding from the life they used to live. If they hadn't dropped out of high school. If they hadn't dropped a few frequencies . . . lower.

"Let's introduce ourselves," Duncan says. And because he's said it, they must.

Barb sits on a half-wall made of bricks, a half-block farther into the light. She wears black pants, a black shirt, has black hair. David has heard the term "goth" before, but he doesn't know if that's what she is. Her eyes are on the concrete sidewalk.

What does she see there? David wants to know.

"Hello there," Duncan says.

The girl looks up.

"Yes?" she says.

"Just saying hi. Saw you over here."

She tilts her head in a way that will haunt the boys for a long time. They'll all want to see that tilt again.

"Hi," David says. "I'm David, this is Duncan, Jonathan, and Larry. We're just hanging out. Saw you doing the same."

She nods. She seems to react well to this direct, factual approach.

"Do you go to school?" Larry asks.

"No more than you do," she says.

"Did you drop out, too?" Jonathan asks.

This she ponders.

"I never went."

"Never?"

"Nope."

"Why not?"

They all want to hear this answer. It's all they've been talking about at the head of the alley for days; school. Who needs it?

The girl stands up.

"I'm gonna go now. Nice to meet you."

Jonathan looks to David like he might save them. Might get her to stay.

"Wait, what's your name?" David asks.

"Barb," she says. "Like," she raises her hands like claws, "*barbed wire.*"

The boys don't laugh. Then Barb does. It's so wonderfully out of place, it adds so much character to the little they know so far, that it's as if the sun got hotter.

"That was a joke," she says. "Maybe not a great one. But still."

David smiles. This girl, Barb, she's cool.

Barb gives them a little wave and heads up the street.

"Where are you going?" Larry asks.

Barb turns back.

"Just walking," she says. "It helps."

"Helps what?" Jonathan asks.

But David feels like he knows what it helps. He can't explain it exactly, but he has a flash, a quick memory of throwing up in the Chaps High library. Walking away from it, forever, sounds good.

"Listen," she says. "If you wanna walk, too, that'll be fine. But let's do it already."

The boys look back to the alley. As if they are somehow committed to staying close to it. As if they have a connection with any one place at all in this whole world.

"Okay," David says. "We'll walk with you, Barb."

"Great," she says. "But not so many questions, deal?"

They all heartily agree. Sure. Okay. Sorry. It's just, a girl! Walking alone in Chaps! The middle of the day! You understand, right, Barb? Oh, that's another question, isn't it! Laughter. Are you always like this, Jonathan? Haha. But she remembered his name! She remembers all their names! Yet, while this stroll through the industrial parts of Chaps ought to electrify the four boys, the only lightning David feels is the kind that darkens the sky before bolts strike the earth. Sure, they're young. Yes, they're in the company of a girl (though, she seems more like a woman after all). And yes, it feels like they have the city to themselves, but still . . .

Frequencies. It took a horrifying event David can barely make sense of to send him and his friends to the place where Barb exists. What did she see to send her here? It's not a requirement that "birds of a feather" have similar tastes, similar sense of humor, similar style. Most people meet because they're traveling along the same frequency. Tuned into the same station. And David isn't sure he likes the one they're on.

It's just a feeling he can't quite shake.

Nor can the boys shake their questions. And Barb, it turns out, is more willing to answer them than she first let on. With each sliver of her life revealed, the sun lowers, and the boys attempt to make sense of their warring emotions.

It doesn't take long to worry about Barb like they would an old friend.

David understands immediately: this isn't a romantic story of a glorious autumn in which four teenagers learn the meaning of life from a lone fifth. This isn't the story of outcasts coming together, discovering joy at last. This is the boys and Barb, Barb and the boys, most of their time spent together actually spent apart, both figuratively and literally, as the boys talk endlessly of her at the head of the alley, especially on the days she doesn't pass by. They do not speak of crushes. They don't see Barb that way. It's silently understood, from the start, that Barb is untouchable, she exists behind glass, they are lucky to know her, but only lucky to a point.

"I always feel like the last time we saw her is the last time we'll ever see her," Larry says, uncharacteristically philosophical.

The others feel the same. David doesn't know how to express what he's thinking; that it's not Barb herself that feels always out of reach, but the frequency they've tuned into. How can anybody really connect if they've met in a place like this, feeling like this?

They know Barb's story now. They know her parents suck. Her father is MIA and her mother is MIA and she's home alone a lot when she's home at all. She hasn't told them everything, David can tell. But he isn't sure he wants to know the rest. It's enough to feel where she's at, the same place *he's* at, using all his youth and strength to resist a life spoiled too soon.

Barb knows more about the world than the boys do. She's been in it longer.

She also knows Mr. Addison.

When she spoke his name the first time, the others avoided each other's eyes. David felt a sickness rise in him that quickly subsided. But the nerves remained. Barb said the Chaps Police found her drunk in Blankenship Park and escorted her straight to the Edsel House. They had no follow-up questions when she said she didn't know where her parents were, didn't go to school. When they pulled up the circular drive, Mr. Addison was waiting outside. Bearded and big, he asked what she'd had to drink and how much of it. Barb spit on the concrete. Mr. Addison asked her again. Told her he could arrange it so she was stuck in a place like the Edsel House for a long time. Did she want that? Of course not. Did she want to tell him what the fuck she had to drink instead then?

"He said that?" Jonathan asked. By then, the boys were wearing jean jackets. At sixteen, it wasn't yet embarrassing, dressing the same. "He said *fuck*?"

"He did."

Barb told them how she had to register. Had to sign her name and address. Her parents' names, too. She said she made them up. The boys thought that was cool. She told them she sat in a waiting room for four hours before a woman told her she could go.

Larry asked what the woman looked like. He tried to make it sound like any old question, but David knew he was asking if she'd seen Mrs. Addison.

Barb didn't remember.

So, yes, they know her story now. They also know a bit more. Barb made contact, after all, with the husband of the source of their confusion. Yet, despite hearing Mr. Addison described, the boys don't talk about him, and they sure as shit don't talk about his wife after Barb leaves them for the day. Or the week. Or forever, like it always feels like, whenever she heads up the street again alone.

By now, Brian is letting the boys into the Million Dollar Shot. Maybe it's the jean jackets. Or maybe he believes a few more bodies will bring a few more yet. They're not allowed to drink, of course, but they pretend their Pepsis are half Jack Daniel's, like they heard the Rat Pack used to drink. They like those guys. Learned about them from the walls in the Million Dollar Shot. Sinatra's mug shot is framed at about the fifty-yard line of the pool table. Duncan quotes

Sammy Davis Jr. jokes. Jonathan has taken to claiming Joey Bishop. David thinks it's because he likes the name. It's a good name.

They're having so much fun in the Million Dollar Shot, playing pool all afternoon, chatting with the regulars, sneaking shots of Crown Royal when Brian steps into the office, that they hardly realize it's been ten days since they last saw Barb. It had gotten to about twice a week, her slouched form passing the front glass like the Bat-signal, sending the four clamoring outside to greet her. But they are distracted now. Or, perhaps, because of the surname Addison, they are intentionally avoiding thinking of her. They haven't mentioned her absence, nor do they plan to. But, at a frequency like this, they don't need to plan.

A friend of Barb's brings news of her instead.

It's a bright midday in Chaps when David spots a redheaded girl standing outside the front glass of the Million Dollar Shot. He elbows Duncan, who raises a Pepsi to the girl like he read he should do in a book about the Rat Pack. The girl surprises them by waving the duo outside. They're quickly joined by Larry and Jonathan because, at sixteen, everybody moves together.

The girl's name is Lynn. She says she was in the Edsel House with Barb. That's where Barb's been. The boys realize then that she hasn't been around, and that maybe they should've noticed. Lynn says Barb doesn't want to be there. Barb got caught drinking again in Blankenship Park and was driven back to the Edsel House and Mr. Addison locked her up in a room there.

"He can do that?" Duncan asks.

"No," Lynn says. "No, he cannot do that. But he has done that."

"So, what do we do?" David asks.

Lynn sighs likes she's annoyed, like they're missing the point. Mr. Addison isn't even the problem, she says. It's the man's goddamn fucked-up wife.

The boys stand up a little straighter. They don't look each other in the eye.

"Mrs. Addison watches her eat," Lynn says. "The lady sits alone at a table in the corner of the cafeteria and watches Barb eat. Three times a day. Barb said she sees her in the hallways at night. Believes she was hiding in the shower one night when Barb had to pee. Barb didn't check. She doesn't like her. And she thinks the woman is getting closer to her."

"Closer?" David asks. "What does that mean?"

"I don't fuckin' know," Lynn says. "Inching her way toward her, I guess. Every day. She's scaring her is what matters. Barb asked me to come fetch you four. Asked you to bust her out."

"What?" David asks.

Lynn rolls her eyes.

"Do what you do. Break some laws. Be bad. Make it happen. She's in there right now. That lady is perched on her goddamn bedframe by now for all I know."

David feels chills.

"Did she say Mrs. Addison was perched on her bedframe? Did she *say* that?"

It's the first time he's spoken her name since the Chaps High library.

"I don't know," Lynn says, bothered. "She might have. Who cares? I just got out of there myself. Came straight here. Told her I would."

The boys finally look at one another. Something's starting, no? It feels like something bad has begun.

Or perhaps it's been on its way for a while.

"Did you ever see her there?" Jonathan asks.

"Are you dense?" Lynn says. "She sent me."

"No, not her," Jonathan says. "Mrs. Addison."

He's said her name now, too.

"I don't think so," Lynn says. "No picture comes to mind when Barb talks about her. Sounds like a psycho to me. Glad not to know her. But you guys . . . do what's right."

With that, she nods to each in turn, then leaves them, up the street into whatever life she lives on this frequency. The four friends stand by the head of the alley again, only now they move over, suddenly not wanting that length of shadow behind them.

"Let's drink," Larry says. He knows they won't, technically, drink. But that's what they call it.

The boys start to head inside but David doesn't move. Not yet. And when they turn to face him, Jonathan looks scared. Because he knows what David is about to say.

"We gotta bust her out," David says.

And the high sun doesn't remove any of the chill the statement delivers.

Okay. But how? They know nothing about the Edsel House, nothing practical. Nothing about security, locks, orderlies. They have no concept of what obstacles stand in the way between themselves and Barb, a prisoner inside. How prepared do they have to be? What will happen to them if they get caught? Is it a federal building? Can they go to jail for life if they break in? Are there armed guards? Could they get shot?

Ultimately, none of this matters. Any four members of the real Rat Pack would've busted out their fifth. So, David, Duncan, Jonathan, and Larry will do it, too. They have youth on their side. That's something. They're still at an age where authority, real authority, bends a little. If they get caught breaking into a drunk house? Forget it. Kids being kids. They'll receive more than a slap on the wrist, okay, but the risk is worth saving their friend. They couldn't live with themselves if they don't at least try.

For Barb.

Yet, for all the talk of potential obstructions, none have yet mentioned the real concern.

Mrs. Addison is in that building.

Or she *could* be. Could be watching Barb eat, sitting Medusa-stone still at a corner table. Could be watching Barb nap. Could be perched above her on a high shelf, on a vent, wedged where the walls meet the ceiling.

Yes, breaking into a city building is one thing, a rush all its own. But a woman capable of making you believe you're somewhere else is inside that building, too.

Youth wins in the end.

"Three doors," Duncan says, rounding the Edsel House, rejoining the others under the shade of the boundary of Werther Woods. "Well, four since the front is really two."

"Three ways in," David says.

"I didn't say that." Duncan smiles. He's sweating. Partly for having rounded the place on foot. But also because he's nervous. "Windows galore. And I'm sure there's a way in on the roof."

The four look up the length of tall bricks leading to the top.

"Are they locked?" Larry asks. "The doors?"

Duncan doesn't know. He didn't try.

"Okay," David says. "I say we try the back door. There's gotta be some kind of check-in desk at the front. Less chance of being seen through the back."

"We don't know that," Jonathan says.

Well, of course they don't. They don't know anything. Least of all where Barb is inside.

"We could each test a door," Jonathan says. "One of us plays lookout here. Waits for the other three to come back."

"You're scared," Larry says.

But Larry is, too.

"Dude," Jonathan says, angry. "I'll check the back fucking door myself."

He's up and walking. The others follow. They leave the cover of the trees and move purposefully across the mowed grass out back. They look quickly to the dozens of windows. The sun glares off each. Somebody must be looking back, right? An orderly, a secretary, a patient? A cook, a clerk, a counselor?

Mrs. Addison?

"Hurry," David says.

They do.

Before trying the back door, they press their faces to the glass. The inside is poorly lit, but they can see enough to determine there's no people. Just an unused plastic chair against a cold blue wall.

Duncan grips the handle.

"Wait," David says. "What do we with her?"

"What do you mean?"

"When we find Barb. What the hell do we do with her?"

"We bust her out," Jonathan says.

"We get her the hell out of here," Larry says.

David is wise enough to think they need more of a plan than that, but young enough to agree.

"Okay," he says, "try it."

Duncan pulls.

It opens.

Muzak greets them. The music of every grocery store and mall.

"Shhh," David says.

But he doesn't have to say it. The boys are quiet as they inch through the hall, the sound of a far-off typewriter joining the plain music. Their sneakers squeak but there is enough activity, deeper in the place, for cover.

At the hall's end, they look left. A dead-end wall. They look right.

It's a long way to what looks like the lighted foyer. A woman passes in high jeans, glasses. The typewriter continues.

The boys walk up the hall without speaking, looking into the small rectangular windows above each doorknob they pass. They do not speak, they do not plan. At the foyer, David sees a desk. But nobody behind it.

The unmistakable sounds of a cafeteria come from a hall past the desk.

The boys move slow, they pass the desk, take the hall.

At the door to the cafeteria, a man speaks to them.

"You guys new?" the man asks.

He sits alone, sipping orange juice.

"Yes," David says, his heart hammering. "Do you know Barb?"

The man squints. He's suspicious. But he smiles.

"One floor up. Room six. She's cool."

"Yeah."

"Are you helping her out of here?"

The question is so on point, it startles David silent. The man lifts his hands to say he doesn't give a shit either way.

"Don't answer that. Only, I hope you do. No place for a young person."

"Why are you here?" Larry asks.

"I work here."

"Oh shit."

"No. Don't worry. She's upstairs. Go on. Get her."

"Where do we take her?" David asks. "How do we sneak her out?"

"I can pretend I didn't see you, but I can't pretend I didn't plan it out for you. Know what I mean?"

David nods.

"Go on."

They move quick to the foot of the stairs, up the stairs, moving like they live here.

They do not stop as they take the hall.

Room 1. Room 2. Room 3. They're almost running, but still quiet. Still cool. David is in the lead. Room 4. Room 5.

Room 6.

It's empty.

A bed. A shelf. Blank walls. No sign of Barb at all.

"Shit," David says.

'Cause now they have to search the building, now they have to stay longer.

"Where is she?" Jonathan asks.

Larry and Duncan exit. David steps to the window. Looks outside.

Sees Mrs. Addison dragging Barb into Werther Woods.

He opens his mouth to speak, can't believe what he's seeing.

Yes. It's Mrs. Addison.

Dragging Barb.

Into Werther Woods.

"*She's got her!*" David yells.

He's already out of the room and running up the hall before the others can ask what he saw. He tells them as he takes the stairs two at a time. Three.

"Mrs. Addison took Barb into the woods!"

The boys pass people who might work here, might not. They barrel toward the back door, then out the back door, across the grass. David is in the lead. But not for long. Duncan is faster. He overtakes him at the boundary of trees, just as the four friends enter a forest they do not know the scope of.

It occurs to David that they also don't know what lives here.

What lives at this frequency.

They are young, sixteen, they move with more bravado than fear. The scale tips in their favor. There is no other way to do this. Duncan up front, then David, Jonathan, Larry. They move through thick trees, squeeze through smaller openings, leap fallen trunks, rise with the hills and stumble with the drops. Their matching jean jackets make them a stream of blue in this brown and gray world.

Duncan is so far ahead the others lose sight of him. They run, sweating now, thinking of Barb. Recalling (without admitting it) the image of Mrs. Addison crouched on the bookshelf, her eyes silver as spoons.

"Duncan!" David calls. Because he's worried about his friend. None of this feels right. None of this feels safe. The gray in here. The sense of something crawling up your arms, your back. The smell.

Ahead, smoke?

Duncan?

"Duncan!" David calls.

There he is, standing still, his eyes on his feet.

By the time they catch up, Duncan is mumbling. Talking to himself.

"Duncan," David says, out of breath. "What's wrong?"

Because something's wrong.

"I served my time," Duncan says. David doesn't like the look in his eyes. Like Duncan is talking to people who are not here. "It's been a helluva time in AA, but I'm gonna go celebrate. With a drink!"

He laughs. Like he made a joke others, unseen, will get.

But there are no others. Only his friends.

David grabs his arm.

Duncan turns on him fast, eyes wide.

"David?"

"Duncan, what's going on?"

"David?" he asks again. "I just got out of rehab. I just . . . didn't I just get out of rehab?"

David and Jonathan exchange a quick look. They, too, experienced the unreal in the presence of Mrs. Addison.

Is she near?

"Did you see her?" Larry asks. "Did you see Barb?"

Duncan looks to Larry. He slowly turns, exposing a clearing in the trees the others had yet to notice.

In the center of the clearing is a hole in the ground.

"I think . . ." Duncan says. "I think they went . . ."

The boys step closer to the edge.

They peer over its rim.

They listen.

"No way they went down there," Jonathan says.

But, why not? The shadows below are no different than any. Certainly no different than the shadows that hung at the far end of the aisle of books in the Chaps High library.

"Barb?" David calls.

There is no echo. Only the flat thud of her name.

"This is insane," Duncan says. "I was . . . I just got out of rehab."

He says it with a smile, but there is no humor there. He's scared. David can tell he still believes it.

And he will. For years. Here and there. As the boys recede back to their lives, back to high school, when even the alley and the Million Dollar Shot no longer feel like safe havens to stop them from thinking about Mrs. Addison. Or thinking about Barb. By returning to their former lives, they will never run into Barb again. Never cross the streets. They fool themselves into believing they are living, once again, at a higher frequency.

But what did become of Barb? Did she still wander the industrial streets of downtown Chaps? Did she get help in the Edsel House? Did the boys leave her to rot in a nest in the forest floor?

They tell the police. The police assure them they will look. But the boys never check up. Never call the station. Never call the Edsel House, either.

Barb was a blip on their life arc. An anomaly now.

It's all too much to think about. None of them talk about it at all. They do not theorize. They do not look for Barb. Every now and then Duncan references his time spent in the Edsel House. As if he were a patient there. As if he went through rehab, successfully, after all. In these moments, David reminds his friend that he's never attended a meeting at the Edsel House. But David is not always there to do this. No. Fifteen years flow between then and now and the four disperse the way even best friends do. None move out of town. None entirely leave Chaps. They move on without ever saying so.

David comes close to convincing himself that he did not see Mrs. Addison dragging Barb into the woods. Because if he *did*, if he saw what he thought he saw, then not only has he turned his back on a young woman who might've been saved, but their deep-rooted suspicions of what Mrs. Addison is could be true.

Life goes on.

The boys go on.

They drive out of the way to avoid the Edsel House.

They bowl.

They drink.

They meet women and they watch sports and they hunt.

They grow up.

And with growing up comes leaving sixteen behind. And the insane things you believed when you were that age. For this, they get by. They adjust. They carry on.

Until . . .

Until one night at Blowers Bar in downtown Chaps, when David adds a surprise round of shots to the first pitcher they order. At age thirty-one, the men know it means something when shots start the night. Something to celebrate? The others don't think so. There's nothing festive in David's eyes.

They wait for him to speak. There's no use pretending he has nothing to say.

"I saw her entering Werther Woods yesterday. I was working on paving the road outside the courthouse. I saw Mrs. Addison entering Werther Woods alone."

"It's not her," Duncan says.

Because it's too terrible if it is. How long has it been? Fifteen years? A decade and a half? There would be no coming back from a discovery like that; to find out that, as the boys did finish school, as they dated and drank, bowled and bow hunted, Barb's been in this hole the whole time. It suddenly feels (overwhelmingly, horribly) like they could've done so much more. *Should've* done so much more. Should've dedicated their lives to finding her.

But they told the police. The police said they'd look into it. What more could they have done?

"But I think it *is* her," Larry says.

Is he crying?

David wants to move. Either closer to or farther from the hole. But this standing still and staring at it cannot end well.

Mrs. Addison wheezes from down below.

Barb (if it's her) lies half-in, half-out. Her face is obscured by the dirt and her own hair. The part that chills David the most is that her hair almost matches that dirt. Both being gray. Is it just the light, the lack of true light, in Werther Woods? Or has Barb aged below?

"She couldn't have survived years down there," Jonathan says. "Not a chance."

"Ready your guns," David says. "We're going to the rim."

Mrs. Addison wheezes below.

David moves first and the others follow, as close to synchronization as they can get, four men stepping, afraid, guns leveled at their target.

"Come out, Mrs. Addison," David says, his voice distorted by tears. For Barb, yes, whether that's her or not. But for him and his friends, too. For the constant shadow they've grown up under, the shadow of a witch flying on a broom by the moon.

"*Come out, Mrs. Addison,*" David yells this time. He does not look to the form of Barb at the rim's edge. They are close now.

Ten feet.

Nine feet.

Does he want Mrs. Addison to spring out? To make a break for it? Does he want this to come to an end?

Eight feet. Larry is yelling. Facing it.

Seven feet.

Six feet.

Jonathan starts yelling, too.

Five feet.

Four feet.

David is shaking, isn't sure he could even hit a hole this wide with the gun.

Three feet.

She's gonna erupt out of the hole. He knows she is. She has to.

Two feet.

Duncan yells now, too, readying himself.

One foot.

David pisses himself. His pants go warm.

At the rim, the four peer over the edge. The gray earth looks like a giant's throat, ashen tissue leading to a black end below.

But not entirely black. Two small silver ovals look back up at them.

"*Fire!*" David says. He thinks he says it. It doesn't matter. The boys unload their rifles, everything they got, into the hole in Werther Woods. Jonathan is screaming like he's firing on his youth, his fear, everything that's ever done him wrong. Through the lights and smoke, David sees Larry's face lit up, a mask of horror and hate, firing, firing, firing. One man reloads as another shoots again. An endless pouring of metal into the gullet of Mrs. Addison's nest.

Eventually, they run out of ammo.

Jonathan's yell lasts longer than the shots do.

David waits for the smoke to clear.

They should run, he thinks. They should back up.

But he has to know. He has to see if those two silver ovals are still looking up.

Jonathan still yells. It seems to be going on forever. Too long. Impossibly long.

David looks to his friend and sees he's seated at a table in the Chaps High library.

David sits at one of his own next to Duncan's.

Larry is here, too.

David looks ahead. Sees an empty table facing theirs.

He knows they did something wrong, but he can't remember what exactly. He thinks to look to his arms, something about a note there, a reminder. But his arms are covered in dirt and smoke.

"Duncan?" he asks.

"Yeah man."

"Where are we?"

"Detention, man."

"For what?"

"For blowing shit up."

"Shhh," Jonathan says.

He says it like he's scared.

David looks to the front table, to a dark aisle of books just past it.

What's back there? He doesn't remember.

"How long have we been here?" David asks.

"I don't know," Larry says. "But we're gonna get in trouble if you keep talking."

David looks to a clock, sees it has no numbers, no hands. Just a big silver oval on the wall.

The color reminds him of something.

Reminds him of eyes.

He hurriedly wipes the dirt from his left forearm. There are words! Yes! A note, after all.

It says:

REMEMBER WHERE YOU ARE

But . . . where?

He wipes the other arm. Something there, too. One word:

DETENTION

David slumps into his seat. Detention? But they aren't kids anymore. He can plainly see Larry's blond beard, the gray at Jonathan's temples, his own strong arms.

"A little gang," a voice says. A woman's voice.

David grips the table.

She speaks again, from the darkness of that aisle:

"I have you for one hour. You will remain seated and quiet."

The men do not speak.

But David gets up.

He can't remember why he should be as scared as he is. Maybe it's Mrs. Addison's voice. Maybe it's the fact that she's not showing herself. He looks to the top of the bookshelf, as if, insanely, she might be up there.

He continues. Towards the darkness. Believing, somewhere deep inside, somewhere buried, it's the right thing to do.

He sees he has a gun in his hands.

He raises it, aims into the darkness he approaches.

"Mrs. Addison," he says. "We're not really here, are we?'

There is only wheezing from the shadows. And the sound, suddenly, of his friends behind him. Yes, David is not alone, heading into the black. Duncan, Jonathan, Larry all follow.

It feels right and wrong at the same time. Does this make sense, he wonders? Can something feel so perfectly righteous and terribly wrong at the same time?

At the very reach of the shadows, David pauses.

He looks down to his arms again.

REMEMBER WHERE YOU ARE

Jonathan passes him just as David makes to look at his other arm.
He sees his friend slip into the shadows, swallowed whole.

Larry's next.

Then Duncan.

It's like they planned this. All of them, David included. But
David simply cannot remember the plan.

His friends all inside, he breathes deep. He knows he's supposed
to enter this aisle, this nook, this nest. But he cannot remember why.

He looks down at his other arm. Reads the words there:

WERTHER WOODS

A vision of smoke and bright bursts comes to mind. Him and
his friends, shooting into a hole.

Why?

Were they practicing for this moment? David thinks maybe
that's so. Maybe they were readying themselves for whatever lies
ahead in the shadows. Whatever spoke to them.

He enters at last, following the others inside.

Because, remaining out here alone is definitely not the in the
plan. Whatever happens next, they will experience it together.
David knows that much. Whatever this is, they've gone through
it together.

As the shadows lap him up, David sees a spot of silver ahead.
And it feels, right now, like a good omen. Like the eye of something
good watching over him and his friends.

He lowers his gun.

"Duncan?" he says. "Jonathan?"

But there is no echo, no sense of distance, no time or place,
here in the dark aisle of the Chaps High library. Here in Mrs.
Addison's nest.

CHALLAWA
BY USMAN T. MALIK

"There's a ghost in the hut," said the guide, smiling. "Better watch your back in there." He paused, hand on padlock, one foot on doorstep, to allow me to snap a picture of him, perfect white teeth shining beneath a handlebar mustache.

Ed looked at me. "What did he say?"

I re-angled the camera and took another shot. "Ghosts of burnings past," I murmured.

"The hut is haunted, sir." The guide switched to an accented, flawless English. "Be careful when you go in," but his kohl-lined eyes held no humor now. When he turned to lead us into the hut, his lips pressed into a thin line.

The hut was cozy. Two rooms separated by a low arch. In one a woven jute charpai, a low chair, table, and a mirror hanging on the wall, in the other pots and clay utensils lined up on the bottom shelf of a mud-baked oven. Two cups under the faucet and a hookah with ash in the coal bowl indicated active occupancy of the room.

"The hookah is mine," said the guide, "but the cups are for the ghost."

Local lore then. "A water offering?"

"This close to the cremation ground he is always hot," he said. "Water does him good."

"Whose ghost is it?" I said, taking out my notebook to jot notes. "Ed, don't, okay?"

Ed dropped the sorghum broom he'd picked up.

"Place is an historical landmark. Let's not mess around. These things might be irreplaceable."

"Well, they are mostly props," said the guide. "The stuff with actual historical value is in Dr. Singh's private collection. You cannot trust visitors with artifacts." He was watching Ed.

I felt a twinge of irritation, the kind a parent might feel when someone else yells at their annoying child. "The matchboxes—those are props too?"

"Replicas." The guide retrieved a wooden box from the oven's bottom shelf and popped it open on the table. He pulled out a matchbox and offered it to me. The front was a sky-blue swirl centered by a Mughal king in profile. akbar-e-azam, read the label. "A vintage print from a hundred years ago. Dr. Singh had these specially made so the originals could be preserved. You won't find it anywhere else."

"Who?"

"Dr. Harcharan Singh. Businessman and heritage worker. His family's been custodians of Mai's hut for nearly a century, ever since Mai died. And we hope to continue the tradition for another century." This time his smile was warm. He was a tall, broad-shouldered man in his forties with a green turban that made him seem taller. Throw a suit on him and he might even be dashing. "Dr. Singh was my grandfather."

"Oh." I stared at him, feeling guilty. That explained his hookah in the hut. When I called the Heritage Division's office earlier, I assumed they'd send a peon to meet us at the cremation grounds. Our guide's simple attire—shalwar kameez, wool chador, a squat turban, and Peshawari sandals—had cemented my assumption. "I didn't realize—I'm sorry. What was your name again?"

"Gurpreet Singh, madam, and it is okay. I'm perfectly fine to be thought a chowkidar. A most important job. I enjoy showing visitors around here."

"Show 'em what?" Ed said, running his finger along the charpai's wooden frame, and snickered. "This here ain't worth shit."

"Ed," I said. He'd been bitching for three hours and I was pretty much done with it, even though I knew the reason. Maybe knowing made me even angrier. "Stop being an ass."

He shrugged. "You dragged me here, Karima. You knew I didn't want to come."

"Sorry I presumed a little bit of culture and history might do us both good. What was I thinking?"

"You mean, do *you* good. You're not here with me. You're here on a mission with that thing." He gestured at the pen poised above my notebook. "We could've gone to Fairy Meadows last night with the tour plane, but no, you wanted to take notes on this pile of trash—" He caught sight of Gurpreet's face and stopped. "What's your problem?"

"Mai Bhago was my great-aunt and this place belongs to my family, sir." Gurpreet's face had darkened. "We're hospitable people, but we do appreciate respect."

Ed gave him a withering look. When we met in college, Ed was a stout, muscular linebacker with a jawline that could cut glass, but years of office work had made him pale and doughy. The guide dwarfed him.

"You wanna go back to the resthouse," I said. "Be my guest. I'll Uber back or something," and turned to the guide. "I'm so sorry, Gurpreet sahib. Please accept my apology on my husband's behalf. He's tired." I shifted my foot, dismayed by how uncomfortable labeling our relationship felt. I shouldn't be afraid of the guide's judgment. I'd crossed that bridge years ago with my family. "Could we please go to the cremation grounds?"

"Sure, madam," Gurpreet said.

"This was a mistake." Ed strode to the door, then looked over his shoulder. His face had drawn in on itself. "I can't believe you're so removed from it all, Karima, so cold. I thought coming here'd help."

"What are you talking about?"

"I don't give a shit about Fairy Meadows, you know that. Today was the day, Karima."

Was that sadness in his voice? I stared at him hunched in the doorway, his back to me now, and I didn't want to stop him. There would be time later, I told myself.

Then Ed stepped out and walked away.

"Sorry you had to see that," I said, trying on a smile. "We got in three days ago and he's still jet-lagged. He tends to get a little grumpy when he's sleep deprived."

"No problem, madam." Without meeting my eyes, Gurpreet led me to a back door. "This way, please."

We went to see the shamshan-ghat.

A few years back when Jack invited Ed and me to his place in Peshawar, the irony wasn't lost on me. Jack's company had been collaborating on a CPEC energy project with a Chinese company and after five years in the area he considered himself a local.

"Come at the beginning of summer and I'll show you guys around," he said. I could hear his smile over the phone. Unlike Ed, Jack had managed to lose what he called his "redneck accent." The cutthroat corporate world made that a necessity, he said. "You can sightsee, trek up the mountains, visit Fairy Meadows in Gilgit-Baltistan. I know you've never been. Plus, Karima, you can visit your mom in Lahore for a couple weeks. Come on, make a month of it. It's not as if you don't know what to expect."

At the time I'd finished graduate school and was tiptoeing my way around my ill-tempered boss at the *Orlando Sentinel*. Ed and his guys were expanding the hardware store and he was drowning in work. We deferred the trip, but the conversation left me with an unpleasant aftertaste. Growing up in Pakistan, I was often taunted by my male cousins for not going to the "hilly areas" with them. Don't you want to travel by yourself to Kalam and Naran and GB, they said. Don't you just wish you could ride a motorbike all the way there?

A white man is living my life in a country I used to call home, I thought, before banishing the discomfort.

Now, four years later, when Jack called to invite us to the groundbreaking of his latest project, I didn't hesitate. It felt like I'd been waiting for the call, and in a way I was. I just hadn't thought up a timeline yet.

"You *must* come, Karima. This is the most extensive development gig my company's undertaken in the country. Hotels with hot tubs in every room, swimming pools, water sports, condos. I'll even pay for your ticket if you promise to write about it in your paper."

"You had me at hot tub." I giggled.

"Seriously! Drinks all around, baby. It's our largest land acquisition."

"Sounds like a hell of a deal. Of course we'll come," I said. "Won't we, Ed?"

"That what you want?" Ed said when I hung up. "Now?"

I shrugged, the good humor leaving me, draining my body. "Sure. I'd love to see Ma, and I can't think of a reason to keep us here, can you?" His jaw stiffened. "Besides," I said. "There's a place in the area I'd like to visit. Supposedly the site of the first ever matchbox factory in India."

He grunted. "You still working on that article?"

"You bet."

"How many months has it been?" We looked at each other cautiously. He considered, then nodded. "Well, maybe you do need a change of scenery. Maybe we both need it. I sure could use some time off too."

The smile on my face felt like it was drawn in hard mud with a stick. It hurt.

At the back of the hut the shamshan-ghat sloped down to Ganeshpur Lake in steps, each step lined with bricks to create a platform for pyres. Surrounded on three sides by sumbal, poplar, and kachnar trees, the lake stretched as far back as the eye could see, its blue-green water twinkling in the late afternoon sun.

Once the waters of the lake were deep and mountain-clean. Thousands of Hindus brought their dead every year to cremate them by the water and set their souls free. Now the cremation grounds were overgrown with weeds and wild grass and the lakeshore was littered with bottle caps and plastic bags that rose and tumbled past us in the early spring breeze.

Gurpreet had switched back to Urdu, obviously more comfortable in the language. "After Partition, most Hindus from around here migrated to India. We still have tiny communities here and there, but they keep a low profile, many preferring to bury their dead in the graveyard that abuts the shamshan-ghat."

I snapped a picture and leapt across a brick rim. "Why'd they change custom?" I said.

"Why do minorities of a country do anything?" He shrugged. "But, here, they remember the horrors of Partition well. One thing that unites the three communities—Hindus, Muslims, and Sikhs—is their dislike of invaders, the white man who tried to take our land from us, and, failing that, divided us before he left."

He pointed to a particularly large platform. "That was once reserved for rich Hindu families. And that is where the hut's ghost hails from."

"What do you mean?"

"Story goes that two hundred years ago a high-caste Brahmin fell in love with a Muslim girl. Their families were not happy. Long story short, the star-crossed lovers tried to elope and were caught by the girl's brothers. For besmirching their honor they made the girl watch as they cut the Hindu boy's wrists and buried him alive in the ground beneath that platform. Then they forced poison down their own sister's throat and set her corpse on fire in the shamshan-ghat at the place where the hut now stands. Neither was, thus, allowed last rites accorded by their religion."

"God, how horrible."

"Legend has it that their ghosts still wander the cremation grounds looking for each other. People have reported sightings of an ash-bride, a woman covered in ashes with a ghoonghat over her head, as well as strange glowing vapors in the graveyard and the ghat. They say the vapors take the form of a boy with bleeding wrists staring wistfully at the hut. He's always thirsty and returns to the place where his love was set aflame. There's even a local word for his kind of wispy ghost."

I shaded my eyes against the afternoon sun and scanned the ghat. No ghosts so far. "What?"

"Challawa. A mercurial creature that shimmers and is gone. A mirage that evaporates when you get close to it."

That rang a bell. Where had I heard that word before?

"Hindus have their own version of this sort of ghost. Vetala, a demon trapped in the twilight zone between life and afterlife. It haunts charnel grounds and possesses dead bodies, making them speak evil secrets."

"Ooh. Love it," I said, smiling. "I love ghost stories."

"Well, the truth's more boring, I'm afraid. Old bones, when burnt, give off a luminescence that can glow for hours. Belches of such glowing phosphorus fumes from charnel grounds can be quite frightening. That's the likely explanation for the rampant challawa reportings at shamshan-ghats."

I started, nearly dropping the camera. "What?"

He quirked an eyebrow. "Khairiat, madam? You look like you saw a challawa."

"Well," I said, feeling unreal. "One of the reasons I came here was to research the Bryant & Stevens matchstick factory and its relationship with a particular disease—"

"Oh? The factory on the highway? That's just a couple kilometers up the road."

"—which, in turn, was due to a particular chemical. Rather, an element. Phosphorus. Once called the devil's element because of its associations with alchemists and glowing skulls. A bit weird to hear of a local monster myth related to that."

"How interesting, madam."

"Yeah." I lowered the camera, let it dangle from my neck, and stared across the lake. "I've been living in interesting times lately."

* * *

My fascination with the devil's element began after my mother's jaw dissolved and fell out. She was visiting us in Florida, and one morning, as we sat on the patio watching geckos do push-ups, she sipped coffee, winced, and mentioned her teeth were hurting.

"Well, my right jaw, to tell the truth," she said, opening her mouth and pointing, "has been hurting for months."

I'd noticed her face was a little swollen, but figured it was another bad tooth. Ma's dental hygiene had always been less than optimal. She was the sort of woman who would take three antibiotics at the first sign of a sniffle and go find a backstreet doctor to pull a rotting tooth rather than pay for an annual check by a professional. It was the mohallah side of her: Rubina paid just a thousand rupees to get all her teeth cleaned by this GP in Samanabad—why should *I* pay more? Buy cheap, you'll cry a thousand times, buy expensive and you cry only once, Ma, I'd say, but it was futile. When I lived at home, before I moved for undergrad, it used to drive me mad, her miserliness, her perennial suspicion that the world was out to swindle her. It had been a relief to move away to a different world, where things made more sense. Or at least they used to.

It appeared her procrastinations had finally caught up with her.

"Probably an abscess," I said, getting up to take a look. "How long have you been putting it off?"

"Not long." She began to close her mouth, but I caught her jaw and tilted it. The molars in the bottom right row were a weird brown color. I looked closer, not believing my eyes. The entire row of teeth seemed *melted*. There remained a brownish mass, which I suddenly realized was not teeth but underlying bone with a pus-encrusted hole in the center. I could see her tongue through it.

"Ma," I cried. "What happened to your mouth?"

"Well, six months ago I had a toothache. Went to see a doctor in Ghari Shahu—nice fellow, good with dental stuff, Luqman told me. He pulled a tooth, said it was infected. A couple months later they all started falling out." She drew back and wiped her mouth.

"It's been hurting since. At my age these things can happen. I've been meaning to—"

"There's a *hole* in your jaw. That shouldn't happen at any age. You must be in agony."

Despite her protests that a couple Brufens would take care of the pain, I rushed her to the dental office by the hospital. They thrust metal clamps into her mouth to shut her grumbling and eventually announced that she had BROJ—bisphosphonate-related osteonecrosis of the jaw.

The masked blond dental assistant pointed at the med list Ma had given her. "The risk is about one in a hundred thousand with this medicine," she said.

"What medicine?" I asked. As far as I knew, Ma wasn't on any meds except the occasional allergy and heartburn pill.

She looked me up and down. "You *never* want to do a dental procedure while you're on it," she said sternly.

Turned out Ma was taking a bisphosphonate. She'd been taking it over-the-counter because Razia's doctor said it was good for bones. If one daily pill strengthened bones, Ma reasoned, a *double* dose would be doubly strengthening.

I wanted to kill her. Instead, I watched them clean out the pus and place aseptic dressing on the area, took the antibiotic and painkiller prescriptions, paid the dental bill—four hundred dollars *without* surgery: they said it'd be cheaper if she got the debridement in Pakistan—and took her home, where I yelled at her till I was hoarse. Silent, she took it, until guilt and remorse filled me and I apologized. This was a pattern we'd repeated for years, a regressive trap I couldn't seem to escape.

Later, when Ed asked me why her face was swollen, I told him it was an infected tooth—would be as good as new soon, I said.

We had Ma's return date changed and got her on the first flight to Lahore.

"Promise me," I said at the airport. "No more back-alley doctors. You need a good surgeon. I'll call Ali, he'll take you."

She held my face in her hands. This close, I could smell both the infection and the dressing in her mouth. "A daughter—" She kissed my forehead. "—is like an Eid moon: you see her only twice a year, but you're always glad when you do. Come visit me, Karima. Come home to your old ma soon."

Her cheeks were wet. For the first time, the thought occurred to me that maybe all her self-wounding, her continual denial of self-care, was a way of punishing herself for driving away her husband and, then, her daughter. Did she believe she was responsible for his behavior, or mine? Baba left because that's what he did, I understood it with a clarity that, sometimes, comes with age. He left because his feet wouldn't stay. The woman he left with was just an afterthought.

And I left for a better future, I told myself. For a better world, where I could wander at will, or, failing that, plant myself and stay rooted forever.

Was it my fault the ground beneath me had been salted and my roots burnt to cinders?

I wouldn't think on that.

Ed was watching TV when I got home. Without looking up, he asked me if all was well.

Yes, I said. I didn't tell him I'd used money from our savings account to pay Ma's dental bill. I wasn't telling him a lot of things in those days.

Not since I read his texts and saw the pictures in his phone.

"Well, you do know your folklore," I said. "Is there a book on all this challawa stuff that I could buy?"

Again, that vague stirring of memory at the mention of the word, slippery like an eel.

We were picking our way across the cremation grounds. No eerie vapors trembled in the corner of my eyes. No shining human bones among the grass and weeds. Minimal littering; whoever managed the shamshan-ghat had kept it reasonably clean.

Gurpreet flashed a brilliant smile. He really was a rather handsome man. I wondered if his childhood had been difficult, insular, surrounded, as it must have been, by a sea of orthodox Muslims. A Sikh kid who wore traditional headgear was a ripe target for bullies.

"The Qissa-Khwani Bazaar in Peshawar," he said. "The Bazaar of Storytellers. My family comes from there. We have maintained oral storytelling traditions. We believe stories, like music, need to be aired—loudly, lyrically, passionately, to come fully alive. You might find some books on challawa in regional languages, but most of these tales have been passed down for generations around hearth fires and cups of green tea. Want to hear another?"

He held out a hand to help me down a boulder. His hand was manicured, long-fingered, surprisingly slender.

"Sure," I said.

"In one version the challawa was an ancient warrior of enormous strength who challenged the gods and, as punishment, was turned into a beast—half man, half ox. Condemned this way, he would neither die nor live, but eternally roam the world. It won't directly pounce on its victims; instead it follows them at a distance. If you're a villager on a deserted, moonlit road you might glimpse it behind you in the shape of an enormous shimmering ox. As it follows you from place to place, it will gather information about your friends and relatives, then call out in their voices at night. If you turn around or stop, it will challenge you to a duel. If you grapple with it and win, you will have good fortune for seven generations. If you lose, it will rip you limb from limb."

A gust of ghat wind burrowed into my shirt. I shivered. "Great story, but, wow, macabre." And suddenly I remembered where I'd heard the term before. "I know a challawa story too," I said.

"Oh?"

I told him.

Children of the nineties growing up in the load shedding-infested summer days of Lahore, my cousins and I would tell each other scary stories in the dark. Tales of jinns, bhuts, and gangs of hathora killers and axe murderers who terrorized urban neighborhoods and killed little kids in their sleep. We frightened each other enough that, for an entire summer, we locked our doors and bolted our windows and used peepholes to prevent strangers from gaining access to our homes.

Like the best urban legends, these stories had kernels of truth.

In 1985 Karachi police were alarmed by a string of murders. The victims were beggars and street kids, all of whom were killed with a single hard blow of a hammer to the head. The moniker "hathora group" began to circulate on the street and the press. Countless theories were cooked up to explain the murders: It was General Zia's men who wanted to suppress political dissidents. No, KGB agents and American spies wanted sow terror for political gain. No, no, it was the work of a single crazed serial killer, a lone wolf.

The killings subsided for a bit, then reemerged in the nineties, at which time the name "challawa group" gained buzz. Supposedly this new group comprised incredibly agile young men who slathered black oil on their bodies, and, wearing only underwear, entered the homes of the rich through high, narrow windows. They injected the inhabitants with a soporific, then killed them, carefully laying out their organs on the bedspread. Then they plundered the house and escaped, their slippery bodies making it impossible for a pursuer to catch ahold of them.

This time the popular explanation involved satanic cults and ritualistic murder.

"Nice," Gurpreet said when I finished. "That should make an excellent addition to my repertoire of tales. You have a storyteller's blood, madam, anyone ever tell you? You take pictures, you write articles, you transmit histories. A rare gift." He touched my arm. "Allow me to repay you with one last challawa story, if you wish?"

"Make it worth my while," I said and leaned in.

In the spring of 1857, at the peak of British Raj in India, Dr. Gilbert Hadow, an army surgeon employed by the East India Company, wrote a letter to his sister in Britain.

"There is a most mysterious affair going on throughout the whole of India at present. No one seems to know the meaning of it. It is not known where it originated, by whom or for what purpose, whether it is supposed to be connected to any religious ceremony or whether it has to do with some secret society. The Indian papers are full of surmises as to what it means.

"It is called the chapati movement."

One morning, Mark Thornhill, a magistrate in a little Indian town near Agra, came to his office to discover four chapatis, "dirty little cakes of the coarsest flour, about the size and thickness of a biscuit," lying on his desk. They'd been brought in by one of his Indian police officers who, in turn, received them from a puzzled village chowkidar.

"A man had come out of the jungle with them," said Thornhill, "and given them to the watchman with instructions to make four like them and to take these to the watchman in the next village, who was to be told to do the same."

Close examination of the unleavened bread cakes was unrevealing: no messages, marks, or secret signals. Yet, thousands of such unmarked chapatis were being distributed to homes and police check posts by runners in the cover of night.

"Pass it on," went the whisper.

Quietly the recipients accepted the offering, baked more, and raced them over to the next village. Thornhill estimated that these "culinary letters" were traveling through the empire at a speed of three hundred kilometers per night—much speedier than the fastest British mail. Within weeks the phenomenon had swept the entirety of India: from the northwest provinces to the Narmada River in the south to the Nepalese border hundreds of miles in the northeast.

The anomalous chapati chain spooked the British because they couldn't make sense of it. Was it a call to arms, a prelude to mutiny? Runners who were caught often turned out to be police chowkidars themselves. Nearly ninety thousand Indian policemen were apparently passing on chapatis concealed in their turbans. When interrogated they seemed to have neither a clue as to the meaning of the chain nor explanation of the compulsion they felt in making the bread and sending it on to its mysterious destination.

Indians, on the other hand, claimed it was the work of the British. A famous prophecy held that the British—who, by proxy of the East India Company, had ruled India for nearly a hundred years—would be unseated at the end of the century. They had recently introduced the infamous Enfield cartridge, which had to be bitten open so the powder inside could be poured down the barrel of the muzzle-loading gun. The cartridges were greased with tallow, which Muslims and Hindus knew was made of pork and beef fat in Britain. Biting the bullet would defile them. Once defiled, the eater would be shunned by his co-religionists, become casteless, and thus be forced to convert to Christianity, they thought.

Perhaps the British were now adulterating Indian flour with a special dust—bone meal made from cows and pigs—and spreading this chapati strain across India, trying to trick the locals into eating them. Another scheme to keep them subjugated to the British will forever.

Whatever its meaning, the chapati movement proved prescient.

Within a few months, the largest and fiercest mutiny the British would encounter in India—the Sepoy Rebellion of 1857—would engulf the subcontinent, threatening the Crown Rule and nearly bringing the Raj to a bloody end.

The British came down hard on the mutineers. The notorious General Neill massacred thousands of Indian sepoys and civilians suspected of supporting the rebellion. They were shot, hanged, even blown from the mouth of a cannon, their limbs scattered all over the depot ground. One Indian historian estimates that nearly ten million Indians were killed over the next ten years as a result of the Raj's policies after the War—an "untold Holocaust," as he put it.

"The 1857 War of Independence failed, but it heralded the end of Crown rule in India: in less than a century the British would forfeit India for good. But to this day neither the white master nor his brown subject really knows what the chapati chain-mail was all about," Gurpreet said.

"Horrifying," I said. "But where's the challawa in all this?"

"There's a well-known peasant ritual to ward off plague. When smallpox breaks out in an Indian village, a large, healthy goat or an ox is procured. One by one the entire village touches a sacred coconut, which is tied to the animal's horns. The village chowkidar then walks the goat to the nearest village; it is not allowed to enter the town but is taken by another villager to the next hamlet, and so it passes on, without rest, to its final destination—which, of course, can only be death."

"Ghastly." I shivered.

"This ritual of 'passing on a malady' was called challawa." Gurpreet turned and looked at me. "Perhaps in the year 1857 the entirety of India took up the magical ritual. Perhaps the very land and its inhabitants *became* challawas in an attempt to dispel the plague that was the white man."

He let the words linger in the air. I savored them. "Intriguing that so much of the challawa mythology—the plague-passing; the warrior who defied the gods and was turned into an ox; the breaking and entering of the sinister trickster thieves into rich homes—takes on notes of defiance that has turned violent. Resistance," I mulled, "that leads to transformation."

"Maybe, like all myths and legends—" Gurpreet tugged at the hem of his turban. "—the challawa is a mirror that takes on the reflection of the world before it. Whether the mirror is supernatural or not, who can say." He smiled.

We were walking back up the slope toward the road. The wind had picked up and despite my cashmere sweater my bones felt cold as ice. A cellphone rang. I pulled out my phone, knowing perfectly well the sound didn't come from me. No message from Ed. I sighed. Was he sulking in our bedroom or sightseeing the city on his own? Then I saw my cell signal strength was at the lowest bar.

Gurpreet was peering at his phone, his face grim.

"You getting a good signal?" I asked. "I'm getting zilch."

"Variable. What service do you have?"

"T-Mobile. I'm on roaming."

"Ah, local networks tend to work better here." He put his phone away, looked at the sky. "We better hurry if you want to see what remains of the matchstick factory."

The factory. Lost in this maze of myth and story, I'd nearly forgotten about it. I glanced up and was startled to see how dark it was. Evening had lowered itself on the receding lakeshore and a thousand bright points, fireflies, flickered across the foliage. In the poplar trees by the lake something hooted and stirred the branches. A monkey perhaps.

"Yes, please," I said. "And on the way you can tell me about Mai Bhago's hut and the matchstick factory."

"Your wish, madam," Gurpreet said, giving me that dazzling smile, "is my command."

I will kill you, then I will kill myself, I told Ed. Were you thinking of her the entire time you were fucking me, even as I carried your baby?

He begged me not to leave. A moment's weakness, Karima, he said. I was overworked and tired. And she texted me out of the blue after years. We met up only once at her place. I made a terrible mistake, but I love you and this baby. Never again, Karima.

I will kill this baby, I screamed. Slumped on the bathroom floor, my shock-whitened hands cradling my belly, I said, You will never touch me again.

In the end I stayed, but his groveling wouldn't melt the cold that boxed my heart. I tried to forgive him, but his face had become the face of my father and in my bedroom mirror walked a woman with a canny resemblance to my mother.

Restless feet, she said, grinning at me.

I love him, he's not like Baba, I told the woman in the mirror. He made a mistake, but he's a good man, I forgive him.

Yet I could taste hatred smoldering in my mouth, like ashes.

There was a time I worshipped Ed. I suppose everyone goes through a phase like that when a glance, a smile, a nod from the boy you're crushing on makes you glow all over. He carried himself like a bull, convinced of his own strength and presence, and his moods would swing wildly, but he could be kind and charming and gracious. He spoke warmly of his passions, he always tipped the waiter well, and I fell for him like a sapling blown over by a gale. Ed picked me up and swirled me around in the orbit of his personality and his friends and relations till the emptiness left by Baba and a childhood wracked by uneasy wanting was filled with my husband's expansive, demanding, enveloping body.

I couldn't remember that Ed anymore. I was naively happy, and he chose to set my innocence on fire. Burnt my roots to cinders. Displaced me from the simplicity of my life. Perhaps a cheater's worst crime isn't betrayal of your trust, but his bisection of your life so there will always be a before and an after. He gives the lie to your faith in your own history.

I took maternity leave from work. Sleepless, I walked up and down the block at night. I didn't want to go inside the house, see the mirror, see Ed. I took up smoking again, two packs a day for a few weeks, then tossed them all; I cried when I did so.

Two months after the cellphone incident, when finally I could *feel* enough to consider starting afresh, we lost the baby. It came out in a gush of blood that filled the toilet bowl.

My screams filled the house. When Ed came running and saw he fell to the bathroom floor and wept.

A late miscarriage, the doctor told us. Perhaps due to excessive stress that she couldn't handle.

As if that were my fault. As if a woman were a perpetual-motion machine expected to tick away the travesties of her life in servitude to men and a breakdown in the mechanism was entirely on her.

Ed wouldn't talk to me. Your smoking killed my baby, he shouted at me once in the ensuing weeks. That he apologized later for saying so was meaningless; I would never forgive him for it. We drifted past each other in the house, preferring dinner in the company of work brought home. I began taking a nightcap, something I'd never done. I began writing again, submitting articles again. A couple were published at respectable venues, but I felt no pleasure. The void in my heart mirrored the absence in my womb.

It would be several months before we could face each other. Ed took the initiative. He didn't want to lose me, he said. We had a history and his mama always liked me. He wanted to try again. I listened to him, thinking of the woman who killed my baby. Her shadow, long and rancid, hung over us. "Ed," I said. "What's her real name?"

For a long moment he looked at me, those baby-blue adulterer eyes staring into mine. How I'd once crushed on them, and his rough blond waves, and that Southern drawl. My own Matthew McConaughey, I'd tell my girlfriends. They made fun of us, scandalized by my breaking of tradition and familial norms. "Blasphemy, bitch," one said and giggled.

"Don't start on me, Karima," Ed said and licked his lips. "This won't work if you do."

I considered, remembering the day when I took a knife and, lying in the bathtub, held it over my wrist, turning it this way and that, watching the blade send shards of light scurrying across the bathroom. So easy, I had thought. It would be so easy.

I didn't tell Ed about the knife incident. I dropped the woman's image from my head, like a stone into a deep well. I let go of the shadow looming above us, or thought I did.

Shortly after that, Mama visited, and I learned the relationship between phosphorus and phossy jaw. Found something new to brood over.

Did you know the word *phosphorus* comes from the ancient Greek words *phōs* and *phoros*: "light-bringer"? Did you know phosphorus was first discovered by an alchemist after he boiled his own urine in his quest to make gold?

Phosphorus is an essential component of life: it holds our DNA together and shapes our bones. But shift its chemistry a little and it becomes highly flammable. Some postulate that spontaneous human combustion can be explained by the reaction of certain microbes with unstable phosphorus molecules in our body. Alchemy, glowing urine, a tendency to suddenly erupt into flame—I was mesmerized.

Night after night I pulled up articles and books on this strange element. Naturally, I wanted to write a piece on it, how the fucking thing had affected my mother's health, but plenty had been written on the subject already. Was there anything left to say?

That was when I stumbled upon the matchstick factory of Ganeshpur and the infamous Ghat Massacre—a discovery that set me on the path that ended at the devil's own doorstep.

This is what Gurpreet told me about the Devil of Ganeshpur's factory.

In 1881, at the peak of the Raj's imperial power, Lieutenant-Colonel James Edmund Stevens, commander of the Eighteenth Battalion of the Indian Defence Force, decided to retire and set up a matchstick factory in India.

Stevens was related to Wilberforce Bryant of the famous Bryant & May factory in the East End of London. He was well aware of the brand-new "strike anywhere" matches that were all the rage in the Western Hemisphere at that time. In an age of sulfur "lucifers" that were trickier to ignite by friction, the phosphorus match head with its highly combustible ignitor caught on quickly.

Sensing ample opportunity and zero competition in India, Stevens made arrangements with Bryant and bought a license to set up a matchstick factory near Ganeshpur, a poplar- and eucalyptus-rich area in the Peshawar Valley.

Pashtun tribesmen of the area, recruited into military units such as the Khyber Rifles, had wives who, because of tradition or domestic reasons, didn't work outside the home. Stevens hired Indian female managers who went door to door, convincing these women to work in matchstick-making "from the safety and comfort of your home." Soon dozens, then hundreds, of women were working up to fourteen hours a day, dipping match heads in white phosphorus, making matchboxes or wrapping them. Initially they worked from home, but later, lured by the promise of more hours, many began working at the factory.

Stevens' operation proved extremely fruitful. By 1884, he was exporting "strike anywhere" matches to Singapore, Japan, and the Middle East.

Then trouble struck.

The brother of a match dipper noticed her jaw was swollen and glowing in the dark. "What's wrong with your face?" he asked.

"I don't know," said the girl, "but my jaw has been hurting for months."

Soon her teeth fell out and abscesses developed within her mandible. Holes opened in her face along the jawline, oozing foul discharge. Steadily, inexorably, the woman's pain worsened until no potion, herb, or opium could touch it.

The girl had phossy jaw from years of breathing in phosphorus vapors. The devil's element had accumulated in her jawbones and necrosed them.

Within months she was dead.

Several dozen cases followed. Many victims were teenagers. Unable to take the agony, one girl went mad and took a razor to her mouth to cut out her hurting gum. Some, disfigured and diseased, committed suicide.

Still the factory machines churned and the white devil who ran them minted his money. "They had better cover their mouth and nose, hadn't they?" Stevens was rumored to say. "Besides, Indians breed like rabbits. So what if a few get the jaw? They'll starve without food my factory puts on their table."

Things came to a head when a matchstick girl threw herself off a cliff and ended up paralyzed from the waist down.

Her mother was Mai Bhago.

Mai was fifty years old and recently widowed when her daughter lost use of her legs. Mai was a proud Sikh woman whose great-grandfather had been a commander in Maharaja Ranjit Singh's army. She had watched the white devil's disease—Stevens' Malady, they called it—sweep across her community and destroy countless lives. Now it had claimed her daughter.

Mai gathered women from her town and others. They held midnight meetings to discuss options. Dozens of matchstick girls were recruited, and together they marched to the factory and sat outside its gates, demanding Stevens reduce work hours and pay medical expenses of the sick workers. Outraged, Stevens sent word to the local magistrate and a curfew was declared. Brandishing sticks and guns, the police arrived and forcefully dispersed the protestors.

Mai Bhago was not to be deterred.

Next week, she along with three hundred men, women, and children camped in protest at the Ganeshpur shamshan-ghat. Dozens of pyres had burnt there lately, courtesy of Stevens' Malady, and Mai thought a sit-in at the sacred site would force the government to take notice.

The British, still seething from the Sepoy Mutiny, were not going to let a bunch of filthy match-makers dictate the terms of their exploitation.

On a fall morning in 1885, a platoon of fifty soldiers arrived at Ganeshpur ghat and barricaded the area. Under orders of General Abbott, a former military colleague of Stevens, the soldiers asked the protestors to leave.

When they refused, the soldiers opened fire.

"It was absolute bedlam," Gurpreet said. "Screams of injured women and children filled the air. Brown bodies tumbled and fell. Some jumped into the lake to escape the hailstorm of bullets and drowned. Others were gunned down on the spot."

The shooting lasted for fifteen minutes. By the end, seventy bodies lay twitching on the ground.

For several hours the soldiers didn't allow medics and doctors access to the hundreds that were wounded. No family would collect their dead until the next morning.

Mai Bhago was badly injured but alive. She was taken to a makeshift hut at the edge of the cremation grounds and imprisoned.

For ten days she was starved, interrogated, and tortured. Asked about collaborators and insurrectionists. Who helped you coordinate the protests? Were rebels from Punjab involved? How did a group of female lowlifes organize such a large protest?

Mai didn't say a word.

They hanged her from a tree outside the hut and didn't allow her body to be cut down for a week.

Word of the Ghat Massacre and Mai's execution spread quickly through the valley, stirring up fury. Indian soldiers who hailed from the area refused orders and were shot or imprisoned as deserters. Skirmishes between the tribesmen and the government were instantly and mercilessly squashed. It seemed there would be no recriminations for the monstrous act, no recourse to justice.

Two months later, a young, pretty matchstick girl smiled at the factory foreman and walked into the chemicals room. Still smiling, she unsealed the lid of a fifty-five-gallon container of white phosphorus, lit up a match, and bent over the drum.

The explosion could be heard for miles. The Bryant & Stevens Matchstick Factory burnt to the ground in hours.

Stevens raged and swore vengeance, but nothing could be done. Word had gotten to a journalist in London about the Ghat Massacre and letters of condemnation had appeared in *The Pall Mall Gazette*. Officers of the Crown deemed it wise to distance themselves from the event and Stevens.

Four months later, in the middle of the night, an intruder slipped into Stevens' palatial bungalow through a high, narrow window. The next morning, when Stevens and his wife wouldn't respond, their servants broke down the door and found the couple dead.

Their throats had been slashed and their mouths filled with matchsticks, which had been set alight.

Darkness had come to Ganeshpur like an assassin, but the town was determined to fight it off. Stalls had been set up on both sides of the highway that curled a finger around the town. Fairy lights hung from tin awnings and doorways of roadside shops. Carts laden with sweets and winter nuts trundled across streets and kutcha roads. Vendors whistled and called to passersby, inviting them to taste their wares.

A festival was in procession.

"The entire town comes out for it. Hindus, Muslims, Sikhs, even a few Buddhists. We have ancient Buddhist sites in the area, you know," Gurpreet told me.

Ed might be interested. I was starting to feel sorry about the altercation. A little space did help put things in perspective. Today wasn't the best day for either of us; I was just better at forgetting.

I pulled out my phone. One signal bar. I tried Ed, but the call wouldn't go through.

I called Jack next. No luck.

I sighed, thinking of what Jack had said when I brought up the signal issue when we first arrived. Wait till I dig in and lay my optic fiber in the area. He had a gleam in his eyes. The entire region will be transformed. We're bringing the future here.

Yeah, not sure everyone here would be as excited about the transformation as you are, I said, laughing.

Think of all the money that'll pour into the area. They'll thank us later!

I tapped my cell and raised it high. Perhaps the valley could use an upgrade, after all.

"Trouble, madam?" Gurpreet said politely.

"Nah. Signal's still awful."

"Yes. Very patchy coverage. You can try the landline at the temple. They have a phone there."

We ambled through town, taking pictures, accepting offerings of rose garlands from a hawker, buying paper packets of roasted chanay from another. We munched our way to the place where the Devil of Ganeshpur had built a matchstick factory. Now a temple stood there, Gurpreet told me.

A little boy with rosy cheeks ran up to me. "Fresh, delicious apples," he cried, his breath steaming.

"Awww," I said, bending to look at his basket. "How much?"

"Free for you, memsahib. Try one?"

"I couldn't! Here, take fifty rupees—"

"No, madam." Gurpreet was shaking his head, smiling. "He won't take anything from you. You're a visitor in the area on a festival day."

Giggling, the boy thrust the apple into my hands and took off.

The temple shone with a thousand lights. A large three-story building with white-marbled terraces on four sides, arched windows, jharokas, and a central dome that could have been Sikh or Muslim architecture. Dozens of turban-clad Sikh children, Hindus wearing orange sashes, and Muslims with long beards and white prayer caps streamed in and out.

"Quite different from what I imagined," I mused.

"Like I said," Gurpreet looked at the building, "one good thing to come out of the Ghat Massacre was the coalition of the communities. Not one episode of sectarian violence in Ganeshpur in more than a century. The temple has become a symbol of resistance and unity for all three peoples."

"And who's the temple devoted to?"

"Jali-Ma."

"Who?"

"Jali-Ma. The Burnt Goddess. Maybe a variation of Mother Kali, or Agneya, the goddess of hearths. It's possible the temple started as a veneration of the matchstick girl who died by self-immolation, but our elders say this was holy ground long before Stevens set up his factory here. Muslims revere her as a saint who walked on hot coals to prove the righteousness of her cause in front of a cruel king. The hymns of the Burnt Goddess praise her as the perfect amalgam of resilience, sacrifice, and resistance to tyranny. What better icon for a place like this?"

We took off our shoes and went up the steps through a high-arched doorway into a tiled courtyard glittering with diya lamps and candles. Excited chatter and sarangi music drifted in the air. We padded across the courtyard, pausing to do ablution at a fountain strewn with rose petals, then proceeded to the main prayer room at the end of the building. Women in saris and shalwar kameez passed by us, smiling and nodding. A pair of men came up to Gurpreet, shook his hands warmly, and went away.

We must look like a pair of happy lovers, I thought, and hid the grin rising to my lips with a bite from the boy's apple.

In the prayer room we stood before a towering bust of the Burnt Goddess placed in the middle of the chamber. Decorated with garlands of marigolds and jasmines, the gold-painted goddess with the blackened face sat in the lotus position, a sword by her left hand. Incense sticks smoked in brass pots around the room, filling the air with a sweet, heady scent. A wizened priest, his chest bare, stood at the statue's feet, blessing worshippers who marched past him and the goddess, ceaseless in their circumambulations.

"Bless her feet, her feet," they cried.

Gurpreet kissed his fingertips and touched them to his eyes. "Bless her burnt, eternally moving feet." He fetched rosewater from the priest and sprayed it over my head and his. We kneeled before the statue, palms joined before our chests, and I thought how surreal it was to be back in Pakistan, unfamiliar yet comforting, and stranger still to be here in this place. The camera dangled on my chest; I lifted it and snapped a picture of the goddess.

Worshippers rang temple bells and chanted hymns. The symphonies of sitar and tabla soared as a door opened, but not before I heard my cellphone ping repeatedly.

I pulled it out. Above the messages icon the number 10 glowed in red. I grinned. Ed must have been trying me, too. Hopefully he'd also have realized how stupid the whole thing was.

I tapped the icon.

Someone touched my shoulder. I looked up to see a tall, smiling woman with silver hair dressed in a sari. She held out a plate of wheat halwa. "Prasad?"

I took a piece. "Thank you."

She smiled. "Welcome home, dear," and moved away.

I looked down and saw the messages were from Jack. All eleven of them.

I frowned and peered closer.

12:01 p.m.: "Lunch at home, guys?"

12:33 p.m.: "When r u guys gettin back?"

1:07 p.m.: "Hello?"

1:57 p.m.: "HELLOOOO!

2:34 p.m.: "Ugh, signal must be shitty out there. Can't get Ed either. Anyhoo, gimme a call when u get this."

4:09 p.m.: "Hey Karima, listen. Just heard there was some commotion at the site. Our work site, I mean. Gimme a call asap. We may have to"

4:22 p.m.: "Can 1 of u pls call? It's kinda urgent."

4:31 p.m.: "Superurgent! Im not fucking around, goddamnit. CALL ME."

4:33 p.m.: "Can't reach either of u. WTF. Call me. PLEASE!"

4:45 p.m.: "Fuck it. I'm callin the cops."

End of messages.

A cold finger pressed into my belly. Did something happen to Ed? But then why would Jack say he couldn't reach *either* of us? I brushed a hair lock away from my eyes, looked around. Gurpreet was talking to a group of men who had carried in a white-sheeted charpai laden with roses. As they lowered it to the ground, he caught my eye and waved. I nodded, chewed on a nail, pulled up Jack's contact on the phone, and dialed.

The call went through. On the third ring, someone picked up.

"Hey, Jack," I said urgently. "Hello."

Silence.

"Jack, that you? Hello? Jack? Speak up, goddamnit!"

Someone breathed into the phone. Then: *beep beep beep.* The sound of a call cut off. The cadence matched my heart beating in my ear.

Quickly I dialed Ed—and the call went through, thank God!

The phone rang. I waited. It rang again, then again.

No answer.

I leaped up and went to Gurpreet. "Something's wrong."

He cupped a hand to his ear against the din of the temple. "What?"

"Something's wrong, Gurpreet. Ed didn't get back home and Jack, his brother, he texted me, said he couldn't reach Ed. And now I . . . I can't reach either of them."

He stared at me, then said, "You look a bit pale. Are you light-headed?" He turned around and shouted, "Can we get madam here some coconut water?"

"No, I just got up too fast. I'm fine, thanks. I'm telling you *they won't pick up.*"

"Try again. If you can't get through, we'll figure something out. Hey, you! Tell Salma to bring in the incense sticks. We're already late . . ."

I couldn't understand how he could be so calm. The temple was so cold, but my hands were clammy. I wiped them on my shirt, tried Ed again. The phone rang, but it sounded different this time. Frowning, I removed it from my ear to see if I'd messed up the sound settings, and cutting through the cacophony of the temple I heard Charlie Pride singing "Kiss an Angel Good Mornin'." Ed's ringtone.

It was coming from the charpai covered with a white sheet.

Holding my cell out, I took two steps forward and stopped. "Gurpreet sahib?" My head buzzed. He was still talking to the cluster of worshippers, gesturing urgently. "Ed?" I said, and felt gooseflesh rise on my arms. Trembling, I reached out and pulled the sheet away from the charpai—and laughed with relief.

Nothing there. Absolutely nothing, except a pile of wheat husk. My ears had been ringing.

They were still ringing.

"Madam?" the silver-haired woman said politely. The crowd of worshippers had ejected her right at the end of the charpai. "Here." She handed me Ed's cellphone. "It's working fine," she explained.

I stared at her, feeling light as a feather, as a swirl of embers. I looked at Ed's cell, then the charpai again.

Not wheat husk. Ash.

A large mound of it.

Panic swept through me like a rough hand sifting the dust that was my body. What the fuck was going on? I didn't know these people, I didn't know Gurpreet. I'd just met him. How was it even *possible* that I unhesitatingly followed him here to this strange temple? I didn't want to be here anymore.

Why was I dizzy?

I staggered. "Easy, madam," Gurpreet said from behind, his strong arms anchoring me. "There'll be time to understand."

"The apple," I said, and licked my lips, they were so dry. I turned to look into his eyes. "The boy's apple."

"A little something to grease the proceedings, yes." He nodded. "It will help later, I promise." The smile was gone, leaving his face shadowed. He dipped a finger into the ash, raised it, and smeared it on my forehead. "Here's to the ash-bride."

"Oh, we're so glad to have you," cried the silver-haired woman, tears running down her cheek. Gently, she pushed me into a chair by the charpai, bent, and raked an ash-touched finger across my left cheek.

"The ash-bride, the ash-bride." The worshippers crowded around me murmuring, their eyes shining. "Oh, how fortunate we are."

"All hail Jali-Ma. Our Burnt Mother sends us her blessing and favor."

"We weren't sure what to do," Gurpreet said. "When they said a white man's company had bought the cremation grounds and Mai's hut. How could it be, we said. History was made here. Written in blood and ashes. How could our people, our very own flesh and blood, sell it to invaders? And now they were pushing to buy the temple site as well? Bribing our people. They'd tear our community apart, we cried."

Ash, ash everywhere. My head swam. Hands painted with henna, forearms ringing with bangles came at me. Bright saris and shalwars and kurtas and turbans. They surged forward, touching me, daubing me with a still-warm dust.

"Today would be the day, we said to each other, when we'd rip up the white devil's machinations and remove him from our midst. But our heart was still uncertain—until we met you," Gurpreet said, eyes shining. "You who followed a flame back to your home. You were a sign from Jali-Ma. All our stories you accepted into your heart and gave us your own in return. You were the flame-head, we knew. Who else could consort with a devil and survive?

"And at last our heart was reconciled, filled with the truth. So, a few hours ago, we went and took care of the pretender, the instigator, at his place of work." He stepped back as the old priest came toward me, took my hands, and kissed them, his lips leaving a smear on my sooty skin.

"They will never take our land again," Gurpreet confirmed, then turning around, he shouted, "Bring it in."

With a gasp, the worshippers drew back from me in a circle, chattering, pointing to the doorway on our left, from which, moments earlier, celestial music had swelled.

It was filled by a large animal.

My vision wouldn't focus. I swayed on the chair. "What is that?"

Four men led the animal in, pulling at ropes tied to its horns and midsection. One of them whipped it with a leather thong and the creature grunted, thrashing its malformed head. Long whiskers protruded from its mouth and its skin was discolored, wrinkled, almost melted. Was it hurt?

The crowd heaved forward, dusty fingers grazing the creature's back, torso, legs, and head, tugging at its horns. Soot and ash and something red fell around the animal in a rain. It shuddered and emitted a choking cry.

"Come, you must touch the fire oxen too," cried Gurpreet, holding my hands. He yanked me to my feet, and I lurched across the room to the creature, its misshapen mouth working this way and that. What was wrong with its back, the strange gash running across it that looked like a line of stitches; what was wrong with its head, its mouth, its whiskers—were they whiskers? They looked like sticks of incense.

I thought, What's that story about blind men patting different parts of an elephant, trying to understand it—and then the disparate pieces of the creature locked together in my head, and I stiffened, the shock of recognition rooting me to the ground.

Flick. Gurpreet held a burning lighter in his hand. "The ash-bride must set the flame." He pressed the lighter into my hand, and guided it to the incense sticks stuffed into the mouth. "The challawa must be passed on from our land."

No, I wanted to scream, but my tongue had curled like a snail in my mouth. My hands, the ash-covered flesh of a goddess, moved on their own.

The creature, blood dripping down its lower animal half, gazed at me, its blue eyes filled with terror. The guttural noises it made rose in intensity; it bucked, as the flame neared its face, to its mouth filled with matches and the incense sticks thrust through the flesh of its lips.

"Ash-bride, ash-bride, lead our sins away."

Dancing and chanting the men, women, and children of Ganeshpur followed me, as I staggered through the courtyard, down the steps, and onto the road, a bleating, flaming, blood-slippery challawa following me on legs neither human nor oxen. We moved between stalls silvered by a sickle moon, and the chowkidars of the temple lashed the creature when it jerked and tried to bolt.

Challawa, I thought, sluggishly, as another meaning from my youth came to me. Challawa is also a fickle lover whose feet won't stay. The lust-filled wanderer who, having ravished one young body, moves to another.

"Ash-bride, ash-bride, send this plague away," the children sang.

Finally I understood the shape of my grief, its star-burnt edges, and the trail of char that stretched from my past into my future.

Immolated daughter. Suicidal girl. Ash-bride forever in love?

The ash on my body stirred and blew in the night wind, and I thought, Today was the day we lost the baby, wasn't it? Wasn't this trashfire of an anniversary why Ed, my unfaithful beast of a husband, had been ruing the day so?

Emptied mother. Burnt Mother.

Am I home? I thought. But I'd hated home. Then, drunk with the idea, and exuberant: I *am* home. I had been run away, put away, but now—

"Ash-bride, ash-bride, take this ox away," the children sang, their eyes glowing with faith.

Jali-Ma, Jali-Ma. Watch-woman to a land threatened by the devil—and his ever spreading, blistering element.

The air filled with the scent of incense and burning flesh. When I looked over my shoulder to ensure I was followed, the fire oxen snapped the binding on its roasted mouth and began calling to me in the sooty voice of my lover.

ENOUGH FOR HUNGER AND ENOUGH FOR HATE
BY JOHN LANGAN

When she had completed her counterclockwise circuit of the lake, Michelle Word turned toward the center of the frozen expanse and began to walk in the direction of the figure seated on the bright yellow bucket in front of the hole in the ice. Walter Ivorsson: the name she had said so often these past weeks its meaning had ebbed and flowed, sometimes reducing to a series of syllables, consonants and vowels yielding sounds of no more significance than the cough of a deer, the scream of a fox, other times expanding to contain all the pain for which this man had been responsible. He was doing his best to ignore the tall woman in the dark green padded coat and jeans drawing steadily closer to him on her hiking boots— or, it was more a case of, he was pretending to concentrate on the short fishing pole whose line he was tugging up and down while secretly taking in everything about her, from the black hair held back by the green scarf wound about her head to the fawn gloves on her hands. She doubted he could pick out the knife clipped to her belt, although his blue eyes returned to her right hip several times. In turn, as she advanced across the scrim of snow covering the ice, which crunched under her boots' tread, she studied him, the heavy tan coveralls over the thick black sweatshirt, itself over two or three additional pullover shirts, the red-and-black-checked hunting cap, the black knit mittens the single incongruous detail in the man's outfit, as if he were attempting to portray himself as possessed of a boyish streak, playful, even, and not

(a monster)

what he was. As if he could hide his nature, when it was there for everyone to see in his pale skin drawn taut to the lines of his skull, the nose hatchet sharp, the eyes a blue so light it was barely a color at all. His scraggly beard and mustache were a blond nearing white, not from age (he was thirty-three), though perhaps from stress. The eyes, Michelle judged, were the principal giveaway, their washed-out regard a mix of simmering hostility and appetite restrained, if just. But it was there in the man's body language, in the way he held himself ready to leap up from his bucket into violence immediate and terrible. She could not see any sort of weapon near him—she supposed the auger lying on the other side of him would do in a pinch—but everything about Walter Ivorsson said he would have no need of an ax, should the occasion arise, an occurrence he would greet smiling, as a great opportunity.

Ten feet away from him, close enough to counter the wind which sometimes raised its voice over the ice, yet far enough to allow a reasonable chance of reaching the knife should Ivorsson move, she stopped. He went on playing at not registering her. She wondered if he noticed her similarity to Toby. If so, he did not appear overly concerned by it. Not for the first time, she wished she were sighting him through the scope of the Winchester with which her father had taught her to hunt and which he had passed on to her now that the Parkinson's had stripped the activity from him. Lining up the sights on Ivorsson's chest from a blind two hundred yards distant would have felt far more secure than this, watching the man's breath steam from his mouth as he continued jigging the rod up and down. She had no need to stare into his eyes as she killed him, to deliver a pithy statement for him to take to Hell. To squeeze the trigger, watch him jerk as the bullet struck him, maybe fall down dead, maybe struggle to keep himself upright, in which case, a second shot would bring to a conclusion the job started by the first, would be fine. Except, according to Dr. Smith, the gunshots would not be sufficient. "Oh, they would make a mess of him, to be sure," she said on the phone, "but not enough to kill him.

Hell, you could stroll up beside him, shoot him point-blank in the face, and it still wouldn't suffice." Having watched a one-hundred-eighty-five-pound buck drop where he stood when she shot it, Michelle found this hard to accept. Yet everything she had learned in the past two weeks had encouraged her to adopt a more flexible perspective. Thus, she was here, at the approximate center of this frozen lake near the summit of a mountain deep in the northern Catskills, the peak rising around half the lake in steep rocky slopes to which spruce stunted by the altitude clung in seeming defiance of gravity, while the remainder of the lake was shored by fields in which stands of spruce, oak, and birch gathered in the snow across whose brittle expanse she had hiked something on the order of a mile and a half, from the pull-off where she had parked her Subaru beside the battered Dodge Ram with the unpainted driver's door. The air was February chilled, the sky a blue equally cold.

There was no need for much conversation—any, really. All she had to do was drop the stones in her jacket pocket on the ice, turn around, and make the trek back to her car. Soon enough thereafter, Ivorsson would discover what had been done to him. Having come this far, however, she could not let pass the opportunity to speak to the man. What she wanted from such an exchange, she wasn't certain. She had no expectation of anything Ivorsson said doing more than confirming what she already knew. In whatever rationalizations he indulged, she had no interest, though she could guess them with reasonable accuracy. It was as if she had been carried here by the logic, or lack thereof, of the narrative in whose currents she had found herself caught. Perhaps she had been mistaken; perhaps there were some final words she was due to deliver him.

Eyes still fastened on the hole in the ice between his boots, which was much smaller than she would have expected, barely large enough, it appeared, to fit anything worth the time and effort of sitting out here in the cold, Walter Ivorsson opened his mouth. As he did, as his lips, chapped by the wind and temperature, parted, allowing her to glimpse the crooked line of his lower set of teeth, she had a brief fantasy of his jaw gaping wider and wider still, impossibly wide, dropping against his overalls' bib and dropping farther, the skin of his face stretching, elongating to accommodate his jaw down to his knees, all the way to the ice supporting his yellow bucket and him. Within was darkness and the stink of blood gone bad. A hellish radiance in his eyes, he swung to face her, to consume her. So vivid was the hallucination, she failed to pick up what he said in his sullen voice and had to squeeze her eyes shut momentarily and say, "I'm sorry. Could you repeat that?" Hardly the opening line she would have chosen for the confrontation.

"I said, your brother was fucking my wife."

Apparently, he had recognized her. "Ex-wife," she said.

"Divorce wasn't final."

"Seems like a bit of a technicality, doesn't it? I mean, you hadn't been living together for almost a year when Toby came along. From what I understand, your marriage counseling crashed and burned before it even got the landing gear up. You only went because your lawyer petitioned the judge to force Karen to give it a try with you. If it hadn't been for your daughter, I don't know if the judge would have agreed. Or if it had been a woman on the bench. I like to think she would have taken one look at your history and not only granted the divorce right there, but issued a restraining order—no, fuck that, those never work in cases like this. I prefer to imagine her throwing your skinny ass in jail, sending you away for the maximum possible time. Still wouldn't have been enough, but it might have given Toby and Karen the chance to get as far away from here as they could and take Rachel with them, to someplace they could have had plenty of warning you were on your way.

"But that wasn't what happened. The judge was that dipshit, Badrebue, and he agreed with your lawyer's request for counseling. For the good of the child, he said. Then after the counseling collapsed and Karen stopped going, it allowed your lawyer to claim she hadn't made a good-faith effort, and everything just dragged on and on."

"Explain it however you like. Fact is, when Karen took up with your brother, she was still legally my wife. Round about these parts, you mess with a man's wife, you'll find the consequences severe."

"Jesus," Michelle said, "exactly where is it you think you are? You're in New York. The middle of Manhattan's a couple of hours south. The nearest town has a Starbucks. The supermarket stocks Greek yogurt and three kinds of veggie burgers. If you're looking for a place where your wife is your property, you're a hundred years and a few thousand miles off."

"Just because you can have your soy latte doesn't change the fundamental things," Ivorsson said. "Your iPhone does not make my marriage any less sacred."

"No, you did that on your own," Michelle said. "I've known enough guys who vote red and you know what? I can't think of a single one of them who would've condoned your behavior. Oh, they would have commiserated with you over a couple of beers down at the local bar, might've rolled their eyes at some of what you described, but when all was said and done, they would have told you to leave, to divorce the woman you couldn't live with anymore, make sure you hired a decent lawyer so you weren't screwed in the settlement. Shit happens, right? I guess you followed the lawyer part, though since you don't appear to have taken most of his advice, I'm not sure what benefit you bought with what you paid him. Although," she added, "no one's charged you with anything, and I have no doubt the cops've been over your place with a fine-toothed comb, CSI'd the shit out of it, and your lawyer's stuck with you throughout, so maybe he's done you some good, after all. No body, no crime, right? No matter how bad the circumstantial evidence might appear. Toby thought you'd murdered her. At first, he wasn't sure, then he was. The same way I'm certain you killed him. Only, I came to my conclusion a bit more directly than my brother did. In all fairness, I had the benefit of evidence."

"Bullshit," Ivorsson said, the irritation he tried to put into the word leavened with uncertainty.

"Wrong." She reached into the left-hand pocket of her coat and withdrew her phone, holding it up for Ivorsson's consideration as if it were an unfamiliar object. "He called me," she said, her voice unexpectedly thick, "at the end. Before you reached him. Had the presence of mind to tell me to save his message. He took a couple of pictures, too, which I'm guessing you were too . . . distracted to notice. Sent those to me, too. Just so you know, there are copies of the call and the images stored on a couple of cloud servers."

For the first time, Walter Ivorsson turned his head to regard her with his nominally blue eyes. There was in his gaze the endless chill of ice fields, of white expanses empty and vast. Michelle let her right hand drop beside her hip, her fingers brush the fringe of her coat, ready to tug it up and reach for the knife underneath. After a long, wintry look, however, Ivorsson returned his attention to the fishing hole. "You might have something on your phone, but whatever it is, wasn't enough to bring the sheriff out here with you. State police, neither."

"Funny you should mention the sheriff," Michelle said. "The man is terrified of you. Didn't want to meet with me, had zero interest in what I had recorded. I played it for him, anyway, but he acted as if what he heard was some kind of prank. He's a bad liar. I wonder what you did to him, what you let him see."

"Don't reckon Sheriff Rudyard saw any more than he wanted to."

"As far as the state cops go, they were more receptive, were willing to listen to Toby's call, to have a look at his pictures. They admitted the recording sounded suspicious, if vague. They were less impressed by the photos, said they were too blurry to be of much use, one way or the other. I figured they would subject them to some kind of computer enhancement, but they decided against it, said the pictures were probably of some animal. 'What kind of animal is that supposed to be?' I asked them. I told them I'd been hunting since I was twelve and the shape in those pictures bore no resemblance to any creature I'd run across in upstate New York, western Connecticut, or eastern Pennsylvania. Had Toby's call been more definite, had he named names, spelled things out in a simple, straightforward way, and had there been a modicum of corroborating evidence, they might have stirred from their chairs. As there was no evidence my brother was anything other than missing, as was the woman with whom he had been having an affair, the state troopers chose a neater, less sinister explanation: the two of them had run off together, staggered their departures so no one would suspect them. Toby's call and photos were part of their plan, intended to divert attention from what had actually happened."

"Sounds reasonable," Ivorsson said.

"Maybe to a bunch of cops who want you to believe they're overwhelmed with all the crime they have to fight. For someone who was talking to her brother every day, who listened to him discuss his girlfriend's disappearance, his suspicions, what you said to him when he confronted you about it, it was obviously false. Not to mention, from everything Toby told me, there was no way Karen would have left her daughter, abandoned her to you."

"Never can tell what a person'll do."

"You don't say."

"Karen and me knew each other when we were kids," Ivorsson said. "I assume your brother didn't tell you that."

"He did not. Can't say I much care."

"She was . . . my ma used to say it was love at first sight for us two. Wasn't for Karen, I know for a fact. Wasn't for me, neither. Not like the words make it sound. Nothing romantic about it. She was the purest thing I had ever seen. Like something amazing, one of those sunsets you have to tell someone else to look at, because it's so surprising and so intense, the sun putting on a show for you right overhead, the deep light and color, red and peach and violet—or like standing out in the middle of a blizzard, with the wind driving the snow straight at you, so you can't see much more'n your hand in front of your face, and any skin you haven't covered up is freezing, and you can feel the storm moving around you, this giant beast raging, which is kind of scary, but mostly, mostly thrilling, because you're standing in it and it's just so big and you're just so small. I don't know if you know what I'm talking about, if you've ever felt anything like this, been in touch with something completely itself, the way those sunsets and storms are. Anyway, this was what Karen was like. Bowled me over; knocked me out. There was nothing I wanted more than to spend every waking second with her." His lips hinted at a smile. "She was . . . terrific."

Michelle said, "You had a strange way of showing your appreciation for her."

"'Cause I lifted my hand to her?"

"Among other things. But yes, that especially."

Ivorsson tsked dismissively. "Wasn't my fault, not really. Hers, neither. It was the Army. Fucked her up, is the way I figure it. She enlisted out of high school, used it to pay for college. The recruiter told her chances were she wouldn't even be called up to serve. Said more people graduate those ROTC programs than they have postings for, so plenty of them never have to put on the uniform after they graduate. Sounded too good to be true to me. We weren't seeing one another then. Only friends. Her family had moved away when we were ten, halfway through fifth grade. Father got this great job in Seattle. Five years later, Karen came back with her mom and sister after her folks split up. The two of us picked up pretty much where we'd left off, friendship-wise. Nothing more, though with the changes the last five years had made to her, *more* was definitely on my mind. Not hers.

"After she graduated Oneonta, Army told her to hang tight, maybe they'd need her. She came back to these parts. Her mom was pretty sick, MS. Sister was no help. She'd gone back to Seattle to stay with Daddy and spend some of his money. Can't blame her, I guess. Would've been nice if she'd sent a few bucks to help with taking care of her mom. Karen had to do most of it; though the insurance paid to bring in a home health aide part-time. Let Karen work the job she'd found. PE teacher at the local grade school. Same one the two of us had gone to. We still weren't together. For a little while, she went out with a professor at the community college. Older guy, taught chemistry. Seemed kind of strange to me—I mean, the guy was going bald, gray hair, liver spots on the backs of his hands. Whatever. Obviously, she had some daddy issues to work out, right?"

"How much longer is this going to go on?" Michelle said.

"Long as it has to," Ivorsson said. "I wasn't the one trailed all the way out here."

"Believe me, I didn't want to. But I couldn't think of any other way to find out what I needed to know."

"What's that?"

"Where my brother's body is." She swallowed. "What's left of it."

Walter Ivorsson's almost colorless eyes did not move from the hole in the ice. "Makes you think I know anything about that?"

"Seriously? Is this what we're going to do? You play some backwoods Hannibal Lecter while I try to trick you into revealing the information I'm after? I already told you, the cops aren't interested in you as a suspect. If I go back to them and say, 'But he knows where my brother's remains are,' they'll chalk it up to coincidence. I tried talking to them before and they weren't any help. I've exhausted that avenue."

"Maybe you have, or maybe you're misjudging the troopers."

"How about this: you tell me where Toby is, I'll go get him, and I'll leave and never return? I swear, on everything I hold sacred. No cops."

"Could be you're lying."

"Come on!" Michelle shouted. "There has to be—I can't believe there isn't a little bit of humanity left in you. Please. If not for me, for my parents. My dad has been torn up for days, walks around distracted, his eyes full of tears. He knows something bad happened to his son, feels it deep in his gut. Mom plays the stoic, acts pissed because she warned Toby not to have anything to do with a woman in the middle of a divorce, says Dad's working himself up over nothing. Toby and this woman probably ran off somewhere, like the police said. But you can tell she doesn't really mean what she's saying. Look her in the face and you see the dread written all over it. She knows, too, but doesn't want to let on in case it makes Dad's health worse."

"Ain't you worried about your daddy's health?"

"If he doesn't find out what became of his son, then yes, definitely. If he does, then I don't think it'll be as bad as Mom fears. I think he'll be relieved."

"Bit of a gamble you're taking."

"It's mine to take."

Nodding, Ivorsson said, "Okay."

"Okay what?"

"Might be I have a notion as to where your brother is lying. Not that I'm saying I had anything to do with how he got there. What was your word? *Coincidence.* Sure. Let's call it that. I was out in the woods and just so happened to come across him."

"Fine," Michelle said. "Whatever you say." Her heart was pounding so hard she felt it at the base of her throat.

"You think you know me, don't you?"

"I never said that, but yeah, I figure I've got a pretty good read on you. You loved this girl from afar for years, watched her go out with all these other guys while you were right there in front of her, waiting for her to open her eyes and see what she'd had the whole time. Sound about right?"

"Close enough," Ivorsson said. "Wasn't as if I didn't have my fair share of girlfriends."

"Ah, but I bet you would have dropped any of them in a hot minute if Karen had told you she'd finally come to her senses. Did you, when she—"

"She came back from Afghanistan," Ivorsson said. "Where the Army sent her when they decided time had come due for her to pay back what she owed them for college. I don't know how these things work, but she was assigned or however you say it to work intelligence. Should have kept her safe on one of the big air bases, Bagram, though she said there wasn't anyplace completely safe over there. She was good at her job, so her CO chose her for a special mission. The details are a little hazy to me. From what I could gather, there were a bunch of guys—our guys—out somewhere in the field who had discovered something important, like papers, plans or maps, I don't know. Anyway, the brass picked Karen to helicopter in to do an on-site evaluation of what they'd found. Had to do with troop movements, I think, soldiers from other countries, like Pakistan or Russia or someplace. The guys she flew to were Special Forces, Green Berets or the like, but maybe you figured that out already.

"Well, she looked at what the Special Forces had turned up and it was pretty important stuff. She called it in, and jets were scrambled to bomb the ever-loving shit out of some poor fuckers. Sit tight, she was told, we're sending another chopper for you. Not long after, the first mortars landed around her. Killed one of the Green Berets right away, sent everyone running for cover. Probably just dumb luck, a case of wrong-place, wrong-time, but Karen always wondered if they'd been set up, stumbled into a trap." Ivorsson shrugged. "I told her it didn't matter. What was important was, she'd survived the attack, which became a real battle. There were twenty, thirty of the enemy moving in on her and the Special Forces, who were already down a man. She walked me through the firefight step-by-step. This was when Rachel was four. She'd had a playdate with a neighbor kid and her toys were all over the place. Karen put her down for the night, we got to talking, and the subject of the ambush came up. She'd told me about it before, but always in pieces. This time, I heard the whole thing from start to finish. As she's telling it to me, she's taking Rachel's toys, her teddies and her dolls, and setting them around the living room—which is where we were—to show me everyone's position. The coffee table was her and the Green Berets. A family of plastic mice got to play them. The couch was the ridge running alongside them, where six or seven stuffed animals manned a couple of cardboard tubes standing in for mortars. On top of the easy chair, which was a mountain peak, a stuffed hedgehog used the view the height gave to snipe at them. The remaining toys, teddy bears of all colors and sizes, Karen spread around the floor in ones or twos. Like the worst teddy bears' picnic ever, right?"

Michelle did not acknowledge the joke.

"Don't mind saying, if it'd been me being shot at and bombed, I doubt I would've remembered much aside from, 'It was loud and I was scared shitless.' Not Karen. She walked me through who was firing at who, how the soldiers' thinking was changing with the situation. What I mean is, at first, they were worried about the guys with the mortars, because they were dropping bombs on them. They'd realized there was someone on the mountaintop with a rifle, but they assumed he was too far away to be a concern. Then the sniper killed a second Green Beret, wounded a third, and suddenly he was a major problem. They had to adjust their positions while calling for air support. Through some kind of million-to-one-odds shit, the planes that had been sent to bomb the targets Karen had reported earlier were still in the air with a couple of undropped bombs apiece. They swept over and lit up the mountain like it was a fucking volcano. Karen swatted the hedgehog, sent it flying into the hallway. Next, the jets turned the top of the ridge into a sheet of fire. Karen swept all the stuffed horses and elephants and dragons off the couch onto the floor. The jets dropped the last of their ordnance as near to Karen and the soldiers as they dared, but it was too far. Still, the jets had cut the enemy numbers by half, maybe more. 'Now it was only three men trying to kill me,' was how she put it, 'instead of six.' For the rest of the day and into the night, she fought those men and their buddies. She called for more help, was told none was coming any time soon. There'd been a much bigger attack on a base and all resources were being diverted there. I guess the Special Forces guys talked a good game, even the wounded one, but this was far outside what Karen had trained for. She was used to studying documents, computer files, emails, not taking a bead on some fellow fifty feet away so she could put a bullet through his head. What else was she gonna do, though?

"The night went on and the enemy moved in closer. On the way, they paid a heavy price. So did the Green Berets. Another one of them was killed. As Karen's going through what happened, she's picking off teddies and tossing them to the side in a heap. A pile of dead teddy bears. The moon rose late, she said. It was full, which was good, because she didn't have any of those night vision goggles. Guess she could've taken them off one of the dead soldiers, but she didn't want to move if she didn't have to. By now, she was out of ammo. Everyone was, both sides. Enemy was still creeping toward them. She didn't know what to do. One of the Special Forces guys, the wounded one, passes her a knife. A clasp knife. Tells her to hold it with the point up, not to ice pick it. She's carried the knife with her since she's been back from the Army. Goes with her everywhere, like her phone and keys. I had no idea this was how she got it. She slides it from her jeans, folds out the blade and locks it. Since the first time she showed it to me, I thought the knife was pretty big. As your last defense against someone set on killing you, it was puny. She picks up one of the remaining teddies. This one we called Darla. Purple, with some kind of glitter in its fur. Stupid expression on its face. A guy I work with gave it to me. Had won it for his girlfriend at the county fair and she didn't want it. May have broke up after that; I can't remember. Whatever. Karen holds Darla by the neck. I know what's coming next. Not because she's ever told me, but because this is where the story's leading. She stabs Darla, right in the bear's roly-poly stomach. Stabs the toy again and again. Karen's still talking, saying how she stood up in front of this guy and before he could react stabbed him ten times, more. She'd never stuck a knife in anyone to kill 'em, and the only way for her to do it was to overdo it. I'm watching her rip the knife into the teddy bear, sending stuffing everywhere, and seeing what it must have been like, the blood on him, on her, on the ground. Blood looks black in the moonlight. No mistaking the smell. She held on to the man until she was positive he was not a threat. Did not want him to get up and come for her a second time. Said she stood with the guy leaning against her like they were at the prom and this was the last dance. She'd stabbed him so many times his intestines were hanging out. Knife was slippery from the blood. But she was ready to stick it into him again if he tried anything. He didn't. Gave a couple of shaky breaths and kind of slid down her. She stepped back slowly, let him drop to the ground.

"While she had been doing the dance of death with this guy, the Green Berets had finished the rest. She went to pass the knife to the soldier who'd given it to her, the wounded one, but he'd died during the fight. Killed a couple of the enemy, then keeled over. Internal injuries from when he was shot catching up to him. His sergeant told her to keep the knife. She did. Carried it with her the rest of her time in Afghanistan and in her pocket after she was home. The knife she killed a man with. I'd watched her use it to slice open envelopes, cut rope, chop a salami into bite-sized pieces when we were on a picnic. Wasn't until I saw her with it in one hand, the remains of Darla the teddy bear in the other, white fluffy stuffing all over the living room floor, that I got what it meant for her to have this thing on her every day.

"So yeah. Karen came back from the war. And the war came back with her. I knew what PTSD was. Who doesn't, these days? Seeing it up close, living with it day-in, day-out was something else. She had trouble with her feelings. Be depressed for days. Get mad—shit, she'd always had a bit of a temper, all the way back to grade school. You did not want to piss her off. But it was like, she'd blow up at you and it was over. Took a lot for her to reach that point. After she came back, the littlest thing could set her off. Seemed like it, anyway. She could stay mad at you for days. Nasty, too, mean-spirited in a way she hadn't been before."

"If everything was so terrible," Michelle said, "why didn't you leave?"

"'Cause it wasn't that way all the time. Sometimes—most of the time—things were fine. I loved her as much as I ever had. More. She loved me, too. I waited my whole life to hear her say, 'I love you, Walt.' I was not about to let it go, how it made me feel. Yeah, she could be difficult, and maybe I didn't always deal with her as best I could, but we were married. Had said, 'I do,' to all the promises the minister read. Plus, there was Rachel. I was pretty in love with her. Felt like she was my own. Which she was, basically."

"I'm sorry?" Ivorsson's words had jolted her, a snowball slapping her on an already cold day.

"Don't know what your brother said, but I treated my little girl like a Goddamned princess."

"Only, she wasn't your little girl, not . . . biologically."

"More to being someone's daddy than knockin' up their mamma. Wait," Ivorsson said, "you mean you didn't know?"

"I did not."

"Huh. Don't matter. But yeah, wasn't my name on Rachel's birth certificate under 'father.' I offered. Karen refused. Said it was important the truth was there for the girl to find, if she ever wanted to. Not gonna lie, I wondered if it wasn't because she was hoping Rachel's actual daddy was gonna show up one day and make the three of them a happy family. She swore she wasn't. She'd made the choice with me and she intended to stick with her decision. Hadn't worked so well when we were first seeing one another, which was how Rachel came to be, but that was then and this was now, over and done with. I wanted to believe her. Mostly, I did. But sometimes she'd be working late, or she'd call to say she and some of the other teachers were going out for wings and beer after school, and I'd get to thinking, worrying. Is it him she's on her way to meet? Has he finally appeared?"

"Did you know him? Was he local?"

Ivorsson shook his head. "Saratoga, these days. Before, Sergeant Robert Dunn was stationed in Afghanistan."

"Was he one of the Green Berets she was ambushed with?"

"Yeah. Their leader. Two of them met up while she was still over there. Had a fling, I guess you'd say. It was finished well ahead of her boarding the plane to fly home. Only it wasn't. Not . . . inside, where it counts. They kept in touch, email, mostly. After she'd been here a couple of months, he emailed her. Said he had some leave coming up, was planning to fly to Athens for a week. Wanted her to join him. Without a second thought, she said she would. Went online and booked the ticket right away. Didn't tell me what she was planning. We'd been seeing one another for a few weeks at this point. After all those years, all it took for her to go out with me was going to war. We weren't living together or anything, though she spent enough time at my place for me to think this might be heading somewhere good. She didn't say she was flying to Europe to meet her ex. Said she was heading the opposite direction, to Colorado, to go white-water rafting with friends from college. I didn't mind. I already had an idea what Afghanistan had done to her, mentally. A few days outside with some friends sounded like it would be helpful.

"Wasn't until a couple of months later, when the home pregnancy test left no doubt, that she sat me down and came clean. Once she returned from what I thought was her trip out west, we picked up where we'd left off. She was some actress. Didn't let on the time she'd had, not in the slightest. Wasn't like I asked a lot of questions. White-water rafting's never interested me. She knew that, said it was the reason she'd picked it for her cover story. So I wouldn't ask about it. There were times she was moody, tearful, but I chalked it up to the PTSD. I guess she wrote to Sergeant Dunn, gave him the news. He wasn't interested in being a daddy. Then it was my turn. We were out to dinner. Burger King, which was okay. She says she's got some news for me. Right away, I thought she was breaking up with me. I knew this was too good to last, and here we were, at the end of it. At first, when she said she was pregnant, I was—I was *overjoyed*. Not what I was planning, yeah, but it was like, I'm thinking things are done, and it's the opposite. We're gonna have a kid together. Only we weren't. Not like that. She laid it all out, as much as I wanted to hear. Felt like I was listening to her from inside a bubble. Minute I understood what was what, all I wanted to do was leave, get in my car and drive home, lock the doors, and never see Karen again. Only, I couldn't, 'cause she was pregnant, and it wouldn't be right to leave a pregnant woman in Burger King with no ride home. I didn't. I sat across from her as she said she wouldn't blame me for doing exactly what I wanted to. She couldn't ask me to stick around. She'd lost the right, forfeited it. But if I wanted to, she'd be grateful.

"I dropped her at her place. Didn't say two words to her the way there. Once she was inside, I headed out of town. Didn't have a

destination in mind. Didn't have anything in mind. Just wanted
to get as far away as I could. Had some money in the bank, couple
of credit cards nowhere near their limits. Ran through all kinds of
plans—fantasies. Most of them were, I was gonna drive someplace
I always wanted to see, like Wyoming, and set up shop there. Send
for my shit when I was ready. Or not at all. Wasn't very much I was
attached to. Might be best to ditch everything, make a fresh start.

"Thing was, I knew it was bullshit, everything I was planning.
I wasn't about to leave Karen. I was pissed, yeah, and who
could blame me?" Ivorsson paused, as if to allow Michelle the
opportunity to say, "I could." When she did not, he continued,
"What I mostly was, was afraid. This . . . situation had come along
and it was gonna ruin everything. Just the latest obstacle, after
her moving away in grade school, and her dating other guys in
high school, and her leaving for college, and her dating the old guy
after she came back from college, and her going to Afghanistan.
Felt like the universe was doing everything in its fucking power
to keep us apart. It was pathetic. Should've had more self-respect,
more dignity. But the farther I drove, the more panicky I got. Lost
track of where I was. I'd been on local roads. Took a wrong turn
somewhere and I was lost. Which was weird. My sense of direction's
pretty good. Plus, I've driven all over the place. There was heavy
fog everywhere. Each road I turned onto was narrower than the
last. On my right, the asphalt fell away. I couldn't see how far. I had
the radio on, some local station. Community radio, the woman
at the mic called it. I'd tuned in in time for the Heartache Hour.
Which went on for at least two. Old timey shit, Hank Williams Sr.
singing 'Your Cheatin' Heart' with his warbly voice, his twangy
guitar. Patsy Cline doing 'Crazy' in her low, deep voice. Finally
reached the point I had to pull over. Needed to piss something
awful. Needed to take a break from driving, too. Felt like forever
until a spot appeared. I left the headlights on, walked a few feet
into the trees to do the necessary. Lights threw my shadow onto
the fog in front of me. Like looking down a long, murky corridor.
From where I was standing, I saw someone moving around out in

it. Couldn't have been anyone there. It was three in the morning. Wasn't hunting season. No sign of any houses around. Should have zipped up, returned to the car, and left. Whoever was in the fog was making the back of my neck prickle. Can't say why. Just too much in my own head, I guess. I decided to investigate. Stupid, yeah. Like every asshole in every horror movie who gets chomped on by the monster. *Fine,* I thought. It would be the perfect fucking ending to the perfect fucking night. I imagined how bad Karen was gonna feel after my body was discovered. Full of regret. 'Oh, what a great guy Walt was. Why did I treat him so shitty?' Would she, though? Really? I wondered. My self-pity turned to anger, which collapsed into self-pity again, until I was moving forward. Straight into the monster's jaws.

"Ground was rocky. Tricky to walk on. Almost dropped me on my ass a couple of times. Twisting my ankle, or breaking it, was a real possibility. Would make getting back to the car a trial. Also, would leave me vulnerable to whoever was out here in the fog. Not that I wasn't now. Wasn't as if I had a clasp knife in my pocket. Or any other kind of weapon. Could grab a rock, I supposed. At least I still had eyes on the person. Sort of. Fog played tricks on my vision. One minute, the guy was so faint, so far away, I figured I might as well head back to the car. Next minute, he was just a few yards ahead. The prickle at the back of my neck had spread to my entire body. I was frightened. Genuinely. Did not want to catch up to whoever I was after, but couldn't stop. I was at the limit of the headlights' reach. Through the fog, I saw shapes. Tall, dark. Bigger than a man, I judged. Couldn't tell what they were, but they made me feel worse. More afraid. Ground was harder to walk on. More rocks—almost all rocks. Clattered and snapped as I stepped on them. Fog thinned enough for me to see I was in a wide ditch, between two low rises. Ground was covered in rocks, none of 'em too big. Flint, as far as I could tell. Lot of the pieces looked like they'd been chipped into arrowheads, spear points, knives, ax heads. The dark shapes I mentioned? They were standing on the rises, every ten feet or so. Outcroppings of flint, each struck into a rough column, maybe eight or nine feet high by two or three wide. Didn't seem like they could be natural, but I didn't know what they were supposed to be. Wasn't anything carved into them, no shapes or symbols. The way the surfaces looked—the way the facets left from where the rock had been chipped away came together, there was almost something there. Faces, but horrible ones. Every last one staring at me.

"Felt like I was someplace old. I mean, ancient. I stopped walking. I had no idea how far this ditch went. Whoever I was following had disappeared. I listened. Couldn't hear any footsteps on the rocks. Should've made me feel better. Didn't. Place between my shoulders tingled, the way it does when someone's spying on you. The flint columns, with their almost-faces, it was like they were watching me. Or something was watching me through them. I'm not putting it right. It's like there was a smile floating behind each of them, a bad smile, except, it was all the same smile. Or—try this. It's like the columns were fingers and I was in the palm of their hand. Ditch was like one of the lines in your hand, grown giant. I crouched, tried to make myself smaller. Less visible to whatever had its eyes on me. Suppose everything I was experiencing could've been from how tired I was. Not to mention, how upset. Squatting in the ditch, though, with all these sharp objects, these weapons at my feet, I had a . . . sense of the ditch filled with blood, of a river of blood running over the arrowheads and knives, the spear tips and the ax heads. Was so vivid, I could almost see it. Reached out my hand and picked up a piece of flint. Knife, the edge still sharp enough to nick my finger, add a couple of drops of my blood to the flood I sensed. Smarted, but I held on to the blade. It was cold, freezing, like it had been buried under six inches of snow, not lying out in the open. Wouldn't warm in my hand. Felt good, the cold. Soothing. What was inside me was hot. I let the cold seep into me, and it brought the hot under control. More. It was like I took a part of winter into me. One of those freezing blasts that comes all the way from the North Pole, barrels down full of ice and snow. Covered the betrayal, the self-pity, the anger in white.

"I stood. Slipped the flint knife into my pocket. Still seemed like the columns were watching me. Didn't matter. Went back in the direction of the car. For a moment, thought I saw a figure walking toward me through the headlights. Wasn't nothing. Got in the car, started it, headed home. Had no trouble finding my way. In fact, funny thing was, I wasn't nearly as far from home as I'd thought. Figured I was out somewhere in the west of the state, Horseheads, that neck of the woods. Nope. Pine Hill, just about an hour south and west. I'd been driving a big loop. Never heard of any place like what I found in those parts. Always meant to look into it.

"Anyway, I pulled in the driveway a little after dawn. Waited a couple of hours til I was sure she was awake and went over to Karen's. She was surprised to see me. Assumed it was over between us. Which was reasonable. Told her I was willing to try moving forward if she was. She asked if I was sure. I shrugged, said yeah. Didn't realize I still had the knife in my pocket until I went home and changed into fresh clothes.

"Sounds sinister," Ivorsson said, "but it wasn't. Not like carrying the knife you killed a man with. Kept my blade on me after that. Was in my jacket on our wedding day. Had it with me when Rachel was born. All the arguments Karen and me had, the out-and-out fights, battles, I never went for it. Never even thought of it. Not once."

"Until you did," Michelle said. A guess, but one rewarded by Ivorsson's glance away. She wondered if the flint knife was in one of the pockets of his coveralls, within easy reach. According to what Dr. Smith had said, he no longer had need of it.

"Wasn't how—" Ivorsson caught himself, shook his head.

"Go on."

He did not. For a long time, Walter Ivorsson remained speechless, his attention so focused on the hole in the ice through which the fishing line he continued to jerk up and down rose and fell that Michelle thought their conversation had reached its terminus. Given her lack of interest in speaking to Ivorsson in the first place, her preference for dealing with him at a distance, the disappointment she felt at the end of their parley surprised her. All she had intended was to draw as near to him as she dared, cast the stones in her coat pocket onto the ice between them, and depart. There had been no need for her to pick up the verbal gauntlet Ivorsson had flung down; there had been less still for her to ask him about Toby. Already, she had reconciled herself to the twin facts of her brother's death and his body's disappearance. Until she had asked Ivorsson about him, she'd been unaware she would; once the words had entered the frigid air, however, they had gained an importance which had rendered her previous acceptance of Toby's loss null and void. Now the prospect of returning to her Subaru with her question unanswered stabbed her like a long, thin needle slid into the thick muscle of her beating heart, an injury insufficient to kill, but more than adequate to cause lasting hurt. Nonetheless, as Ivorsson's concentration appeared to have plunged into the chill water through which sluggish fish drifted in the wintry glow admitted by their icy ceiling, it seemed she would have no option but to leave with more pain than she'd brought. Had this been Ivorsson's intent in speaking to her all along? Her hand slipped into her jacket pocket, where the stones slid against her fingertips. She gathered them together, their rounded sides clicking against one another.

Ivorsson licked his lips with a tongue as washed-out as the rest of him. He said, "Took a while for things to go bad. Between me and Karen." Perhaps he wasn't done speaking, after all; perhaps, now that he'd started, the urge was proving too strong to resist. One by one, Michelle allowed the stones to slip from her grip. "Didn't mean they were over," he added.

"I'd say your divorce argued otherwise."

"That was your brother's idea," Ivorsson said, "*Toby*," giving to the two syllables such venom Michelle could easily believe he would have lunged at her brother, teeth bared, had it been him standing in her place. The anger Ivorsson provoked in her, the heated reminder this man had murdered Toby, was diluted by fear, unexpected and unexpectedly strong. She regretted losing hold of the stones. She swallowed, said, "You're telling me the papers hadn't been filed before Toby met Karen?" struggling not to blanch uttering both names, as if mentioning them in the same breath might stir Ivorsson to greater wrath. Yet she was damned if she would cower in front of this man, whatever crimes he had committed, whatever he had become. If he made a move on her, there was the knife on her belt; ineffectual as it might prove in the end, it would still hurt him, and the chance to inflict any pain at all on Walter Ivorsson had a fine appeal.

Leaving her parents bereft of two children, however, was not in her plan.

"No," Ivorsson said. So distracted had she been by fear, it took a moment for Michelle to recall the question he was answering. "He walked into the middle of that mess. Shoulda kept walking. What kinda absolute fucking *idiot* takes up with a woman with a husband and an eight-year-old daughter?"

"Ex-husband," Michelle said, remembering her many conversations with Toby over phone and Skype after he told her about the woman he was seeing, the PE teacher at the school where he'd accepted a position as school psychologist. Her own first reaction had been unease with her brother dating a woman whose divorce was a work in progress, her nervousness approaching anxiety as weeks built to months, the divorce dragged on, and Toby recounted more stories of the not-all-the-way-ex-husband's belligerent past and menacing present. "You need to be careful," she warned him on multiple occasions, which Toby had assured her he would be, was being, even as the lightness in his voice told her he wasn't unduly concerned with his girlfriend's ex, no matter what threatening behavior he'd just described. In part, this was because her baby brother was a six-three, two-hundred-and-fifty-pound, third-degree black belt in Tae Kwon Do who had shelves full of the trophies and medals he'd won sparring. Beyond that, Toby was fundamentally an optimist, unwilling, despite his considerable training, to credit the full extent of the human capacity for violence, especially when one is confronted by a situation over which they felt themselves losing control. Her work as an insurance investigator had left Michelle with a much dimmer, if to her mind more accurate, estimate of the chasm into which people might rappel, but no matter how much she tried to argue this to him, Toby would not be persuaded. "The guy's the head school bus mechanic," he said. "He isn't going to do anything to jeopardize that. Plus, he has joint custody of his daughter. If he does anything stupid, he could lose it." "If he messes with her mother," Michelle said, "I'm not so sure about you." Worry for his safety had made her wish they were kids again, so she could tell him what to do, leave this woman with her dangerous ex prowling around like a dog working itself up to bite—or, to be more accurate, so she could run to her parents and convince one of them to order Toby away from the woman whose presence in his life had placed it in such jeopardy. Except, she had seen the pictures her brother had posted of him and Karen on social media and texted to her, and she could not deny the look of happiness on his face, the smile she had missed in his photos of the last several years, as he moved through a succession of failed and occasionally disastrous relationships. His smile had been the marker for the bet she took in trusting his optimism.

Ivorsson ignored her correction. He said, "I helped raise that girl. Got up in the middle of the night with her when she needed to be fed. Rocked her back to sleep. Changed her shitty diapers, and man, did she have some doozies. Strangest foods would set her off. Bananas, which is unusual. She'd fill her diaper, and if you didn't realize what was happening straight away, shit went everywhere. Down her legs, up her back—I'm talking, almost to her neck. Ruined whatever outfit she had on. Had to drop it in a bucket with some hot water and detergent and hope for the best. Had to take her into the shower and hose her off. It was disgusting, but kinda funny, too. We'd laugh about it sometimes. Most of the time. We'd say, 'How can something so small make so much of something so horrible?' Times Rachel was hurt—there was this one night, she took a fall off the living room couch. Cracked her head on the floor pretty good. Screamed and cried like hell. No blood, pupils were okay. Had a hell of a lump. We called the pediatrician. She said Rachel was probably okay, but there was a chance of a concussion. To be safe, we should wake her every couple of hours through the night. Karen and me traded off checking her. This other time—Rachel was about a year old, she got this weird bruise on her forearm. Neither one of us could figure out what it was. Didn't look like she'd hit herself or anything. Course your mind jumps to the worst-case scenarios. Cancer in all its flavors. Weird, incurable infections. We found the bruise too late to do anything except leave a message for the doctor. All we could do was wait and worry. Finally, we heard this sucking sound, and there's the baby nursing on her arm. Gave herself a Goddamn hickey. We were so relieved, both of us had tears in our eyes." He shook his head. "Homemade birthday piñatas, summer trips to Lake George, taking her to ballet lessons—hell, I played the fucking mouse king when she was in the *Nutcracker*. What father could've done more? Not fucking Bobby Dunn. Not fucking Toby Word.

"But no, first Dunn reappears, emails Karen saying he realizes what a terrible mistake he made, not having anything to do with his daughter. Says he's living in Saratoga. Out of the service, doing executive protection for some of the bigwigs who live around that neck of the woods. Great pay, flexible schedule. Would be no problem for him to nip down to visit, if Karen thinks it's a good idea. Which she does. Doesn't consult me. Tells Rachel before she tells me. Rachel always knew she wasn't mine. Never tried to hide it from her. Still, she grew up calling me Daddy. Having Dunn enter the picture confused her. She was nine. Didn't need this kind of uncertainty. But her mother had insisted on putting Dunn's name on the birth certificate, hadn't she? Like she knew this was gonna happen. I argued about it with her. Couldn't change her mind. 'He needs this,' she said. Can you—I mean, don't that beat it all? *He* needs this. What about me?" Ivorsson clenched his teeth and jerked his head, a gesture of lingering resentment.

"Read this book when I was at the community college. *The Sun Also Rises*. About this guy who got his dick shot off in World War

I and can't be with the woman he loves. Who's a slut. Anyway, there's a scene where this other guy is talking about how he went bankrupt. Says something to the effect of, a little bit at a time, then all at once. What happened with Karen and me was like that. Starting with her inviting Dunn into our lives, things went wrong. Routines we had, Chinese takeout on Sunday, watching Fallon on *The Tonight Show*, weren't any good any more. With Rachel especially, it was, 'Bob' (which was what he told her to call him) 'and I went out for Indonesian food,' which, there wasn't an Indonesian place nearby. I'd get frustrated at that, at her, 'It's okay,' which she said with a sigh, to let you know it wasn't okay. If I called her on it, on her attitude, she'd walk away from me. Go to her room and refuse to come out. Lock the door. Karen told me I was overreacting, but what the fuck did she know? She was the one who'd caused this in the first place. She emailed Dunn all the time. Sent him pictures of Rachel, Rachel and her. Never pictures with me in them, or almost never. Started calling him, too, filling him in on everything he'd missed. Consulting with him, planning for Rachel to spend even more time with him, for him to come to our place for Thanksgiving, maybe.

"Yeah. There was plenty for us to argue over. Seemed like all the time I'd known Karen, I'd been—not unhappy, exactly, but not all the way happy, either. Always another complication coming up. For once, I wanted to feel like I was at peace with her, her with me. Like the two of us were settled with one another. Like she said she was, when I agreed to stay with her. Direction things were headed, it didn't look like this was gonna be the case, ever. Felt like I was trying to hold on to Jell-O. Stuff keeps slipping between your fingers, and the tighter you squeeze, the more it comes apart. Went from saying stupid shit to her—nasty stuff—to getting in her face. Menacing her, you would call it. Shoved her sometimes. Knew she had her clasp knife on her. Every time I crowded her into a corner, pushed her against a wall, I knew there was a chance this would be the time she took it out, used it on me the way she did the poor fucker in Afghanistan. Didn't want her to, exactly.

Wondered what it would feel like. Seemed if she stabbed me, it would be proof of everything I'd said about the way she treated me. The way she made me feel. But she didn't. Never went for it once, even when I . . . when things got worse. I'd been physical with her before. Slapped her to bring her out of her PTSD states. Stuff like that. Didn't mean nothing bad by it. This was different. First time, we made up. Second, she threw me out. Third, she took herself and Rachel to a friend's house. Next day, I heard from her lawyer. Pretty soon, I had a lawyer, too."

Ivorsson sighed. "Everything was fucked up. Not gonna lie, there were times I wondered if we should go our separate ways. If nothing else, I thought we might have to end the marriage. So we could start over. Put the past behind us, make something new, better. Almost had Karen convinced of it. Then your brother comes on the scene. I was not happy at Karen seeing him. But I told myself it was just a fling. No big deal. Took it as penance, something I had to endure because of what I'd done. Balancing the scales, like.

"Next thing I know, Karen's pushing to get the divorce done. I tried to slow things down. Thought I could outlast the new boyfriend. Was sure he'd get tired of her soon enough, and then what would she be left with?"

"How romantic," Michelle said.

"Didn't work," Ivorsson said. "Son of a bitch was dug in like a tick. Worse, Rachel liked him right away. Talked about him nonstop when I took her for our time together. Yeah, Judge Badrebue hadn't given Karen what she wanted as far as the divorce went, but he agreed Rachel should live with her, especially after she told him I wasn't Rachel's biological father. Meant I saw her every other weekend and one day during the week. Could've been more if Rachel had asked for it. But she never did. Wonder why that was. We'd sit eating ice cream at the Cone E Island and she'd chatter on with Toby-this and Toby-that. Unless she was telling me about the plans Bobby Dunn had for them the next time she went to see him. Between Dunn, and your brother, and school, and ballet, there wasn't any room left in her life for me. I was being squeezed out."

"You don't think acting like a lunatic might have had something to do with it?" Michelle said. "I heard about the shit you pulled. Sitting out in front of the house in your truck at two in the morning. Calling at all hours of the day and night and not saying anything. Showing up at Rachel's school and saying you were there to pick her up. You cannot have believed any of that was going to help whatever case you imagined you were making."

"Maybe I didn't. Maybe I couldn't help myself."

"Bullshit. You didn't want to help yourself. You were wallowing."

The fishing rod stopped its up and down motion. Ivorsson's gaunt face seemed to grow thinner still, the flesh to tighten over the bone. Underfoot, ice crackled.

"What I can't understand," Michelle continued, "is how you convinced Karen to go with you to wherever you murdered her. Because the cops all agree, there was no sign of a struggle, not in her house, at least. Did you con your way inside, then pull a gun on her? Or did you tell her a story, something designed to get past her defenses? Something about Rachel?"

"Something to do with me." The words rasped from Ivorsson's throat. "Got to the point, living lost its savor. Everything turned gray, like. Couldn't find pleasure anywhere. Stopped watching TV, listening to music. Ate less and less. Couldn't taste the food. Was always hungry, but couldn't work myself up to care about it. Finally stopped eating altogether. Weak, light-headed all the time. Figured I was starving myself to death. Didn't care. One morning, just wouldn't wake up. Pictured how upset Karen would be, how full of regret. Serve her right. Only problem was, I wouldn't be around to see it. Shouldn't have mattered, but it did. Seemed like one more disappointment. The final frustration. Guess I could've faked my death. Spied on everyone at the funeral. They did that on an episode of *Little House on the Prairie,* I think. Didn't want to, though. What I wanted was to watch Karen's face as I died in front of her.

"Didn't take long to come up with a plan. Had to be sure Rachel wasn't around. Or your brother. This was between me and Karen, no one else. Fortunately for me, Rachel was visiting with Bob

Dunn the same weekend your brother was away doing something with your family."

"Our mother's birthday," Michelle said. "Toby wanted Karen to come with him, but she didn't feel comfortable going. She hadn't met any of us yet, and the prospect of doing so all together was intimidating. Especially with her divorce not completed, she was self-conscious about showing up as Toby's date. Which was stupid, and got her killed."

"Couldn't drive to her place. Too light-headed. Cut through the woods between the cottage I was renting now and the house that had been mine not long before. Started snowing on the way. Part of me felt like lying down right there in the middle of the trees and letting the snow cover me. Ignored it, kept going. Thought the radio said something about a storm heading our way, but wasn't sure. Wind blew over the treetops. Made a spooky sound, like ghosts crying. Came to the house. *Her* house. The house she and Rachel were living in without me, but sometimes with your brother. Her car was in the driveway. Would've been funny if it wasn't, if she'd gone somewhere, too. Joke's on me! you could've said."

Michelle did not respond.

"Banged on the front door. Best I could, anyway. Nearly passed out from the effort. Karen answered. Didn't act surprised to meet me standing there, all snowy. Just looked tired. Said, 'What is it, Walter?' Like I was a nuisance, same as some asshole going door to door trying to sell you on his church. Rachel wasn't there, she said, as if I didn't know. Can't remember exactly what I said. Something about the snow. Asked her if she was gonna make me stand out in it. She crossed her arms. Didn't move from the doorway. 'So this is how it is,' I says. Reached into my pocket and came out holding my flint knife. That got a reaction. She stepped back. Stuck her hand in her jeans pocket for her clasp knife. Guess I understood why. Still made me sad. Tilted my head back, pressed the stone to my throat. Over the carotid. Blade was sharp as ever. Wouldn't take much pressure to part the skin. Stared up into the snow falling.

Seemed like the prettiest sight I'd ever seen. Thought it would be okay to die looking at this.

"Then Karen said, 'Stop. Please.' And I did. Or didn't, I guess. Kept the knife where it was. But lowered my head to look at Karen. Her hands were empty. No clasp knife. She held them out in front of her. The way she was standing, kind of crouched down a little, it was like she was getting ready to jump at me. To wrestle the blade out of my hands, maybe. Felt something wet on my face. Snow, I figured, melting. Realized I was crying. Started sobbing. Like a kid. Hadn't cried like that since . . . don't know how long. Maybe when my ma died. Not in all the time Karen and me were together. Couldn't stop. Seemed like everything inside me was forcing its way out through my tear ducts. I saw Karen's face. Some suspicion, but mostly pity. Which didn't help my crying none.

"'What is it you want?' Karen says. Like she didn't know. Like I hadn't told her a thousand times. Like my Goddamn lawyer hadn't told her Goddamn lawyer. Like she couldn't see what was right there in front of her and know what it meant. She waited for me to answer. I couldn't, with the crying. Finally, she said she would drive me home. Didn't argue. Waited for her to pull on her coat and boots, grab her keys and bag. Seemed foolish to keep the knife at my throat. Kept it in my hand, though. She started her car. She brushed the snow off the driver's side. I brushed the snow off mine. Belted ourselves in and set off. Wasn't far to my place. Took a while, on account of the weather. Couldn't see two feet in front of you. Felt like we should be having some kind of important conversation. Held the knife in my hand and ran my thumb along the edge. Was done crying. Had the hollow feeling you get afterward. Empty. Hungry, too. So much my stomach hurt. Wished we could keep driving. Eventually, though, we were at the end of my driveway. Karen put the car into park. Kept looking straight ahead. 'Well,' she said.

"I unlocked my seat belt. Leaned toward Karen. Like I was going to kiss her cheek. She went all stiff. I came up with the knife and slashed her throat."

He had said the words. Though she had expected them, Michelle flinched.

"Blood sprayed over the steering wheel, the dash. The smell filled the car. Karen grabbed her throat with her left hand, grabbed for the seat belt lock with her right. I caught her wrist, pulled her hand away from the lock. Her eyes were wide. Blood was leaking through her fingers, running down her neck onto her coat and sweater. She tried to yank her wrist free. Couldn't. I held on tight. She rocked against her seat. Kicked at the floor. Her mouth opened like she was going to say something. But her eyes were losing focus. Strength was leaving her arm. She tipped against the door. I let go of her. She slapped at the seat belt. Eyes rolled back in her head. Hand dropped from her throat. More blood ran out of her neck, but in a trickle. Like a faucet with no pressure. It stopped. I waited. She got very still. I lifted her arm. Felt for a pulse. None. She was gone."

"You mean she was murdered," Michelle said, voice shaking. "You murdered her. Toby was right. My brother was right. You fucking murdered your ex-wife."

The description bothered him far less than she would have expected. One side of his mouth lifted in an expression of dismissal, as if to say, "Well, what can you do?" He said, "You could call it that."

"Is there a better word for cutting someone's throat and holding them in place until they bleed out?"

"Holy," Ivorsson said. "What I did in the car with the snow covering the windows was holy. Felt like I was in a huge space. Like a church. Full of darkness. And something else. Something big, set back in the shadows. Watching me. Like when I found the stone knife. At the streambed full of flint pieces. Where I'd sensed something looking at me. Didn't know if this was the same . . . thing. Thought so. Seemed like it was holding its breath. Waiting to see what I'd do next. Was still trying to figure that out myself when a snowplow went by. Splashed snow and slush over the car. Lit up the windows yellow with its roof light. Came so close, it rocked the car side to side. That made me move. Got out my side of the car. Looked to see if there was anyone else nearby. Just the plow, heading off into the storm. Went to the driver's door. Dragged Karen out of her seat around to the trunk. Found a couple of old blankets in it. Used to keep them in there for Rachel, in case she wanted to stop and have a picnic. Lifted Karen into the trunk, covered her with the blankets. Wouldn't do much to hide her from anyone intent on finding her. With all the blood on the driver's seat, the steering wheel, the dash, I figured that was the last of my worries. Wasn't time to do anything about the mess. Climbed behind the wheel, set the wipers going, turned up the heat, and put the car in gear."

"Where did you take her?"

"Someplace secret. There's secret places all over these mountains. Old houses down long driveways. Logging camps up dirt roads. Summer camps in little valleys. Clearings where someone laid the foundations for something and never finished it. You can run across rusted-out cars with trees growing through them halfway up a mountain. A washing machine sitting at the foot of a cliff. A tuba half in a creek. Caves, too. You find caves everywhere. Some are shallow. Some go down, right into the heart of the mountains. Under the mountains, if you believe some of the stories folks tell.

"Kept to the back roads. Which was tricky, in the storm. Headed deep into the mountains. Weather got worse. Had to slow to a crawl. Put on the hazards. No one else out, but wasn't taking any chances. Couple of times, thought I might be lost. Wasn't. Was just the snow making everything look strange. Finally reached my destination. You woulda seen a gap in the trees beside the road and not thought it was anything. Most people would've thought the same. Put on my damn turn signal." Ivorsson barked a laugh. "Don't that beat all? Here I am, in the middle of a blizzard, with the road empty, with my trunk full, and I'm worried about using my signal." He shook his head in amusement. "Force of habit, I guess. Anyway. Steered off the road, between the trees. Hemlocks. Drove through a grove of them. Came out the other side next to an old tannery. Used to be tanneries all over the Catskills. Wasn't much left of this one, foundation and part of one wall. Went around it. Would've been slow going without the weather. Followed another old road down a steep slope. Wheels slipped. Half-slid the rest of the way. Rolled across a brook. Came to the mouth of a cave. Eased the car into it. Kept going. Place went back and back and back. Cave ceiling came right down to the car's roof. Decided to stop once I judged I'd gone far enough not to be seen by someone standing at the entrance to the place. Wasn't expecting anyone to be there. The storm would cover my tracks pretty well, on top of me driving to a place not ten men knew about, and nine of them in nursing homes. Turned off the engine, but left the lights on. Wasn't ready to be in the complete dark yet."

"'Yet'?"

"Plan was for me to stay with Karen. Until I died. Felt like I was already most of the way there. Couldn't believe I'd had the strength for . . . everything. Managed to fetch Karen from the trunk, sit her against the front bumper. Sat down beside her. Leaned my head on the car. Closed my eyes. Imagined the two of us being discovered like this some day far in the future. All dried out, a couple of mummies. Was a little sad for Rachel, not knowing what had happened to us. Where we were. Seemed for the best, though. Dunn would look after her, I assumed. Wanted nothing more than to let go. Drift out into the dark. Fade like the car's headlights, which were starting to lose juice.

"Problem was, I was hungry. Worse. Couldn't believe one man could feel such hunger. It was like, my appetite was outside me, giant-sized, crouched in the shadow beyond the light. Smell of Karen's blood was everywhere. On her sweater, my jacket. Made my mouth water. Stomach growled like a bobcat. Waited for the feeling to pass. Didn't. Got worse. Drool spilled down my chin. Wiped it with the back of my hand. Realized I was holding the flint knife. Couldn't recall taking it out of my pocket. Gripped it tight. Saw something at the edge of the darkness. A face, hanging in the air. Like a man's, but huge. Broad. Heavy black hair. It was squinting at me. Lip raised on rough teeth. Jagged, the lot of them.

Broken, maybe. Pair of horns stood out from the temples. Thick, like an elk or moose, but weird, warped, like they were diseased. Licked its lips. Tongue was thick, pointed. Rolled out of its mouth and hung there, swishing back and forth. Something moved on the tongue. Maggots. Like it was a length of dead meat dangling there. Some of the maggots fell on the cave floor. Sounded like raindrops. I was sure I was hallucinating. Had to be. On account of the hunger. Seemed pretty real, all the same. Scared me so bad it was like I wasn't in my body. Pissed myself. Might as well have been someone else's jeans getting wet. Was like the face was more real than I was. Fear was so strong, it was almost another feeling . . . joy, I guess. Felt the knife weighting my hand. Came back to myself a little. Found I could move. Move in that greater reality. Turned to Karen. Hunger twisted my gut.

"Seemed like a kind of wind passed through me. Like the face breathed out. Only, the breath was cold. Freezing. There were words in the wind—or, not words, exactly, but meaning. I'm not describing it right. More a case of, I knew I didn't have to die. No reason to starve to death, with all this meat fresh in front of me. The other stuff I thought, about dying next to Karen, didn't matter anymore. What did was eating. Stood and almost fell down again. Legs were asleep. Forced them to walk me to the driver's-side door. Wasn't a hundred percent sure the car would start, but it did. Right away. Headlights glowed. Wanted to make sure I'd have light to last me. For what I was gonna do. The face was gone. Didn't pay it any mind. It—or what it gave me—was inside me. Swear I could feel horns on either side of my head. Had to remove Karen's clothes and then . . . don't suppose you know how to dress a deer?"

"I do," Michelle said, the words weighted and difficult to say, because already her mind's eye was viewing memories of Saturday hunting trips with her father. Having opened the buck or doe they'd shot and removed the wet mass of the organs, saving the heart and liver, they tied its legs together, hauled the deer out of the woods, lashed it to the roof of the family car, and headed back down the Taconic, their gruesome cargo drawing wide-eyed looks from their fellow drivers. Their destination was not the brown and white Tudor in which Michelle was raised; rather, they made their way across Yorktown Heights to the strip mall in which Dad's friend, Van, had his butcher's shop. They would drive to the back of the store, where Van would be waiting for them. Together, they would untie the deer and carry it inside. If the trip had been long, if she and her father had to sit in their blind until almost the last minute before a deer picked its way into sight, they would hang the carcass in Van's walk-in freezer, to await his attentions the following morning. If they had been successful immediately, or near enough, Van would set to work on the remains with the knives he laid out on a small wheeled table he rattled over the tiled floor. From the first moment Michelle had expressed an interest in accompanying her father on his annual hunt, he had insisted she commit to the entire enterprise, from cleaning the rifles, to helping to load the car the night before, to field-dressing the deer, to standing by for this last, bloody chapter, in which Van's knives separated the cloudy-eyed carcass into steadily smaller pieces, until all that was recognizable of the animal her or her dad's bullet had brought to the leaf-strewn earth was its head, its hooves, and its hide. The rest was in stacked packages wrapped in white butcher paper, the identity of their contents scrawled on them in black grease pencil. For his labors, Van retained twenty percent of the meat; the rest went into a pair of large coolers in the car trunk, and from there to the big freezer in the garage.

The methodical, surprisingly quick process by which skin was sliced from muscle, muscle freed from bone, bone sawed from bone, had not bothered Michelle. She herself had been surprised at her lack of any emotion other than a keen interest. Picturing Walter Ivorsson employing a flint knife to perform the same series of actions on the still-warm corpse of his ex-wife, however, was an entirely different matter, particularly as what it was preliminary to. "He will have eaten human flesh," Dr. Smith had said. "Not just tasted it, but consumed it. From what you've said, his ex-wife. I would fear your brother, too." Seated in her cushioned office chair, her cell pressed to her ear, Michelle had felt her arms and neck crawling with horror, her two cups of coffee burning at the top of her throat, at what the community college professor (emerita) had been saying to her. The response was nothing compared to what swept her out here under the sky's bright blue bowl, a revulsion so profound it made her legs tremble with the urge to run, to flee from this man and his depredations. As long as she remembered to drop the stones in her pocket on the way, why shouldn't she let her feet do what they wanted?

Because, she thought, *you don't know where Toby is.* Given the chance of learning the location of his remains, which it seemed she was on the verge of, she had to take it, didn't she? Besides, it was too late. She had heard Ivorsson's terrible confession, been shared secrets toxic as uranium. Some part of her . . . spirit? soul? call it what you would, the interior space where her truest self lived, had been poisoned and would remain blighted forever. A line from a college literature class sounded in her ears: "After such knowledge, what forgiveness?" (From a poem by T. S. Eliot, she was reasonably sure.) At the time, she had read and re-read it, labored over its nine syllables, whose apparent clarity masked a meaning she had been unable to grasp—or, not grasp as much as appreciate, feel. Knowledge was knowledge, she had contended in class, information. How could it be either good or bad? Little had she known the answer to her question was waiting in her future, on the frozen surface of a lake high in the Catskills. And if this was the case, if she was tainted, she might as well remain in place, and see her bitter mission through to the end.

"Not a lot of women know how to clean a deer," Ivorsson said.

"Yeah, well," Michelle said.

"Flint knife worked better'n I woulda guessed," he said. "Got hard to hold at times. Slippery. But I managed to do what I had to. Didn't have nothin' but time. Was so hungry, I wanted to rush. Forced myself to go slow. Do things properly. What was happening was . . . sacred. As much as if I'd been in a church. More. I dressed every last bit of Karen. Then I sat down to table. Never tasted anything so sweet. Brought tears to my eyes. Assumed I'd have to pace myself. But it was like, the more I ate, the more I could eat. Like I was growing gigantic, until I had to lean forward to keep my head from hitting the cave roof. All of her went into my mouth. Was still hungry after. Broke open the long bones and sucked out the marrow. Licked the rest clean. Only part of her I didn't touch was the head. Set it on top of the car, facing into the cave. Reached into the car and shut off the engine. Turned off the lights. Everything went black. Didn't matter. Walked toward the cave mouth. Didn't bother saying goodbye to Karen. No need. She was inside me.

"Reached the entrance at dusk. Snow over everything. Ice hanging from the trees. Setting sun turned all of it red. Had stripped off back at the car. Didn't much feel the cold now. Even though the breath was steaming out of me. Still seemed like I was bigger than I had been. Like the feeling I had while I was eating was right, real. Have to admit, I half-expected a bunch of cops to be waiting for me, guns drawn. Don't know what I would have done. Wasn't no one. Which was a relief, I guess. Mostly what I was was hungry. Not like I had been, but enough so I noticed. Stepped onto the snow. Stung my feet. The wind I felt in the cave raised in my chest, and I ran across the snow. Back up the way I came. Feet burned like they were on fire. I was barely touching the ground. Running faster than I ever had. Climbing up into the air. Through the trees, then over them. Soles of my feet all fiery. Everything sped up. Next I knew, I was at the back door of my cottage, reaching under the doormat for the spare key. No one saw me.

"Which made it easier when the sheriff came knocking. Couple days later. Asking if I'd seen Karen. Told him I had not. Said I'd been sick. Flu, maybe. Called into work about it. Had, too, since I'd been home. Told them I'd been too ill to phone before, and they believed me. Sheriff Rudyard was less convinced. Snow was piled up on my car, though. Driveway hadn't been plowed. He stuck his head through the doorway. 'Come in,' I says. 'You wanna have a look around, go ahead.' Man checked out the entire house.

Went from the attic crawlspace to the basement crawlspace. Kept his hand near his pistol. Only thing he paused over was the flint knife. I left it sitting on the coffee table in the living room. Rudyard stared at it for a long time. Never touched it, never asked me about it. On his way out, he said I should stay put until Karen turned up. Sure, I said. Was just about sure he'd be back.

"Next day, he was. Had a couple of deputies with him. Said he wanted another look at my knife. 'What knife?' I says. 'So this's how it's gonna be,' he says. 'I don't know what you're talking about,' I says. 'I let you have a look around the other day out of courtesy. You won't do so again without a warrant.' Turns out, he had one. No matter. Knife was hid where the likes of them wouldn't find it. Didn't stop 'em from tearing the place apart searching for it. Still had my lawyer's number from the divorce stuff. Called and gave him the lowdown. Not ten minutes later, he was at the end of my driveway. Got right up in Rudyard's face. Sheriff had ideas about taking me into custody. Escorting me down to the station, was how he put it. To conduct a more in-depth interview about Karen's disappearance. Uh-uh, lawyer says, no way. Mr. Ivorsson will be happy to drive himself into town, where I will be happy to sit with him while you interview him. Rudyard was mad. Oh man, was he ever. Went along with it. No choice, really. Our talk was what he woulda called inconclusive. Was obvious he wanted to come out and ask if I'd killed Karen. With the lawyer there, wasn't no way that was gonna happen. Kept my answers short. Honest as I could. Closest Rudyard came to accusing me of anything was asking if I had any thoughts as to what might have happened to Karen. I said I didn't. But also said he should be putting the same question to Bobby Dunn and your brother."

"The cops talked to Toby several times," Michelle said. "Called the rest of the family to verify his alibi. Not to mention, to find out if everything had been okay between him and Karen. I can't say if they checked on Dunn, but I would be surprised if they didn't. Sounds to me as if the sheriff liked you for the crime. Better judgment than I would have given the man I met credit for. You did something to him, didn't you?"

"Day after my visit to the station, sheriff comes by a third time. Around dinner. Says he's giving me one last chance to do the right thing. Spill the beans on what I did with Karen. Says it'll go easier on me if I help locate her. Asks me to think about Rachel. Who's still with Dunn. Did I mention that? When Karen wasn't around for her to come home to, son of a bitch decided to keep her with him. Ran it by Karen's sister—the one in *Seattle*—who said, Yeah, sure. Not like there's anyone else she could stay with. Like, say, the man who raised her. Who's still supposed to have some rights.

"Anyway. Answered Rudyard's same questions same as I had sitting next to my lawyer. Didn't go over any better outside my front door than it had in the station. Rudyard's hand was on his pistol. Could see him thinking about taking it out, waving it around. Reckless. Might go off. Was already pretty sure it wouldn't hurt me if it did. Wasn't in a hurry to test the theory, though. Have to admit, him showing up made me—not nervous. Antsy. Pissed off. Mostly, I was hungry. Always. Like I had been in the cave. Like the emptiness in me now was a bridge to the emptiness in me then. To what had flown into me there. To what I had become. Just like that, I brought what I had been across that bridge to this moment. Felt like a storm blew up around me. Sheriff looked like he was shrinking. Old Rudyard had no fucking conception what was going on. His eyes bugged out. His mouth opened and a high-pitched sound came out: Eeeeeeeeeee. Backed away from me. Missed his footing, fell on his ass. Forgot all about his gun. Crawled to his car and took off with the driver's door hanging open. Heard he had a heart attack later the same night. Kept him in the hospital the better part of a week." Ivorsson made no effort to hide his grin. "Didn't see him again after that.

"Your brother—Toby—he was another story."

"You want to know what's funny?" Michelle said. "He thought you were innocent. At first. Said it was too obvious; there was no way you would do anything so dumb. You would have to know you were the first person everyone would suspect, the estranged, soon-to-be-ex-husband with a history of domestic 'problems.' Not that he liked you personally; he was afraid the cops had wasted precious time on you while whatever had happened to Karen was receding further into the past. Since there was no sign of the car, he thought she'd gone out for a drive, decided to take a day trip somewhere, and had an accident, run off the road and not been found, yet. I told him in all the cases I'd worked, ninety-nine times out of a hundred, when someone goes missing, a family member is behind it."

"'Cases'?" Ivorsson said. "Didn't figure you for a cop."

"I'm not," Michelle said. "Insurance investigator. Some overlap as far as the ringside seat for human folly—and occasionally worse."

"Sounds like you aimed your brother in my direction."

"I talked over the details of Karen's disappearance with him. Walked through different scenarios. From the start, we dismissed her running away. Well, Toby did. He couldn't believe she'd abandon Rachel. What he really meant was, he couldn't believe she would abandon Rachel and him. I wasn't as sure. People can surprise you in all sorts of unpleasant ways. Based on everything I knew, I admitted it sounded unlikely. The car accident theory, we pursued for a while. Toby compiled a list of locations Karen had been to and enjoyed, and a list of places she'd expressed an interest in visiting, and plotted out the most likely routes to each and every one. Any on main roads, he crossed out. Any on back roads, or that you had to drive on back roads to reach, he highlighted. He took a couple of days off work and spent them driving these routes, eyes peeled at every twist and turn for evidence of a crash. He had a fantasy of finding her car buried in a snowdrift at the bottom of a gulch, Karen inside, unconscious, possibly comatose, but clinging to life. For his sake, I wanted it to be true, but I wasn't optimistic. By the time he decided you were worth considering, after all, it sounds like you'd had your final . . . encounter with Sheriff Rudyard, because the man was in the hospital. His deputies weren't any help. I wanted him to go to the state police, which he did, only to have the guy he spoke with inform him they were aware of the situation and offering assistance to Sheriff Rudyard as he requested it. In other words, not at all. By this point, Toby was in a low-level panic. He'd left so many messages on Karen's cell, the mailbox was full. None of her friends or family had heard from him. He considered hiring a private investigator, went as far as to call a woman in Albany. She listened to him and said it sounded as if he'd done a lot of what she would have. She could go over the same ground he'd covered, see if she noticed anything he'd missed, but she was reluctant to take his money if she wasn't going to be able to contribute to the search. Much as I respected the PI's honesty, I can't help wishing she had been just a little less scrupulous, because then she would have been the one to knock on your door. It might have led to her death, I know, but I would still have my brother."

"Nah," Ivorsson said, "things were always gonna heat up between him and me."

"You're saying you were bound to murder him?"

"Don't know as I murdered the man . . ."

"Oh, come on," Michele said. "You already admitted to killing your ex-wife."

"Wife. And killing her, yes. Murdering her, no."

"What word would you prefer?"

"Karen was a sacrifice."

"To whom?"

"Face I saw in the cave. What came into me there."

"You didn't know about any of that when you cut her throat."

"You forget," Ivorsson said, "the place I found the knife. The flint river. First time I was aware of it. The presence."

"Is this what Toby was, another sacrifice?"

"He was more in the way of," Ivorsson searched for the correct term, "prey. Don't talk about murdering prey. Don't make sense. Being killed's what prey's for. What makes it prey."

"Prey and provender," Michelle said. "That means—"

"I know what provender is," Ivorsson said with pique. He did not say if Michelle's use of the word was correct.

"Toby called me the night he confronted you. He was . . ." She recalled the emotions fighting for control of her brother. She had heard anger quivering in the first thing he said to her: "He did it, Shelly. The fucker murdered her. He fucking *murdered* her," the trembling continuing as anger crumbled to anguish and he said, "She's dead. Oh my God. She's gone. I'm never going to see her again," the shaking subsiding, his volume diminishing as anguish gave way to something like wonder and he said, "He isn't human." Of course he wasn't, Michelle had said, he was a monster, but where she had been speaking metaphorically, her brother had not. She caught the thread of what she had been saying to Ivorsson, continued, "He was upset. He was sure Karen was dead and you had murdered her. I tried to get him to tell me what you'd said, what had convinced him you were responsible for Karen. Depending on what it was, I thought we might be able to take it to the cops, force them to do more than they had. He wouldn't say. Or he couldn't. He was too overwhelmed by something else, something he'd seen. He didn't make any sense, not to me, at least, not at the time. He kept repeating, 'I saw him, Shelly, I really saw him.' You were tall, he said, so tall. Thin, too, as if you were starving. There was something about your head, but he had trouble describing it. Like horns, he said, which sounded ridiculous, insane. He couldn't talk about your face, just said what he saw there made him run to his car and leave as fast as he could. He said you followed him part of the way, walking on air."

Ivorsson smirked. "Can guess how that went over."

"No," Michelle said, "I didn't believe him. Can you blame me? You knew—you knew you could show him what you were and as long as there was no one else there to corroborate his story, you were fine. You were more than fine: the narrative someone like Toby, or the sheriff, would've told sounded so crazy there was no way anyone would believe it. Instead, it would seem like you were the object of a delusional person's obsessive fantasy."

Ivorsson nodded. The smirk had stretched to a grin, which would not have been out of place on the muzzle of a wolf.

"Afterward, he said you were following him. Stalking him, right? Every time he turned around, there you were. In the Price Chopper, at the other end of the meat counter. At the McDonald's, eating your Quarter Pounder a couple of booths away, your lips smeared with ketchup. Standing outside his kitchen window in the middle of the night, when he got up for a glass of water. Watching him get in his car from across the school parking lot. None of it was anything he could tell the cops. It would have gone even worse if he'd told them everything he'd seen: your tongue flopping past your lips, impossibly long and crawling with maggots; your mouth opening wider than any man's could; you with the soles of your boots three feet off the ground. You watched him from high up in the branches of tall trees. You floated on the other side of his bedroom window, scratching at the glass and whispering to him.

"Yeah, I thought he was having some kind of extended breakdown, brought on by the stress of Karen's disappearance and likely death. I had no problem believing you were responsible; like I said, the odds, not to mention, what I knew of the facts, argued in favor of it. The other stuff, you as a supernatural monster, was harder to accept, to put it mildly. The thing was, Toby didn't come across as out of his mind. At this point, we were on the phone with one another every day, and what I heard was confusion, my very smart brother struggling with information which couldn't be true but all the same was. Since he disappeared, I've become a lot more sympathetic to what he must have been going through."

"All my life," Ivorsson said, "it's been me on the receiving end. Of Karen's bullshit, mostly. At work, too. Always the butt of someone's joke. Was the same in high school, middle school. To be the one giving shit, instead of taking it, was great." The smile had decayed to a sneer. "Didn't hurt it was the guy who'd been fucking my wife."

"He figured out what you were," Michelle said. "Not immediately. At first, he was worried he was losing his mind. Eventually, he decided to do research, to see if he could find a connection between what he was going through and anything in the real world. Such as it is. It took him a little while, but with Karen gone, time was one thing he had plenty of. Online, he found a couple of articles in an academic journal which seemed to relate to what he was experiencing. He reached out to the author, and she was willing to speak with him. He didn't tell her the truth. Instead, he said he was working on a horror novel set in the Catskills, and he needed help with the monster for it. She listened to him enumerating your various activities and gave what you are a name."

"Oh?" Ivorsson said. "What is that?"

"Wendigo," Michelle said. *Or Stone Coat,* Professor Smith had said. *Or Chiroo. The native peoples of this land had different names for the same figure, a giant who eats human flesh but is not filled. It has cousins as far afield as India—the Rakshasa—and as far back in time as ancient Greece—the Laestrygonians, who destroy most of Odysseus's ships and consume most of his men. It is monstrous, evil, the end result—usually—of a great crime, a profound betrayal, typically cannibalism.*

"Wen-di-go," Ivorsson said, drawing out the syllables. He shrugged. "If you say so. Didn't help your brother none. He came for me, you know. Wasn't ready to be done fucking with him yet. But he's waiting when I come from work. Didn't see where he was hiding. Back of a big willow in the front yard. Must've walked, 'cause there was no car in the driveway. Holds on til I'm at the front door, then steps out and points the gun he's carrying at me. Big thing. Three-fifty-seven. Says I'm gonna tell him exactly what I did with Karen. If he doesn't like my answer, he'll blow a hole in me with his hand cannon. 'Tell you?' I says. 'Shit, son, I'll go one step better. I'll show you!' And I did. Credit where credit's due: he didn't run. Not right away. No, he lifted the pistol, steadied his wrist, and pulled the trigger. Got off four shots. Two missed me. Smacked the cottage. Other two hit me. Full in the chest. Felt like being kicked by a horse. Staggered me. I'd had a hunch a gun wouldn't kill me. Turned out to be true. Hurt, all the same. Pissed me off. Made me roar. Like, I don't know, a bear. Or the wind. That was it for your Toby. Turned tail and ran. Straight into the woods. Situation might've turned out differently if he tried for the road.

Especially if he flagged down a car. In the forest, he was mine. I didn't bother walking on the air. Wanted to run him down. Already was pretty far ahead. Fast."

Michelle heard herself saying, "He ran track in high school, sprints," which was absurd but somehow important to say now, as the story of her brother's life was reaching its end.

"Took me a little bit to catch up to him. Right as I was nipping at his heels, he stopped, turned, and shot the last two bullets in his gun. Surprised me. One went wild. Other caught me straight in the head." Ivorsson released the fishing rod with his right hand and raised it to point at a spot over his right eye, a location which would have been incapacitating, if not out-and-out fatal, for anyone else. His mitten traced the skin there, in whose pale surface Michelle could detect no hint of a scar. "Took the wind out of my sails for a good couple minutes. Who knows? Maybe if he'd had an automatic, he coulda done more damage. Or if he brought extra bullets. In one of those speed-loader things. Instead, he tossed the three-fifty-seven. Went back to running. Stopped one last time. Took a couple of pictures with his phone. Didn't get much farther. Tried to run and do something with his phone. Guess he was sending the photos to you."

"Yes." She had been out with her friends when her phone chimed to announce the arrival of a new message. A glance at the screen had shown a pair of attachments from Toby. The images tapping the phone brought up were blurred, poorly lit, and would have been difficult to discern even had she not been standing in a crowded club whose sound system was thumping so hard it was making her beer dance on the table. Toby must have messaged her by mistake, she thought. (Though whom he could have been sending such pictures to was unclear.) Before she returned the phone to her pocket, she set it to shunt directly to voicemail, and so missed the last communication she would have from her brother until it was a message from a ghost.

"Should've used the knife," Ivorsson said. "If I had time to plan, I would've. Happened too fast. Plus, I was pretty mad. Head was a mess. Pieces of it hanging in front of my eye. I was hungry, too. Felt like I spent my days with my stomach hurting. Surrounded by the food I really wanted." Ivorsson's milky tongue licked his lips. "No knife. Still, had my hands. Teeth. Wasn't as neat as the flint would've been. All the same. Managed to keep him going for a good hour or so. Not nearly long enough for me. Expect it was a lot longer for him."

Here at last was the worst part of Walter Ivorsson's tale, the detail Michelle had been hoping not to hear even as dread rose in her like icy water. Toby's death, she had been led by her investigation of the last weeks to conclude as likely—Karen's, too, although the probability had not affected her as deeply. While she resisted it, every skill she had learned at her job, a decade and a half of observation, analysis, induction, and intuition, had delivered her to the same destination, the one where her brother's remains lay under a thin layer of dirt and snow. If his death was quick, if it had occurred before he understood what was happening, if he had not suffered, then she could clutch at this as a kind of mercy, albeit, of terrible stripe. For him to spend his final moments in agony and terror, however, was intolerable. For twenty-eight years filled to the brim with canoeing on Lake Taconic, with playing acoustic guitar at Sunday folk mass, with a semester abroad at Oxford, with medium-rare cheeseburgers at his favorite restaurant, encyclopedic knowledge of every *Simpsons* episode, the first Ph.D. in the family, with all the minutiae that gave his life its particular shape and texture, to be reduced to flesh ripped open and torn away, blood steaming on snow, organs wrenched from their places, nerves alight with the same idiot message—PAIN—blinking on and off, on and off, made her throat constrict with horror, even as another emotion rushed underneath, sorrow of such profundity it threatened her eyes with a lifetime of tears. She sniffed them back, because this was neither the place nor the time for weeping.

Ivorsson had set his abbreviated fishing rod on the ice and was rising to his feet. Despite herself, Michelle retreated a step, fumbling in her pocket for the stones. At a certain point, when he described murdering Karen, he had made it inevitable he would not allow her either to leave or to live. The time had come, it appeared, for him to enact his latest plan. The stones slid maddeningly around her fingertips. Ivorsson leaned down to the yellow bucket on which he had been seated and placed a mittened hand flat on either side. Michelle ran the stones through her thumb and index finger, counting them, *One, two, three, four, five,* or was that one again? There was no time. Ivorsson was raising the bucket carefully, the way you might lift the plastic cover from a store-bought cake in order not to smear the frosting. Michelle brought her clenched hand out of her jacket and opened it. The stones—all five, yes—fell to the ice at her feet with the glassy clatter of marbles on pavement. If Ivorsson noticed the sound, he ignored it, focused on the object his seat had concealed.

It was a human head—it was Toby's head, resting slightly askew on the ragged stump of its neck. All the breath left Michelle's lungs. Toby's skin was gray, his eyes rolled up under his lids. His lips were gone, from the look of his mouth chewed away, as was a piece of his left cheek, through which bone flecked with muscle showed white flecked with dull red. A loud ringing filled Michelle's ears. The edge of Toby's neck was crusted with blood turned black. Due to the damage to his face (*the bites the fucking bites the bites*), it was impossible to ascertain her brother's expression, but Michelle thought it was one of terror, of fright so commanding it had swept Toby to death. Dark spots flickered in front of her eyes. Ivorsson bent over and seized Toby's hair with his left hand. As he rose, he threw the head to Michelle with an underhand toss. She caught it reflexively, wrapping both arms around and hugging Toby's poor, mutilated head to herself. It was cold, heavy, as if sculpted from ice. Michelle did not look at it.

Instead, she watched Walter Ivorsson, whose face rippled as if it were behind a sheet of glass across which a spray of water passed. Wind gusted over the ice, whirling snow around him. Within the snow, he seemed—no, *was* taller, much taller, so tall she had to crane her head back to see his face, which had expanded, broadened, eyes pale fires, enormous mouth brimming with blackened teeth like a wolf's fangs. A coil of tongue flapped over the lips, tiny white forms crawling on it. From either temple, a misshapen web of bone flowered, the horn of an elk or moose distorted by some dire sickness. The Wendigo's white skin stretched tight over the rack of its misshapen bones. White flame danced around feet halfway to hooves, rushed over the ankles, up shins and calves. Under other circumstances, her mind would have reeled at the thing leering at her, ravenous. It was fantastic, unbelievable, an affront to the world as she knew and understood it. With Toby's head clasped to her chest, though, the beast Walter Ivorsson had revealed himself to be was only another manifestation of the crack that had split open the center of existence. She went to speak, found her mouth too dry. She swallowed, said, "I guess this is you keeping your word."

In reply, the Wendigo's tongue lashed, spraying maggots across its face and chest.

"The Wendigo isn't new," Michelle said. "They were around when there was a land bridge connecting Siberia and Alaska, hunting the people who crossed it. Those people learned how to fight them. An especially powerful shaman could seek them out and kill them. A brave warrior might do the same thing. I think this is what Toby was trying to do. The problem is, my brother wasn't a warrior. I'm not, either. What I am is thorough. He had sent me the pictures he took of you, the audio of you . . . savaging him. The photos were too blurry to make out. I had to take them to a guy I know who specializes in cleaning up these kinds of images. Even then, I didn't understand what I was seeing: a monster with a bloody hole in its forehead. The recording of his screams was enough to tell me what had happened to him, but I needed to understand the connection between Toby screaming and those pictures. I ran through his emails, his texts, until I found his communication with the person I mentioned, the scholar. I reached out to her and she agreed to talk to me. We went over what she and my brother discussed, some of which I already knew. After she was finished, I told her the real reason Toby had been in touch with her. She didn't believe me—or, let me put that another way. She was prepared to accept my brother had been harassed and stalked by someone pretending to be a supernatural creature, who maybe even believed he was this creature. But the things Toby had described to her were not possible. I shared the cell phone pictures, the originals and the enhanced versions I'd had made. She refused to accept any of it, said photos can be faked, which, God knows, they can be. For me, the opposite was happening. I was understanding how everything fit together, at least, everything I knew. Profess—the scholar became very agitated, accused me and my brother of playing a weird joke on her, threatened to hang up. I begged her to give me five more minutes. I apologized for dumping all this on her. Maybe I was wrong, I said. What if we forgot all my assertions? What if we went back to Toby's story, to the novel he said he was writing? Imagine we're inside the novel, I said, and there's a Wendigo. What do we do about it?

"She repeated the information about the shaman and the warrior. Those didn't work, I said. Do we have anything else?"

Ice creaked as the monster shifted its weight. It was growing impatient—was already impatient, eager to add the taste of her flesh to that of Toby's and Karen's. There was no need for Michelle to tell Ivorsson—what had been Walter Ivorsson—any of this; she would have been as well to turn and start back across the lake. Yet with the moment arrived, she was possessed by the urge to let him know what was about to occur here, in this secluded spot high in the Catskills on a February afternoon. She said, "The people who started to visit this area at the end of the last ice age—the scholar called them the Clovis—had ceremonies for dealing with the Wendigo, rituals dating to when their ancestors hunted in Siberia. Those practices were handed down over millennia. The one she knew of came from the Iroquois, who lived a little ways north of here. Maybe you learned about them in middle school. This ceremony consisted of walking counterclockwise around the Wendigo until you had returned to where you started, chanting a spell as you went. Then, you approached the monster and cast five stones at it. There were details the scholar couldn't remember. She knew the chant was calling on the god the Iroquois call Flint. He's associated with monsters. She thought the stones were made of granite, carved with important symbols or characters of some kind. I asked her if she could find out the exact information and email it to me. She said she would, she did, and I got what I needed for this, our confrontation."

The Wendigo tilted its horned head back and howled, a high cry which echoed off the hilly amphitheater. Michelle heard mixed in it the mournful wail of the coyote and the shriek of the winter wind. Snow belled around it as it took one giant step forward. The ice shuddered.

Michelle glanced down and saw the frozen surface of the lake had turned from opalescent to transparent, allowing an only slightly distorted view of the fish throwing off their winter torpor to crowd it. Although no fisherman, she recognized bass both large- and small-mouthed, crappie, pumpkinseed, bluegill, muddy catfish, pickerel, a scattering of larger fish, pike, all pressing their mouths to the ice like goldfish eager for their flakes. She looked up from the mass of scaled bodies in time to see the corona of snow fly away from the Wendigo in all directions, with a noise like a great fire being extinguished all at once. The monster paused, sniffed the air as if scenting something new, and although it was difficult to read the creature's expression, its features relaxed in such a way as to suggest confusion, indecision, perhaps fear.

A moment later, it dropped to the clear ice, its great form jerking as if all its nerves were firing. Its flesh seemed to liquefy, to slide back and forth across bones losing their size. It cried out a second time, but the sound was more that of a man attempting to scream with a mouth whose shape kept changing. Its right horn cracked off and shattered on the ice; the left contracted into and against the head, stopping as a kind of bony tumor. All at once, the Wendigo was gone, leaving only Walter Ivorsson writhing naked on the ice. If he had appeared thin before, now he was truly emaciated, skeletal, as if his body were so far along the path of starvation it was consuming itself. His mouth opened and closed, trying to seek sustenance from the air itself.

Beneath her feet, the fish had turned on one another, attacking each other with a savagery Michelle could scarcely credit. The ice trembled with the violence of their heads and tails striking it. Blood bloomed in the cold water as, without regard to species or size, fish bit chunks out of each other's sides, tore away each other's fins, shredded each other's tails. Even suffering from tremendous wounds, mortal wounds, half of their heads bitten away, their bellies open and guts trailing after them, the feeding frenzy continued. Nor would it stop until the lake's inhabitants had consumed themselves.

From his position on the ice, Ivorsson glared at her.

"What I did—the ritual traps you here," Michelle said. "Although it doesn't look like you're in any kind of shape to leave. Without the Wendigo inside you, I doubt you'll last very long. According to the forecast, the temperature's going to drop tonight. I believe the weatherman's exact words were, 'dangerously cold.' From what I understand, not many people ice fish here. Too difficult to get to. I bet this is why you like it. I imagine someone will find you, eventually. If the coyotes don't eat you, first. I wish there were some way for everything you've done—for the truth to be known. I can't think of one, so this will have to do."

Ivorsson's teeth had started to chatter.

"I guess there's some doubt as to whether you'll remain confined to this place after you die, or go to whatever hell is waiting for you. I've thought about it, and either is fine with me."

There was nothing more to say. Her dead brother's brutalized head in her arms, Michelle turned away from the man who had killed him and the woman he loved and began the long walk off the lake beneath whose glassy surface the bloody remains of fish spun in the diminishing currents of their awful death.

For Fiona, and for Brian Horstman

AFTERWORD
DARKENING THE DARK

My old friend Kirby McCauley was crucial to the development of horror fiction from the early seventies onwards. He was important to fantasy too—he chaired the first World Fantasy Convention, and George R. R. Martin has celebrated Kirby's support for *A Game of Thrones*—and to science fiction, but horror was always the fiction we enthused about most when we met. On my first trip to America I'd scarcely landed in New York when Kirby rushed me across town to see *The Texas Chainsaw Massacre* and relished my reactions. I still recall Kirby telling me there was a new writer in the field he thought I'd like, and so I sought out that black paperback with the discreet drop of blood on the cover. I did indeed like *'Salem's Lot*, but that's the start of a saga for another book.

I initially heard from Kirby in December 1962, not long after my first professionally published tale appeared. He was then a salesman for Sears Roebuck, living in Minneapolis, and much given to contacting writers he admired (even when, in my case and at that time, they'd provided precious little evidence of worth). He corresponded copiously with quite a few of us, and eventually concluded that so many of the British authors could use American representation that he undertook to provide it, moving to New York to set up his agency in a basement flat at 220 East 26th. As well as commanding the British invasion and agenting a new generation of Americans he revived the careers of pulp veterans—Manly Wade Wellman, Frank Belknap Long and others. With such a list of clients he might have been forgiven for drawing heavily upon it once he turned to editing anthologies, but he ranged far wider. *Dark Forces* is the most ambitious of his three books, into which, alongside old masters and newer voices in the field, he succeeded in scooping Joyce Carol Oates, Davis Grubb and Isaac Bashevis Singer (to whom, in one of his typically compendious letters from the early years of our friendship, Kirby devoted an entire closely handwritten page). He enticed Steve King in too, expecting a short story that burgeoned in the telling to become *The Mist,* the centrepiece and by far the longest story in the book. How appropriate, then, that the present volume— composed in tribute to Kirby's anthology—should encourage its contents to breathe and to take as much space as they need.

Caroline Kepnes transports us into the last century, where a phone in your pocket or your bag was still the stuff of science fiction for most of us, but even the most modern technology wouldn't save her characters from the fate that gathers insidiously around them. They live vividly, these people—they come so close to us we feel their heartbeats and their tears, and the story is raw with adolescence and with authentic emotional awkwardness. When the fraught relationships lead to darker developments, they're only the preamble to a resolution that's as disquietingly truthful as it's unexpected, certainly by this reader.

Alma Katsu conjures up tradition in her opening sentence, but in just a few more paragraphs she makes plain that we're being led into the thrillingly unknown and the bleakly psychological, both of them expertly and gradually revealed. The latter aspect in particular refreshes a theme we might feel has been drained bloodless, but that would be to reckon without the author's considerable originality. Not the least of the elements she reinvents is the sense of terror, too often absent these days from stories about the kind of creature that lurks in the lair of her tale.

In less than a page Josh Malerman lets us feel we're safe only to pull a world out from under us. His quartet of characters and the presence from their past they must confront could easily be the stuff of a novel, but instead the story distils the essence of uncanny fear in his typically wiry prose. It's a breathless read, but then you wouldn't want to breathe around his monster in case you attracted attention. In a nightmare an hour can be eternal and perhaps inescapable, or is there a note of hope?

Livia Llewellyn wastes not a word in seizing us by the guts. Her poetic prose never falters in its clarity, nor in its irresistibly compelling narration and emotional directness. How can the story she's telling lead back to that headlong preamble? A sense of wrongness gradually gathers in the best classical tradition, to explode into a vision of cosmic terror that doesn't eclipse the tortured humanity at the core of the tale.

I talk about my contribution later in the book. I imagine Priya Sharma's story has some roots in her own experiences as a doctor, but the mythic secret of her lonely island feels equally authentic. Like all the best legends, invented or otherwise (and can even the author always tell the difference?), it resonates like a folk memory we may have forgotten until now. It's as disturbing as, and perhaps because, it's beautiful, though painful too—but then the truth, whether symbolic or direct, often is. Who would know this better than a doctor?

Stephen Graham Jones confronts the challenge many of us may feel we have to face as writers—how to deal with the pandemic that surrounds us while this book takes shape. His nightmare arises from it and then mounts above it, but into utter terror. If, as Lovecraft had it, the oldest and strongest emotion of mankind is fear, perhaps the buried essence of some of us is our earliest experience of that oldest strongest element. Perhaps each of us is still our inner child—the terrified one that's hiding in there, hoping never to be noticed. We may certainly hope never to experience the inexorable fate of Jones's characters except by sharing his powerful imagination.

John F.D. Taff's poignant opening pages carry a tinge of unease that doesn't lessen the power of his exploration of grief. Like Stephen Graham Jones, he acknowledges the pandemic, by now a fact of life. The familial relationships central to his story have the ring of absolute raw truth and lived experience, common factors in our book. They make the relentless advance into bleakness and terror all the more disturbing. It's a tale that leaves us desperate to hope.

Gemma Files revels in the possibilities of a fruitful form, the hardboiled fantastic—in this case, the British forensic procedural grown fabulous. Her story brings a lost superstition up to date, not least in its literally visceral vividness. I don't think it's paradoxical to describe the tale as microscopically cosmic. It's a magical story in more than one sense, however dark. Science fantasy has fallen into disuse as a term, but here it fits like a skin and is vindicated by the tale.

Chesya Burke jazzes things up in the best senses, incidentally celebrating the poignant ephemerality of unrecorded performances. Her vision of the afterlife is unusually benign for our field and, I imagine, the one we would like to be real. Perhaps we've had hints of our own if we trust them. Dark things may stray from it, but so does inspiration that battles self-doubt, though the optimism the story offers is hard won. Such, so often, is life.

Usman Malik evokes not just a place but a culture with deft strong strokes of prose and with an unerring eye for telling details. His ugly American tourist could equally realistically easily be English, and the tensions of the intercultural marriage epitomise a situation far more widespread. I take the uncanny elements to demonstrate the richness of Usman's imagination, and ring so true that I searched online for the actual legend. The historical horrors of which he reminds us lead to solidarity, but horror— however merited—lies beyond.

John Langan compels with the richness of his prose and intense specificity of detail, all of which helps render his story compelling. It's a classic two-hander in which the monologues very gradually reveal the mystery that underlies it, along with the personalities of the participants. When the supernatural seeps into it, the images are hauntingly unfamiliar. Beyond them lies real horror and a gruesome kind of awe. It's an unusual combination, but then the entire tale—like its companions between these covers—is admirably fresh. I believe my old friend Kirby would be honoured by this tribute—by the entire book. As a contributor to the original anthology as well, I'm honoured to be in both.

Ramsey Campbell
Wallasey, Merseyside
3 February 2021

AUTHOR NOTES AND BIOS

As a reader, I've always loved authors who include notes to their stories, those little insights into where the author was when they wrote the story, in a writerly sense. Where the idea came from, what it meant to them to write it. So, I asked each of the authors to provide me with just a bit of how the story came to be. Hope you enjoy this little pulling back of the curtain to see backstage.

CHESYA BURKE, "TRINITY RIVER'S BLUES"

Trinity River is a young woman caught between many worlds. Not just the obvious worlds of the living and the dead, but also between the education that her Grann's rootwork has afforded her and the humble, socioeconomically disadvantaged roots of her people. Trinity spends her nights and weekends longing to be a famous jazz musician, like the greats of her grandmother's day, but she has neither the talent nor the drive. She feels guilty for "killing" her mother in childbirth. She doesn't know who she is. And her best friend is a dead jazz musician.

Trinity River may be different, but she is not The Other in her community. Neither her black skin, belief in rootwork, nor ability to see the dead marks her as strange. Instead, it is her inability to see other things—the importance of secrets—that harms her the most. "Trinity River Blues" is the song of despair, but this is the story of forever.

Chesya Burke is an assistant professor of English and U.S. Literatures at Stetson University. She has written and published nearly a hundred fiction works and articles within the genres of science fiction, fantasy, noir and horror. Her story collection, *Let's Play White,* is being taught in universities around the country. Poet Nikki Giovanni compared her writing to that of Octavia Butler and Toni Morrison, and Samuel Delany called her "a formidable new master of the macabre."

RAMSEY CAMPBELL, "A LIFE IN NIGHTMARES"

The central idea of my story—a set of nesting nightmares with reality as the innermost—had been slumbering in a notebook for a while, sleepily encouraging me to wake it up, but seemed to need developing at a length that finds few takers. I was happy to write it and have it find a home. I see that it started life as "No End of Nightmares", although it was written as "Beyond Every Nightmare", but at last I lit on the title it bears now. Not too usually for me, I incorporated most of the notes I made without finding them significantly altered by the process of writing. For the record, I appreciate my own nightmares so much that I've asked my wife never to waken me from them—they're free immersive horror films, more inventive than many, and I believe they contain their own release mechanism when things become too frightening. Just now the notion of wakening from a nightmare only to find that reality is worse seems all too topical.

The Oxford Companion to English Literature describes Ramsey Campbell as "Britain's most respected living horror writer." He has been given more awards than any other writer in the field, including the Grand Master Award of the World Horror Convention, the Lifetime Achievement Award of the Horror Writers Association, the Living Legend Award of the International Horror Guild, and the World Fantasy Lifetime Achievement Award. In 2015 he was made an Honorary Fellow of Liverpool John Moores University for outstanding services to literature. His most recent novels are *The Wise Friend, Somebody's Voice* and the Brichester Mythos trilogy, consisting of *The Searching Dead, Born to the Dark* and *The Way of the Worm. Phantasmagorical Stories* selects sixty years of his shorter fiction in two volumes. His nonfiction is collected as *Ramsey Campbell, Probably* and *Ramsey Campbell, Certainly.* He is working on a book-length study of the Three Stooges, *Six Stooges and Counting.*

GEMMA FILES, "THE SANGUINTALIST"

I love paranormal detective stories, pretty much universally—it's the *John Constantine, Hellblazer* fan in me, though I'll also settle for versions modelled on narrators as disparate as Carnacki the Ghost-Finder, Dancy Flammarion, Carl Kolchak or Silver John. So for a while, I'd had this idea about how someone could use the old tradition of cruentation ("blood evidence") in a modern forensic context, but not much else; then I got this anthology invitation, and all of a sudden Lala Mirwani started talking to me inside my head. That's basically it, that's the whole story. Or rather, this is.

Formerly a film critic, journalist, screenwriter and teacher, **Gemma Files** has been an award-winning horror author since 1999. She has published four collections of short work, three collections of speculative poetry, a Weird Western trilogy, a story cycle, and a stand-alone novel (*Experimental Film,* which won the 2015 Shirley Jackson Award for Best Novel and the 2016 Sunburst Award for Best Adult Novel). Her new story collection from Grimscribe Press, *In That Endlessness, Our End,* was published February 2021.

STEPHEN GRAHAM JONES, "ALL THE THINGS HE CALLED MEMORIES"

About half of the story ideas I scribble down are ideas for psychology experiments that no funding body would ever approve, as they leave victims behind. So I have to stage those experiments on the page, in fiction. This, I guess, is one more of them. Please note too that I had to cut about two thousand words of more experiments out, as they finally weren't contributing. But they're still going on in my head, don't worry, and with people who are only, for the moment, real to me. And, as for where this couple comes from, I think they spawned from some chairs I saw on Craigslist, that maybe needed re-covering, and I considered how complicated that would be, re-covering a chair, and then this big sewing machine I used to work with in a seed outfit surfaced to recover that chair for me, but I needed someone to run it, and someone to push him into places in his head he didn't want to go, and . . . that's how stories happen, right? That's how they happen for me, anyway. But still, it took three runs to get the end down, on three separate days. Each time I thought I had it, but then, hours later, I'd realize it could be worse, and then worse still. And, Bo, with his phones and dice and certainties and fears, he's someone I know very-very well, let's say. Someone I've lived with for years, walking in my own footsteps.

Stephen Graham Jones is the *New York Times* bestselling author of *The Only Good Indians*. He has been an NEA fellowship recipient and been recipient of several awards including the Ray Bradbury Award from the *Los Angeles Times*, the Bram Stoker Award, the Shirley Jackson Award, the Jesse Jones Award for Best Work of Fiction from the Texas Institute of Letters, the Independent Publishers Award for Multicultural Fiction, and the Alex Award from American Library Association. He is the Ivena Baldwin Professor of English at the University of Colorado Boulder.

ALMA KATSU, "THE FAMILIAR'S ASSISTANT"

The inspiration for "The Familiar's Assistant" was *The Talented Mr. Ripley* by Patricia Highsmith. I loved *Ripley*'s damaged, manipulative main character. Sociopaths are so much fun to write. People tell me I write sociopaths well. I should: I've been surrounded by them for most of my adult life.

"Let's write *Ripley* but with vampires," I thought. Who doesn't like a vampire story? Imagine my surprise when the Ripley character turned out not to be a vampire (and they all must be narcissists, mustn't they? Always *me, me, me*) but the man who aspires to be the vampire's familiar. Because the real monsters, the ones you have to watch out for, are not the ones hiding in the shadows but the ones standing right in front of you in their chameleon clothes, lying to you even when the truth would better suit. Lying because they themselves cannot bear the truth.

Alma Katsu is the award-winning author of seven novels, including historical horror (*The Hunger, The Deep,* and *The Fervor*) and, most recently, *Red Widow,* her first spy thriller, drawn from a long career in intelligence. She is a graduate of the master's writing program at Johns Hopkins University and earned her undergraduate degree in literature and writing from Brandeis University. She lives in the Washington, D.C., area with her husband, musician Bruce Katsu. For more information, please visit her website at www.almakatsubooks.com.

CAROLINE KEPNES, "THE ATTENTIONIST"

A writer friend and I were speculating about what it must be like for teenagers dealing with social media during the pandemic. There is something timeless about the desire to be desired, and after this "When I was that age . . . " conversation, I wanted to revisit the social landscape of my youth. Summer jobs. Landlines. The angst of watching so many romantic, memorable movies where young women were in love triangles with a very obviously bad guy and a very earnest puppy of a good boy. Oh that life was so simple.

Because I write books about social media, I've had people ask me if Joe could do what he did in earlier times and this story is basically a big fat scary yes. This time, I wanted to explore how this young woman weaponizes her first brush with male attention, the horror of finally getting that call that she so wants so desperately, except it's violent and menacing. What if the reward is a punishment? What then? The emotional and physical claustrophobia of a family plus the emotional and physical claustrophobia of a stalker combine for maximum . . . emotional and physical claustrophobia. It grew from there and I loved showing how these sisters navigate the world in their own ways. I hope the story makes you feel transported into that house, to a time before caller ID, when stalkers could still do their thing, even without access to the internet.

> **Caroline Kepnes** is the *New York Times* bestselling author of *You, Hidden Bodies, Providence,* and *You Love Me.* Her work has been translated into a multitude of languages and inspired a television series adaptation of *You,* currently on Netflix. Kepnes graduated from Brown University and then worked as a pop culture journalist for *Entertainment Weekly* and a TV writer for *7th Heaven* and *The Secret Life of the American Teenager.* She grew up on Cape Cod, and now lives in Los Angeles.

JOHN LANGAN, "ENOUGH FOR HUNGER AND ENOUGH FOR HATE"

In a lot of ways, this story began with the ending scene of Philip Roth's novel *The Human Stain,* in which Roth's narrator, Nathan Zuckerman, confronts the man he is certain is responsible for the death of Zuckerman's friend, Coleman Silk. He does so on the surface of a frozen lake high in the Berkshires, where the man has gone to ice fish. It's a remarkable scene in what I think is a remarkable book. The image of the lone man sitting on a sheet of ice surrounded by snow-covered mountains stayed with me, it haunted me in a way few others in recent memory have, to the extent I decided I would have to include a version of it in my own writing at some point in the future.

I reached for the image not long after receiving a request to write a story about a Wendigo. It came from Brian Horstman, who had supported a fundraiser for Robert Wilson's excellent Nightscape Press by choosing the option I had volunteered: donate a specific amount of money and I will write a story about the monster of your choice. Brian selected the Wendigo, a selection I found both exciting and intimidating. Of course, the monster—or a version of it—features in Algernon Blackwood's famous story of that name; not to mention, another variety of it is present in Stephen King's *Pet Sematary*, one of the formative horror novels of—well, of my life, I suppose. Visually, I knew the monster as a villain in Marvel Comics' *Incredible Hulk* title; the Hulk had faced this Wendigo (whose design I was quite taken by) alongside Wolverine. In more recent years, the monster has shown up in the Hellboy sister comic, *The B.P.R.D.,* as a kind of monstrous set-dressing in the *Hannibal* TV series, and in a couple of Larry Fessenden's films (*Wendigo* and *The Last Winter*).

In my take on the monster, I incorporated aspects of several versions of the Wendigo. If you're into this kind of literary investigation, you'll find references to Blackwood's "The Wendigo," King's *Pet Sematary,* and the *Hannibal* show in the story. My brief mention of the Catskill community of Pine Hill is a nod to my friend Chelsea Goodwin's novel, *Pine Hell*. The story's title came from a mishearing of a line in a poem by my dear friend and mentor, Bob Waugh. The story's basic structure, the confrontation between Michelle Word and Walter Ivorsson, emerged from Roth's novel, with the not insignificant exception that my characters' conversation is more wide ranging and direct than the one in his book. (Not to mention, full of supernatural materials.) As I was writing, though, what surprised me most was Walter Ivorsson's character, his self-pitying and self-justifying psychology, which, I came to see, drew on my reading of the great Russell Banks's novels, especially *Continental Drift* and *Affliction*. In those books and others, Banks excavates the

psychology of a certain type of male insecurity and self-destruction
to powerful effect. (Banks also showed up as an influence on the
beginning of another recent story, "Natalya, Queen of the Hungry
Dogs," which makes me think either that he's becoming more
important to me at this moment in my writing or that he's always
been in the background and I just wasn't aware of him.)

Much of the research I did for this story involved the figure of
the Wendigo and its place in the cultural stories of a number of
Native American peoples. I drew inspiration from the Iroquois's
connection of the monster to the god, Flint, and when my reading
on the area turned up the existence of an ancient flint quarry in
Greene County, one county north from me, which appears to have
been visited for something on the order of ten to twelve thousand
years, beginning with the Clovis people, a number of seemingly
random elements fell into place. The binding/exorcism ritual is, of
course, my own invention.

This story is among the more gruesome I've written, which is
due in part to a friendly jibe from Brian Keene, who mentioned
on social media a dream he'd had in which I wrote a splatterpunk
story under a pseudonym. This provoked a stream of smart-assed
remarks from friends and acquaintances, to which I replied that
I would write such a story, and when I did, it wouldn't be under
a pseudonym. I wouldn't call this story splatterpunk, exactly, but
certainly, I allowed myself to embrace its more gory moments.

So thanks to Brian Horstman for prompting me to write about
this monster.

John Langan is the author of two novels and four collections
of stories, for which he's received the Bram Stoker and This Is
Horror awards. He's one of the founders of the Shirley Jackson
Awards, for which he serves on the board of directors. He lives
in New York's Mid-Hudson Valley with his wife, younger son,
and a small, German Godzilla.

LIVIA LLEWELLYN, "VOLCANO"

The origin of "Volcano" was an image of an open door in a silent, darkened basement, an image I'd been carrying around in my head for decades. Like a lot of images, I just let it live there, bumping up against other ideas and then drifting back away where it would be forgotten again for a couple of years. Eventually, that image found its plot, its protagonist, its setting—all of those separate elements finally came together last summer, and I was finally able to write the story that had been floating like a half-formed ghost in my thoughts for over a decade.

As for what "Volcano" means, or might mean—I'm sure some of you know I don't like to go into those details too much. What the story means to me, what it's about, is really up to each reader to decide. I know what the story means to me, but I don't want my interpretation to become yours. "Volcano" truly is an open door in a silent, darkened basement, and what lies beyond that door is undefinable, indescribable, and unique to every person who passes through it; and each of you must enter it alone.

Livia Llewellyn is a writer of dark fantasy, horror, and erotica, whose fiction has appeared in over eighty anthologies and magazines, including *The Best Horror of the Year, Year's Best Weird Fiction,* and *The Mammoth Book of Best New Erotica.* Her short fiction collections *Engines of Desire: Tales of Love & Other Horrors* (Lethe Press) and *Furnace* (Word Horde Press) were both nominated for the Shirley Jackson Award, and her short story "One of These Nights" won the 2020 Edgar Award for Best Short Story. You can find her online at liviallewellyn.com and on Twitter and Instagram.

JOSH MALERMAN, "MRS. ADDISON'S NEST"

I've always been into the "hunt" in horror stories. Stories in general, really, as *Moby-Dick* is an all-timer for me. But sometimes the actual standoff is the fun part. Why not start a story there?

Also fun: a hole in the woods that a witch calls home.

Her nest.

"Mrs. Addison's Nest" begins at the standoff, as four ne'er-do-well friends (now grown men) have finally tracked down the hiding place of the monster who scared them deeply way back in high school. Problem is, this monster messes with your head. Makes you think you're someplace else, gives you illusions, so that our quartet of anxious witch-hunters might have forgotten they were in a standoff in the first place.

That's a serious disadvantage.

So it's a good thing they've tattooed the truth on their arms. To remind themselves of the fact that they're standing in a circle around a monster's den: Mrs. Addison's nest.

If only they'll remember to look at their arms . . .

Start a story at the standoff, I say. Let's hit the ground running. We can flash back, or not. Explain things, or not. Because what really matters is that eventually, all things that hide in a hole gotta come out. And all people eventually must face their fears, whether they recognize when that's happening or not.

> **Josh Malerman** is the *New York Times* bestselling author of *Bird Box* and *A House at the Bottom of a Lake* as well as one of two singer/songwriters for the Detroit rock band the High Strung, whose song "The Luck You Got" can be heard as the theme song to the Showtime show *Shameless*. He lives in Michigan with his soulmate Allison Laakko and countless animals.

USMAN T. MALIK, "CHALLAWA"

I have been wanting to write a story on the mercurial monster challawa from Indo-Pakistani mythos ever since I heard of its eerie similarities with Spring-heeled Jack. When I began researching it, though, I stumbled upon ancient magical rituals centered on it that I'd never heard of—rituals that seemed to personify the Indian resistance movements against British colonization.

Usman T. Malik's fiction has been reprinted in several year's-best anthologies including *The Best American Science Fiction and Fantasy* series. He has been nominated for the World Fantasy Award and the Nebula Award, and has won the Bram Stoker and the British Fantasy awards. Usman's debut collection, *Midnight Doorways: Fables from Pakistan,* came out in early 2021, and has garnered praise from Brian Evenson, Paul Tremblay, Karen Joy Fowler, Kelly Link, and other luminaries. You can find him on Twitter @usmantm and Instagram @usmantanveermalik.

PRIYA SHARMA, "PAPA EYE"

The island of Papa Eye is part of a fictional archipelago in the North Atlantic Ocean. Each island has its own cultural and economic identity, as well as its own peculiar magic. The sister story to this, "Maw"—published in *New Fears 2,* edited by Mark Morris—is set on the neighboring Little Isle. I'd cite George Mackay Brown as an influence. His writing is full of ancient myths, early Christian mysteries and the landscape itself.

I once saw a skip outside a nursing home filled with a resident's belongings. The framed photos were the most poignant. It shocked me that those precious moments had been discarded. Lost forever. That's what "Papa Eye" is about. My dad's fond of saying people live on in our memory. I hope so, but even memory is finite. After the indignities of death, the final insult is that we are forgotten.

Priya Sharma's fiction has appeared in venues such as *Interzone, Black Static, Nightmare, The Dark* and *Tor.com.* She's been anthologized in many best-of series. Her short story "Fabulous Beasts" won a British Fantasy Award for Short Fiction. *All the Fabulous Beasts,* a collection of some of her work, won a British Fantasy Award and a Shirley Jackson Award. *Ormeshadow,* her first novella, won the Shirley Jackson and British Fantasy awards. You can find out more at priyasharmafiction.wordpress.com.

JOHN F.D. TAFF, "SWIM IN THE BLOOD OF A CURIOUS DREAM"

Does your love for your children, your desire to be with them, end when you die? I'd like to think not, and this is my meditation on that theme. The story came about, as most of mine do, with a fragment of an idea. This one concerned a rest stop where a few people are trapped. A man and his young son, a guy who pukes a lot, a young woman. Maybe the man's wife has died, and he and his boy are on a road trip to a new home. I wanted a confined space, a small cast of characters and increasingly dangerous weather outside to heighten a sense of isolation and claustrophobia in the piece. But the idea really took off when I combined it with the thought that death is kind of like a divorce, isn't it? A separation, a loss, hurt feelings on both sides. And then how to you share the children of the marriage?

That got me thinking about how that might play out, even when the divorce is *actual* death. How would the parties navigate this? And what would it mean to the kid? Anyway, there it is. I can't take credit for the title of the story. It's part of a line from a song by one of my favorite bands, Guster.

John F.D. Taff is a multiple Bram Stoker Award nominated author with more than thirty years in the horror genre, one-hundred-plus short stories, five novels, and three collections in print. His apocalyptic novel *The Fearing* was published serially in 2019 to critical and reader acclaim. Robert R. McCammon called it "A powerful and epic trip into the land of feardom"! Look for more of his work in anthologies such as *The Seven Deadliest, Gutted: Beautiful Horror Stories, Shadows Over Main Street 2,* and *Behold: Oddities, Curiosities and Undefinable Wonders.* Taff lives in the wilds of Illinois with three pugs, two cats, and one long-suffering wife. Follow him on Twitter @johnfdtaff.

ACKNOWLEDGEMENTS

No book like this comes about on its own, and I have many people to thank. First and foremost, thanks to Josh Malerman for letting me bounce this idea off him in its early stages and sticking through to write the Foreword and a fantastic story. Ditto to Ramsey Campbell, who I approached to write the Afterword, not even thinking a new story from him was an option until he stunned me by offering one. He truly is the connective tissue between this book and *Dark Forces*. I should also hasten to thank the late Kirby McCauley, editor of *Dark Forces*, and all the legendary authors who appeared in that seminal collection. That book was formative for me, as it was for the entire horror genre. I hope we've done you all an honor here.

Thanks also to Usman T. Malik for making the introduction to Diana Pho, formerly with Tor/Nightfire and now with Realm Media. Thanks to her and Nightfire Senior Editor Kelly Lonesome, both of whom—and Tor!—have been terrific to work with. My gratitude also to artist Jeffrey Alan Love for giving us a cover worthy of the spectacular authors and stories contained herein. Also thanks to Ellen Datlow, who needs no identifier, for invaluable input from her exhaustive, expert anthology experience when I needed it, even if it wasn't asking her directly, rather simply saying to myself, "What would Ellen do?" She was always gracious and patient with me.

Horror is a diverse, emotional, empathetic genre, and I hope the authors featured here demonstrate that. Thanks to them for helping me layout that argument and then hammer it home.

Thanks as always to my wife Deb for allowing me to do this, and to my kids Harry, Sam, and Molly.

And thanks, finally, to you, the readers for taking the opportunity to expand your horizons and see that there are no boundaries in horror. If you see unfamiliar authors out there with horror books, take a chance, give them a read and see what dark corners they lead you to.

For more fantastic fiction, author events,
exclusive excerpts, competitions, limited editions and more

VISIT OUR WEBSITE
titanbooks.com

LIKE US ON FACEBOOK
facebook.com/titanbooks

FOLLOW US ON TWITTER AND INSTAGRAM
@TitanBooks

EMAIL US
readerfeedback@titanemail.com